THE
ORPHAN ANGEL

By

ELINOR WYLIE

With an Essay by

MARTHA
ELIZABETH JOHNSON

First published in 1926

British Library Cataloguing-in-Publication Data
A catalogue record for this book is available
from the British Library

To
WHOM IT
MAY CONCERN

LIFE OF ELINOR WYLIE

AN ESSAY BY
MARTHA ELIZABETH JOHNSON, 1936

The work of no poet has achieved fame in such a short time as that of Elinor Wylie. Her growth has been like a series of steps taken in rapid strides, each one carrying her a little higher than the proceeding one. She seems to have emerged from a background of no preparation into a vast field of poetry, as a full—fledged poet.

She produced, in an unbelievably short time, four volumes of poetry and four prose, and these books have placed her among the most accomplished of American poets. These books were all written within a period of eight years; none before her thirty—fourth year and none after her forty—second, which was the year of her death.

She was born Elinor Hoyt. She came from a brilliant American family of English origin and was reared with every social advantage, making her debut in Washington society at the age of twenty. In 1907, when twenty—one, she was married to Phil Hichborn, son of Rear Admiral Hichborn of the United States Navy. This marriage was broken up because of her elopement with Horace Wylie, to whom she was later married after her second elopement with him. At the time of her death she was the wife of William Rose Benet, the poet.

As a girl she loved literature and wrote some poetry when she was eight years of age. Much of her background of classical reading she got in her childhood while living with her parents at Washington. From fourteen to twenty—two she wrote poetry but not really in earnest and then stopped writing for seven years while she was having her escapades and going through the aftermath that made her want to withdraw from public view.

She went to England to live but to the surprise of those who knew her, she soon returned, and the following poem appeared:

> Now why should I, who walk alone,
> Who am ironical and proud,
> Turn when a woman casts a stone,
> At a beggar in a shroud?

She could not adjust herself to her home in England and she did not desire to return to Washington. She was unhappy, alone and unoccupied, so she decided to go to Maine. There she lived alone with her typewriter in a small room over a grocery store, in 1919, and wrote verse that resounded with a sad and mournful note. She had given up a life of luxury and excitement to live in this way and it has been questioned whether

> "It was life's enrichments or life's deprivation that tempted her to write."

Here in Maine she was inspired by the woods and by the sea, but she was dissatisfied — restless — and after a short time she went to New York where she settled down to writing in all earnestness, in her thirty—fourth year. She was probably inspired by her last husband, Mr Benet, the writer, to write with the powerful determination that produced great results. So we find her at the age of thirty—four just discovering the literary gift that was here, after she had been through the most tragic experience, which probably was the thing necessary to call it forth.

Her first published poems appeared in *The Century Magazine,* in *Poetry* and in *The New Republic.* There were some poems she classed as *Incidental Numbers* written in 1921, which was a small collection and they were never reissued because she considered them the work of a juvenile. In 1921, also, appeared the first book of poems that she was proud to claim authorship of *Nets to Catch the Wind*. This book made her reputation as a poet of great prominence. It won for her the Julia Ellsworth Ford prize that was awarded by the Poetry Society of America for the best book of poems published in the United States in the year 1921. *Black Armour* followed close on the heels of *Nets to Catch the Wind* and this book tended not only to hold her reputation but to increase it. In this second book her expression is more intellectual, and her feeling is more profound. She was more interested in the thought that she had to express than how she should express that thought.

In 1922 her third book of poems came out - *Trivial Breath*. It was written in the same intellectual strain, but her thought is expressed in a more subdued tone and is more variable than in her two preceding books. The contents of her three books to date are just one hundred poems and most of them are quite short. Possibly two or three consist of as many as fifty lines and her longest poem has about two hundred.

Her fourth and last book of poems has been published under the titles of *Angels and Earthly Creatures*. It is so named after the finest poem in the book. It is her heart and not her intellect that speaks through the poems of this collection and they reflect her deeper understanding of herself and of life in general.

When we give careful attention to her four books of poems we invariably conclude that her growth was as sudden as it was remarkable. In the chronological arrangement they show a series of marked advancement.

The proceeding outline of her writings has not included her first four poems, which she called her *First Acceptor*. These were printed in 1820 before her first book *Nets to Catch the Wind* and even these poems are considered as capable of forecasting her master of arts. As she wrote from time to time her poetry gained not only in depth but in simplicity. The outstanding characteristic of all her poetry is clarity and this is noticeable especially in her later poems. Her clarity was the outcome of her carefully striving to attain that end. Although her work was cleverly done, it never seems labored. Peregrine a good example of this:

Loved a city,
And street's alarums;
Parks were pretty
And so were bar-rooms
He loved fiddles
He talked with rustics;
Life was riddles
And queer acostics.

The noose draws tighter;
This is the end;
I'm a good fighter,
But a bad friend:
I've played the traitor
Over and over;
I'm a good hater
But a bad lover.

As a more careful study of her books is made, it may be noted that *Nets to Catch the Wind* does not show the working of a grave and melancholy mind altogether.

There are instances of playfulness and strains of emotion run along through a large number of her poems. She conceieved the idea that our senses are nets which are not strong enough to stop and control the emotions that are all about us and a consequence of this fact we learn but little from our experiences.

PREFACE

Genius comes among us in many ways, but sometimes as suddenly and sharply as a new star. The course of the average writer — even the very good writer — is, often enough, fairly easy for the critics to plot, looking backwards. There are the first attempts and the juvenilia, the fumblings and false starts, the slow or swift development into strength. To be blind to this process is to sentimentalize art — to complain of it is to complain of the apple-tree because it bears leaves and flowers before it bears fruit. Only sometimes, as I say, it happens otherwise. The tree grows before our eyes like an Indian magician's — we look at the familiar patterns of heaven and there is a new and burning dust between Rigel and Altair.

It was so with Elinor Wylie. It is true that she had written before, it is true that she had published privately and suppressed a small book of verses before " Nets To Catch The Wind." But when that book appeared, in

Preface

1921, the usual critical adjectives reserved for first books of verse simply did not apply. It was not " promising " or " interesting " or " creditable " — it was the work of a scrupulous and inimitable artist. And " Jennifer Lorn," with its complete command of style, its extraordinary wit, beauty and finish, is as different from the average " first novel " as if it came from another world.

In the eight, packed years of her writing life, Elinor Wylie wrote four novels. Of these, " The Orphan Angel " is the third, the longest, and the only one that has an American background. It was, to its author, a very personal book, for in it she drew at full length the mortal image of that one of the English poets to whom she gave an entire devotion.

I have heard people speak of that devotion as if it were a pose, a hobby, or a blind worship. It was none of these things. She was entirely sincere about it but she was also entirely mature. In " The Orphan Angel " she could and did show her hero, Shiloh, as sometimes pedantic, sometimes naïve and often difficult. She could laugh at him a little with no diminution of love and make of him no less an immortal because he was sometimes preposterous. As a result, in a work of fiction, a work entirely and necessarily outside of the real events of his life, she has probably come nearer to the essential character of Shelley than any of the critics. For that, too, is genius, that clairvoyance that sees beyond fact and circumstance into truth.

Preface

There are three strands woven together in the fabric of the book — a spirit, whose ruling passion is a passion for liberty in a world where liberty is the unpermitted thing — a knight-errant, whose fatal habit it is to rescue princesses from dragons, with no thought whatever of the necessary dangers of that pastime after the dragon is dead — and that lost America of rivers and forests, of wild turkeys and buckskin riflemen and the red shape in the wilderness which lies somewhere at the back of all our minds.

The whole search for Sylvie La Croix is a green-and-silver arras that could hang in a long chamber at Knole or Amboise and be taken, from a distance, for some hunting-tapestry, woven these many years. For the style is not " modern," in our contemporary sense — it deliberately employs the full resources of a language — and the architecture is nearer Wren than Wright. And yet, the first glance would undeceive the eye. These hounds and horses are of another breed, they are not the King's or the Duke's — these riders and runners and walkers have the high cheek-bones and the drawling, salty voices of a new world. The sun may hang in the heavens like an heraldic shield and the evening fall softly as a fall of snow whose flakes are shadow instead of shining crystal, but when we come to the feast, there is baked ham and roasted turkey, pot-pie and custard-pie.

" ' Fiend, I defy thee! With a calm, fixed mind, all

that thou canst inflict I bid thee do,' said Shiloh, bravely, but in a rather faint voice.

'Which remark don't butter no parsnips,' replied David, with some impatience, ' First place the bastard can't hear you and second place it wouldn't do no good if he did.' "

The tone of the book is a little exaggerated, in those two speeches, but they are very characteristic. They give an inkling of that mixture of luminous beauty and wild earth which gives " The Orphan Angel" its peculiar charm.

For the book is fine and ghostly as a tea-clipper under its cloud of white sail, but as solid and seaworthy, too. Beneath the incantation and the spell lie an admirable knowledge, an admirable craftsmanship. Elinor Wylie was a great lyric poet — she could also have been a great scholar, for she had many of the scholar's gifts, including an extraordinary patience and thoroughness in research. We are all of us familiar with the sort of people who profess such extreme devotion to a cause or a personality that they cannot bear to have it tainted by fact. They lie in the warm, relaxing bath of their own emotions and murmur, " Oh, don't tell me who wrote that beautiful thing — don't tell me he limped or was married — you are spoiling my dream."

Such an attitude is one of the marks of the permanent adolescent. It was not Elinor Wylie's. She knew every small incident in Shelley's life as thoroughly as any com-

mentator, she knew what he ate and drank and how much money he had in his pocket, but she knew these things without dryness or pretense. She knew them, not as one knows a lesson, but as one remembers a past. She would talk of them as casually as of a personal reminiscence. And, similarly, the whole journey of Shiloh and David, across the continent, from Boston to San Diego, may seem to the reader, at times, like a fantastic fairy tale. But every stage of that journey could be plotted on a map of the period — and each stage would be right and probable, down to the number of days it took to traverse it and the means of locomotion used. The transmutation of the material is magic; but the little details of food and drink and gear that make a past live again were sought for and gathered from a hundred sources by a mind that seemed to know by instinct where its necessary victual lay.

The pilgrimage in search of Jasper Cross's sister across the America of the Eighteen-Twenties is the twisted silver plait that holds the book together. On this are strung the bright and diverse beads of adventure and incident — the river-ark and the rifle-match, the wilderness-wedding and the Indian stake. And, always, there are certain ladies who appear, from Melissa of the small clear singsong, Shiloh's most touching worshipper, to Anne the singular child with hair like a magical bronze bell who would have felt such genuine pleasure in giving Shiloh the head of his enemy, if Shiloh had only wanted it. And always, as there are ladies who appear, so there are ladies to be left. With exquisite courtesy, with amiable recollection, sometimes even in sheer though by no means unmanly panic, but, nevertheless, to be left. For ladies are, somehow, inconsonant with liberty, and yet, the instinct to rescue persists in spite of the facts.

" ' But I am afraid that I am an excessively poor hand at rescuing people,' said Shiloh and opened his eyes upon reality." And yet, with the next lady, he forgets, though his author does not. The book ends, and ends in grave beauty, but the soul's comedy is unfinished. It cannot, indeed, be finished — for its essence is the disparity between an ideal and the world.

Here is a head-dress of eagle-feathers taken from an Aricarax chief and a volume of Condorcet, read by candle on a flatboat. Here is The Missouri Intelligencer *and Tom O'Bedlam's song. And here, in a frame that has the hard bronze of Latin within it as well as the silver, is the picture of a lost America and, wandering through it, two strange companions, a Yankee boy called David Butternut and another who walks as swiftly as the West wind. Here are many adventures and one that is always the spirit's. And here is a prose that was unique in our time.*

I have written around and about this book and yet, it seems to me now, I have told little of it, though I hope I have said enough to make the reader impatient to be through with this preface and beat out of Leghorn har-

bor with the Witch of the West. *But, perhaps, on my
part, such a course was inevitable, for the look of the
printed pages is bound up in my mind with certain recol-
lections and the sound of a voice, reading, a little hastily,
a little scornfully, as if impatient with beauty and fire
themselves because they were not a beauty beyond all
mortal conception, a fire that fed on something lighter
and more pellucid than air. I have heard that voice many
times. It had the accent of greatness. I shall not hear it
again. But the words remain, and these were some of
the words.*

STEPHEN VINCENT BENÉT

NEW YORK CITY, 1933.

CONTENTS

I

WESTERN WAVE

On the eighth of July, 1822, at half past six in the evening, the American clipper-built brig *Witch of the West* was beating out of Leghorn Harbour, close-hauled upon the increasing wind. She was a smart little vessel; beneath the varnished black of immaculate paint a new copper bottom glittered bravely as she leaned over nearly upon her beam-ends in the racing glass-green sea.

In place of the dried codfish, furs, and Virginian tobacco with which she had put forth from Boston seven weeks before, the pretty ship now carried a luxurious cargo of wine, olive oil, and candied tropic fruits; her shining surfaces and slender compact proportions concealed an appropriate core of honeyed essences and spice. Yet, as she struggled under naked and singing shrouds against the force and violence of the summer hurricane, she wore an air no less valiant than graceful, like the aërial composure of a cloud.

"If we spin her round upon her heel, as we oughter, and put back to port, you'll hang, Davy, or I'll eat my oilskins," said the skipper, a red-haired Yankee from New Bedford; he spat an impatient expletive and a thin stream of tobacco juice within an inch of young David Butternut's excellent sea-boots. The captain had shipped upon an old-fashioned whaler, in the capacity of cabin-boy, during the most formative period of his youth; his manners were often rough to the point of boorishness, but a soft heart beat under the horny tarpaulin of his seaman's coat.

"You'll hang, I calculate," repeated the skipper pessimistically. "And mebbe you'll burn too, for you boys picked the quarrel in the porch of a church, and that's what these Eyetalians call sacrilegious, I reckon. You've attracted the notice of the authorities, and I doubt that I'd have power to help you, my lad. We got our clearance papers just in time to save your skin, otherwise I'd never have sailed into the jaws of this dirty weather."

"I know it, sir," replied the youth with becoming modesty, "and trust me, Cap'n, to be properly grateful." David Butternut was a tall muscular stripling from the coasts of Maine; the changing fortunes which had uprooted him from a forest to set him upon the slanting deck of a brig appeared to have fitted him into his surroundings as neatly as any shipbuilder transplants a pine-tree to carry spread of sail. "Not that I'd have you drown the other boys along of me; I don't see as there's such an almighty difference betwixt hanging and drowning, after all. Go back if you've a mind to, sir, and don't never bother about me; I'm not worthy of any such kindness, and I don't rightly know as I'd rather not hang; it's a fine dry death, when everything's said and done."

"No, no, Dave my boy, you're wrong there," the captain insisted with an indulgent smile, "as you'd realize full well if ever you'd been strung from the yard-arm, like I was once in the good old days. Cut down in the nick of time, by the special intercession of the first mate, but my throat was sore for a week, I do assure you. No, it's a damned uncomfortable death, lad, and I hope it's not necessary that you should hang this voyage. Jasper Cross was a nasty customer, for all his pleasant gentlemanly airs, and there's some of us as knows you only acted in self-defence; yet the law's a pretty crank thing to handle, and I'd

2

not give a wooden dollar as the price of your neck in Leghorn to-night."

David shot an appreciative glance towards the captain, in whom he had long recognised a true if an untender friend. "Thank you kindly, sir, I'm sure," he whispered huskily, brushing the sleeve of his pea-jacket across his ingenuous blue eyes.

"Now, boy," said the captain in a brisk business-like manner, "seeing as you've left us kinder short-handed with that there fist of yours, mebbe you'd better attend to reefing the topsail, and quit worrying about murders."

Butternut turned cheerfully enough to this change of employment, and good Captain Ffoulkastle remained for a moment lost in reverie, gazing out over the tumultuous sea, where all the elements of sublimity and terror raged unseen behind a descending veil of darkness.

Suddenly, with the amazement of a thunderclap, he beheld a human countenance emerge from this sinister obscurity to float upon the dark like a drowning star, without mortality or substance.

"Man overboard!" cried Captain Ffoulkastle in a tremendous voice; he spoke to himself in an awe-struck murmur. "Strike my timbers if I didn't think it was that sarpent Jasper, come aboard to pester us, but here's Jasper's corpse still a-rolling in the bloody scuppers, lads not having time to tidy up along of this blasted storm. Still, I'll stake my soul it's Jasper's ghost I seen . . ." whispered the captain nervously. Another great wave lifted the mysterious face well-nigh to the level of the vessel's plunging side, where it shone brighter and whiter than before in a flash from the larboard lantern.

"Man overboard!" shouted the captain a second time, and in response to his call young David Butternut leaped from the mast as from the summit of a swaying forest tree and sprang into the blackness of the ocean.

"Didn't even wait to kick off them heavy boots of his," observed the captain philosophically. "Well, there goes another of my able seamen!" Aloud he bellowed "Ready about!" and "Helms down!" and was about to add "Lower the boat!"

3

when he perceived that David, by some miracle of superhuman strength and agility, and by the material aid of a rope flung by his affectionate comrades, had indeed regained the deck, bearing in his arms a singular and unearthly burden.

"It's Jasper's attendant angel!" breathed the captain, surprised into a momentary pang of pure mysticism.

The scene was solemn to the extremity of awe; upon the deck, illuminated by the faint glimmer of a lantern, lay the blood-stained corpse of Jasper Cross, and above this tragic indication of impermanence appeared, supported in the arms of David Butternut, a veritable image of the same figure, but brighter, clearer, fairer, as if from the blessing of another planet. The creature's eyes were closed, but its countenance wore a look of beatitude and innocence infinitely touching to behold, and the composure of the brow was childlike and serene.

"Cap'n, I don't know what I've snatched from the fury of the waters," said David simply, "but I do know this: it's something good and something beautiful, and if I've preserved its body from destruction, I think it's saved my soul from everlasting death!"

In his own face was mirrored a reflection of the preternatural light shining upon the stranger's forehead, and as he gazed from one to the other of these curious visions, this the secular portent of mortality, and that the embodiment of spiritual grace, he trembled and wept as if he had that moment come naked into a legendary world.

"Give Davy a tot of rum," said the captain compassionately. "The poor boy must be chilled to the bone. And some of you lazy lubbers look to the stranger and see whether there's any life mixed with the sea-water in his innards."

Captain Ffoulkastle had satisfied himself that the unknown was a human creature, and as such singularly innocuous, but to the superstitious sailors he was still an object of fear; not until the blustering second mate had led the way with a laugh and a brutal jest did any dare to lay his hand upon the body, now lying tranquilly along the blood-stained deck.

"Our Jasper's twin, by the pretty face on him," cried the mate with a coarse chuckle. "And both of them deader nor

doornails, damn their silly eyes; we won't pour good Demerara
after stinking sea-water down the throats of no drowned men,
will we, boys? "

He was about to spurn the motionless form with the toe of his
great tarry boot, but David Butternut sprang forward in time
to prevent this act of cruelty, and the indignant murmurs of
the men soon warned the mate that such sentiments were un-
suited to the hour and the grave occasion. Swallowing a curse,
he applied himself with tolerable interest to the problem of
ascertaining whether or no life yet lingered in the stranger's
breast.

"Gone, I do declare," said the mate casually, dropping the
cold hand and shrugging his shoulders. "Well, reckon there's
nothing to do but pitch him back into that pesky tea-cup where
he come from."

"But, by graminy," cried David in horror, "we're a-going
to try to bring him round, ain't we? I know in my heart he's
some kind of messenger from God, and if we reject him now,
indifferent-like, what's to become of us all? I asks you honest,
is that the face of an angel, or ain't it? " None cared to contra-
dict him; without another word he unscrewed the flask of rum
which the captain had given him and attempted to pour a few
drops of the fiery liquid between the colourless lips of the unconscious stranger.

Presently the captain's repeated cry of " All hands ahoy!"
left the young sailor the sole occupant of that retired portion
of the deck, but still David knelt devoutly beside the mysterious
visitant, forgetful of the storm and its attendant pandemonium,
and searching with an agonized attention the peaceful face of the
unknown.

Meanwhile his mind was full of confused prayers and images,
in which the continued life of this mortal, snatched by his
strength from the blackness of annihilation, seemed the dear
embodiment of something lost and infinitely cherished.

"To make up for Jasper! " he muttered to himself with a
shaking mouth, " oh, to make up for Jasper! Please, please, come
back, and I shall be forgiven! "

2

As if in answer to David's low entreaty, the stranger stirred, and, opening large blue eyes, gazed with an expression of innocent bewilderment straight into the small blue eyes of his preserver.

With a cry of joy, David caught the living creature's hand in a strong salty grasp, and, to his own and the other's extreme amazement, covered the cold wet fingers with religious kisses.

"Thank God! " he cried, while the tears mingled with the bitter spray upon his cheeks. "Thank God you've come back! Now everything will be all right, I reckon; I thanks you with all my heart for coming, and I bless you for ever and ever."

"Where am I? " asked the stranger in a very faint voice; his voice seemed to travel from tragic distances, and yet he was smiling a little at David's vehemence. "And where is Edward, and what has become of that poor boy, Charles Vivian the sailor? "

"I am that poor boy David Butternut, a sailor and a murderer," declared David with fierce humility. "Leastways, I reckon as I'm a murderer, though not going for to do more than bust his head for him when he ups and draws a knife on me. But I've a goldarned heavy hand, more's the pity, and there he lays as cold as so many pounds of salt cod, and 'twas me as killed him, and I won't deny it; no, never to you, whatever tale I tells the police when we lands in Boston. Can you be friends with a murderer, young fellow? 'Cause I want for you to be my friend, and yet I'm a terrible sinner to ask for friendship from the likes of you."

"The likes of me! " repeated the stranger softly and ironically. "The likes of me will not refuse your friendship, David Butternut, nor fear to shake the hand which all unwittingly has sent another man to unravel the ultimate enigma of the grave." He essayed weakly to offer his own right hand to David, who took it with a cry of gratitude,

Western Wave

"You know I was so lucky as to save your life, don't you?" asked David a moment later with renewed cheerfulness. "Yes, stranger, I hopped into that there dirty old sea, and I pulled you out as easy as rolling off a log in the Kennebec. But now tell me, seeing as we're friends, are you an angel or a man, and are you any kin to Jasper there? for you're alike as two peas, only he's a rotten black pea and you're a brand-new silver one. Who are you, young feller, and what might be your name, and do you happen to come from heaven or anywhere along those coasts?"

"No, not precisely," answered the stranger gently and a little sadly. "I do not come from anywhere along those coasts, nor am I any kin to Jasper there, save as all men are brothers. As for my name, it is . . ."

But here the stranger's voice failed him so completely that David Butternut, bending low, could with difficulty distinguish any sound, and that perplexing and dispersed upon the wind. At the same time he noticed with alarm that the other's countenance had assumed an excessive and sorrowful pallor, and that his large blue eyes were closed as if in sleep.

"Are you all right?" he inquired sharply, a chilly sensation contracting his heart almost to suffocation. "Hey, there, young feller, are you all right, or are you a-going to die after all?" And he shook the other by his thin shoulder, as one who rouses an obstinate and beloved dreamer from oblivion.

A slight smile was discernible upon the stranger's pale and composed lips, and he contrived to enunciate, slowly, but with exquisite politeness, a few words of amused reassurance.

"I am exceedingly sorry to constitute myself a nuisance, and I would not for the world have you distress yourself upon my poor account, but I believe, my dear David, that I am about to solve the great mystery of dissolution."

Apparently suiting the action to the word, he lay relaxed and motionless upon the deck, while David, with a loud cry of dismay, ran headlong towards the lighted cabin.

The captain, in dripping tarpaulins and very high boots, was filling his pipe by the fitful illumination of a brazen lamp sus-

7

pended from the ceiling by chains and shaken violently by the motion of the ship. Under the falling alternations of flame and shadow his weatherbeaten face was intent and tranquil.

"Well, what is it now?" he called testily, in response to David's frantic knock and immediate entrance. "I calculate those lazy dogs are skeered of this capful of wind, and want me to sing them to sleep. But who in hell told you to come in here?" he demanded irascibly, recognising his visitor.

"Oh, please, sir," David began in agitated accents, "that there young stranger has been and died again on deck, and I want for you to come along and look at him, and mebbe give him just a drop of that special peach brandy that we had on the Fourth of July. Aw, Cap'n, I'd be that grateful if you'd spare him just a little drop!"

"Come, come, Dave my lad," said the captain calmly, presenting to these agonised entreaties the impassive front of a carven storm-scarred fragment of hickory wood, "keep cool and I'll spare you a minute for this business, though it's sheer waste of time fussing over a dead boy with all you kicking live ones on my hands. It's the time and not the brandy that I grudge him, Dave, but it's worth it if we can bring him round and put him in the starboard watch to take Jasper's place. And that reminds me," said the captain indulgently, his eyes on David's simple honest countenance, "I have a fine scheme for saving your precious neck, my lad, when we land in Boston."

David paid no heed to his remarks, watching instead with the most fascinated attention the decanting of a minute quantity of peach brandy into a thick blue tea-cup, which feat the captain performed with amazing delicacy and skill. Without another word the two sturdy sailors made their way through unnoticed prodigies of wind and thunder to that part of the ship where the mysterious stranger lay entranced or dead.

To the captain, and in a far greater degree to David, there appeared something obscurely moving and magical in the scene now presented to their view. The ultimate curtain of the sky was split at intervals by hieroglyphs of lightning and the immense profundities of cloud seemed audible in thunder. Above their heads, the rigging of the ship was plucked to an intense thin music by the hurricane, and driven sheets of green and silver water drowned them in cold and phosphorescent brilliance.

Upon the slanting deck two figures were disposed, miraculously still in the midst of this delirium. Jasper, with the bruise darkening at his temple and blood upon his brow, stared upward with an angry questioning insistence, but the other lay as if asleep, with quiet eyelids and dark hair drenched with spray, and the locks of hair were folded about his forehead like a spiked and ghostly crown.

3

" They both look just about equally dead as drowned rats," said the captain, shaking off the atmosphere of supernatural awe with an impatient movement of his massive shoulders. " But I reckon as this one can be revived with a little judicious encouragement, and a mite of creature comfort. Then," said the captain briskly, for he was after all an eminently practical man, " you'll be safe as a landlocked harbour, according to this plan of mine. Once get this fellow on his sea-legs, and slushing down the mainmast from the royal-mast-head," said the captain with anticipatory gusto, " and you won't be able to tell him from Jasper, and no more will the Boston police, or my name ain't Abner Ffoulkastle! " And he gave David a hearty punch in the ribs before kneeling down, with becoming gravity, to feel the stranger's pulse and to force between his lips the entire contents of the thick blue tea-cup.

" There's life in the young dog yet," he informed David, who waited breathless in an agony of fear. " Yes, he'll be hauling at a hawser by to-morrow morning, with his ribs lined with good salt beef and sea-bread. Now, Dave, I want you to understand that it's all to your profit to learn him the ropes, as they say, and make a useful sailor out of him, for by this means you'll save yourself from the gallows and the other boys from a deal of extra work. Do you catch on, my lad? "

" Yes, sir; I think so, sir," murmured David in confusion. " You want for me to learn this stranger to take Jasper's place on shipboard. . . ."

"Yes, and on shore too, when the time comes," said the captain with a kindly chuckle. "Jasper was an orphan, and a black sheep, from some God-forsaken high-and-dry hole out west, and I hardly look for much trouble from his relatives. If we can satisfy the port authorities in Boston that we come home with the same crew that we shipped on sailing, that'll be enough for your purposes. Your mates won't split on you, and as for this young fellow, he seems by his face to be a gentle obliging sort of chap, and one that would be glad enough to help a friend in a little emergency. Wouldn't you, my lad?" he added, with a smile at the unknown, who at this moment opened his eyes and gazed inquiringly about him.

"I shall be most happy to help my friend David by any honourable act which lies within my powers to perform," he answered at once, in a firm if somewhat far-away voice, with a quick surprising flash of blue from his large intelligent eyes. At the same time he essayed to rise, but the captain thrust him down again with a brief peremptory gesture.

"No, you lay there, stranger, till we've done our little transformation act," he said cheerfully. "Here, you David, run and fetch Jasper's Sunday clothes, while I strip these wet rags off this lad and shove 'em overboard. But no — I've a brighter idee than even that — we'll rig Jasper out in the stranger's suit, and then if any body is found, by bad luck," said the captain with a jovial laugh, "they'll think it yours, mate, and nobody's likely to suspect our Davy of killing *you!*"

While David hurried below in search of Jasper's Sunday outfit, the captain busied himself in peeling from the stranger's slender limbs the cold and dripping garments which had clothed them. A pair of black pantaloons, a short black jacket, somewhat the worse for wear, a white shirt unbuttoned at the neck, and the customary quantity of underlinen completed their number, and by the time that David arrived with the necessary covering, the unknown youth lay naked and shivering in the chilly wind, protesting feebly against the captain's forcible removal of his property.

"Please be careful of the books; I do entreat you to be careful of Keats and Sophocles," he cried faintly, but the captain heeded him not at all, and proceeded calmly upon his course, stripping Jasper's body and methodically reclothing it in the short black jacket and the shabby pantaloons.

"Never saw such a pair of fools as you two boys in all my born days," he grunted contemptuously, seeing David's averted face and the stranger's wild and stag-like eyes shaded by a thin cold hand, and hearing their united murmurs of horror and surprise. "Are you scared of poor Jasper's dead corpse, David Butternut, you that had the guts to strike him down, and are you, my lad, who lately faced the raging ocean without particular signs of fear, hiding your eyes from a mere harmless murdered body? For shame, I say to both of you; your conduct's unworthy of men and sailors. Turn to, and help me, David, for Jasper's a damned dead weight to heave over, I can tell you."

At last, and without the aid of his young companions, the captain's self-imposed duty was completed, and, lifting Jasper's corpse in his mighty arms, he carried it to the rail, and balanced it there above the turbulent and racing sea.

"My Keats, my Sophocles!" cried the stranger in an agonized whisper. "Oh, I do beg of you not to throw my Sophocles into the ocean!" His large blue eyes were full of tears.

"He means the books he has in his pockets, sir," explained David. "Leastways, they're Jasper's pockets now, I suppose, but the books belong to the stranger, and I can see he sets great store by them."

"I can't be bothered with no books!" shouted the captain with magnificent scorn. "Now David, I'm going to shove your messmate overboard, and if you want to bid him good-bye, here's your last chance. Well, I can't stand here all night waiting for you to make up your mind, my lad; here goes, Jasper Cross, and may the Lord have mercy upon your soul!"

The body descended through the darkness into the whirling pit of the waters, and its phosphorescent track was a moment visible and then no more. The captain and David removed their caps; the stranger closed his eyes and seemed to meditate or pray.

"I could find it in my heart to desire for this poor fellow's mortal remains a more classic dignity of requiem," he said at length with some emotion. "And yet is it not, after all, singularly fitting that a sailor's clay should be thus committed to the vaulted caverns of the crystal wave? I have frequently observed . . ."

"And I have frequently observed that you young rascals talk too much," said the captain shortly. "Moreover, you're shivering fit to shake your teeth out, and if David doesn't hustle you into those dry warm clothes you'll take your death of cold. Now, Davy, look alive, and let's see how this lad appears in a proper outfit. Rub him down a bit with this here bandanna, and button him up smart in them Sunday togs, and I dare say he'll be a decent enough looking chap when you've done with him."

4

THE storm had by now somewhat abated, and an occasional gleam of tarnished moonlight lit the swift procession of the clouds. By this illumination, and by the rays of the larboard lantern, David Butternut noticed with compassion the stranger's pallor and evident exhaustion, and with the utmost neatness and dispatch he proceeded to clothe him in the comfortable garments from Jasper's locker, and to chafe his frozen hands into a condition distantly resembling warmth.

"When you've finished, bring him along to my cabin," called the captain, disappearing down the deck. "Get the cook to dry Jasper's old clothes in the galley, and they'll do him for every-day. I'll see that he gets a drop of hot grog from the steward, for he looks as if he needed it."

"How do you feel now, stranger?" asked David solicitously when the two found themselves alone.

"Oh, I shall do very well, I think," returned the other evasively, as if unwilling to be led into complaint. "I shall probably be none the worse for my experience, after a crust of bread and a good night's sleep. But tell me, David, was Jasper a wicked man?"

"Not what you'd really call wicked," replied David charitably. "He was a queer mixture, was Jasper, with a face like a choirboy's, half the time, and half the time like a devil's; with beautiful manners, gentleman's manners, and no book-learning at all, savage and revengeful, in a way of speaking, and yet with a soft heart for any woman as cared to fool him; free with his money, when he had any, and a good enough friend when he was sober. But he was hardly ever sober," added David with a burst of honesty, " and he was so ignorant, stranger, if you'll credit me, that he couldn't hardly write his own name. Funny, to think of your books in poor old Jasper's pockets, down there where even the great fishes ain't got no eyes! "

The stranger shuddered a little, but David went on unheeding, driven by a painful excitement into the appeasement of confession.

" 'Twas his craze for women killed him in the end, you might say, though I suppose I killed him right enough with this fist of mine, only I never meant for to do it, I'll swear on a stack of Bibles — and God strike me dead if I'd lie to a friend, a kind friend like you, and you believe me, don't you, Shiloh? "

" What is that curious name by which you have just addressed me, David? " asked the stranger, a look of keen intellectual curiosity lighting his wan countenance.

" Shiloh? Why, Shiloh out of the scriptures, to be sure; 'twas you yourself told me to call you that just before you fainted. Then I knew for certain what I had somehow suspected all along; that you were sent by God to save me from damnation. I can't explain it, but I know your coming has made it all fair and square about Jasper, and because I raised you up out of the devouring sea I'm no longer a murderer, praise be to heaven! "

" But who was Shiloh? " persisted the unknown. " I seem to have encountered the word repeatedly during my career; Byron called me Shiloh before he called me the Snake, and I know of course that the name occurs with frequency in the Scriptures; but I retain a strong impression that Shiloh is a place rather than a person."

" Sometimes it's a place right enough," David admitted. " But don't you remember the chapter in Genesis where old Jacob is a-scolding of his sons, and almighty mean the old man is to some of them, how he says as the sceptre shall not depart from Judah until Shiloh come? That's you, stranger, I reckon, and you knew

13

it yourself a while ago, but has most likely forgotten it on account
of being cold and tired and sorrowful. Come with me now, Shiloh,
my dear friend Shiloh that has saved my soul, and I will find you
food and a place to sleep, and to-morrow I will teach you to be a
sailor."

So saying, he very tenderly assisted the stranger to rise, and
the two young men stood face to face in the intermittent moonlight, and tall and slender as twin pillars of some temple of the
sea. The stranger swayed a little, but David stood strong as stone,
and where the other's blowing hair was darkness shot with silver,
David's was close and curly like a golden cap, and where the
other was pale, David was ruddy like his namesake, and his blue
eyes met the wilder, wider eyes with infinite humility and trust.

"Just about my height, you are," said David happily. "And
now catch a-hold of my arm, and come along to the captain's
cabin for a nice glass of hot grog."

Captain Ffoulkastle looked up with frank curiosity as the two
companions knocked and entered. Without a word he waved his
hand towards a locker, where they seated themselves side by side
in attitudes of respectful attention and courteous patience. He
handed the stranger a large glass of steaming rum punch, which
the young man regarded silently and with apparent disapproval.

"Drink it up, son," said the captain in an authoritative voice.
"Orders is orders aboard the *Witch of the West,* and you're ordered to drink that toddy without making any ungrateful faces.
Don't be dainty, but get it under your belt double quick; now,
then, down she goes with a yo-heave-ho, my hearty!"

The stranger obeyed, swallowed the scalding drink with an
expression of acute agony, and leaned back rather limply against
the panelling, exhausted by the unnatural effort.

"Take the glass from him, Davy; I don't want it broken," said
the captain. "Pour yourself a nip from that jug on the table, and
then go out on deck and wait there until I call you. I've got this
Jasper business to attend to with our young friend here, and perhaps it might embarrass you a bit; also he may have family affairs
to discuss with me, and for that we need privacy. Run along, and
don't sit there gaping like a stuck pig."

David, his eyes fixed admiringly upon the stranger's dreaming countenance, sidled slowly from the cabin, closing the door cautiously behind him, and the captain turned to his guest with a brisk and kindly question.

5

TEN minutes later, Captain Ffoulkastle realized with sincere regret that he was shouting the fiftieth of these questions, briskly indeed, but not at all kindly, into the pale and distressed visage of the weary and bewildered unknown, who remained unknown in spite of a number of polite, painstaking answers with which he had met the captain's inquiry. The poor young man had visibly reached the end of his powers, and his sad self-command was the more surprising inasmuch as he looked quite ready to weep, to faint, or to expire in the event of further confusion; yet, withal, his dignity remained somehow unimpaired.

" Oh, hell," cried the captain at length. " You're plumb worn out, and so am I, and all to no purpose so far as sense is concerned. It comes to this, in the main: you say you're so and so, and frankly, I don't believe you, but even if it were true — and mind, I'm not admitting that it is — I couldn't put back into the port of Leghorn for all the poets in Christendom, nor for all the philosophers in heathen parts, nor for all the wives and children in Italy. Understand that, and take it as final; my first and only duty is to the owners of this ship, and they're already sick of waiting for a clipper that's been as slow as molasses in January. So back to Boston we must go, and you must come along with us, working your passage as best you can, since you have no money, and submitting yourself to my discipline as I think fit. Davy will help you; he's a good-hearted boy, but it's a hard life, and you must make up your mind to it."

" It is not the hardships which I anticipate with dread," said the stranger gently. " It is rather the thought of the suspense and terror that my absence must engender in the hearts of my loved ones, and my own extreme anxiety as to the fate of my friend Edward, under which my spirit sinks to desolation."

" As to the fate of your friend Edward," said the captain with

15

inexorable firmness, " you may well feel regret, but anxiety is unnecessary; by now he is comfortably drowned. The same thing applies to this sailor chap, Vivian; I have already told you that your escape was a damned miracle, and there isn't one chance in a million that the others were snatched up by any similar providence. Be a sensible lad, now, and accept the plain truth from a man old enough to be your father; the others are dead, and you're alive, and bloody lucky, if you ask me, so give thanks to God for his manifold mercies and be prepared to haul on a rope with a stout heart and a strong pair of hands."

The stranger stared at his slender hands, which were sufficiently sunburnt and sinewy to have attracted the captain's favourable attention; then, with something very like a stifled sob, he covered his stricken face and leaned mute and trembling against the wall.

" How can I believe that Edward is dead? " he demanded presently, in a broken voice. " He, the best and bravest of men, the kindest, cheerfulest creature under the broad sky? Such an one should never pasture the abhorrèd worm . . ."

" It's not worms, but fishes, as will make a meal of him," said the captain consolingly. " And now, to turn to brighter subjects, how about this here murder business? The case stands, roughly, like this: here's Davy, a good boy if a bit hasty, has killed Jasper by means of a clip on the head, not meaning for to do it, but along of impetuosity and a heavy fist, as you might say. Jasper got ugly back in Leghorn, because Dave give a coral necklace or some such fal-lal to a young Eyetalian girl with whom he was keeping company, for Jasper was a brass sarpent with the women, and he'd had his weather eye on this little craft ever since the day he landed. But she preferred master Dave, and they walked out together very nice and proper every Sunday afternoon, quite as if the piazza had been Boston Common, and she took him round to supper with her folks, and everything was all serene. Until last night, that is, when Jasper picked a quarrel with David just as he and his girl were coming out of one of these popish churches, and the boys went at it hammer and tongs, and the Eyetalians begin to chatter like monkeys, and a couple of women had hysterics, and then before you could say Jack Robinson there was a crowd of these little gibbering policemen on the scene, and I had hard work getting my lads back on board without a spell of jail for one or both of them. I knew Dave was fighting mad, but Jasper seemed cool enough until six o'clock this evening, jest as we were beating out of the harbour in the dusk; suddenly he was on top of young David like a tiger cat, and I saw the glitter of one of them thin Tuscan knives as he whipped it out of his pocket and struck to kill. I'll swear to my dying day that Jasper struck to kill, and Dave hit back at him in honest self-defence, as you or I might do, stranger, if six inches of steel was a-tickling of our ribs. Well, sir, the blow cracked Jasper's head like a bloody walnut-shell, and there he laid on the deck, deader'n mutton, and there warn't nothing to do about it, as I could see, and I says to the boys, 'Swab down the deck, and straighten out Jasper,' but just then the storm come up, and I reckon you know the rest as well as I do."

6

"Certainly the sympathies of any just and virtuous person must be entirely with David," said the stranger meditatively. He had perfectly recovered his composure, and had listened with a kindling glance and a brightening cheek to the captain's recital. Seen thus, with the swaying radiance of the lamp dispersed over his countenance, he appeared to be about twenty-five years old, very slim and graceful, with a deceptive air of delicacy veiling an uncommonly strong and active body.

"Clipper-built, or I'm a flying Dutchman," said the captain to himself with satisfaction. "Worth any two of these broad-beamed fellows ballasted with too many pounds of plum-duff."

The stranger's face was now illuminated by a pure healthy colour, and a fine sunburn somewhat obscured the inherent transparency of his complexion. He wore the unmistakable air of one who has lived companioned by the elements, and his dark blue eyes had the clarity and brilliance of a sea-gull's gaze.

"Pretty coat of tan he's got," said the captain to himself with increasing approval. "And sailor's eyes; sailor's eyes if ever I seen any."

The Orphan Angel

" Now David Butternut," the captain continued aloud, " runs considerable risk of being hanged unless you'll consent to my proposal. Briefly, the plan is this: that you should try your luck with the rest of the boys for the remainder of the voyage, and that you should land in Boston in the character of Jasper Cross for the simple purpose of saving Davy's neck. After the port authorities are squared, there's no need for you to hang around any longer, and you can ship for Leghorn on the first ship that offers, or take passage like a fine gentleman if you can find the money. If you can't, you'll be a fairly able seaman by that time, and can always get a berth on your merits, and my recommendation. By this means, my lad, you'll be rescuing a comrade from a disgraceful death, and at the same time earning an honest living. Don't forget, either," added the captain impressively, " that David has already rescued you from death by drowning; seems to me that the least you can do in return is to be obliging, and help him out of this very tight hole in which he finds himself, which is neither more nor less than the hangman's noose, my hearty."

" Since you plead so eloquently for this excellent young man, I know not how to refuse your humane request," answered the stranger with an air of mild perplexity. " Yet the circumstance of a voyage to the New World at this particular moment may conceivably embarrass my future, as it certainly complicates my present state. Nevertheless I should be overcome with humiliation, in withholding from David the brotherly aid which on his part was so generously expended in the preservation of my life; I therefore cannot longer hesitate in consenting to your proposal, and here is my hand upon the bargain."

" Then you'll do it, and keep mum? " said the captain in some confusion, feeling himself adrift in a tidal wave of words. At the same time he took rather gingerly into his own broad palm the other's outstretched hand, examining its nervous shape and flexible sinews with professional interest.

" Stick these arms of yours up to their elbows in a tar-bucket, and they'll look more like it," he said with a judicial squint. " Still, it's done a lot for you, even the make-believe business of navigating that pretty toy which has just capsized. Crank as an egg-shell, she must have been, but at least her ropes have hardened your hands into a proper sailor's, my lad, and I reckon you'll be a real addition to the starboard watch."

"I trust so, indeed," the stranger replied politely. "But one stipulation I must make before undertaking my duties: that you will regard the relinquishment of my will to yours as a voluntary act, honourably based upon a desire to benefit a fellow-being, and not merely as the compliant submission of a coward and a weakling. Superior strength shall never daunt the independence of my spirit — while tyranny . . ."

"Easy now with that there talk of tyranny, my young cockerel," said the captain with good-humoured authority. "There ain't no tyranny aboard the *Witch of the West*, so long as you obey orders and keep a civil tongue in your head. Do your duty like a man, and you'll fare well enough; so long as we pull together, you'll find me a clever fellow, and if the second mate is a bit rough in his methods sometimes, you'll live to thank him for his trouble one of these days. Now, boy, I'm going to call Davy; have you anything more to say to me?"

"Only this: that since you doubt my identity I should infinitely prefer to be addressed by some name other than my own," said the stranger softly and rather haughtily. "I suggest therefore that I be known as Shiloh; David already believes that such is my true title, and the word pleases me with its curious antique music. And now, Captain Ffoulkastle, I have the honour to bid you a very good night, and to assure you of my devotion to the welfare of this noble vessel, of my loyalty to yourself, and of my disinterested friendship for David; farewell."

Shiloh, for thus must our narrative continue to know him, rose to his feet upon the completion of this speech, bowed slightly, and then, assuming an attitude of dignified detachment, stood with folded arms awaiting the captain's further commands. He looked very tall under the low beams of the cabin, very slim and strange and foreign to the scene, with his preposterous elegance, his romantic grace, and the aristocratic attenuation of his frame. At the same time, he wore the indubitable air of an athlete; even the captain's critical gaze granted him muscle and bone, agility and strength and lightning quickness of the faculties. His face was bronzed, save where the exceeding whiteness of the forehead betrayed itself under the tumbled hair, whose dark eccentric exuberance was flecked with silver.

"Queer, about his hair," thought the captain. "For the lad don't look a day over twenty-five. But it's his eyes that make me wonder; sailor's eyes, and something more that I can't rightly recollect; seems as if I'd dreamed about them, mebbe, or heard tell of them in a tale."

"Davy," he called aloud; and then to Shiloh, "Well, my lad; so long; Davy will look out for you." Moved by a sudden impulse of pity, he laid his great hand familiarly on the stranger's shoulder. "Don't be downhearted, boy; you'll see the Fortezza Vecchia again before six months are out."

"Perhaps," said Shiloh, as one who dreams a dream, and that intolerably sad, "perhaps you are right; who shall foretell the future? To my own eyes it is shadowed; I am no prophet, but my heart is singularly shaken by foreboding, and my mind is troubled. Yet I say again to you, perhaps you may be right, for doubtless you are wiser than I, and I am very tired."

7

"You'll do now, Shiloh; you haven't at all the look of a green hand," said David a few moments later, giving a conjuring and peculiar twist to his friend's black silk neckerchief. "We must manage to shear away some of those crazy locks of yours, but otherwise you've a decent cut to your jib, and them things of Jasper's fits you like a second skin."

Indeed, David Butternut might well feel proud of his handiwork, for he had contrived to create the illusion of custom in Shiloh's appearance; the trousers, belted tightly about the narrow loins, and hanging loose and baggy around the feet, the checked shirt negligently ample, the low-crowned varnished hat, shiny and black, with half a fathom of black ribbon falling over the left eye, all these details confessed the master's touch in their arrangement.

"Shove your hat a mite farther to the back of your head, son, and we'll go below," said David with lively satisfaction.

"David, have you ever seen an albatross, and have you read

Western Wave

The Ancient Mariner? " asked Shiloh as they proceeded to the hatchway. " I have called Coleridge a hooded eagle among blinking owls, but perhaps he is rather . . ."

" Shiloh, for pity's sake stow that talk about reading until we're alone," whispered David in desperation. " There's some of the boys ain't never learned to read, and they'll think as you're putting on lugs. Of course I seen lots of albatross when I was rounding the Cape, but it don't do to mention them silly things too much on shipboard. As for ancient mariners, you're a-going to meet old Zebulun Cary in a minute, and he's so ancient that they say he's got barnacles growing on his . . ."

But before David could conclude this curious exposition of natural science, the two had reached the steerage, where the starboard watch slept. It was now past eight o'clock and, the second of the dog-watches being over, the men were preparing for rest. There were no berths in the steerage, and very little light; the scene was one of indescribable confusion to any unaccustomed eyes. Mattresses, chests, blankets, and boots seemed mixed inextricably upon the tilting floor, with coils of rigging, spare sails, and ship stores not yet stowed away. A pervasive fragrance of bilge-water clogged the brain as the darkness obscured the vision, and the low growling murmur of speech was equally confusing to the senses. David had a sudden misgiving; he glanced anxiously at Shiloh, but in the heavy twilight the stranger's face was admirably composed and clear. Curiosity, and the eager friendliness of simple good breeding, informed his luminous gaze and the quick question of his smile.

" It's all right," said David immediately, as much to himself as to the other. " And now, Shiloh, you take my mattress for the present; this roll of canvas will do for me. Mates, this is Shiloh, that you seen me fish out of the water a while ago; he's come to take Jasper's place in the starboard watch. I'm going up to the galley to get him a mug of tea and molasses and a hunk of bread, for I reckon he's almighty hungry; say a word to him, boys, to make him feel at home, for he come damn near to laying down to-night along with the bones of poor drowned sailors in the depth of the sea, and mebbe he feels sort of strange and lonely-like among us."

21

The Orphan Angel

The sailors subjected Shiloh to a prolonged scrutiny, in which inquisitive wonder was mingled with suspicion and doubt; nevertheless one or two of them made shift to address him in kindly rallying tones, and even to slap him on the back with rough jocularity. These advances he accepted in a spirit of happy simplicity; he was palpably both tired and hungry, and he yawned frequently and rubbed his eyes with a childlike lack of self-consciousness, yet all the while he was alert and shining with a sympathetic interest in his queer surroundings. He talked little, but when he did he was frank and outspoken like a well-conditioned boy, and presently the sailors perceived his essential good-will, and smiled at him in spite of themselves.

" Not a bad youngster; better than Jasper, if you ask me," said old Zebulun Cary, and a subtle spirit of peace pervaded the steerage, warming poor Shiloh's soul as the hot tea was even then warming his vitals.

" What very excellent tea, and what truly magnificent bread you have brought me, David," he said at last. " Thank you for the loan of your case-knife, but I do not believe I shall require any of Mr. Cary's plug tobacco. And do you tell me that this beverage owes its superior flavour to the introduction of molasses? I must remember that, I must indeed. Water bewitched, I perceive Mr. Cary calls it; a charming name, and one most germane to my fancy! But I must no longer detain you from your slumbers; I trust that you will not stand on ceremony, and as I am myself amazingly sleepy, perhaps I had better bid you all good-night. Good-night, my best David, and a thousand thanks for your unprecedented kindness. For my own part, I was never more comfortable in my life, and I feel sure that the morning will discover me completely restored. Good-night; no, I would not dream of taking your other blanket, David; no, not on any account. Good-night, good-night to you all."

" Does the poor innocent imagine that he's going to be let to sleep the long night through without a hail? " inquired old Zebulun Cary of David. " I fear he's got some sharp surprises coming to him, along of Mister Murdoch and what-not. Pity he's not in the larboard watch, for the chief mate's a kindly gentleman and a true sailor, but Murdoch's a different story, and this lad's just the

22

sort of high-mettled youngster he loves to come it over. Did you warn Shiloh, David, or is he still unsuspecting-like as the babe unborn? God knows he looks a perfect infant a-laying there! "

" Shiloh's kind of worn-out at present, what with being drowned and everything," said David with an almost paternal pride, " and of course he doesn't look very old, I'll allow, but he's quick and strong as they make 'em; I seen him stripped, and I do assure you, Zebulun, he's like a young Indian brave from the primeval forest. Mister Murdoch, with his precious belaying-pin, had better not try any of his tricks on Shiloh, or he may find he's roused a proper wildcat. Yes, sir, Shiloh's an uncommon sort of fellow; you can see that with half an eye. What's more, the cap'n said as how he could sleep till seven bells in the morning, and there ain't nobody going to wake him while I'm around, not all the Mister Murdochs this side of hell! "

" Easy now, Davy; don't get excited," the old man replied soothingly. " Cap'n's orders is cap'n's orders, and Murdoch's not the kind of fool to dispute 'em. He'll leave Shiloh sleep till morning, I make no doubt, and then have his revenge subtle-like and sly with a kick in the ribs or some such deviltry. I advise you, lad, to hold hard and steer keerfully, and not be asking for trouble; you'll be a better friend to Shiloh in so doing. Oh, you young stripling limbs of Satan are altogether too rash and mutinous by nature, too prone to contention and revolt, for a peaceful man like me! Now for God's sake let me get a mite of rest, and quit tucking up Shiloh like a blooming baby; you'll only wake him, and that would be a pity, seeing how tired he is."

" I don't think he'll wake," said David, preparing for repose. " He must have had an almighty lot of liquor, first and last, before the cap'n and I were finished with him, and he has the look of a very sound sleeper."

So saying, he turned upon his side, and closed his eyes, but slumber eluded him, and against the darkness the stranger's countenance still floated like a drowning star. The roll of canvas under his head was hard enough, and his thick woolen garments were clammy with salt and spray, but David, in the admirable vigour of his blood, remained profoundly indifferent to these things. Rather he was disturbed by a vague melancholy abnormal to his mind, a hint, an evasive whisper of despair. He knew with the clarity of intense conviction that Shiloh's presence was his own release from guilt, that Shiloh's life atoned obliquely for another's murder, and that in saving Shiloh he was himself delivered from a deeper annihilation of the soul. Now suddenly he felt that perhaps he had been less than kind in his insistence, since Shiloh was so very tired.

" Seems lunatic and outlandish, but I keep on asking of myself if he wouldn't of rather drowned," whispered David in the darkness. " He was so peaceful, and I made him come to me; I cried to him to come, and he heard me. Well, mebbe I've done wrong; mebbe by now he'd be in some high gold house in heaven, laying asleep between fine white linen sheets, with the moon and the morning stars singing together outside the window like birds upon a bough. Mebbe I've asked too much of him, mebbe life'll be too hard for him to bear. But I'll try to make it up to him; I'll do my level best; I'll be like one of these here faithful dogs you hear of, running at his side through the world, loving to him, but fierce as a wolf to his enemies. And that," said David with his eyes on the dim radiance of Shiloh's forehead, " and that, I reckon, is what they call a vow."

Afterwards he slept, until the cry of " All starbowlines ahoy! Eight bells there below; do you hear the news? " roused him from dedicated and heroic dreams to stagger up on deck with the rest of the starboard watch. The skies were clear as black crystal now, and the toppling waves slid by in glassy brightness. David drank the cool winds as if they had been the waters of some airy spring, and the taut ropes wetted with spray quivered under his hand like the sinews of a flying horse, winged and monstrous and unreasonable, which sprang ever towards the west along a smooth white valley of the sea.

II

PURE ANTICIPATED COGNITION

" Seems as if I'd like to climb a hill, along about moonrise to-night, and see the earth spread out below me," said David to Shiloh upon the last evening of the voyage. It was a tranquil twilight hour, and the crew were sitting on the windlass or lying comfortably on the forecastle, smoking, singing, and telling curious yarns. A violet sky contained a few frosty stars, and from the quarter-deck the rhythmic footsteps of the captain and the first mate sounded small and far-away upon the measureless quiet of the atmosphere.

The two friends were momentarily occupied with a large tin pot of tea and a kid of salt beef, and the calm of appeased hunger had lately descended over their spirits like a pleasant cloud. David's ingenuous face wore a look of the liveliest satisfaction, and ever and anon he turned his curly head to stare proudly at his companion, whose long slender limbs were disposed in an attitude of easy grace upon the forecastle's weather side.

" It certainly does beat all, the way you've looked up aboard ship," remarked David parenthetically. " I remember when I first seen you, Shiloh, I thought as how you was sort of an unearthly critter, but now there ain't none of us can touch you for nimbleness and spunk. To see you on a yard I'd swear you'd been bred to the trade of knotting a reef-point, and you swing down them

25

The Orphan Angel

shrouds and back-stays like a blooming monkey. And my stars, how the victuals seem to suit you, Shiloh; you're hard as hickory and cat-gut, and brown as a copper penny! Cap'n says . . ." continued David boastfully, but Shiloh stopped him with a brotherly hand upon his arm, and David saw that the other was blushing furiously under the clear bronze colour of his cheek.

"Really, David, your partiality is so kind that it overwhelms me with a sense of my profound unworthiness," said Shiloh, laughing. "You must not praise me so warmly, my dear friend; your admiration is far in excess of my modest capabilities. Yet it is true that I have succeeded beyond my most sanguine anticipations in performing my duties on shipboard, and I have rarely experienced a keener joy than in the reefing of the fore-topsail during the last storm. The frenzied elements appeared obedient to my hand, and in the howling of the gale I heard the voice of a baffled host of kings. But I fear I have interrupted you, David; pray go on with your meditation upon mountain-peaks."

"Oh, I was just saying as how I'd like to climb a hill to-night, and watch the moon rise over the spread-out land," said David rather shyly. "You see, Shiloh, I was born down in Maine, and there's plenty of hills in them parts, sightly places, standing tall above the pine-trees. Sometimes I don't hardly feel that I was meant to sail the seas; I get so homesick for the hills, and I asks myself: *David, what are you doing on this lonesome waste of waters?* Shiloh, if you would come with me, I believe I'd go stepping westward, to the great mountains that I've heard tell of ever since I was a child."

"David, do you know that you have unconsciously quoted Wordsworth?" asked Shiloh eagerly. "That is a most interesting example of a naturally poetic impulse informing a simple mind. Now if you would only try your skill at composing even the least elaborate hymn to Liberty, I feel sure you would be miraculously repaid. Your noble country must inevitably inspire such vehement longing to express in words. . . . But forgive me, I perceive that I am boring you with my enthusiasms. We were speaking of the hills."

"Yes, we were speaking of the hills, and I was wishing that you'd come with me to climb them," cried David earnestly.

Pure Anticipated Cognition

"Wouldn't you admire to be a pioneer, Shiloh, like that wonderful and famous old codger Colonel Boone, and seek out strange places full of wild bears and buffaloes and mountain lions, and kill 'em with your naked hands, mebbe, and trap the eagles, and hunt the savages? I don't want you to think me downright bloodthirsty," said David timidly, "but ain't you ever sort of hankered after them things, Shiloh?"

"Assuredly I have desired these things, David," said Shiloh with his customary gentleness. "I love all waste and solitary places, as I have affirmed ere this; power dwells apart in its tranquillity. Could you have come with me to the vale of Chamounix, to behold Mont Blanc . . . ! But enough; we will have adventures wilder, holier even than this. Bear with me, my friend, for a little while, and we will perform prodigies together."

"Shiloh," said David suddenly, in an agitated whisper, "there's something that I feel I'm bound to tell you; something that troubles me turrible at times. I hadn't exactly meant to tell you, Shiloh, you being so good and kind to me, and I not wanting to bother you with foolishness. But it's this, Shiloh: Jasper had a twin sister."

Shiloh turned his large blue eyes towards David with a look of mild surprise, for the lad's voice had broken upon the words, and an expression of superstitious fear convulsed his lips and brow.

"A twin sister!" and "Jasper!" cried Shiloh blankly. Watching David's face, his own grew rather pale, and his gaze widened as upon a vision and a mystery.

"Yes, Shiloh; Jasper's sister," David answered slowly, staring into the other's eyes. "And I feel in my bones a most powerful conviction that I must go west to rescue her; it's the least I can do for poor old Jasper."

"But is she in any imminent peril?" inquired Shiloh, an expiring gleam of worldly wisdom contending with the chivalric fever of his mind.

"Well, I don't know exactly as you'd call it peril," said David candidly. "But I'm sure she's in constant danger of being stolen by the Indians, and then of course she's almighty poor; poverty-stricken and forlorn. The girl's an orphan, too, and with her

27

brother dead and done for, I can't help feeling that she's sort of
unfortunate. Mebbe I'm too soft-hearted, but the thought of that
girl has haunted my dreams, Shiloh, and I've about made up my
mind to wander out west in search of her."

"But don't you know where to look for this interesting young
creature, David?" asked Shiloh in amazement. "To employ a
homely simile, would not your quest resemble the hunting of a
bright silver needle in a savage subfuscated haystack? By what
shining clue do you propose to unravel this riddle?"

"Funny, your calling her a silver needle," David commented
thoughtfully. "Because that's the name that Jasper used to give
her: Silver. It's a queer name, and I reckon she's a queer girl;
more like a sperrit than a mortal woman. But beautiful; Jasper
always said she was very beautiful. He loved his sister, did poor
old Jasper, and he never showed me her portrait without tears in
them angry eyes of his, and a shake in his voice."

"Silver, Silver, a silver sister in a valley alone," repeated Shiloh
dreamily, his eyes upon the arch of the evening sky.

"I don't think she lives in a valley; Jasper always spoke of
mountains. But I know her name was written on the back of her
portrait, and mebbe it tells where she lives too; I'll look for it in
Jasper's ditty-box."

David rose to his feet and hurried toward the steerage, but
Shiloh appeared indifferent to his errand; indeed it is doubtful
whether or not he had remarked his friend's departure. He lay
very still, his slender hands clasped behind his head, his gaze profoundly fixed upon the stars. At intervals he murmured to himself the name of Jasper's sister. "Silver, Silver," said Shiloh to
his own heart, whispering the word aloud like an hypnotic
incantation.

The violet sky, withdrawn as it darkened, was pierced now
by innumerable stars, its purity of colour holding an even in-
tenser purity of light, so that the luminous distance trembled like
water, and was no more stable than the sea; yet in the moving,
wavering brightness was composure, and the clear dignity of
peace. This brightness and tranquillity fell from the air like dew,
and echoed in the absence of any sound, to lie cool and musical
upon Shiloh's spirit.

Pure Anticipated Cognition

2

PRESENTLY David returned panting, a little parcel clutched tightly in his sunburnt hand, and the close gold rings of his hair dishevelled by haste.

"Here it is!" he cried triumphantly. "I found it between a pack of cards and a velvet prayer-book, laying next to Jasper's big Spanish pistol. All that truck is just like Jasper, a crazy mixture of good and bad, but here's the little portrait right enough; and now tell me what you think of Silver, Shiloh, and whether or not I had better go in search of the girl."

Shiloh took the little object carefully in his slim brown fingers; he regarded it with a rapt and dreaming attention while unfolding the crimson handkerchief and opening the shagreen case. Within, the portrait lay revealed; he stared at it in silence, his eyes large and preternaturally radiant in the starlight.

"Silver," he said again, very gently, "must we go in search of you, Silver? What do you say, *animula, vagula, blandula,* little soul like a cloud, like a feather?"

The starlight was no more than twilight, and the ivory oval upon Shiloh's palm glimmered uncertainly, as if faintly lit with inner phosphorescence. The pictured face was small and pale, the shining hair was silvery pale, the eyes alone were full of a soft darkness, like the patterned eyes upon the wings of moths.

"You see, David," said Shiloh with a curious smile, "Silver has told me that we must come and find her; she has told me with her eyes, but very plainly, and I dare not disobey."

"Oh, Shiloh, that's what I've been a-hoping all along, only I dassn't ask you myself, it seemed so kind of unreasonable! But if you come too, we'll be bound to find her, I'm certain sure of that, and the poor girl will welcome you like a brother, you being the dead spit of Jasper, and him no more. Not but what you're far finer and stranger than Jasper, somehow, but with a sister's partiality she may be forgiven for taking note of the likeness. Yes, it'll be a wonderful happy day for Silver when you ride out of the east on a wild pony, with your eyes like saucers of blue sea-water and your hair like a capful of north wind. Oh, I know I'm talking kind of crazy; forgive me, Shiloh, but I'm so pleased that I reckon I'm nearly out of my mind, and I can't keep a-hold of the sense of what I'm saying! "

Indeed, the honest fellow's eyes were full of tears, and he wrung Shiloh's hand with fervent and tempestuous joy. Shiloh sat up, restored the portrait to its case, and, wrapping it in the crimson silk handkerchief, slipped it into his own pocket.

" Very well," he pronounced calmly, " that is quite settled, then; we travel west in search of Silver. I have other duties, other dear and necessary devoirs to perform, but this comes first, as it is the most poignant and burning cry of all. By the eloquent patience of those lips, by the deep entreaty of those eyes, I swear that I will come. Silver, do you hear me, even across the world? I swear that I will come."

He ceased, and thereafter was silent for so long a time that David grew restless, teased by a thousand questions of how and when and where, and longing for the warm reality of words. Nevertheless the boy preserved a laudable peace, out of respect for Shiloh's hushed and exalted countenance and the enchanted fire of his eyes.

It grew darker; eight bells were struck, the clear notes dividing the quiet atmosphere with measured cadences. The log was hove, the wheel relieved, and the other men of the starboard watch went below, but still Shiloh lay upon the forecastle, his eyes importuning the stars, and in each of his eyes a fire brighter than a star was pointed and apparent.

"Shiloh," said David at last, " Shiloh, didn't you hear the watch going below? It's your trick at the wheel to-night, Shiloh, and you ought to get some rest while there's time. Furthermore, if we land to-morrow there'll be an almighty lot to do, and we've a long journey ahead of us, a long journey into the west. Better come below, Shiloh, and try to sleep."

Shiloh rose quickly and noiselessly, and with admirable docility followed David to the hatchway. He ran his long fingers through his blowing locks, lifting his face to the heavens with a look half bewildered, half entranced.

Pure Anticipated Cognition

" Do you really believe that we shall land to-morrow, Davy? "
he asked in a voice of wonder.

" I do," said David decidedly, " unless Boston has taken a
running start and jumped back into the tall timber. Yes, we'll see
the three hills by to-morrow at sundown, and I'll show you the
sights of the town, and we'll eat a proper meal of good fresh beef
and onions and apple pie and cheese, washed down with punch
and Philadelphia porter. That's something to hearten your innards, my boy, after all these weeks of scouse and biscuit."

" David," said Shiloh with profound solemnity, " David, I
wish to ask you an important question." His bright eyes transfixed the other with a piercing scrutiny.

" Ask away, Shiloh," replied David valiantly. " You know I
ain't so very learned in history and such-like subjects, but I know
Boston was discovered from the Indians by Cap'n John Smith,
and I've heard tell of the tea-party and Paul Revere, and I visited
the Old South Church and two distilleries last time I landed. I
reckon I have a pretty fair idea of the town, and I'll answer you
honest to the best of my powers."

" David," said Shiloh with an increased solemnity, and his
words were audibly shaken by some obscure emotion, " David,
tell me only this: do you believe we shall be able to buy penny
buns in Boston? "

3

NEXT day the *Witch of the West* passed Castle Island as the sun
was setting, thus terminating a swift and prosperous voyage with
peculiar fitness, along a smooth broad path of molten gold. Shiloh
sniffed the mingled fragrance of the land with rapture; he
smelled freedom in the abstract, and more particularly his romantic senses detected spices from the India Wharf, while his fastidi-
ousness noted soap and candles from Boston Pier and his country-
bred nose was aware of the distant aroma of new-mown hay.
As for his eyes, they were full to overflowing of new visions
and revelations, so much so indeed that they spilled a little
of their brightness in tears upon the altar of liberty, and the

gilded pine-cone crowning the State House dazzled them like a flame.

Later, as the ship lay alongside Hancock's Wharf, her riding-lights yellow against a fine blue dusk, Shiloh and David sat in Captain Ffoulkastle's cabin and shyly discussed the future. With-out, under a constellation of lanterns, the men were already break-ing bulk, for a consignment of candied fruits and Chian claret must reach the hands of a certain Salem merchant on the morrow. Captain Ffoulkastle had been with the owners in their magnifi-cent warehouse on Broad Street, and Shiloh, in the character of Jasper Cross, had casually wandered ashore and supped with David in a waterfront ordinary without attracting a notice more peculiar than that which must inevitably be accorded to any tall young sailor with large and luminous blue eyes. The police had betrayed no interest in him, but several pretty girls in simple calico had gazed upon him kindly, and a benevolent white-haired gentleman had offered him a glass of excellent cider.

Therefore he felt at peace with the whole world; he leaned back against the mahogany panelling of the cabin, his long legs stretched out in front of him, his hands clasped loosely in his lap, his face composed to a delicate mask of pure tranquillity and good will. The captain detected a slight relaxing of discipline in this nonchalant attitude, but Shiloh was so clearly innocent of offence, so friendly and so exquisitely courteous, that it was impossible to find tyrannical or bitter fault with him. David, divided between loyal apprehension and admiring pride, kept glancing from one to the other of his two companions; the captain looked at Shiloh, and Shiloh looked at the ceiling as if it had been hung with stars.

"Well, my lads," said the captain at last, "I'm sorry that I can't dissuade you from this wild-goose chase. Nobody can say as I'm a hard-hearted man, and I feel most tenderly towards Jasper's poor little orphan sister, but you can be of no practical use to the child, not even knowing where she lives, and you'll be wasting precious time over plain foolishness. You young rapscallions should stick to the sea, and not go rampaging over the western prairies, running after a lost girl that neither of you never saw. Davy here's a smart fellow in a gale, and Shiloh has done wonders considering what a green hand he was when he come aboard.

Pure Anticipated Cognition

Now take my advice, and sign on with me for the return voyage. Leghorn's the port for you, Shiloh, if you've got a wife and child down Lerici way."

At these words David emitted a curious hoot of laughter, causing Shiloh to turn to him in mild annoyance and the captain in unconcealed surprise. He blushed, and ducked his head in embarrassment, as the others stared at him.

"Beg pardon, cap'n, and you, Shiloh old friend," he mumbled, "but it always makes me laugh something cruel to think of Shiloh there with a wife and baby. Why, he's only a baby himself in a manner of speaking, for all he says that he's twenty-nine years old, and it don't seem hardly proper for him to be a husband and a father and have all this ballast of duties and sacred obligations, as he names 'em. There he sets as if sweet butter wouldn't melt in his mouth, and he's always pitching me yarns of mud turtles and sarpents and supernatural monsters, and yet he says he has a wife and child; it's plumb ridiculous, and I don't believe him!"

"Nevertheless it is true," said Shiloh with gentle dignity. "It is true, David, although to a boy of twenty-one it may seem strange. At your age I had been already twice a father; a fortnight ago I celebrated my thirtieth birthday amid the profound solitudes of the Atlantic, and these silver locks above my brow may attest my absolute veracity. It grieves me that you should not accept my word, David; but some day you will understand."

David, speechless with shame, held out his hand with a look of imploring apology, and Shiloh took the hand and its amending message with a smile.

"I'm sorry," said Shiloh; "I didn't mean to scold you, David. You see, I am somewhat weary of being taken for a child, since the years have taught me so much of sorrowful wisdom."

"Then, my lad," the captain interpolated briskly, "why don't you apply a bit of that wisdom to the present case? If you keep on this wild western tack you'll be calmly deserting your wife, who you tell me is a lady of breeding and sensibility. How can you reconcile that with your conscience, Christian or no Christian? I was raised a good Calvinist, and never had no dealings with Unitarians nor free-thinkers, so it's hard for me to take your

33

meaning, but why should you think it necessary to run off after this here Silver girl when you have a lawful wedded wife at San Terenzo? "

4

THE DELICATE mask of tranquillity upon Shiloh's face was shattered in an instant; he became very pale, and his brow was troubled above darkened eyes. A singular look of apprehension crept into these eyes, tired, yet painfully alert and brilliant. He had all at once the air of a hunted thing, a wild deer, fragile and untamed, and the brightness of his eyes was amazing.

" I must decline to discuss my domestic affairs with a stranger," he said in a tense contemptuous voice, and as he spoke his whole slight body trembled. Captain Ffoulkastle was surprised to perceive that the boy was both wounded and angry, and forgave him the more readily inasmuch as Shiloh had never before given evidence of either of these regrettable states of mind.

" Steady," said the captain in a warning tone. " I didn't intend to pry into your private life, my lad, but I hate to see you behaving like a fool and a knave without a mouthful of friendly advice from your elders. I know you're a good boy, I might almost say a very good boy; you're brave as a lion in the face of danger, and you've a soft heart for any sort of trouble among your mates; I've watched you, and I know. But you're inclined to be hot-headed and what the schoolmasters call idealistic, and that never did nobody no service," said the captain with a comprehensive sweep of the arm.

" I wonder," said Shiloh softly. He had completely regained his composure, and was at all points his charming self, save for a slight pallor and a fainter shadow upon the eyelids.

" You must understand," he continued with a sweetly reasonable air, " that I have been much persecuted at the hands of authority, and I am therefore unduly sensitive to any hint of despotism. I was mistaken in my resentment, and I entreat your pardon. Touching the matter of my return to Italy, the case is strangely complicated by circumstance, which, being assured of your benevolent intentions, I will here pause to elucidate."

"Shall I go on deck, Shiloh, and leave you and the cap'n alone?" asked David rather miserably, torn between curiosity and the desire to spare his friend at all cost to himself. He was immensely relieved by Shiloh's permission to remain, implicit in a quick gesture of the hand.

"Know, then," said Shiloh to Captain Ffoulkastle, "that my situation is one of peculiar difficulty and peril. I speak not of bodily peril; to that I am indifferent, as you have rightly judged, but of those spiritual dangers and blights which beset the soul upon the slopes of time, and to which I am particularly susceptible. I am not certain," said Shiloh in a shaken voice, "that my wife desires my return."

"Fiddlesticks!" cried the captain, and "Oh, rats!" ejaculated David with the same accord. Indeed, Shiloh's evident grace and distinction, his nervous strength, and the strange deep colour of his eyes rendered the thing incredible. He was too completely the bright embodiment of an ideal to be unwelcome in reality, and both David and the captain rejected the notion with simultaneous scorn.

Shiloh accepted the interruption as the compliment it indubitably was. A sad smile played for an instant about his expressive lips, and his face was grave again.

"Yet it is but too true, my friends," he assured them with gentle melancholy. "Nor is it so unnatural a suspicion as you appear to believe. I am not one profoundly to engage the affections of a feeling heart, I fear, nor has nature bestowed her choicest workmanship upon my form and hue. I have long perceived that my presence was wearisome and my faults offensive to her whom you have named; let us not name her again, but dash the tear from the eye and the memory from the mind of sorrow. My present thought is this: that I should indite a letter to this lady, and dispatch it by the faithful hand of Captain Ffoulkastle, thus insuring its certain and immediate delivery. In less than a month it will be in her possession, when she can come to a decision at leisure and free from the agitations of soul which must inevitably attend my personal reappearance. In a word, I shall permit her to choose, untrammelled by aught save her own desires, between a future of complete independence and one spent by my side amid the austerities of the new world."

"A pretty rough choice for a lady, my lad," the captain replied thoughtfully. "Is your mind entirely easy on this point, taking into consideration the stormy passage, and the foreign land, not to mention Indians and snakes and such vermin as the females never precisely cotton to in America? Because you must remember there's a sight more sows' ears than silk purses west of the Alleghanies."

"My determination is irrevocable," said Shiloh with proud simplicity. "I shall never return to that theatre of tyrannies, the continent of Europe, and my greatest content would be to retire with my wife and child to some cabin in the wilderness or solitary island in the sea, and, utterly deserting all human society, to shut upon our retreat the flood-gates of the world. Nevertheless, as I have said, the decision rests with her; if the die be cast against me, henceforward I must live alone, and devote either to oblivion or to future generations the overflowings of a mind which, timely withdrawn from the contagion, shall be kept fit for no baser object."

"But Shiloh," cried David in honest distress, his heart wrung by the sad nobility of these words and the resignation of the broken voice which pronounced them, "you won't never need to be alone; you'll have me always, and mebbe you'll have Silver too."

"'Tain't likely, far as I can see, that you'll ever find that girl," said the captain with crushing common sense. "But then, it's just as well, what with one thing and another, and you being a married man, and David no more than a silly boy. For silly you are, Davy, to leave this ship that's been more than father and mother to you. and go r'aring and ramping over the earth with this atheistical son of Belial. Oh, I've said he was a good lad, and I'll stick to it that he is, but only look at him there, a-shutting of his eyes — and them sailor's eyes at that — to all save vanity and the chasing of rainbows! I've no patience with neither of you," said the captain explosively, striking the table a resounding blow with his great hairy fist.

"And if I may make so bold," he went on presently, with heavy sarcasm, "I'd like to inquire what provision in money you've made for this poor lady that was unlucky enough to marry you some time back. I suppose you'd thought of that, even in the midst of your precious plots and plans for improving the world."

" Assuredly I had considered that question," Shiloh answered with imperturbable politeness. " And since I perceive your interest to be an unselfish one, unsmirched by vulgar curiosity, I may inform you that I shall suggest in my letter the simplest of all solutions: namely, that my own income be transferred to my wife in the event of a separation. Does this arrangement meet with your approval? " he asked, with light and amiable irony.

" That's fair enough, I'll allow," the captain grudgingly admitted, "and I reckon it might even be called generous if the whole crazy scheme were not so damnably unnecessary. What's all this talk of a separation? I don't credit for a split second your notion that your wife's grown tired of you; why should she, for the Lord's sake? You're a handsome young devil, quick as a catamount, and them eyes of yours might strike any girl plumb silly. I'm weary, bitterly weary, of your foolishness, and I wash my hands of the whole affair."

" And that, if you could but comprehend it, is precisely my wife's sentiment in the matter; she is weary, bitterly weary, of my foolishness. But, washing your hands like Pilate, you will not stay for an answer, and as the whole subject is infinitely painful to a sensitive mind, I suggest that we abandon it forthwith and for ever. The letter I will presently compose, counting upon your friendly offices for its safe delivery into the lady's hands. For the rest, I need not further assure you of my unalterable esteem for yourself, nor of my never-ending gratitude for your benevolence."

" Oh, shucks," protested Captain Ffoulkastle, touched in spite of himself by the other's evident sincerity, " I don't deserve none of them fine phrases, having done no more than my duty by you, boy. You've been a clever lad about the ship, too, and worth your salt beef with the best of 'em. And that reminds me: since you're both so stubborn sot in your ways about going west, here's your rightful pay, Dave and Shiloh, and a little extry something to help you out of the tight holes you're bound to fall into now and again. Oh, a dollar or two more or less won't break me this voyage, and I don't want no thanks for it, only I hope to find you two young idjits a-languishing here on Boston Pier when I return, waiting and thankful to be signed on again. Meanwhiles, the *Witch* will lay alongside Hancock's for another fortnight, and you can bring me the letter any day, Shiloh; you know it's safe in my keeping. Mebbe the answer will be a mite more cheerful than you seem to calculate."

"I trust so, indeed, but my mind is a prey to the gloomiest forebodings," replied Shiloh with an ambiguous shake of his romantic locks, and a glance of darkling fire.

"Now, lads," the captain continued pleasantly, "you can sleep aboard the ship to-night if you've a mind to, only give me a hail in the morning before you're off for good or bad, as the case may be. If I'm not here, I'll be over with Mr. Russell in the warehouse, or in the Broad Street ordinary across the way. Run along now, and lend a hand with them crates, and mind you don't go feeding candied citron and Chianti to the flounders, you young scalawag of a Shiloh."

When Shiloh and David had departed, the captain sat for a while lost in profound reflection; sometimes he frowned, and several times he laughed aloud with a robust guffaw, but in the main his look was puzzled and indignant, and he rubbed the hair above his brow into a veritable cockatoo's crest of flaming interrogation in unwonted agonies of thought. Finally, with a portentous shake of the head he sought his couch, nor did slumber in the least enlighten the baffled course of his obscure ruminations.

5

"First things I want to buy me are a bottle of cherry brandy, a yeller silk neckerchief, and a new jack-knife," cried David cheerfully, jingling a double handful of coins.

"And I," said Shiloh, with a deeper, dreamier fervour, " must purchase a loaf of fresh bread, a few raisins, Calderón's *Magico Prodigioso*, and, if possible, the works of the Greek dramatists in pocket editions."

It was a flawless morning of mid-August, and the docks presented a picture of the liveliest activity under an amber super-

Pure Anticipated Cognition

fluity of sunlight. The breeze was sharply flavoured with salt and the exotic fragrance of spices from the India Wharf, and overhead the bland white clouds of summer preserved a stately leisure of their own. The splendid warehouses of Broad Street were bright with white and pumpkin-coloured paint, and far away the State House dome hung like a shining bubble above Beacon Hill.

"How passing fair the world appears to-day," said Shiloh in measured accents. "The senses alone, unaided by the mind, might discover in this scene a new world, unsullied by the blots which disface the elder. The very countenances of the people unite a Republican simplicity of morals with that politeness and delicacy of manners which render virtue amiable. The good cloth coat habits the man; calicoes and chintzes adorn the modest unassuming beauty of the woman and the blue-eyed babe. To crown my happiness, I observe none of those livid wretches, covered with rags who in Europe, soliciting our compassion even from the foot of the altar, seem to bear testimony against religion and the order of society. With what pleasure do I contemplate this enchanting town, and enjoy the spectacle of liberty where nature, education, and habit have engraved the equality of rights upon the hearts of the multitude!"

"Boston's a sightly spot, I'll allow," agreed David with a moderated ardour. "Not but what there're prettier places down in Maine, if you know where to look for 'em. I ain't much of a hand at stringing words together, such shiny words as I'd need to make you see it as it is, Shiloh, but believe me that it beats this city hollower than an old snare-drum. Yes, sir, you ought to see them mountains setting right up out of the bright blue sea, Mount Desert and Isle au Haut and Grand Manan, covered with a kind of pearliness in the distance, and mebbe with another range of hills a-floating over 'em in the heavens. Mirage, they call it, same as mirrors, I suppose, and sure enough there's a looking-glass colour about it all, wavy and clear as water. Oh, I can't put such notions into speech, but I wish you could see them mountains in the evening, under the moon, rising up out of a smooth sea."

"I wish I could, indeed," said Shiloh rather wistfully. "But

39

The Orphan Angel

I suppose there is no possibility of finding Silver in the hills of Maine. Yet I would dearly love to see your home, David, and share the golden pageant of your childhood's memories."

"We have an elegant house in Castine," said David, "a fine modern house, painted white like these here Boston houses. But when I was a little shaver we used to live in a log house; a fort, it was really, for fighting Indians. The British burnt that place in 1812; I was only eleven, but I was almighty mad, and I know I went for the sergeant like a crazy wildcat. My daddy was to sea at the time, taking part in the war, you understand, and I had my mother kind of on my mind. Well, mebbe it was all for the best, as the new place is so neat and tasteful, but I think I liked the log house better."

"It was consecrated to you by the blood of your ancestors, who had fought for freedom, and bedewed the lintel with their sacred lives," suggested Shiloh.

"Some were scalped, but not a one was ever killed," David confessed, "so I reckon they fought to save their precious skins. French used to give 'em a sight of trouble, too, and they say the French love freedom. But I guess they were different in those days."

"A happy augury of the perfectibility of the human mind!" cried Shiloh. He had removed his varnished black hat, and the fresh breeze from the harbour lifted the dark abundance of his hair and made the silver in it shine like the rippling silver on the under side of willow leaves. He strode along with an amazing airy speed, and his bare brown throat and brighter forehead were washed to coolness by the wind of it.

Presently he began to intone the words of some high incantation of the soul, by which the names of oceans and elemental storms and the processional seasons of the year were influenced to music. And this chant resounded with an illimitable and solemn exaltation, so that it was no mere artifice of speech, but deserved rather to be numbered among the natural and vital forces, like a whirlwind or a meteoric flame.

So speaking, or perhaps singing, Shiloh passed along the clean and sunny streets of Boston, and all who beheld him marvelled at his beauty and the singular triumph plain upon

40

his brow. Some thought him mad, but few forbore to love him, and into the hearts of several his image entered that morning to remain always, the bright wound of an arrow pointed by a star.

"I ain't never heard that hymn before, Shiloh, but it's real uplifting," said David at his side.

Suddenly Shiloh darted into a small grocer's shop and emerged with a loaf of bread and a twist of brown paper. He looked more triumphant than ever as he shook a dozen raisins into David's hand.

"Sustenance for the inner man, Davy," he cried. "Not by bread alone shall he live." And he made a pun upon a certain passage in the Testament, which, being Greek, was doubly Greek to David.

Nevertheless David was supremely happy; he purchased his yellow neckerchief and his jack-knife, and, as a temporary substitute for the cherry brandy, some fine ripe peaches and a great sheet of gingerbread. On this simple fare they made their noon-day meal, seated under a tree in Franklin Place.

"'Tain't exactly my idea of a square meal, but I suppose we must get used to roughing it," said David, philosophically, swallowing the ultimate crumb of gingerbread. He drew the jack-knife from his pocket, and began to carve a peach-stone with meticulous care.

"Can do mighty pretty things with cherry-stones, but this ain't the season for cherries," announced David, squinting at his intricate handiwork.

Along the shady turf, Shiloh had composed his graceful limbs as if for slumber, but suddenly he sat up with a start, and, producing pencil and paper from some unapparent hiding-place, he prepared to write.

The grassy square, chequered in amber and emerald by the lengthening afternoon, was very quiet; only above the neat red roofs the plumes of smoke were set in motion by the air, but all else was tranquil in a plenitude of light and warmth. David sat with his curly golden head bent over the carving; and the sun fell upon him like a stream of sunny water, but Shiloh lay in shadow, and the shadow too was coloured like water, the

deeper colour of the sea. Each after his peculiar fashion was
absorbed by the work of his hands and brain to forgetfulness of
all else, and the hours slipped swiftly by into the west, and the
work went on, in delicate periods of creation.

At last David rose and stretched himself with a yawn, his
flushed face burnished to copper by the sunset. Shiloh rose also;
he was pale, and the locks of his hair were disarrayed as though
by prodigies of invisible speed.

"You look kind of like you'd come from the moon," said
David laughing.

"That was a good long lazy afternoon," he went on. "We
didn't do nothing, of course, only sit and fritter away our time
like a couple of truants out of Sunday School, but it was pleasant, wonderful pleasant. And there's your paper all covered
with squiggles like the acrostics in the *Advertiser,* and here's
my peach-stone, carved with a funny little face. Shall I chuck
it away, Shiloh, or save it to give to Silver when we find her?"

"By all means save it, David," Shiloh said gravely. "I shall
save my squiggles, as you call them, to give to her also. They
are magic squiggles, only waiting to sing her to sleep with the
voice of a Mediterranean wave and a Tuscan nightingale. I wish
they might sing myself to sleep, and at once, for I am amazingly
tired."

"I know you are, by the way you blink your eyes and ruffle
your hair," replied David in surprise, "but why you're tired
beats me completely, for you've done nothing but rest for three
mortal hours! However, most likely you're hungry and don't
rightly realize it; come along with me and get a bite of hot
supper under your belt and you'll feel better. You can't expect
to live on dry bread and raisins in a free country, my lad, whatever you may do in Italy. Steer for the Broad Street ordinary,
and I'll set you up to a steak and kidney pie and a pint of porter."

6

LATE that night, in their modest lodgings, Shiloh sat long in
meditation by the light of a single candle. In the near-by bed,

Pure Anticipated Cognition

David slumbered below the cheerful rainbow of a patchwork quilt, and sounds without were hushed to the tranquillity of darkness. Finally Shiloh opened the little attic window and leaned out under the stars; he shivered slightly in the keen wind from the sea, and the brightness of his eyes was full of tears as he looked eastward.

Afterwards he wrote a letter to his wife, sitting hunched over the rickety table and seeing the great shadows flicker like ghosts upon the whitewashed walls. The quill pen trembled in his hand, and its feather made another flying shadow above his head. A tear fell upon the sheets of the letter, and he brushed it away in anger at his own weakness, for he had ever studied to be brave, and now he had need of all his faculties of courage. Beyond the four white walls the greater shadow of a greater wing engulfed the sky.

At last the letter was finished; Shiloh sealed it carefully with red wax, and leaned back exhausted.

" It is finished," he said aloud, with a vague recollection that the words were not his own but another's.

He leaned against the whitewashed wall, below the steeply sloping roof of the attic, and he was so tired that he forgot to think or even to suffer. The deep conviction that he was unloved had entered his soul like mortal iron, but now the agony was past, and he was only a little breathless and confounded and faint as he sat and listened to the strokes of midnight falling through the air and watched the candle burning to its end.

Before its uncertain light had reached the socket, he had found the hidden portrait of Jasper's sister; he turned to it in his weariness as a scolded child turns to a picture-book. Indeed its cool pure colours and gentle looks were a consolation to his drowsy mind, and suddenly he knew that he could sleep.

" A silver cup of cold water," said Shiloh to himself sleepily. With infinite reverence he kissed the small pale lips of the portrait.

In another moment he was slumbering by David's warm and comforting humanity, under the homely rainbow of the patch-work quilt.

III

LOVE IN DESOLATION

" SHILOH," asked David, with his mouth full of johnny-cake and fried ham, " where is it that a man is half horse, half alligator? "

A lion-coloured sunlight enriched the long pine tables at the Broad Street ordinary, gilding their beeswaxed surfaces with an imperial varnish. Curtains of scarlet cotton fluttered against a clear blue sky, and the gaiety of a good breakfast pervaded the air. It was impossible to be melancholy after the third cup of China tea, and Shiloh looked up with an enchanted smile.

" ' Dog-headed, bosom-eyed, and bird-footed,' " he murmured reflectively, spreading honeycomb on a slice of new bread. " But your image is even stranger, David, and your monster of a more prodigious brood. Is he a riddle, or the beast out of Revelations? "

" He was Jasper," David explained gravely. " Leastways, that was Jasper's manner of speaking about his friends. If I could only remember what part of the country had a name for rearing such unholy critters, we might chart our course for Silver."

" For that matter, there is a vast variety of charts and atlases in the adjoining room," said Shiloh helpfully. " I observed them this morning while you were bargaining with our host, and I was especially attracted by a seventeenth-century map of the Cau-

44

Love in Desolation

casus. But I believe that there is an American geography among them."

"Then we'll lose no time in finding it," David said firmly, finishing his porter in one prodigious gulp. "The missis won't mind your admiring her parlour, since you've already made yourself civil to her, and old man Fernald has often told me I might inspect his library. He's proud of them books of his, and he likes us to take an interest in them. He's all for educating sailors, and some of his books is French."

"Seems as though I'd know the name when I see it," he went on a moment later, in the hushed seclusion of the front room. It was a pretty little chamber, panelled in white; the walls were hung with coloured maps, and upon the chimneypiece, within bubbles of bright glass, bloomed a profusion of delicate wax flowers.

"Now," said Shiloh, depositing a large atlas upon the round mahogany table, "here is an opportunity for refreshing your memory. This map represents the states and territories of your noble land. Here must the monster dwell, among these impenetrable forests or upon these sublime and awful pinnacles of rock."

"H'm," pondered David, knitting his brow. "'Twas mountains where he lived, I'll take my oath, but then, why the alligator? Stands to reason an alligator means water of some sort, a lake or a river. Keep a sharp lookout for a country of hills and rivers, Shiloh, where a man might run like a horse over the upland and dive like a fish into the valley swimming-hole. That's the country where we'll find Silver."

"I wish it might be the Rocky Mountains, David." Shiloh's nose was within an inch of the map, and his voice trembled with eagerness. "As for a river, I cannot be satisfied with a lesser flood than that of the Father of Waters, as the redskin names the Mississippi. Unfortunately that mighty river flows at some considerable distance from the peaks of the Rockies, and we cannot hope to discover a junction of their several immensities. It is a pity, but there are other mountains in America. There are mountains in Virginia, mountains in the Carolinas."

"No, no, it wasn't none of them ladies' names, Shiloh," David

45

protested impatiently, turning over the leaves of the atlas with
a determined hand. " It was some fine queer word that I always
liked, some Indian word it was, that sounded kind of rough and
brave to me. I remember that Jasper used to say this place was
once the common hunting-ground of many tribes of Indians,
and that even now these savages, driven from it long ago, have
a sad lamenting song to remember it by. But the name; what
was the name? "

" Was it New Connecticut, or Ohio? " asked Shiloh. " Was it
the Illinois? " David shook his head disconsolately, thumbing
the broad pages of the book.

" Was it Indiana? " Shiloh persisted. " Was it Indiana, or
Kentucky? "

" By jiminy, you've got it! " David leaped from his chair in
strong excitement, and slapped Shiloh upon the back with such
triumphant violence that the other's slight form swayed like a
sapling in a September gale. " Trust you, Shiloh, to strike the
very word; you're the smartest chap alive, I do believe, and anyone'd think you'd been raised down East, for you've got proper
Yankee brains and gumption! Yes, by cracky, that's it! Kentucky,
old Kentucky, Jasper's old Kentucky! Now it's all plain sailing
to the port of this Silver girl, and shall we start to-day, Shiloh,
for we've a fair wind setting from the sea? We'll tell the captain
where we're going, and be off."

" By all means let us go to-day, David," Shiloh answered,
closing the atlas with a light gesture of finality. He rose to his
feet; the fingers of one long brown hand ruffled his hair into
the blown feathers of predestined speed; his other hand sought
and found the miniature of Silver. He stared at the shut shagreen
case as if it had been an holy talisman.

" ' And the souls of whom thou lovest walk upon the winds
with lightness! ' " said Shiloh, and with this surprising remark,
glided swiftly from the chamber into the volatile golden airs of
noon.

Love in Desolation

2

" LET us never go west with a deacon again! " cried Shiloh, escaping from the vicinity of the meeting-house with a sigh of relief. The bright-plumed birch-trees closed around his flight, and he turned to David panting a little, and vehement with laughter.

" The privilege of riding in an excessively heavy waggon is hardly worth the dangers of the prayer-meeting, Davy; another minute, and those gloomy portals would have received us with a groan! Here, in the forest, we are safe, but the peril was appalling, and we have need of sustenance to restore our shattered nerves."

From his pocket he drew an apple and a hard-boiled egg, and, seating himself under a lofty festoon of blackberry vines, he proceeded to devour this ingenuous fare with neat celerity, plucking his dessert from the darkly jewelled garlands above his head, and refusing David's flask with exquisitely courteous obstinacy.

" No; a crystal spring must soon be forthcoming, if these sylvan vistas redeem one-tenth of their promissory charms. You'll make a drinker of me yet, I have no doubt, amid the parched and desiccated horrors of the plains, but these lovely honey-flowing hills and valleys quench my thirst with falling dews and deep cool springs of atmosphere. It is enough; such hunger as I still can feel involves the soul alone. But why did we ever deliver our bodies into the hands of the Westchester deacon, Davy? "

" Because he offered us a lift up a long hill, and we was tired, and the sun was hot," said David reasonably, demolishing an apple-core with a thoughtful air. " Truth to tell, he warn't such a bad old codger, Shiloh, if you'd have let him stick to the history of his rheumatiz, and hadn't got him started on religion. Of course its being the Sabbath sort of druv him on, but folks doesn't mostly expect sailors to go to meeting; it ain't natural, and 'twas your being an atheist got him enraged-like, and set on saving you from hell-fire. If I was you, Shiloh," said David with feeling,

47

an imploring look in his small blue eyes, "I'd go sort of easy, leastways with deacons, on that there atheist tack of yours."

"I shall endeavour to amend my conduct according to your kind suggestion, David." Shiloh's docility was complete and disarmingly gentle; he continued to eat blackberries and to smile into the azure distance between the delicate colonnades of birch-trees.

"One thing the old catawampus told us that come in handy for our health, leaving hell out of the question," David went on, "was that news of his about their having yaller fever in New York; we can go round by the ferry to Hobuck, and run no risk of catching it, but 'twas an almighty fortunate providence as sent him along with the tidings. Yaller fever's no laughing matter; I've seen it in New Orleans and the Indies, and I don't want to see it no more. We'll cut across Jersey to Pennsylvania like greased lightning and be in the high Alleghanies, out of harm's way, before you know it, but I should have hated to leave your bones a-bleaching on the Battery, Shiloh."

"Nevertheless, I question whether we are morally justified in avoiding the plague-stricken city," said Shiloh with stubborn meekness. "My own best content would be rather to venture boldly among its cankered multitude, in an attempt to alleviate somewhat the rigour of their agonies. Surely this were the part of that humane and charitable valour by whose impulse we would seek to live! Can we hesitate, when expiring voices call?"

"I can," replied David with commendable decision, "and I'm not a-going to let you catch the yaller fever, Shiloh, not for all the expiring voices in the whole tarnation town of New York. Besides," he added hastily, observing the fanatic brilliance of his companion's widening eyes, "don't go forgetting Silver, for pity's sake; what would Silver do if you were dead, Shiloh?"

"True; she might have some cause to regret my premature demise," Shiloh admitted in tones of marked disappointment. "Yet it seems a base and cowardly dereliction of duty to preserve our own lives at the expense of our brothers' suffering. I cannot forget those hollowed eyes I might have closed in peace, those fevered throats I might have slaked with cold fresh water.

Love in Desolation

For Silver's ultimate happiness, it must be so, but I shall turn sadly enough towards the wholesome summits of the hills."

"Well, I can't say as I will," said David cheerfully. "I'll be all-fired glad to climb a mountain again, and to get a breath of good pure air after all that stuffy sea-fog."

Ten days of wayfaring had set a deeper tint of bronze upon our young friends' faces, and put a lengthier swing into their step along the sun-powdered road. A smell of September was in the air; Michaelmas daisies and a feathery saffron flower unknown to Shiloh bloomed profusely in the hedges, and a rose-red plume upon a maple confessed to a glitter of frost at daybreak. Nevertheless the weather was incomparably fine; Shiloh had seldom beheld such sunsets, even in Italy, and the winds were perfumed with wild grapes and apples. Indian grass was fragrant in the marshy hollows; scented fern and juniper were fantastically sweet upon the hillsides. All the thickets were ambrosial with blackberries, and the outcroppings of granite among the higher meadows were savage gardens of blueberry-bushes, warm between walls of rock. There were very few mornings when David did not find a handful of mushrooms for breakfast.

They walked in the vivacious early hours, and through the long delicate decline of day; the stillness of noon surrounded them until they lay moveless as flies in amber under the profoundest shade. David was of a piece with the landscape, indigenous to its trees and stones; he was a chip of these blocks of hickory and granite. His colours, too, were manifest in every field; if you had to match his eyes with the blue mountains you need go no farther than apples and pumpkins for the honest brightness of his cheeks and hair. But Shiloh shone exquisitely alien to the earth; you looked for wings upon his heels, and his mercurial rarity was so marked that the very dust silvering his shoulders might have been the eccentric metal of another planet. Yet none the less he appeared the stronger for this singularity; he had shed lassitude and dejection like an effete and heavy mantle flung from tameless speed. And, although his eyes were still the stars of a wilder heaven, he was brown and ruddy as David; his tints were fiercer, partaking of the subtlety of flame, and his feet burnt up the long white miles like magic.

On rainy nights they found a tavern, if no hospitable barn threw wide its hay-loft, but such nights were happily infrequent, and their customary slumbers were sheltered by ricks and the woven trellises of trees. Sun-warmed hay is notoriously sweet, and while few leaves had fallen, David covered the bare ground with balsam boughs and springy heaps of fern, and they slept soft enough even in the forest. The hour before dawn was cold; David burrowed deeper into his rustic couch, and if Shiloh woke shivering, he had only to lift his eyes to the sunrise to be kindled into divinity again.

Besides the seasonable fruits of the earth, bread and cheese and beer were cheap at every tavern; on frosty evenings David might sup on ham and johnny-cake, and Shiloh indulge a fancy for a well-peppered mutton-chop.

"It is an infallible remedy for muscular fatigue," he would say gravely. "I had the hint from Peacock, years ago, and it has stood me in good stead under a variety of circumstances." And he would call for blueberry pie and pineapple cheese to follow in a fashion which, for him, was well-nigh imperious.

That Sunday afternoon, as the ferry carried them towards the Jersey shore, they both confessed to a tender sadness in abandoning New England.

"It's home to me," said David. "Though Maine's the top-notch part of it, Connecticut ain't so bad. Even wooden nutmegs taste kind of good on custard pies."

"It is a fair land, New England," said Shiloh sighing, "and the cradle of the infant Liberty." He dashed a tear from his eye, moved perhaps by high imaginings of freedom, and perhaps by the thought of his own child.

3

In the quiet town of Philadelphia a Quaker boarding-house received the two companions; the good woman who kept it had been upon the point of refusing lodging to the dusty ragged sailors, when a glance from Shiloh's large blue eyes had effectually softened her heart, and wrought the miracle of much broadcloth and fine linen. Upon the brick pavement of Mulberry Street a pretty lady in a leghorn bonnet and a white merino shawl had smiled at the pair; a kindly shopkeeper, lounging under his great striped awning, had offered them hot cinnamon buns and coffee at the price of a penny roll. The city seemed a pleasant place in which to linger, and Shiloh would fain have seen the celebrated waterworks at Fair Mount, with their catalpa trees and marble naiad, but the sultry weather and the advancing season alike suggested haste, and David advised an immediate flight into the cooler hills.

"No use dodging yaller fever to pick up malairy here," he said, and the friends went forth into a region of stone farmhouses and rolling meadows.

"Blow the man down!" sang David a little later, in the teeth of the west wind, but Shiloh sang another song, of his own making, as he sped like the shadow of a cloud across the golden land.

"You could do your thirty miles a day regular even on a corduroy road, I truly believe," said David admiringly. "Flying Shiloh; that's what I call you to myself. Like a ship, you are, close-hauled upon the gale; I do admire to see you go so fast and nimble, even when I'm near breaking my neck to keep up with you."

The length and agility of Shiloh's legs, and David's dogged determination not to allow the lateral rolling of his own step to interfere with the general pace, had indeed resulted in a very fair rate of speed for the journey. Trusting to shoe-leather and human sinew, the pair had proceeded almost as rapidly as if they drove a light buggy or shandrydan, and although they accepted with gratitude an occasional lift from a friendly waggoner, such interludes were rather in the nature of delays, for the companions could easily outwalk any brace of cart-horses hitched to a lumbering van. By the time they crossed from Pennsylvania into Maryland they had found themselves under the necessity of purchasing new hobnailed boots, but their muscles were in superb condition, and they had learned to sleep peacefully under the hood of the heaviest waggon that ever rattled over rocky streams or stirred the thunders upon covered bridges.

The Orphan Angel

They arrived in Cumberland excessively ragged and brown; their spirits were buoyant as the bright autumnal air, and their bodies had hardened into thin contrivances of fiddle-strings and steel. They had managed, by Sabbath-breaking and audacity, to make nearly seventy-five miles for every three days of their pilgrimage.

"Can't go lickety-split up them mountains like you'd want to, Shiloh," said David, eyeing the sober beginnings of the great National Road. "Mebbe we can't even beat the stage-coach into Wheeling, unless we sprout wings like a turkey-buzzard."

"Oh, stage-coaches be blowed!" cried Shiloh robustly; association with David had enriched his vocabulary with several vigorous expletives. "Stage-coaches are for old women suffering from elephantiasis and a plague of bandboxes; we need not concern ourselves with such chimæras. My only regret is that we must descend to the level of a common steamboat on the Ohio, instead of continuing this wild free existence in an Indian canoe or pinnace, along the lucent waters of *la belle Rivière*."

September among the Alleghany hills wore deep transparent tints of auburn and amber, veiled in azure haze; the maples and the sumachs showed the colours of roses, and Shiloh went drunk with loveliness and new cider. The nights were delicately chill, but the sunburnt days were hot and sweet at the core, and wholesome as apples. Sometimes a deep green Pennsylvanian valley invited them to slumber beside a chuckling mill-wheel or a spring-house comfortable with cream; sometimes a level meadow in Virginia lay above the evening clouds, hiding a stone cottage bright with candlelight and firelight. There were breakfasts of coddled eggs and waffle cakes, and suppers of wild turkey and mountain venison. The land flowed with milk and melted butter and honey in the comb.

Shiloh was happy, taking no thought even for the most auspicious morrow, vivid and careless as the wind itself. The money that the captain had given him seemed inexhaustible, because the more earnestly he pressed it upon the farmer's wife or the country storekeeper, the more darkly and profoundly must his blue eyes speak to their inmost hearts with a peculiar spiritual grace, so that they were constrained to refuse payment for their hospitality. And not infrequently he would draw forth his little books and read to them before the fire, while David chopped kindling by lantern-light in the back yard, or helped the hired man with the milking.

The books which he had bought in Boston were ever in his hands; he attained a high degree of proficiency in perusing them while he walked, without in the least moderating the rapidity of his step, and David soon became familiar with the sublime mysterious rhythm of certain scenes from Sophocles, owing to Shiloh's habit of declaiming them aloud upon the summits of the loftier Appalachian hills.

4

"GOLDARN it, Shiloh, you're enough to make a sea-cow laugh," cried David one radiant afternoon, as the two descended into the cool emerald depths of a mountain valley. A slight eccentricity was indeed observable in his companion's appearance; the bright bronze column of Shiloh's throat emerged from the tattered collar of his blue cotton shirt, his pantaloons were secured about his slender waist by part of an old saddle-girth, and his fantastic locks were crowned by a wreath of scarlet Virginia creeper. He seemed half fawn, half panther in his grace and savagery.

The ashen-coloured peaks above them were covered with a profusion of azalea and rhododendron bushes, intermixed with the lacquered viridian gloss of cedar and hemlock, and the coppery luxuriance of oak and beech. A variety of mosses and creeping plants carpeted the ground with woven leaves, and fruits of blue and crimson dangling from the wild vine and the brier rose were lovelier than flowers. Below, the clear waters of the Monongahela, fringed by romantic piles of rock, mirrored a golden picture of the scene.

A shadowed pool lay deep under the shelter of a cliff; Shiloh cast his dusty garments from him with cries of joy, and leapt into the cold revivifying stream. Afterwards he sat naked upon a broad black stone, reading Herodotus in the waning rosy light.

"A practice," said Shiloh, "excessively refreshing in the hot weather." And presently he laid down his book, and began to twist a bit of brown paper into the mimic likeness of a boat, whose sail was a gossamer skeleton leaf.

"You're real handy at that, Shiloh," David commented admiringly. He drew forth his own jack-knife, and busied himself about the manufacture of a very superior type of willow whistle. "Silly, for two grown men," grinned David, slipping a section of pith from the smooth willow bark with exquisite precision. He put the whistle to his lips and blew one long shrill note.

"A voice," murmured Shiloh dreamily, "heard from some Pythian cavern in the solitudes where Delphi stood. Your flute is extraordinarily Hellenic, Davy. By its music we are transported to the banks of Peneus, and linger under the crags of Tempe, and see the water-lilies floating on the stream. We are with Plato by old Ilissus, under the sacred plane-tree among the sweet scent of flowering sallows, and above there is the nightingale of Sophocles in the ivy of the pine, who is watching the sunset so that it may dare to sing."

"That there's a catbird," said David, "and this here's not a flute but a plain whistle. Still, you do talk most beautiful, Shiloh, and the sound of them words is like bees around a locust-tree at noonday. I do admire to hear them Greek names; tell me some more, out of that old boy Hummer, and a hummer he was, I reckon, in his own time, too."

Thereupon Shiloh, sitting naked like an image of bronze above the golden pool, subdued his voice into the whispering of waves among sea-weed, and stretched it taut into the very cord of Apollo's bow, which vibrated and sang. And David listened entranced, unmoving save when now and again he blew a single note, clearer and shriller than a bird's, upon his willow whistle.

A small moon rose over the treetops; the night was warm, and the tranquillity of the forest was unbroken below the falling dew; the pool turned slowly from gold to silver under the moon, and a tender wind stirred the water into flakes of brightness.

Suddenly, on the extremest margin of the farther bank, a dim ethereal figure was visible in opalescent mist; the figure was slight and wavering, and its floating garments were without colour and apparently without substance.

"By golly, it's a girl," cried David, "and she's a-going to jump into the river if we don't get to her in double quick time. Scramble over them stones, Shiloh, as lively as ever you can, and I'll swim to her in a jiffy."

He was already kicking off his heavy boots, when the more impetuous Shiloh passed him like a long bronze javelin flung into the broken pool, and in another instant David saw him attain the opposite bank and emerge dripping with moonlight upon its terraced rocks.

"So it done some good my chucking him head-first into the Susquehanna," thought David as he dived. "I knew I could teach him to swim, if he only give me a chance, and he struck out real pretty across that creek."

Meanwhile Shiloh had gained the side of the young girl; he stood before her charmingly unconscious that his only garment was a glamour of silvery light, and his eyes were grave and luminous with solicitude.

"Please do not think me impertinent if I assume that you are in distress, and so inquire," said Shiloh with a slight chivalric bow, "whether or no I may have the felicity of assisting you."

The young girl fixed her gaze upon Shiloh's large and radiant eyes; the element of the unconventional in his appearance doubtless for this reason escaped her notice, and she spoke without surprise, in a voice of considerable emotion.

"Pappy tried to choke me 'cause the hoe-cake wasn't crisp," said the young girl, and began to weep bitterly, covering her face with a pair of small pale hands.

Her face, when at last she lifted it, was also small and pale; a quantity of soft dark hair surrounded it with shadow, under which the grey glimmer of enormous eyes was evident through tears. She appeared to be about fifteen years old; her beauty was immature and fragile, but exquisitely refined. She was no more than skin and bone, but the delicate texture of the one and the graceful proportions of the other made them sweet as the stem and petals of a slender flower. A gown of thin white muslin, frosted by moonlight, showed fresh and pure in spite of several fantastic patches and rents; her little feet were bare among the cold green tendrils of the ground pine, and as she wept she shivered like a silver leaf.

"For the land's sake, Shiloh, take these if you're a-going to talk to a lady," David cried in an agony of shyness, hastily divesting himself of his own pantaloons and diving back into the pool. The chilly water cooled his blushes, and Shiloh calmly proceeded to don the borrowed garment, meanwhile continuing to address the weeping girl in tones of affectionate and consoling warmth.

"You must really stop crying, my dear young lady, and tell me more about your cruel parent," he said at last, fastening his belt with a business-like air, and hanging a magnificent garland of Virginia creeper around his gleaming shoulders in lieu of a shirt. "While David and I are near you, no man dare lay a finger upon your safety, and if you will but confide in me as a friend, I feel sure that I shall be able to relieve your immediate melancholy." And he took her hand between his own beautiful strong brown hands.

5

"STRANGER," said the child, in a soft little drawling voice, which was at once illiterate and delightful, "if you don't mind I'd sort of like to sit down on that big log, and lean against the china-berry tree, for I've got a heap of queer things to tell you, and Pappy shaked me so that I'm all of a tremble. They's been powerful dark doings to-night down to Pappy's cabin, and even now that he's rode off to the Dutchman's tavern at Little Washington I don't hardly dare to breathe above a whisper. Yes, I'll be right glad for you to hold my hand, for I'm cold as early morning and scairt as a rabbit."

Shiloh, with his air of romantic courtesy, led the child ceremoniously towards the mossy log; they seated themselves upon its crumbling surface, and as the china-berry tree was hard and narrow, Shiloh's shoulder seemed a more natural resting-place for his companion's curly head. She settled herself thus with a sigh of tired contentment, closing her eyes, upon whose fringes bright tears still glittered in the moonlight.

Love in Desolation

"My name . . ." began the child, in her soft slow drawl, but Shiloh gently interrupted her.

"Is Silver; surely it is Silver, and we have found you by enchantment," he said tenderly, raising her hand to his lips.

"No, sir; I'm mighty sorry, but my name is Melissa, Melissa Daingerfield," said the child apologetically. "Pappy comes from a grand family, kin to all the quality in Virginia, but he's shiftless, is Pappy, and he won't work when he's in liquor. Ma was a lady, a lovely lady like a lily as I remember her, but he bruk her with his cruel ways, and she fell down into the dust and died, jest like a lily that you've trod into the dust. I was only seven years old when she died; I went with her into the green yard and we laid down in the shade of the laurels; she couldn't bear to stay in the cabin, 'cause it was full of smoke and dust and smashed whisky bottles, and she smiled at the sun between the green laurels, and pretty soon I knew she was dead. I kissed her, and I cried, and Pappy come raging and swearing into the yard and looked down at us both, and then he flung hisself on the ground beside Ma and cried fit to break his heart for a long while, but when I put out my hand to comfort him he pushed me away and cursed me with an awful curse. Since that day he's always hated me, and he's been powerful unkind to me for seven weary years. Oh, sir, I beg as you will help me, for Pappy's a bloody-minded man when he's been drinking, and I'm scairt most to death that he'll murder me some day."

During this tragic narrative Shiloh's countenance had become pale with horror, and his eyes appeared supernaturally large, and brilliant with agitated light. His sensitive and passionate nature was ever profoundly moved by the thought of cruelty, and now he had difficulty in commanding his voice even to a shaken murmur of pity and reverential affection.

"Did you but hear her, David," he demanded in a firmer tone, turning to his friend, and at the same time clasping the child Melissa more closely to his furiously beating heart, "and do you stand by unmoved by this recital of unprecedented suffering, or is your soul convulsed with indignation like my own?"

David had returned by way of the slippery rocks, and waited in respectful silence at some little distance from the others. He

57

wore Shiloh's pantaloons and his own shirt, and carried Shiloh's shirt carefully over his arm.

"I reckon I ain't exactly what you might call unmoved, Shiloh," he protested with considerable heat, kicking violently at the inoffensive ground. "In fact, if this young lady will give me her kind permission, I'm moved to go to Little Washington and wallop her parent good and plenty no later than to-night. The infernal swine, if I may say so, of course meaning no discourtesy, to lay his dirty hand on a pretty little slip of a thing like her, God blast him, and I hope you'll excuse me, Miss, as he's your father, but I never, no I never in all my born days heard tell of such wickedness before, and her with no mother, and such beautiful hair, and no man could bear it calmly without busting loose, and oh, damn, damn, damn!"

With which unwonted ebullition of feeling David subsided once more into silence, broken only by an occasional cough or a suspicious snuffle. Shiloh made no attempt to conceal his tumultuous emotion, and tears shone in the profundity of his eyes as he turned again to Melissa.

"You see," he said with a reassuring smile, "you see, my dear child, that you have two very brave champions, who will nevertheless do nothing to alarm you."

"I sure is glad to hear you say so, stranger," Melissa answered solemnly, "for Pappy kin break you gentlemen like a couple of sticks of kindling if you rouses him to wrath. Pappy kin spit further, curse worser, and hit heavier than any other man around these parts, and I don't want him to bust your head nor black your handsome eyes for you."

To Shiloh's amazement, a very true pride was apparent in Melissa's words, and she raised her curly locks from his shoulder and faced him with a flashing look of defiance.

"Do not appeal to my cowardice, my dear," he said rather haughtily. "It is at best an uncertain quantity." The irony in his voice was lost upon the child, but she saw that he was hurt, and caught at his hand in a gesture of humility.

"I asks your pardon, stranger, if I spoke hasty," she whispered, bending her head against his breast. "I'm kind of fond of Pappy, and it riled me to hear you talk of champeens like you was pu-

Love in Desolation

gilists and Pappy jest nobody at all, him that has knocked out heavyweights from Kentuck and Missoura. I reckon you can't fix a man's hog-meat and mush fer seven years without gitting mighty attached to him, spite of being banged about a bit when the corn liquor's extry powerful in his sperrit. Forgive me; it's jest family pride and filial vanity, I reckon, but Pappy's a gentleman born, and you should see him lift my grandaddy's old flintlock musket jest by sticking one finger into the barr'l of it! "

"You are a darling child, and a very loyal daughter," said Shiloh, touched to the soul by the girl's simplicity. "But you know you really must not run about the country at night attempting to drown yourself; I shall never have a moment's peace of mind if you do not promise me to desist. Furthermore, I shall consider your future as my especial care; I must lose no time in arranging for a suitable education for one of your undoubted talents, and your material welfare must be secured immediately. Your charm and fragility demand certain refinements; true taste hires not the pale drudge luxury, I admit, but you need a sufficiency of simple food and a pair of pretty slippers at once."

At these words, spoken with exquisite sympathy and respect, Melissa clapped her little hands in ingenuous delight.

"Oh, glory, glory!" she cried, jumping to her feet and executing an impromptu saraband upon the ground pine. "They's the beautifulest slippers in Wheeling, like Miss Marianna Grimes wore at her wedding, and that's no more'n twenty miles away, and we kin walk it in one day, I reckon! Oh, glory hallelujah, stranger, I thanks you with all my heart for them kind sentiments, and mebbe you kin knock Pappy out if you tries hard enough, and oh, you are the generousest gentleman in all the world, and I love you!"

It was impossible to help laughing at her pleasure, and yet her pleasure was curiously pathetic. David made a peculiar grunting sound; Shiloh's large eyes brimmed alike with tears and laughter, as he received a glancing kiss of gratitude upon the tips of his fingers.

"One moment, my dear friend," he said to David, drawing him aside into the shadow of the china-berry tree. "The thing I am about to propose may in all probability surprise you, since

59

The Orphan Angel

it runs counter to my declared convictions, yet I believe that for once instinct must prompt a charitable action, setting logic at defiance. Much as I abominate the galling customary chain of matrimony, I am nevertheless aware that a journey to Wheeling in our company might involve Melissa in embarrassments both painful and humiliating, unless one of us were in a position to protect her from flagitious calumnies and insulting abuse. I, as you know, am already wedded, but you are fortunately free; in brief, had you not better marry the poor child? "

"Who? Me? " cried David in sincere alarm. "Now, Shiloh, you're never a-going to make me get married just for the sake of buying a girl a pair of slippers! That's plumb plain foolishness, that is, as you'd know if the moon wasn't shining and Melissa didn't have such pretty curls. Besides, I'm already half promised to little Bianca over in Leghorn, what with walking out with her Sundays, and even lambasting Jasper all on account of her, and then," David concluded, blushing furiously the while, " and then, Shiloh, you see there's always Silver."

Shiloh, his face pale as a dawn of moonlight in the shadow of the china-berry tree, remained for a long moment without answering; his voice, when at last it broke the silence, was noticeably strained and weary.

"True, David," he said gently. "There is, indeed, always Silver; I had not forgotten, but she shines to me ever as a holy sister, and I suppose I am a fool. I had not perceived, I had not imagined, that you felt . . . but no matter, I will speak no more of this madness. I am sorry; the fault is my incurable simplicity. Help me now to contrive some more pragmatic scheme, serviceable to employ for the relief of this young creature, fallen so strangely, and as it were from the clouds, upon our casual mercies."

David, feeling himself touched upon the tenderest strings of his heart, blushed more hotly than before, and stammered in confusion.

"Oh, well, I guess we can manage somehow without marrying her, Shiloh, though I have no wish to treat the poor thing mean, nor be stingy with our money, if it comes to that. We ain't spent hardly anything lately, what with folks along the road being so hospitable and open-handed, and I should calculate

60

as we might be able to spare her five dollars anyway, even if we can't have the fun of knocking down that rotten father of hers and stamping on his ugly head, like I'd admire to do. And mebbe we can find some kind lady hereabouts as'll bring the child up like a Christian, and see that she has shoes and stockings and her hair in decent braids. The Lord knows I don't want to desert a fellow mortal who's in trouble, but marry her I won't, and that's final," said David with emphasis.

"My dear David, let us say no more about it, I beseech you," Shiloh replied in a low pained voice. "Above all, we must not allow Melissa herself to overhear our discussion; imagine the mortification of a sensitive spirit under such circumstances! Melissa, my child," he continued, turning to the girl his most winning look of gallantry, "since you are to accompany us to Wheeling, have you no relatives in that town who may, while unluckily depriving us of the joys of your society, nevertheless supply a more fitting refuge to your inevitable fatigue than our poor though devoted efforts can achieve?"

Melissa laughed merrily, and reseated herself upon the log, curling up her little bare feet under the tattered ruffle of her muslin gown.

"Stranger, you do talk a heap of furrin words, don't you? I reckon I knows pretty well what you're trying to say, all the same, Ma having spoke French something beautiful, and Pappy hisself being a powerful fine scholar when he's sober. So I answers you, yes; I've an own aunt in Wheeling, my Ma's second sister, only I've never laid eyes on her along of Pappy swearing to murder me cruel if I did, but Aunt Juliana her name is, and she's a Sunday-school teacher in the First Methodist Church!"

"Dear me," said Shiloh regretfully, "I am indeed sorry to hear you say so; I should have preferred a secular schoolmistress for the instruction of youth. However, all now depends upon this lady's personal character, and since we have no cause to credit aught but good of your beloved mother's close relative, we must hope for the best. To-morrow we go to Wheeling; it shall be my dearest care to place you unharmed under the protection of this excellent female. Meanwhile I suppose we must part until the morning; the forest will afford sufficient shelter to David and myself, and doubtless your father's cabin may serve as your asylum for a single night."

"Oh, Lordy, yes," Melissa answered cheerfully, "I reckon I shan't take no harm from another night under Pappy's roof, though if he catched you there he'd kill you same as he would a fly. But he don't never leave the Dutchman's tavern till daybreak, and you-all had better come along home with me and git a bite of corn-dodger and mebbe a mite of bacon. Plenty of clabber there is, too, and liquor for them as likes it. Then you can sleep in the corn-crib, and be ready to start at sun-up, before ever Pappy gits back from Little Washington."

"Don't sound extra safe to me," said David cautiously. "But then again, I'm goldarned hungry. Guess we might as well go with the young lady and get a proper supper; I'd rather risk having a skinful of buckshot than starve to death, and we had nothing but apples at noon. Only, I never could abide clabber, and the liquor's real good in these parts," he concluded plaintively, with a glance at Shiloh.

6

HALF an hour later the three were seated about a square pine table in Mr. Daingerfield's cabin; a fire of oak logs had smouldered into rosy ashes upon the hearth, where several dishes of coarse blue and grey crockery companionably steamed. The table was spread with a clean chequered cloth, and upon this was set a generous platter of fried pork, a pint bowl of apple sauce and another of pickles, and a vast pile of corn-dodgers. There was also a saucer of fresh butter, two pitchers filled respectively with buttermilk and new cider, and a large honeycomb. A water-bucket and a jug of whisky were placed with admirable impartiality side by side upon a bench in the corner of the room.

"I don't generally git time to eat," said Melissa happily, with her mouth full of honey and corn-dodger, "'cept when Pappy goes off on a bust, and then I'm mostly so lonely that I cries all night and hasn't the heart even to swallow a bite of mush. Now this is mighty different; it does me good to see you-all tuck in your victuals, and I could sing for joy to see your faces a-smiling

Love in Desolation

at me so kind and grateful-like. Oh, glory be to God, I'm so joy-ful that I could fall down on my knees and pray, 'cause I've got two loving friends, and I'm going to Wheeling to visit my aunty, and buy me a pair of prunella shoes! "

A tallow candle stuck in a green glass bottle illuminated the table; by its light Melissa appeared lovelier than ever, with vivid cheeks and small vermilion lips. The grey of her enormous eyes was shot with emerald and amber, in a complicated maze of colour, and Shiloh thought of her honey-sounding name, and wondered whether Silver's eyes were hazel or pure brown, like the patterned eyes upon the wings of moths. And he remembered another pair of hazel eyes, which might even now be mournful by the shores of the Gulf of Spezzia, and he sighed profoundly, above his cup of new cider. He did not perceive that the girl was watch-ing his own face, his own luminous eyes, with an adoring con-centration, and he flushed shyly when she said good-night to him, standing on tiptoe and lifting her mouth to be kissed as if she had been a child of seven years.

"I reckon I like you best, Mr. Shiloh," she whispered. "David's a right sweet boy, and I wish he was my brother, but they's some-thing about you I love with all my heart. I reckon it's your eyes, Mr. Shiloh; you've got powerful pretty eyes."

"Good-night, Melissa," said Shiloh, kissing her as gently as if she had been a child of seven years. "Please believe that I love you too, and that I shall endeavour to serve you, by virtue of that love." And he went very softly from the house, without another word or backward glance, and the small silver moon, which hung over the western hills, was like an aureole about his head as he departed.

"Good-night, Miss Melissa," said David, following him, "and thank you for an elegant supper, not to mention the finest drink of corn whisky as I've had in Virginia." And he too disappeared into the night, fading as a glimmer of yellow hair and the sound of a strong young voice singing "Blow the man down."

The two went at once to the corn-crib; it was quite dry and comfortable, and within five minutes they were both deep in dreamless slumbers upon rustling mattresses of corn-stalks. The moon dropped down behind the hills, and in the darkened night their tranquillity was unbroken even by the shadow of a dream.

Melissa said her prayers as usual, to her mother's portrait, which hung in an obscure corner out of reach of Mr. Daingerfield's familiar wrath, with a pink calico curtain artfully disposed over its pensive countenance. Then she curled herself up in her little low truckle-bed, and at first she wept, because Mr. Shiloh had such powerful pretty eyes, but at last she fell asleep smiling, because in the morning she was going to Wheeling, to buy her a pair of prunella shoes.

7

THE MORNING dawned cold and rainy; an equinoctial gale seemed to smell of the sea even among these inland hills, and the twenty miles to Wheeling stretched sinister and clammy with mud under the inundation of the clouds. Melissa waked her two friends at five o'clock; in the pale unnatural light her small face glimmered like a sick pearl, and she appeared unsubstantial as the dim etheric double of the jocund creature who had laughed over the supper-table. Even David felt a chilly stiffness in his magnificent sinews, and Shiloh, although he would not for the world have mentioned the circumstance, was suffering from a slight attack of neuralgia in the left temple. Nevertheless, they greeted each other with affectionate cheerfulness, in which a faintly plaintive quality was mingled, and the sight of a superb fire leaping upon the cabin hearth warmed them all three into smiles again.

" They's roasted eggs in them ashes, and coffee in the big tin pot," said Melissa quickly. " And now, gentlemen, I'm afeared we must hurry jest a mite, so's to be gone afore Pappy gits back from Little Washington. I wish I could 'a' cooked you a sure-enough breakfast, with wheat bread and chicken fixings, but mebbe I kin do that when I gits to my aunty's house. Make out the best you can with hoe-cake and hot coffee; they's a cupful of cream on the table. You look kind of froze, Mr. Shiloh, so sit down by the fire and warm yourself while I bring you your breakfast. David, put another log on the fire so as Mr. Shiloh kin warm hisself nice and comfortable while he drinks his coffee."

Love in Desolation

Melissa was attired in a man's drab woolen greatcoat, worn over a short frock of faded indigo and yellow homespun; even these shabby garments failed to conceal her delicate prettiness, but she looked the most pathetic of orphans as she trotted about the cabin, her little bare feet blue with cold against the hard clay floor. Shiloh stared ruefully at his own stout shoes; at last he took them off and set them side by side upon the hearth. Now Shiloh had beautiful narrow feet like an Indian's, but he was six feet tall and his shoes had been made by a country cobbler, who was incidentally a Dutchman. The shoes seemed absurdly large ever to be laced over Shiloh's aristocratic insteps; as a substitute for the prunella slippers they were preposterous.

"Do you think," asked Shiloh, in a humble, doubting voice, "that you could possibly wear my shoes, little Melissa? I should say Cinderella, for the notion is obviously farcical, now that I observe the minute proportions of your toes, and yet I cannot reconcile my mind to the prospect of miles of mud, with the winds of autumn howling about your slender unprotected ankles. Will you be so good as at least to make the attempt, out of the charitable kindness of your heart?" And he stooped and lifted the shoes from the stone hearth, as though they had been some novel form of sacrifice and he the acolyte of a new religion.

"Oh, Mr. Shiloh, indeed and indeed I couldn't!" cried Melissa in sincere distress, falling to her knees by his side; her spirit laid oblations counter to his upon the fire-warmed stone, and she took the shoes very firmly from him and placed them before him on the hearth. He saw to his amazement that she was crying.

"It's not that they's a bit too big," she protested through her tears. "They's mighty fine shoes, Mr. Shiloh, a heap too fine for me. Put 'em on quick, Mr. Shiloh, and I'll lace 'em up for you; please let me lace 'em up for you! I love you, Mr. Shiloh, and I couldn't let you go barefoot in the rain!"

"If you refuse to wear the shoes, Melissa, I certainly shall not do so," Shiloh answered with gentle obstinacy, preparing to sling the clumsy contrivances around his neck by their buckskin laces. The two gazed at one another, drowned in mutual glances of admiration, and deadlocked in a stubborn self-denial.

"Can't you see the poor girl could never wear them things,

Shiloh?" David demanded with some impatience. "I'd be happy to lend her mine, for the matter of that, but look at the size of the brutes; fit for a giant. Seven-league boots they may be, but they weren't cobbled on a lady's last. Now put on your own like a sensible fellow, and we'll steer clear of this Daingerfield before he comes a-hollering after our blood for breakfast."

"You're a gentleman, Mr. Shiloh, but I'm jest a child that's used to running barefoot," cried Melissa, skipping along the road with rain-drops in her curly hair. She had tied up her slender hoard of treasures in a bright silk handkerchief, and it now dangled from Shiloh's stick beside a bandanna heavy with Greek tragedies and Albemarle pippins. She had left her father's great-coat behind, and her gown was kilted about her little waist with a leather thong. Hot coffee and exercise had warmed them all to merriment, and Melissa was as playful as a kitten and as innocent as a fleecy lamb.

She proved to be, as Shiloh prettily remarked, a heaven-born traveller; her small curvetting feet had no difficulty in keeping up with his long strides, even upon the ascending slopes of hills, or along their steep and perilous declivities.

"I'll allow the girl is goldarned nimble; nimble as a squirrel!" said David, and Shiloh laughed and spoke of the Acroceraunian mountains.

Melissa talked very little, but she sang a vast variety of hymns, in a small soprano voice in which the notes were clear and cool and pure as drops of rain.

> "God moves in a mysterious way,
> His wonders to perform;
> He plants his footsteps in the sea,
> And rides upon the storm."

Thus Melissa sang upon the mountain-tops, and as she sang she fixed her eyes upon Shiloh's countenance, while Shiloh in his turn stared radiantly into the valleys of the west, where the clouds were already lifting.

Love in Desolation

8

PRESENTLY the land began to fall away into rolling meadows and low hills; the road crossed a long succession of stone bridges, and there were farmhouses among the trees by the stream. They halted at noon before the door of a modest dwelling, whose mistress refused payment for a pitcher of milk and a bowl of pickled peaches. The travellers' pockets were full of cold bacon and corn-bread, and they made a sufficient if somewhat chilly meal under the shelter of an enormous apple-tree. When Shiloh returned the empty bowl and pitcher to the farmwife, she looked at him pityingly and offered him a silver quarter and a tin cup of whisky, both of which benefits he courteously declined.

The rain had now ceased, and as the afternoon lengthened the sun emerged from watery mists, coloured in the softest tints of rose and amber; a rainbow spanned the opposite heaven with an arch of flame. The hearts of the three friends were simultaneously lightened and infused by hope, and they paused upon a broad stone bridge to rest for a moment, and to admire the opalescent clouds reflected in the stream, which with the sky itself formed the two hemispheres of a circle of living pearl. Toward the west lay Wheeling, invisible as yet, but imagined vividly as a cluster of white spires and evening lamps, inviting the weary to repose.

Presently the hoof-beats of a horse were loudly audible along the road whence they had come, and Melissa clutched at Shiloh's hand in instinctive alarm, and trembled in some quick prevision of despair.

"It's Pappy; I knows it's Pappy," she breathed shudderingly, pale as the smallest dying rain-cloud in the sky. " He's borrowed Jesse Bryan's horse and he's a-chasing us with murder in his heart. I knowed it was too beautiful to last, Mr. Shiloh; to-day's been jest a dream to me, walking with you and David in the peaceful rain, and seeing the face of my Redeemer upon the high hills, and the rainbow, and the promised land. Now I reckon I've got to go back to Pappy's cabin, and git more beatings than ever because I tried to run away. Good-bye, Mr. Shiloh, my darling

Mr. Shiloh, and now run, run for your life, before Pappy catches you and kills you!"

Shiloh and David did not move; they stood leaning upon the low stone parapet of the bridge in attitudes of admirable composure, and only a faint reflection of Melissa's extreme pallor was apparent upon their faces. Shiloh's eyes were very bright; David had set his lips into a grim Puritan line; they stared along the muddy road, and each one hoped that the other could not hear the hurried beating of his heart.

Suddenly a horseman appeared around the turn of the road; he was bent forward over the neck of an iron-grey horse, and he rode as if for a wager, madly, and with loud and profane exhortations to his steed; he wore a red shirt, and his streaming sable hair was uncovered to the wind.

"It's Pappy; O sweet Jesus, help us, 'cause it's Pappy sure enough!" cried Melissa, collapsing in a little heap against the coping of the bridge, and hiding her eyes with her shaking hands.

At this instant the rider perceived them; he reined in his horse with a violent imprecation, and leapt to the ground beside the panting animal. Steam rose in wreaths into the moist air; the horse hung his head, labouring for breath, but the man showed no evidences of exhaustion, and he faced the two friends with a savage sneering laugh.

"So," he drawled in a husky voice, which was nevertheless that of an educated man, "you gentlemen have seen fit to run off with my little girl, have you? I presume you know the penalty for that in the great state of Virginia; I presume you know that I am about to shoot you down like the curs you are, unless you can convince me of your honourable intentions. Now pray explain yourselves, and be quick about it, for by heaven you have neither of you many minutes to survive if you've harmed a hair of this little angel's head. Image of her sainted mother, she is, and the sweet snow-apple of her father's eye! Now, sirs, I am waiting, as your most impartial judge, but, I have a shrewd suspicion, as your righteous executioner to boot."

He drew a gigantic pistol from his holster, cocked it, and stood regarding Shiloh and David with a cold distasteful stare, Mr. Daingerfield was a singularly handsome man; he had a fine thin aquiline nose, a quantity of raven-black hair, and a pair of magnificent grey eyes set under beetling brows. It was not difficult to believe that the best blood of Virginia informed the arteries of his splendid frame, but his temper appeared to be irascible, and he had the unfortunate habit of picking his glittering white teeth with his pocket-knife. He now produced this instrument, employing it in the manner described; Shiloh watched him in a species of sinister fascination, and for fully a minute there was no sound save the plashing of water under the little bridge.

"Well, speak up, sir, or you will compel me to shoot you unheard!" said Mr. Daingerfield irritably, caressing the trigger of the pistol with an absent-minded touch.

"My dear Mr. Daingerfield," began Shiloh politely, "I must emphatically assure you that you have mistaken our intentions. We are not curs; my natural resentment at this insulting term must yield to the respect in which I hold a father's sacred anxiety as to the welfare of his child, but I repeat, you have mistaken our intentions. Only the desire to be of service to this young lady has led us to accompany her to Wheeling, and it is our purpose to place her under the protection of a superior female relative when once our journey is accomplished."

"Then am I to understand that your purpose was not matrimonial?" Mr. Daingerfield inquired with perfidious calm; Melissa, peeping from between her cold fingers, saw his smile, and the manner in which he softly teetered back and forth on his toes, and she knew the peril imminent in the pistol-barrel.

"To my profound regret, I could not contemplate such felicity," said Shiloh with trusting candour. "You see, I happen to be already married."

In the next instant, three several events providentially conspired to save Shiloh from annihilation: Mr. Daingerfield's pistol flashed in the pan, Melissa rose from her apparent swoon and flung herself like a frail shield upon Shiloh's bosom, and David cleared his throat and spoke with portentous solemnity.

"It's me as wants to marry your daughter, sir," he said deferentially, turning his varnished hat in his broad muscular hands, and looking a veritable model of bashful and deserving love. "My friend here is just giving us the pleasure of his company as far as

The Orphan Angel

Wheeling, so as to make it more seemly-like for Melissa and me until we get to Miss Juliana's. Melissa took a fancy to buy her wedding-dress in town, and she thought as how her aunt could advise her about biases and ruchings and such-like fal-lals, her being young, and unlearned in these matters same as me. I hope, sir, as you'll forgive us being a bit hot-headed and impatient, and not waiting for you to come back from Little Washington. Mebbe you'll come along with us now, sir, and give us your blessing when the minister of the First Methodist Church splices us up right and tight and proper to-morrow morning; we'd admire to have your blessing, Mr. Daingerfield, on our wedding-day."

Mr. Daingerfield appeared considerably mollified by this speech; nevertheless he looked rather regretfully at the slim aristocratic figure of Shiloh, who seemed to him better suited to any romantic rôle, whether of seducer or bridegroom, than the earthier David. Within the corded veins of his forehead the blood of the Daingerfields throbbed protestingly, but David was strong and comely and well-formed, and Mr. Daingerfield resigned himself to a plebeian son-in-law with a sigh of appreciation for an honest workingman's usefulness in the hog-pen and the corn-patch.

"I suppose you realize that you are scarcely a fitting match for my daughter," he replied proudly, twirling his opulent mustachios. "However, you are doubtless a worthy fellow, and although it is a pity that you are a common sailor and a Yankee, you have the air of possessing the domestic virtues, I will therefore consider your proposals for my little Melissa's hand, nor can a father's heart fail to be softened by the evident preference evinced by her maidenly confusion."

David's down-cast countenance turned slowly to a sumptuous copper tint; he glanced furtively at Melissa, and perceived that the girl's face was hidden against Shiloh's breast; she seemed half-fainting and completely forlorn. Shiloh supported her with the most reverential tenderness; he bent his head, and whispered words of comfort and advice above her tumbled curls. At that moment Shiloh appeared, even to his friend's simple eyes, as very knightly, very noble, very pale, polished to a scrupulous image of pure chivalry; David wondered miserably what high exalted

70

Love in Desolation

arrows of unwisdom he was feathering for Melissa's little ears. Nevertheless, the devoted fellow felt a pang of happiness in considering that he had indubitably saved Shiloh's luminous existence from an ugly shattering death, and he felt that no sacrifice, not the very nightmare of an early marriage, was too painful in the light of this consummation. And, even now, he could not help hoping that he might himself be saved.

"Melissa, my little darling," said Mr. Daingerfield fondly, "why don't you raise up your lovely eyes and look your poor old father in the face? Don't be timid, my precious treasure; come to your daddy's arms and kiss him good-bye. I'm losing my one ewe lamb in losing you, but I can't destroy the pretty pastoral idyll of your love, or rub the bloom from your morning joy. And so I say to this exemplary young man, ' Take her, my boy, with a father's blessing and a father's tears, and may the brightest of good luck be with you both, my children! ' "

Mr. Daingerfield pronounced this edifying speech with a beaming smile upon the company; his consternation was extreme when his daughter lifted up her drooping head to say with surprising finality, "I've changed my mind, Pappy; I don't want to marry David nohow. I reckon I'd ruther go along home with you; seems as if I'd kind of lost my taste for matrimony."

9

SHILOH gave a low shocked cry of horror, but David's heart leaped up like a wild creature released from a trap, and as he looked at his friend his eyes were passionate with a mute entreaty.

Melissa gently extricated herself from Shiloh's absent-minded embrace, and walked bravely up to her tall father; her little face was as white as the plume of some lost impossible crusade, her eyes were shrines of a perpetual devotion.

"Pappy," she said in a small clear singsong voice, as if she were repeating an austere and delicate admonition of the soul, "Pappy, I reckon you'll have to take me home with you to-night; I reckon you'll have to keep me with you always. I done made

71

a mistake 'bout loving David; I don't love him, and I won't marry him. I love somebody else, and there can't nobody git me to name his blessed name, but I reckon I love him forever."

"What does the girl mean?" demanded Mr. Daingerfield indignantly. "Is she moon-struck, or have you been taking her to religious revivals? This is either the language of lunacy, or that of salvation; in my experience the two come to much the same thing in the end."

"I ain't crazy, Pappy, and I ain't been a-follering no preachers," said Melissa with simplicity and pride. "I'll be a good daughter to you if you'll jest leave me alone to keep the counsels of my own heart in peace and quiet." She folded her small hands over some secret, locked in her breast below the shallow breathing, and looked imploringly at her father.

"Well, I am totally unable to understand the vagaries of the feminine soul," sighed Mr. Daingerfield, "but I suppose it is a lady's immemorial prerogative to change her mind; I can only apologise to my young friend here, and perhaps bid him not completely to despair, since your affections are still malleable and mobile. Doubtless in a year or two," he said consolingly to David, who writhed in an agony of embarrassment, "my daughter may be persuaded to look more kindly upon your suit; she is after all little more than a child."

"Yessir," stammered David, "yessir, mebbe so, sir; I'm sure I hope so, sir." The varnished hat revolved so rapidly in his hands that it threw off points of light like those scattered from the circumference of a Catherine's wheel.

"But, Melissa!" exclaimed Shiloh wildly, his blue eyes brilliant with amazement, "what is this insanity? In the name of heaven, pause ere it be too late; you cannot mean to plunge once more into the gloomy pool of solitude and fear which has engulfed your youth these many years! Oh, my dear little friend, consider well what you are doing, and even if you will not marry David, pray, pray be advised to seek the respectable aid of your Aunt Juliana!"

"Really, my good sir, you presume upon my leniency when you dare thus to address my daughter," said Mr. Daingerfield angrily. "Who are you, may I ask, and why do you make so curi-

Love in Desolation

ously free with the intimate family cognomen of my deceased wife's sister? If you knew Aunt Juliana, as you call her with such singular impertinence, you would hesitate before advising an innocent child to cast herself upon the ambiguous mercies of as dark and bigoted a soul as ever crushed the resilient laughter from the heart of youth. Oh, sir, you speak very glibly of solitude and fear, but what is an honest occasional black eye or a stormy uncompanioned midnight compared to the monstrous panic of the revival or the saturnalia of the camp-meeting, where young creatures in the gay dawn of existence are seized upon by a sinister madness, horror-struck, and rendered feeble and enervated for ever? It was for this reason that I forbade my poor wife to hold any communication with her unhappy sister; it is for this that I have kept Melissa herself aloof and untrammelled in our mountain fastness, and, believe me or not as you will, you would abandon both her body and her delicate spirit to destruction, if you conveyed her within the power of that appalling woman! "

Mr. Daingerfield paused exhausted, and wiped the sweat from his brow; it was plain that he did not love his sister-in-law.

" I reckon as Pappy is right, Mr. Shiloh," Melissa interposed softly, slipping her hand into Shiloh's, and looking up at him with sad adoring eyes. " I reckon I better bid you good-bye, and go back to the cabin with Pappy. Aunt Juliana must be a holy terror, and I'd be scairt to death of her, worser than I am of Pappy. I'm powerful happy to have known you, Mr. Shiloh, and I won't never forget you s' long as I live, and ever after, if they is an ever after."

She put up her face to be kissed; she could not speak of the prunella slippers, nor of her love for Shiloh, which burned in her eyes like two perpetual tapers in a most single-minded shrine. The small face that he kissed was cold with tears, and for a moment he held her against his heart, but was unable to feel the little beating of her own.

Mr. Daingerfield had been busily dusting his great hip-boots with his heavy riding-crop; at last he seemed to steel his courage to some disagreeable duty, and he turned to Shiloh with a look of positive shyness in his fierce grey eyes.

" Sir," he began ceremoniously, " I owe you neither explanation nor apology; the fault lies entirely with you, and I am surprised at my fantastic weakness. The fact remains, however, that I feel a strong desire to assure you of my profound affection for my daughter, and of my recently taken determination to amend my ways for her benefit. She may have mentioned," said Mr. Daingerfield rather self-consciously, "that I am perhaps over-fond of the good corn liquor of my native state, and that my temper is at times uncertain. I marvel at my own folly, yet somehow I would not have you go from me without these guarantees of my good faith towards my child, and even—but indeed, I blush for my irrational dementia as I speak—and even, sir, I would fain shake your hand in parting, and call you, however foolishly, my friend. There's something about you, sir," said Mr. Daingerfield with unwilling warmth, "by gad, sir, I swear there's something about you that I like! Will you have a drink of whisky?" He produced a fine silver flask of Jacobean workmanship, and unscrewed the top with accustomed celerity.

"No, thank you," answered Shiloh, distaste chilling the words to faint hauteur. "I wish," he went on, "that you would not drink . . ."

"Corn liquor!" shouted David in the nick of time; Mr. Daingerfield's brow had darkened again alarmingly. "He has a fancy for French brandy, has my mate, and he won't never stop singing its praises, in season and out of season. He wants for you to take to that, Mr. Daingerfield; he thinks corn whisky's bad for the digestion. I tell him that's all moonshine, but he will have his little joke."

"How absurd you are, David!" Shiloh was slightly annoyed; he did not know that his friend had saved his life for the second time within half an hour. Mr. Daingerfield restored the flask to his pocket with an indulgent smile, wiping his lips upon a fine linen handkerchief.

"You young fellows are always silly about French kickshaws," he said in a tone of pleased superiority. "Brandy may be all right for boys, but it isn't a gentleman's drink; it has no fire and passion in it. However, if you'll follow me into Wheeling, and meet me at the residence of my friend Judge Poindexter, I can promise you as pretty a glass of *fine Champagne* as was ever

smuggled out of France. Darkness has descended upon our con-
ference, and I propose an adjournment to the Judge's hospitable
parlour. It is too late to return to my home this evening, and I
am sure my daughter must be considerably fatigued. I will furnish you with the Judge's address, and ride on with my little girl
upon the pillion of my saddle; you will follow me as soon as you
may find it convenient, and the remainder of the night may be
profitably spent in determining the relative merits of French
brandy and the rarest corn whisky in Wheeling."

Shiloh appeared aloof and pensive; he felt all at once very
tired, and he would have given his hope of supper for the privilege of sleeping under a hedgerow fresh with early moonlight,
but Melissa's eyes implored him, and David shook his arm and
muttered in his ear long eloquent prophecies of beefsteaks and hot
toddy. He had not the heart to disappoint them, although he desired with all his soul to be alone in the companionship of burning
indignations and fastidious dreams.

"Very well," he said wearily, "we shall be most happy to accept your friend's kind hospitality for to-night. To-morrow we
must depart upon other business, but for to-night I am at your
service."

10

LITTLE more than an hour later, Shiloh and David sat in the dim
and tranquil elegance of Judge Poindexter's parlour; oak logs
glowed between high brass andirons under the white mantelpiece,
and the wine-coloured surface of the mahogany table reflected the
subdued brilliance of the flame. It reflected in addition several
cut-glass decanters and steaming plates surmounted by silver
covers; the cloth had been drawn before the friends' arrival, but
Judge Poindexter had insisted upon calling for freshly broiled
chops and freshly opened Burgundy, and the stiff and foot-sore
travellers were expanding under the benign influence of his fire,
his generous food and drink, and his benevolent smile.

Shiloh, relaxed in the smooth fragrant depths of a great leather
arm-chair, regarded the judge with unconcealed approval; he was
forcibly reminded of his childhood's guide, the venerable Dr. Lind

of Windsor. The judge was tall and spare; his upright figure and the frosty abundance of his locks accorded well with a face of singular refinement and humane power. His low voice, warmly coloured by the accent of his country, charmed the listener no less by its quaint and pleasant modulations than by the high and fearless opinions which it so felicitously expressed.

It was clear that the judge entertained a distinguished regard for Mr. Daingerfield in spite of that gentleman's eccentricities and foibles; in the course of the conversation it became evident that the eminent jurist had been the devoted friend of Mr. Daingerfield's father, and that he still cherished this friendship's memory in preserving an affection for the son. Shiloh was amazed to observe the amelioration wrought in Mr. Daingerfield's manner and mood by the judge's society, and he thought of the perfectibility of mankind, and condemned himself for an impatient and undisciplined spirit.

Melissa had been sent to bed; she lay in the judge's wide white guest-chamber and dreamed, between waking and half-asleep, of Shiloh riding upon a mountain storm. She was neither happy nor unhappy; dimly she perceived that the variations of a single day had given her the ultimate sum of experience; the fact that this experience was of the soul alone troubled her tired body very little.

Both Shiloh and David were thinking of Melissa, as their minds grew drowsy under the gentle influence of the fire and the fragrant wine. Because they were each essentially generous and merciful, although in different spiritual degrees, each thought of Melissa tenderly, and hardly of himself, David because he did not want to marry her at the First Methodist Church, and Shiloh because he could not make her happy for ever in some golden sanctuary of immaculate innocence.

Presently they both heard with relief the judge's clear pronouncement of her name; they listened, and their drowsy careworn minds were suddenly at peace.

"Hector," said Judge Poindexter in his warm and cordial voice, "you'd better leave your little girl with me this winter. I'm lonely in this great house, and it must be lonely for the child in that wild valley of yours after the snow falls. I'll send her to a seminary for young ladies if you like, but personally I should pre-

Love in Desolation

fer to turn her loose in my library, with an occasional tutor to help her over the hard places. My old 'Rastus and 'Mandy will take care of her as if she were a spun-glass fairy doll, and I'll see that she has companions of her own pretty age as well as my senile devotion. You'd better do it, Hector, and make an old man happy."

"The offer is like your invariable kind heart, Judge," said Mr. Daingerfield, an added huskiness in his tones, "and for my poor child's sake I shall accept it, without blinding my eyes to its charitable nature. But from you alone such charity is not an humiliation; rather indeed, when your hand confers it, do I account it honourable alike to you and to me. Melissa is fortunate in possessing such a friendship; it is the only legacy which my dear father's poverty permitted him to leave, but it is more valuable than a miser's millions. Your health, sir, pledged in your own soul-warming whisky and my undying gratitude!"

Mr. Daingerfield drained his replenished tumbler; he drank whisky without stint while the rest of the company drank wine, and sparingly at that. Shiloh had relaxed his usual abstinence in compliment to the judge's gentle urbanity; a single glass of Burgundy had proved, together with the well-peppered mutton chop, a perfect panacea for muscular fatigue, and since the natural mood of his soul was universal benevolence and lovingkindness towards all men, he now floated in an aureate cloud of contentment towards the haven of sleep. To be sure, he had not touched the delicate amber decanter of French brandy which his host had set at his right hand, and he watched Mr. Daingerfield's libations with a sensitive shiver of alarm, but his mind was at peace concerning Melissa, and a delicious langour held him immovable in the great leather chair.

David was no less happy; his supper had exceeded his most sanguine expectations, and he did not share Shiloh's scruples about the generous wines of France. He was warmed through and through, and he felt almost sleek with pure comfort and the consciousness that it was no longer necessary to marry Melissa, or even to horsewhip her father. A lazy self-satisfaction made him stretch his superb muscles and yawn deliberately into the fire. He considered the excellence of the judge's *cuisine* and the ele-

77

gance of his old-fashioned parlour, and he knew that the child Melissa had found a safe anchorage and a sweet untroubled harbour.

Shiloh lifted his bright sleepy eyes towards the towering rows of books which lined the panelled walls; he perceived that the judge's library was well chosen, and he rejoiced for the sake of his little friend. Among the richly bound volumes he recognised the names of the French philosophers, and was happy in identifying the familiar bulk of *Political Justice* besides the *Republic* of Plato. He realised with poignant relief that the judge must be a person of liberal and enlightened views, and in spite of his extreme weariness he rose from his chair to draw from among its closely packed companions Locke's *Essay on the Human Understanding,* in whose pages he was presently profoundly lost.

" So, Mr. Shiloh," said the judge, smiling indulgently at his guest's graceful and fantastic figure and the intent beauty of his face bent upon the book, " I suppose you've come over here, as the ode puts it, ' From kings who seek in gothic night to hide the blaze of moral light.' Very right and proper for a fine young fellow like yourself, and if you have a fancy to establish yourself in Wheeling I can furnish you with some valuable introductions to leading citizens of our fair town. I hope you may decide to settle among us, sir, for you would be a delightful addition to our intellectual society, which is select, indeed, but unfortunately limited."

Shiloh shook his wind-blown hair in courteous regret; he looked a trifle wistfully at the richly ordered rows of books, the clear bright fire, the comfortable curtains of crimson brocade against the white-panelled walls, but his eyes sought a chink in the wooden blind through which a silver lancet seemed to pierce; he knew it for the thorny brightness of a star, and his heart tore at his ribs like something savage and imprisoned.

" Alas, no; I fear it is impossible," he said with calm politeness. " To-morrow we must prolong our journey still farther into the west; it grieves me that we must bid farewell to Melissa, but doubtless we shall return. Please believe us sensible of your kindness; I have no words wherewith to thank you."

He was palpably moved; the judge knew him to be weary, and

Love in Desolation

guessed him to be perplexed and sad. Indeed, melancholy had suddenly taken possession of Shiloh's mind at the thought of parting from Melissa; he was eager to be gone, and yet he longed to stay. He felt the familiar pity divide his heart, and he grew pale with the purely moral pain of it.

" I am sure that you gentlemen are ready for repose," said the judge humanely. " Come; 'Rastus will show you your bed-chamber, which I trust you will find comfortable and quiet after the fatigues of your journey. I have given orders that you are to be called betimes, and you will find breakfast prepared against your rising; I regret profoundly that the Cincinnati steamboat departs at so ungodly an hour, but you would be ill-advised to miss this opportunity of travelling by water along that beautiful natural avenue of traffic, the Ohio. I shall give myself the pleasure of joining you at breakfast, but I fear you must bid good-bye to Mr. Daingerfield to-night, as he is not an early riser. To Melissa I will myself convey your affectionate adieux; I know she will be sorry not to see you, but the poor child is sadly tired, and it will be more merciful to let her sleep until nature is restored."

Cheerful good-nights were exchanged between Mr. Daingerfield and the two friends; the judge followed them into the hall to see them safely into the respectful custody of old 'Rastus. They took their shining brass candlesticks from the table and ascended the low broad flight of stairs to the charming, old-fashioned room prepared for their reception. A cordial blaze welcomed them from its hearth; there was a bowl of late yellow roses upon the marble mantelpiece. Shiloh gave a sigh of unconscious pleasure at sight of the embroidered linen sheets, turned down in a cool smooth triangle over the blue counterpane. His elevated mind abominated the luxuries of an effete civilisation, yet he had suffered all his life from an obscure unapprehended homesickness for the decorous comforts of his father's country house, and a long exile among the majestic draughts of Italian palaces had sharpened this ache to poignancy. The simple yet spacious amenities of the judge's guest-chamber were as balm and oil upon the throbbing of a neglected wound.

"I swan!" said David appreciatively, preparing for slumber.

"Now this is something like and no mistake. 'Tain't exactly pioneering, but it suits me down to the ground. Yes, sir, this beats cock-fighting, I do declare! So hurry up, Shiloh, and hop into that handsome bed, for you look clean tuckered out, and I'm so sleepy I could sleep standing up like a hoss, only thank God there ain't no need for such carryings-on in this elegant mansion."

11

Shiloh paid no heed to his friend's advice; he stood staring into the fire in an attitude of thoughtful melancholy. His brow, supported by his slender sunburnt hand, was shadowy with meditation; his eyes absorbed the flame into their burning blue.

"David," he said at length, "I must say farewell to Melissa."

"But you can't," David objected promptly. "You heard what the judge said about her being tired; she ain't coming down to breakfast to-morrow morning, and I for one don't blame her, seeing as we have to eat at the outlandish hour of four o'clock."

"I shall not wait until to-morrow morning," Shiloh answered with wild and dreamy enthusiasm. "I shall go to her to-night, alone, and in the very hush and suspension of mortality I shall give her a single parting kiss, thus mingling for a moment our extremest souls in hallowed chaste communion."

"Plague take you, Shiloh," cried David in a panic, "you can't mean them crazy words; I know you can't, not if you set a fippenny bit upon your life, with that rearing tearing Daingerfield right down the hall! Why, man, he'd shoot you full of bleeding holes as soon as he'd take a chaw of tobacco, and then there's this grand old codger the judge, that's used you like a prodigal son; you ain't never going to abuse his kindness like that, are you? Goldarn it, Shiloh, it's too bad, that's what it is, and I wouldn't have believed it of you."

"Precisely what is it that you do believe of me, David?" asked Shiloh gently. "Do you think that I would lay a finger upon this innocent save in an exalted reverence of love?"

"Of course not, Shiloh; I couldn't think ill of you, never," replied David blushing hotly. "I didn't mean nothing wicked;

Love in Desolation

I know blooming well as you're a kind of saint, and you wouldn't harm a mosquito, much less a little orphan like Melissa. But there's such a thing as common sense, and there's such a thing as caution, and you haven't got neither. What would those two gentlemen imagine, I ask you as a sensible man, if they caught you coming out of the child's room?"

"I am unable to conjecture," said Shiloh proudly. "I prefer not to probe the corrupt and pitiful suspicions which convention engenders in maggot-broods within the human mind."

"Then are you really set on going?" David inquired desperately. "Because if you are, I shall come along, just to see that you aren't shot without a proper trial. I'll stand outside in the passage, and if I hear any one coming I'll whistle a bar of 'Shannandore' to warn you. Why, man alive, there's no earthly use in your arguing; I'm not a-going to let you be murdered all by yourself, so hold your hush and leave me come with you as I say."

Shiloh proceeded along the passage with quick and noiseless steps; David followed him in a more hardly achieved silence, the floor creaking beneath his stockinged feet.

Outside Melissa's room they paused; Shiloh entered, leaving the door slightly ajar, while David waited in miserable anxiety, leaning against the wall of the passage, and listening to the jovial voices from the parlour, and to the heavy beating of his own pulses as the darkness weighed upon his heart.

Moonlight floated like a frosty bloom upon the white guest-chamber where Melissa lay; the wide white couch was spread with a delicate coverlet of moonlight, and beneath this thin silver Melissa slept, and woke, but not to cry, and slept again to dream. Now she awoke from happy sleep to a consciousness of peace, and she saw Shiloh plainly, and without surprise, as he approached her softly along a path of silver.

"Melissa," said Shiloh simply, "I have come to kiss you good-bye." He leaned above her in the moonlight, and the flood of silver poured from his shoulders in feathery flakes like the bright cataract of archangelic wings.

Melissa lifted up her lips to his kiss, with an invisible lifting of the heart; she did not speak, and although her enormous eyes were open, she still appeared to move in some miracle of sleep. She permitted him to take her small cold hand in his, without the faintest pressure of farewell, and he could not be sure that she had recognised his presence, or returned his kiss. Yet in that instant, in that soft and fleeting breath, the perfect essence of her soul went forth, to be drawn like a little pulse of sighing air into Shiloh's breathing, and set free again into nothingness.

It was not that she died; it was not even that she grieved, aware of any deprivation. She remained indeed singularly tranquil and composed, and when at last Shiloh passed gently from the room, she lay unmoving in a meek passion of relinquishment, tranced in accepted sorrow, and dedicated to the wonder of her loss for ever.

Afterwards she slept; when the pearl-coloured fogs of the eventual morning interposed their veils between her slumbers and Shiloh's departing form, she lay unconscious of his going, her cheek upon her folded hands. So was she to sleep, peacefully enough and perhaps even happily, throughout the long superfluous nights of the years to come; these were nevertheless not interminable, having a limit and a consummation set to their loneliness, and it were futile to affront the dignity of that consummation by prophecies of pity or of hope.

IV

BROTHER LIZARDS

DAWN found the travellers among the river wharfs of Wheeling; David stared rather scornfully up at the vast luxurious shape of the steamboat *Lady Washington*. He had never plied his trade upon a power-driven vessel, and he did not scruple now to display a true sailor's contempt for such new-fangled devices.

"With all due respect for the judge, who was surely a grand old Roman, I don't think much pumpkins of that there top-heavy plaster ark," he said, eyeing the towering eminence of fresh paint and gilded curlicues with strong disfavour. "May be all very well for rivers, but you won't get a clumsy tub like that to beat a Salem clipper at sea, like they claim some of them have done. No, sir, she'll waddle along like a blooming mud-turtle all the way to Cincinnati, and by graminy I don't like the look of her. But come aboard, Shiloh, and we'll get our bearings; we don't have to decide yet for certain, for I see she's still taking on cargo, and she can't sail for another hour at least."

Shiloh followed his friend on board the steamboat; while David explored the possibilities of its lower deck the other leaned upon the rail, and watched the morning break over the noble bluffs which fringed the Ohio. Autumnal foliage glowed richly in the augmented light, and every withering tree bore a brief

The Orphan Angel

enchanting harvest of pure rose-colour under the sun's ascension. The river, flushing to responsive red, was thronged with curious and outlandish craft, keel-boats, broad-horns, and French batteaux, mingled with flimsier canoes and dinghies. An unsubstantial but populous city rose from the shining water; there were floating shops, floating taverns, and floating gambling-saloons, and from the stove-pipes of innumerable house-boats domestic plumes of smoke suggested coffee-pots and bacon and the pleasures of family life.

In the cabin above his head ladies and gentlemen were sitting down to an early breakfast; the savours of beefsteak and Mocha were wafted upon the freshening air, and David reapproached, unwrapping the large packet of sandwiches with which the judge's kindness had provided them.

"We did eat so goldarned previous," he explained apologetically, setting his broad white teeth into the generous layers of bread and butter and Virginia ham.

Shiloh was nibbling an apple, and watching the faces of his prospective fellow-travellers with admiration, wonder, and alarm. Here for the first time he perceived something vaguely approximating to his provisional hopes of a mighty race of pioneers inhabiting the primæval forests of the west. Shiloh had never beheld such a magnificent redundancy of beard as decorated the countenances of the men; even Trelawney's corsair mustachios faded into sparsity by comparison. Nor had he previously imagined that there was so much tobacco grown in the whole luxuriance of the New World as seemed necessary to these worthy persons' satisfaction; every whiskered cheek contained a formidable section of plug-cut, and the surface of the dark and narrow deck was not the cleanlier in consequence. He managed to curb a quite undemocratic disgust by a private meditation upon liberty, and while gently withdrawing himself into a less maculate corner he was consoled by a quotation from Lord Byron, which enabled him to finish his cool sweet apple in comparative peace of mind.

"Certainly they are surprisingly dirty, but then, 'corruption could not make their hearts her soil,'" thought Shiloh, still loyal to his dream of freedom.

Brother Lizards

His reflections, which contained perhaps the faint flavour of bitterness lacking in his apple-core, were somewhat rudely interrupted by a loud cry from David, who had seized his arm, and was endeavouring to drag him towards the rail under the influence of strong excitement. Shiloh feared for a moment that a suicidal impulse had overcome his friend's reason, and he attempted without success to oppose the forceful and persuasive grip of David's hand, but presently he realised that the latter's emotion was pleasurable in nature, and he discerned, among the swarm of river craft, the object of David's pointing forefinger and of the delighted scrutiny of his small blue eyes.

"Looky there, under our bows, Shiloh," shouted David ecstatically. " Now that there vessel's the spit and image of what a river-boat should look like, leastways according to my notion. By thunder, ain't she pretty, built on that elegant log raft, with her stove-pipe sticking up so pert and chipper out of her deckhouse, that's like a real little pioneers' cabin a-floating down the stream? See the men with their fowling-pieces, Shiloh, and the kegs that I calculate must be full of whisky and gunpowder, and the good old yaller dog laying asleep in the sun! Oh, that's the vessel for us, matey, and we're going aboard her this tarnation minute, 'stead of pottering about on this ornamental mausoleum for three-four enduring days! Come along, son, and we'll be signed on before you've cotched your breath."

Indeed, Shiloh was quite breathless with surprise and hurry by the time they had reached the wharf, and he permitted David to hire a row-boat from a negro boy and to pull out into the current of the stream without a single word of remonstrance. Finally he reached for the second pair of oars and placed them in the rowlocks with dexterous rapidity.

"Very well, David," he said with a laugh. " If you like the river-boat better, I can agree unhesitatingly with your romantic choice. I did not find the *Lady Washington* in the least degree prepossessing, and I shall welcome a change with all my heart. I have a shrewd suspicion that we are about to encounter adventures more manfully in keeping with our intentions than any by which our travels have been previously enlivened. But here we are under the bows of the noble ship; let us try our luck with her commander."

A few more vigorous strokes brought them alongside the raft, which was formed of gigantic logs most durably lashed together, and covered by a timber flooring; in the centre of this rectangle was a sort of cabin, built of scantlings and planks, and provided with an arched wooden roof, which gave it a grotesque resemblance to the ark of biblical mythology. At the sides this superstructure was almost flush with the edge of the raft; rude wooden fins projected from opposite apertures into the water, and served to navigate the clumsy craft in the absence of a tiller; both fore and aft the plank deck extended for some distance beyond the cabin.

An excessively lanky individual with a short dust-coloured beard lounged upon the forward deck; another and younger man, clean-shaven and with a look of the scholar in his deep-set grey eyes, sat hunched beside him, a fowling-piece across his angular knees. A nondescript yellow dog dozed near them, his wet black muzzle twitching in the sun. The scene was almost idyllic in its implications of leisure; a primitive checker-board occupied the top of an inverted keg, and several tattered books lay within reach. Shiloh noticed with heartfelt relief that both of the men were smoking corncob pipes; although not himself addicted to the use of tobacco, he was aware of the impracticability of smoking and chewing at the same time, and the evident enjoyment wherewith these persons inhaled the fragrant fumes of the Virginian weed seemed an earnest of their preference for the more agreeable habit. The clothing of the pair was reduced by exposure to the elements to a uniform earthen tint, their locks were long and untidy, yet withal there was something of queer distinction in their appearance, and their calm and thoughtful eyes interrogated the newcomers with a frank and cordial curiosity.

In response to David's jovial hail the elder of the two rose and leaned from the side of the ark; Shiloh saw that his warm brown eyes were surrounded by a network of amiable wrinkles, and when he smiled similar wrinkles involved his entire countenance in a map of pleasant past amusements and tolerant scorns. He removed the pipe from his mouth with extreme deliberation.

"Well," he inquired affably, "what do you youngsters want aboard the *Prairie Flower?*"

David, for whom this pretty name had a pronounced appeal, nudged Shiloh surreptitiously and replied in his best able-seaman manner.

"Beg pardon, sir," he said respectfully, "but me and my mate was a-wondering whethei you mightn't have a couple of berths for us aboard your vessel; we'd like to sign on regular, but if you don't need no extra hands we'd be ready and willing to pay anything as you might say in reason for our passage to Cincinnati. We're real strong and handy about a ship, sir, and you won't never regret it if you take us on, I do assure you."

"I couldn't take you as far as Cincinnati, my lad, for we are ourselves abandoning this noble galleon at Limestone," answered the unknown gentleman with the warm brown eyes; his wrinkles charted promises of excellent good-humour. "My friend the professor here, who is incidentally both first and second mate, happens to be betrothed to a young lady of Louisville, and it is our intention to strike across country to that Athens of the west without wasting time in other exploration. I am myself bound for distant Illinois, but a desire to be present at my learned colleague's nuptials has led me to accompany him to Kentucky. If you wish to come with us to Limestone, I have no objection, and as captain of this ship I believe I can guarantee an equal complaisance on the part of my crew."

He grinned humorously at the younger man, and Shiloh had a swift conviction that the nondescript yellow dog was the crew in whose friendly spirit the captain reposed such confidence. As if to affirm this supposition, the yellow dog opened one amber eye and winked with slow and indolent facetiousness.

"And couldn't you use us, sir? We're goldarned useful in a gale," said David eagerly; he had taken an immediate fancy to the captain, and his fingers ached for the touch of tarry ropes.

"Well, I'll be delighted to have your services in the arduous matter of agitating those oars about once in twenty-four hours," the captain replied. "They are solely for the purpose of steering,

87

and we rarely trouble to employ them unless our craft is completely reversed by the current; I believe our stern is a trifle blunter than our bow, albeit I have never verified the point. For the rest, you will discover little to do beyond the ordinary domestic duties customary for the preservation of life; I trust that one of you is a passable cook, for indeed neither myself nor the professor is precisely skilled in that branch of science. Your nautical knowledge will, I fear, be somewhat more esoteric than is strictly necessary; we do not sail or steam, we simply drift, and I would rather you played a good game of checkers aboard the *Prairie Flower* than that you were past masters in the knotting of reef-points. But tie your boat to that staple, and swarm up the side, both of you, and I'll show you our beautiful vessel."

Shiloh and David lost no time in complying with his request, and a moment later they stood on the broad planks of the *Prairie Flower,* examining their new surroundings with an ecstatic and uncritical excitement.

" This," said the captain politely, " is Professor Lackland from Pennsylvania; he has recently been instructing the youth of the country in mathematics at Washington and Jefferson College, and is at present honourably employed as my first and second mate. I am Captain Appleby from Massachusetts, brevetted by the double virtue of a British rifle-bullet at New Orleans and my current command of this ship. And now whom, in your persons, have I the satisfaction of addressing? "

"My name's David Butternut, and I come from Castine in the state of Maine," replied David with equal courtesy, " and this here's my friend Shiloh; we're both able seamen, and we purpose to be pioneers. We're prospecting through the west in search of a messmate's sister that we fears is in trouble, and we're in a tarnation hurry to reach Kentucky. Any way as we can be useful aboard of the *Prairie Flower* suits us elegant, and we hopes as you'll find us proper sailors and clever fellows at checkers. About cooking we don't rightly understand so much, but we can try, can't we, Shiloh? "

" Assuredly we can try," said Shiloh with his frank disarming smile, which was so electric a matter of large blue eyes and universal benevolence.

Brother Lizards

Captain Appleby and Professor Lackland examined their guests with interest; they had from the first been favourably impressed by David's ingenuous countenance, and now they revised by a shade their initial observation of Shiloh, granting him less eccentricity and a greater degree of distinction. The captain noted that his body was a model of athletic lightness worthy of the Grecian heroes of antiquity, and the professor was aware that his brow was loftier and more illumined than that of a stoic philosopher or an Athenian poet. Each was conscious of a strong personal self-congratulation in the thought that henceforward the stranger was to be the companion of his voyage.

"As David says, my name is Shiloh," he informed them pleasantly. "I am a poet, and an adventurer upon the face of the earth. My native land has most unhappily of old been the enemy of yours, but time has healed the poignancy of that ancient wound, and my own convictions are so liberal that they cannot clash with your devotion to freedom. Much as I deprecate my country's conduct, so much so indeed that I have long sought relief from oppression in the kinder Italian clime, I nevertheless will not insult your patience by apologies; let our own friendly and untrammelled relations be sufficient earnest of our mutual good faith. I am honoured, sirs, in your acquaintance; the fact that one of you is a scholar and the other a soldier of unvanquished liberty adds exaltation to my delight."

"I thought you were an Englishman, by your accent," said the captain smiling. "Well, we shan't agree any the worse for that circumstance, my boy; I'm getting along in years, and in spite of the ounces of British lead in my game leg, I have to-day an admiration for your country probably considerably in excess of your own, which you tell me is non-existent. You are young and uncompromising, but the day may come when you'll be glad enough to go home and settle down in the Thames valley or the Weald of Sussex."

"How under the sun did you know . . . ?" began Shiloh rather wildly, but the other interrupted him with a paternal laugh.

"Never mind, my boy; don't agitate yourself about it, I beg of you. I haven't the faintest notion who you are, except that you're a man of breeding and cultivation; I've never visited your ancestral home, and if I made a lucky shot it was a sheer fluke, I assure you. I have no desire to pry into your personal affairs; forgive me if I have said anything to disturb the tranquillity of your spirit." He extended his lean corded hand in a gesture of deliberate kindliness.

"Excuse me, but are you not a graduate of Oxford, sir?" asked the professor in a dry precise voice. He was a thin young man with a pallid intelligent face and a pair of singularly piercing grey eyes, and there was something about his narrow elongated nose and the domed benignity of his forehead which reminded Shiloh of William Godwin.

"Not a graduate; I spent a couple of terms at Oxford in my unseasoned youth," replied Shiloh with dignity. "I was, as a matter of fact, expelled from the university owing to a boyish prank which was," explained Shiloh blushing, "of a purely intellectual character."

"We shan't like you any the less for that, son," said the captain. "We're sick of all colleges, aren't we, Lackland? But we're not sick of scholars and gentlemen, I can tell you, and you'll be a veritable godsend to the poor professor if you can talk Greek with him on the long autumn evenings; I'm sadly rusty since I took to navigating an ark among the snags and planters of the Ohio."

"Is that a volume of Condorcet which I perceive upon the deck?" asked Shiloh of the professor with companionable eagerness. "Because, if it is, I should be infinitely obliged to you for lending it to me for a few hours."

"It is," said the professor with all the warmth of which his curiously frigid voice was capable. "Take it, by all means, and keep it as long as you please. Captain Appleby is disposed to be facetious when he speaks of my fluency in the dead languages; I am unfortunately a wretched Greek scholar, but I am not wholly unlearned in the higher mathematics, and I have amused myself occasionally in my leisure moments with metaphysics and the philosophies of the elder civilizations. If you find any of these subjects in the least amusing, I shall be most happy for your company."

Brother Lizards

"But what radiant and incredible good fortune!" cried Shiloh in delight, seizing the professor's whitey-brown hand and wringing it with fervour. "You shall teach me the more advanced branches of mathematics, in which I am sadly deficient, and I shall be overjoyed to impart to you all that I know of the divine language of Hellas, although I dare say that your knowledge is not in truth inferior to my own. Oh, this is indeed felicity, to come upon such treasures of wisdom and philanthropy in the very wilderness itself! David, is not this amazingly lucky, that now we shall be able to talk about the calculus of variations?"

David eyed the pale professor with some suspicion; he was obviously relieved when the captain clapped him on the back and addressed him with a jovial laugh.

"I'd far rather that you learned to make flapjacks, for my personal convenience," said the captain decidedly. "Come now, David my lad, and I'll show you the rest of the noble ark of the covenant, as I call her. We have a superb state cabin amidships, and our kitchen is provided with a real hearth of mortared bricks, to say nothing of a Dutch oven and the largest iron pot and skillet this side of Pittsburgh."

Shiloh was soon deep in the professor's dog-eared volumes; he speedily abandoned Condorcet in favour of Cauchy's new treatise, and an expression of reverential pleasure made his blue eyes luminous as the kindled brain behind them. The professor's colourless and desiccated features glowed pallidly with a transmitted spark of this same fire, and the silvered darkness of one head and the rough and dusty-flaxen fairness of the other were bent in a single fascination above the mesmerising page.

2

MEANWHILE the captain and David explored the deck-house together; David was enchanted by innumerable miracles of ingenuity and convenience, and presently the captain had drawn from him the shy admission that he used to be quite a hand with the frying-pan and the hunter's kettle away back in the Maine

woods before he run off to sea like the goldarned scalawag he
was, by graminy.

"We'd ketch trout and fry 'em with a bit of bacon," said
David reminiscently. "And in the big kettle — sugar-kettle as
Ma had thrown out it was, really — we'd have mostly just plain
stews, such as mebbe a good chunk of bear-steak or venison,
with a rabbit or a pa'tridge or a brace of quail to make it tasty-
like, and a handful of scallions for seasoning. That was simple
and easy, but kind of good all the same, and when we didn't
have no venison we'd fix up a mess of chowder with nice fresh
cod and onions and potatoes, or mebbe if we'd find a few extra
lobsters in our pots, that we didn't need to sell, we'd cook 'em
on the rocks in red-hot sand and sea-weed. You'd laugh, sir, I
suppose, at such childish notions, but it ain't so bad when you're
real hungry and the lobsters is young and tender. You eat
'em with potatoes roasted in the ashes."

The captain's lean countenance assumed a look of positive
starvation, and he regarded somewhat ruefully the arid un-
succulent bags of coffee and corn-meal, which, with a quantity
of dried apples and about half a bushel of smoked sausages,
composed the entire stock of comestibles aboard the *Prairie
Flower*. He laid his hand caressingly upon the consoling ro-
tundity of a five-gallon keg, and addressed David in tones of
measured firmness.

"My boy," he said with decision, "you and I must form
a defensive alliance aboard this ship, in sheer self-preservation. I
think I perceive in your friend Shiloh certain qualities only too
familiar to me from my acquaintance with the excellent professor; the chaste and abstracted intellect of the scholar refuses
to concern itself with material considerations, and the mind
flourishes at the expense of the emaciated frame. This would
be all very well if the professor alone were involved in the privation, but while he is perfectly content to gnaw a fragment of
bacon-rind or a morsel of dried apple, I am reduced to a state
of semi-starvation which is far removed from my natural desires
and appetites. I feel sure that you have experienced similar suf-
ferings as the price of your affection for the poet Shiloh. I believe that an English singer of like convictions has noted the

phenomenal fact that chameleons feed on light and air; very probably they may, poor little creatures, but ordinary mortals cannot follow this ethereal example without a tragic diminution of their vital force. David, let us conspire together against these children of a sunnier star; let us insist upon a sufficiency of food! "

David's face brightened conspicuously upon this suggestion; at the same time his loyalty to Shiloh was too complete to permit him to give an unqualified assent to the captain's critical remarks.

" I don't think as you hardly understand Shiloh as yet, sir, if I may make so bold as to say so," he said modestly. " Shiloh's a most surprising feller, a thundering wonder in more ways than one. He's what they call a genius, I reckon, and he just plumb forgets to eat now and then, but oh sir, it isn't as he's disapproving or superior like I guess the professor might be, judging by the long sniffy shape of his nose. He's humble as a child, is Shiloh, and he's tarnation thankful when I remind him to eat his dinner, and so pleasant and gentle-like about it all that it fair brings the tears to my eyes to think of it. 'Twould be so goldarned easy to cheat him, and by jiminy I wish I could have the everlasting licking of the man as tried it! Now the professor, I calculate he's different; he has a look of my old schoolmaster back in Castine, and I reckon he could be real nasty if you blew the dinner-horn just as he was a-studying out a terrible problem in arithmetic."

" You do not entirely do justice to the manifold excellences of my friend the professor," replied the captain. " There is some truth in what you say, yet he is undoubtedly a most amiable young man, as well as an elegant and distinguished scholar. Your temperaments may be somewhat uncongenial, David, but you will soon learn to like as well as to respect him, and his companionship will be a boon to Shiloh, I feel sure."

" Mebbe," said David dubiously; he found it hard to believe in a fervent passion for the higher mathematics, and he was glad when the captain began to talk of venison hams and mallard ducks.

" I'll tell you what you must do, David," the captain explained eagerly. "You must take the skiff and row back to shore, towing that hired tub of yours behind; then you can visit the markets and select everything we require, the best of everything, my boy, and plenty of that. Spare no expense; I intend to reform the culinary mechanics of the *Prairie Flower*. Here's some money; you'll find it ample, but if you prefer to contribute something towards your passage to Limestone, let it be in provisions; a nice pair of chickens, say, or a few dozens of fresh eggs. We already possess the more ordinary utensils, but perhaps you'd better lay in a proper assortment of plates and spoons; the big lead spoons are the best, and that Pittsburgh Liverpool ware is cheap and durable as well as pretty. Now off with you, and don't forget butter and cheese and milk, to say nothing of sugar and spices and preserved fruits. I would prefer to have a share in the expedition, which is after my own heart, but I fear that our studious young friends might sink the vessel upon a sawyer during my absence, in some fit of sublimity or intense contemplation."

3

WHILE David rowed back to the wharf, the captain again sought the deck where Shiloh and the professor sat absorbed; he lounged idly against the rail, smoking his corncob pipe and scratching the yellow dog between the animal's drowsily twitching ears.

"The principle of virtual velocities," Shiloh was saying gravely, "employed by Lagrange to elucidate his theory of the libration of the moon . . ."

The captain listened dreamily, lulled almost to slumber by the chanting eloquence of Shiloh's voice; he smiled as the professor's dry clipped tones cut sharp across his reverie.

"But my dear sir, I know little or nothing of astronomy, yet surely I am right in believing that in Laplace's memoirs published in the volumes of the French Academy, it is demonstrated that, independently of any save the most general consideration as to mass, the mutual action of the planets could never largely affect the eccentricities and inclinations of their orbits."

The captain now perceived that Shiloh held Cauchy's treatise

in one hand and in the other an open quarto of Lagrange, while
the professor was similarly burdened with Gauss's *Disquisitiones
arithmeticæ* and the third volume of Laplace's *Méchanique céleste*.
While the one discoursed pedantically of planetary mean motion,
or surveyed with a glazed grey eye the theory of probabilities, the
other contrived to varnish with romantic glamour even the chilly
calculus of finite differences, and to make of mechanical truth
a lucid and harmonious revelation of serene and rigorous loveliness.

" The elimination of the unsatisfactory conception of the infinite from the metaphysics of the higher mathematics . . ." said
Shiloh with passion, and the captain observed that his eyes were
like portions of the midnight sky itself burning through the
hollow sockets of a noble mask of exaltation; the mask was pale
as snow or stone, but the eyes were bright pieces of infinity.

" Good heavens above! " cried the captain appositely, " what
a precious pair of theorists you are, and how thankful I am that
I have the delightful David to support me in my more ponderable
incarnation of hungry flesh and blood! I realize that I am the
basest of materialists, yet I own to a lively curiosity about the com-
ponent parts of my dinner. But here comes David with the skiff
full of charming provender; I discern a pair of my favourite mallard ducks, and, as I live, I believe he has succeeded in obtaining
the venison ham of my Lucullan dreams! "

It was true; David bounded to the deck with his arms full of
bundles and his face aglow with simple triumph, and as the captain praised him warmly for his sagacity and initiative in discovering so many rare and exquisite viands in the markets of
Wheeling, Shiloh came forward with an air of generous and unselfish pleasure lighting his abstracted brow.

" My dear Davy," he said affectionately, " I have missed you
even in the midst of the intellectual raptures of the last hour,
but I have excellent good news for you, my friend. I had feared
that you would be unable, owing to your unfamiliarity with the
French tongue, properly to appreciate the rich and delicate satisfaction prepared for us by Lagrange and Laplace, yet behold, the
professor has but just informed me that several of the latter's
most celebrated works have been translated into English by a

The Orphan Angel

Mr. Pond. See, here is one of them; shall not the professor explain it to you, David, so that we may all three share the delights of this mental ecstasy? "

David appeared so ridiculously alarmed by this kind proposal that the captain took pity on his distress, and sent him off to the kitchen, much to Shiloh's disappointment. The latter was far too polite to protest, but he gazed rather wistfully after his friend's departing form, sure that David had been cheated of a sublime and fearful joy, and his eyes were sorrowful as he listened to the captain's excuses.

" I quite understand that it is necessary to serve mallard ducks with an accompaniment of hominy and currant jelly," he said at length with extreme seriousness, " and I am certain that my good David possesses a skill capable of dressing these dishes to perfection, but might he not have had a moment's leisure in which to taste the true Pierian crystal? But no matter; he is too magnanimous a creature to repine, and I will not dull his bright example by spiritless complaints. I dare say, sir, that your experiences in the army have made it difficult for you to comprehend that boundless liberty of the soul which gives even a poor sailor a right to the treasures of high research, although you yourself fought with such valour to preserve that very liberty for the least of your countrymen. I crave your pardon if I am too severe in my strictures upon the discipline to which David has been subjected; I rely upon your honourable and charitable heart to forgive me, and to release David from his duties as soon as it is humanly possible to do so."

The captain contented himself with a courteous inclination of the head and a humorous and twisted smile; he presently joined David in the warm seclusion of the kitchen, where culinary operations of the most elaborate description were immediately begun. The two did not appear again until dinner-time, and then as the victorious heralds of so inspired a repast that even the scholar and the poet were startled into enthusiasm by the refined perfection of its flavours.

"Speaking of geniuses, David, Vatel might own a natural master in you," said the captain cryptically to his flushed assistant. " We should have had wild rice for the ducks, but this

hominy is really very palatable. Shiloh, will you have a little more
of the currant jelly? It is put up in glass jars by a worthy old lady
of Wheeling, and upon my soul it is nearly equal to my own
dear mother's delicate concoction."

The afternoon was flawless; as the ark drifted softly between
the towering bluffs of the Ohio, the four companions lounged
upon the deck in different attitudes of contented relaxation; the
yellow dog dozed on the warm pine planks, and Shiloh dozed
also, his head in a patch of sunlight. The others sucked sleepily
at their corncob pipes; David and the captain had begun a game
of checkers with red and white corns, but presently they grew
too lazy to play, and there was no longer any sound except the
lapping of water against the moss-grown sides of the *Prairie
Flower*.

The season was the honeyed heart of Indian summer; the
trees upon the lofty banks of the river were sumptuous in all the
colours of the nobler metals, with here and there a higher plume
of sanguine or of flame. Shiloh stretched himself as he dozed in
the sun, and in the golden twilight of his drowsy mind a strain
of music shaped itself in words, lucid and harmonious as the
calculus of variations, and sumptuous as the processional colours
of the forest.

He put his slim brown hand into his breast pocket, and very
quietly drew forth pencil and paper, and there, while the others
dozed, he wrote down certain words in a certain magical order of
his own contriving, and put the paper back into his pocket, and
slept, with his head in a bar of golden twilight.

The ensuing days were truly idyllic in their gentle progres-
sion; a life of idleness and innocent duty endured upon the
Prairie Flower, and both Shiloh and David flourished in its foster-
ing sunny air. Perhaps the very fact that the unhurried ark was
drifting with the current instead of plunging forward animated
by wings or the impetuous breath of steam, may have laid a pro-
founder peace upon the spiritual atmosphere; it is certain that
this peace existed, and that it was beneficent and dear.

David and the captain pacified the actual hunger of the body
by a succession of almost incredibly savoury and appropriate
meals, and Shiloh and the professor laboured untiringly in the

starry vineyard of the higher mathematics to distil such wine as must appease the extremest mortal thirst of any soul.

Their material wants were few, and liberally satisfied; their duties were definite and simple, and the performance of such communal operations was drudgery to no one. The captain and David did the marketing, rowing ashore every second day for the purchase of provisions; the more prosperous hamlets along the river-banks furnished an endless plenty of fresh eggs and butter, chickens and ducks, and the kindly cultivated fruits of the earth. In their capable hands reposed the responsibility for sending these delicacies to the deck-house table well dressed and seasoned, a task most cheerfully and successfully accomplished. Upon Shiloh and the professor devolved the business of occasionally and violently agitating the vessel's gigantic oars; this they appeared to regard rather as a jocund form of sport than a serious employment, and often the professor's arid chuckle echoed upon the chime of Shiloh's fiery laughter as the two pulled desperately at the great leather-bound handles. They compared the callouses upon their palms with pardonable pride, and had there been even an ounce of superfluous flesh to pad their muscular slenderness, it must have been consumed like candle-wax in the flame of this singular exercise.

Theirs, too, was the slight innocuous toil of sweeping the cabin floor and tidying the primitive wooden berths with which this apartment was provided. Each was by nature fastidious and active, and their quick dexterous performance won the admiring praise of David and the captain. On the whole the domestic arrangements of the *Prairie Flower* were above reproach; a democratic peace and good-will reigned in all the labours of its daily life, and the four companions became firmer friends with each rising and setting of its rich autumnal sun.

The long amber afternoons were spent in recreation; Shiloh and the professor wandered happily among planetary perturbations, while the captain and David played at checkers or indulged an ingenuous taste for marbles. And not infrequently it came about that these enthusiasms grew vocal with excitement, and a curious chorus of strophe and antistrophe made musical the aureate descending hour.

Brother Lizards

"Knuckle down!" David would shout in his agreeable baritone. "Toy bone! Go to baste!" and the captain's booming bass would roar its answer like replying cannon, "Man-lay! Clearings! My first, I believe!" until the bluffs of the Ohio echoed with innumerable Titanic voices, as if a monstrous warfare lay concealed behind the copper ramparts of the forest.

At the same instant the lighter, less substantial tones of Shiloh and the professor might be lifted in ethereal cries concerning the commensurability of the mean motions of Jupiter and Saturn, or in sudden poignant exposition of the nebular hypothesis, spoken in a thrilling whisper that trembled with its own intensity.

One day the several sciences of astronomy and marbles discovered a definite point of contact in the shape of a charming sphere of azure glass, whose orbed circumference was interlaced with mazy convolutions of pale and silvery threads. David had won this lovely bauble from the captain in honourable combat, and Shiloh, perceiving it, had desired it passionately, because of its beauty and its vague resemblance to a universe in miniature.

"But I could not deprive you of your delightful plaything, David," Shiloh protested nobly, with a veritable longing in the large blue eyes that gazed at the large blue marble. "I really should not consider it right to accept the gift of your unselfishness, much as I admire this enchanting toy. See, it is indeed the universe, the true colour of heaven, streaked with wandering planets and divine emanations; the wonder of it is that it has grown so small that I can balance it upon the palm of my hand."

"Oh shucks, Shiloh, I want for you to have it!" said David. "I can buy me another in the next village. I'll learn you to play if you like, though them big ones ain't so good as the little black alleys."

Shiloh and the professor rejoiced not only in their mutual passion for astronomy and metaphysics; they spent many profitable hours in the discussion of ancient and modern poetry, and the professor brought to birth a very pretty talent for the composition of classical odes in the Augustan manner. Shiloh was continually busy with a pencil and a scribbled fragment of brown paper; the product of these activities went into his breast pocket, where various folded sheets lay secret against Silver's likeness.

The Orphan Angel

He had already showed the little ivory oval to the other, in compliment to the professor's amiability in exhibiting the portrait of his own fiancée, the lovely Miss Rosalie Lillie of Louisville.

Professor Lackland wore his lady's picture in a flat locket of engine-turned gold, suspended by a black silk ribbon over the region of his heart. Shiloh was never weary of marvelling at this circumstance, nor at the apparent opposition existing between the professor's calm and chilly deportment and the internal temperature of this heart. In a thin precise voice more suitable for the expounding of algebraic functions the lover grew eloquent in praise of Miss Lillie's virtues and the splendid velvet of her eyes, until Shiloh longed to behold this paragon of tender brilliance, and stared rather wistfully at Silver's pale and evasive smile and the moth-wing darkness of her gaze.

The professor took a not unnatural delight in his Rosalie's accomplishments, and he informed Shiloh with vicarious pride that she was a gifted poetess and an elegant performer upon the Spanish guitar. Both Shiloh and David were determined to dance at their friend's approaching wedding, even though David should be capable of no more than a sailor's horn-pipe, and Shiloh of some airy and improbable *pas-seul* of his own invention.

At night the ark was invariably moored to a convenient tree; such storms as visited their voyage raged exclusively during these intervals of inactivity, and so hardly constituted a real annoyance, much less a danger or a problem. The tie-rope was admirably reliable, and the studious pair of steersmen developed a curious instinct for avoiding snags and planters among the waters of the majestic stream.

It is clearly impossible to give a detailed account of all the batter-cakes and biscuits, eggs and fried ham, steaks, stuffed chickens, and mysterious puddings' produced by David and the captain with the aid of the Dutch oven and the enormous iron pot and skillet; suffice it to say that their quantity was unequalled by the stock of an average Covent Garden stall and their quality unsurpassed by the masterpieces of an exceptional Parisian chef. David grew sleek as a comely gold-curled ram that has feasted on honey-flowers and thyme, and even the lean dust-coloured captain blossomed into new vigour, and his twisted smiles

were like a surprising pattern of foliage upon the dry stick of
Aaron's rod.

The yellow dog basked in sunlight within a circle of beef-
bones; the professor had rescued him from an unhappy Pittsburgh
slum, and the creature believed that the river ark was a canine
paradise created for his particular benefit. He was a placid contented beast, and everyone called him Log; the captain said that
this was the diminutive of Ship's Log, but the professor insisted
that it was obviously a contraction of Logarithm. David, whose
vocabulary was racy of the soil, was convinced that Bump on a
Log was the proper appellation; neither Shiloh nor the animal
itself ever ventured an opinion on the subject.

Now all too soon the darling argosy approached its haven,
and upon a softly melancholy evening of pale clouds and pearly
river mists the *Prairie Flower* drew near to its destination, and
the travellers beheld the lights of the little town of Limestone
gleam faintly through a thin curtain of rain. Even the professor,
who would presently be in the bright company of his beloved,
owned to a mood of sadness; the others were frankly despondent,
and the yellow dog whimpered in sympathy, a brute Adam dis-
possessed of paradise.

"You'd far better come with me, boys, and settle down
in Illinois," said the captain, sucking pensively at his corncob
pipe. "Then Shiloh can send for his wife and child, and David
can marry Miss Silver and found a Butternut family in the pro-
ductive soil of Pike County; this will save me the trouble of be-
getting any sons to be the comfort of my declining years; yours
can maul the rails for my fence and hoe my truck-patch in the
spring. I'll gladly turn over a part of the bounty lands I've bought
up to any brisk young fellow who'll consent to populate the west
in the interests of patriotism. Here's your golden opportunity as
the servant of mankind, Shiloh, and do you, David, meditate
upon your duties as an American citizen and perform what is
required of you by a loving country."

Both Shiloh and David laughed in rather an embarrassed
fashion; they shared in common a curious childlike innocence of
speech and thought, and the captain's kind suggestion appeared
slightly indelicate to this mutual taste for modesty. They did

ample justice, however, to the complete benevolence of his intentions, and only an unswerving devotion to Silver prevented them from accepting his magnanimous offer. They shook their heads with stoical decision; the captain and the generous bounty lands of Pike County pleaded in vain against the sorrowful entreaty of Silver's eyes, which were after all no more than shadowy blots upon a small circle of ivory.

"David, David, how can I contrive to exist without your beautiful cooking?" cried the captain despairingly. "Here was I, beginning actually to take on flesh and to feel the replenished blood sparkle in my veins like April sap, and now I suppose I must go back to bacon and dried apples, with an occasional dreadful experiment in corned beef and cabbage. Lackland will miss his mathematics, I have no doubt, but his bride will be on hand to console him, and after all there is very little succulence in the integral calculus. My case is much harder, yet I will not weary you with my lamentations; I only hope that we may have a good supper to-night, to prepare us for the morrow's parting."

"But you are all coming to my wedding; I insist upon your presence at my wedding," said the professor eagerly, adding in a faintly dubious tone, "I am convinced that Rosalie would desire it above all things; she is the soul of hospitality, and my friends are to be her friends always, and by her own heartfelt wishes."

"We'd be rather a ruffianly crew to introduce into a lady's parlour, Lackland," the captain objected; he had small faith in Miss Lillie's ability to be friendly with a trio of ragged tramps. "You must remember that we can none of us afford new clothes, and although Shiloh's so particular about shaving his practically non-existent beard, David and I have somewhat the air of minor Hebrew prophets, and we're all disgracefully tattered and weatherworn. Your fiancée must be a remarkable girl if she can consent to receive us."

"She is a remarkable girl," explained the professor proudly. "She is a talented, liberal, lovely creature, and her father's financial reverses have unfortunately familiarized her with poverty, and softened a heart which adversity was powerless to shatter. I believe that the family is at present residing in a species of log

cabin in the remote environs of Louisville, and although they have
been since birth accustomed to the niceties and refinements of
affluence in that metropolis of the west, I know that their hospitality is as exquisite when dispensed from four rude walls of
unhewn timber as when the noblest mansion on Third Avenue
sheltered its grace. Come, my dear comrades; my Rosalie will
welcome you with joy, and her charming parents will endorse
the pleasure of their child in your acquaintance. Surely you will
not permit a few sartorial deficiences to cheat us upon this auspicious occasion."

"By graminy, Shiloh, I agree with the professor," said David.
"I don't see as we look so tarnation terrible, anyway, and Cap'n
and I could borrow your razor and smarten up a bit before the
wedding. I'd admire to meet the professor's young lady, and I
think a fine old-fashioned reel or country dance, with a few fancy
liquors, would do us all a power of good, loosen our joints like,
and put ginger into our spirits. Myself, I'm real handy with a
needle, what with being raised a sailor and all, and I reckon I
can set a stitch here and a stitch there in these wild raggedy garments of ours as'll spruce 'em up considerable in a brace of shakes.
Then Shiloh and I can borrow a cake of that elegant brown soap
and wash our shirts in the river like we did last week; I fetched
the collar off'n mine pounding it with a big rock, but it was
goldarned clean when I had done with it. At the same time
we'll have a chance to scrub ourselves most particular, and I war-
rant we won't disgrace the professor when once we gets to the
party, will we, Shiloh?"

"Certainly we shall endeavour to make ourselves presentable
in honour of our friend's felicity," Shiloh answered gracefully.
"If Miss Rosalie Lillie will allow us to pay our respects to her,
even in this woefully dilapidated condition, she must indeed be
the daughter of nobility and gentle tolerance; Professor Lackland is profoundly happy in uniting his fortunes with one so
virtuously gifted and so sweetly bred."

"Well, I dare say we shall not actually invalidate the ceremony," said the captain with a philosophic yawn. "And yet I
confess to a flavour of scepticism in my faith in your fiancée's
liberality, if that liberality must embrace a bearded villain like

The Orphan Angel

myself. However, I will investigate my stock of outmoded necker-chiefs and antique flowered waistcoats, and we will all come forth like the celebrated Incredibles of Bonaparte's Directory. I believe my lieutenant's uniform is in the large portmanteau under my berth; when I was brevetted a captain in 'fifteen I steadily set my face against the purchase of a new set of regi-mentals, in spite of my poor old mother's tears, and her only con-solation lay in embalming the war-worn remnant of the other in a superfluity of gum-camphor. Shall I resurrect its glories, pro-fessor, in compliment to your nuptials?"

Shiloh and David warmly seconding this proposal, the cap-tain was persuaded to repair to the cabin in search of his uniform, and presently he emerged in the full magnificence of threadbare blue broadcloth laced with tarnished gold. The sword which clanked against his long bony thigh seemed the pattern of his own soul turned to steel, slender and fine and durable, yet rusty, and sad-coloured with disuse.

"A captain's sword, you see," he said, smiling cynically. "I managed to afford this dainty lethal instrument, although I could not afford a new uniform. My choice was perhaps unwise, since the fighting was over, and a prosperous coat covers a multitude of follies."

"I swan, Cap'n, you're a perfect picture in them clothes!" cried David delightedly. "I calculate as how you'll clean knock their eyes out at the wedding, a-swaggering in with that grand pair of gold epaulettes on your shoulders, and that sword a-rattling by your side. I'm proud to know you, sir, and you'll be a credit to the professor in the eyes of his stylish friends, I'll bet my bottom dollar as you will!"

"You do indeed approximate closely to my conception of the ideal warrior," said Shiloh in an awe-struck voice. "You are aware, Captain Appleby, how irrevocably I am fixed in my disapproval of bloodshed, but there are certain struggles, like the present conflict in Greece and the lofty strife in which you won your own well-merited laurels, to which no ordinary standards may fitly be applied; their very nature exempts them from con-demnation. You are doubtless familiar with Wordsworth's noble poem upon the Character of the Happy Warrior; I think I can recite a portion of it from memory, if you will permit me to do so in salutation to a soldier of freedom."

" It's more than kind of you, my boy, but I beg you to spare my blushes," replied the captain, laughing. " You regard me through the medium of your own romantic mind; the only part of that very fine poem which applies to me is the line about the unfortunate person who was left unthought-of in obscurity; that's my portrait to the life."

" Good heavens! " cried Shiloh in distress, " how can you possibly suggest anything so supremely ridiculous? The moment you strode out of the cabin door, looking so tall and exalted, you reminded me forcibly of the line, ' Happy as a lover, and attired with sudden brightness, like a man inspired.' "

" And that," said the captain rather bitterly, " is because, my dear Shiloh, you are an incurable idealist. But perhaps," he added quietly, stroking the hilt of his sword, " you may have the right of it, after all."

And indeed the captain was a sufficiently splendid figure, as he stood upon the deck of the *Prairie Flower* with the expiring glimmer of a rose-red evening piercing the pearly river-mists to paint his shabby coat to the colour of dragon's blood; forgotten lions raged suddenly in his untidy earth-tinted hair, and his beard was tawny in the sunset. It is somewhat more than possible that Shiloh may have had the right of it, but since the question involves enormous mortal issues, it is not the privilege of this simple tale to attempt to disentangle them.

4

NEXT day the travellers set off through a wild region of bear-brakes and thickets; the roads were a succession of corduroys and mud-holes, and although no more than a hundred miles divided them from Louisville, they could not hope to make the journey in less than six or seven days. They had abandoned the *Prairie Flower* at the rude riverside wharf of Limestone; David and Shiloh had bedewed the worn planks of her deck with actual tears, and when the captain succeeded in selling her to an old gentleman who was contemplating a trip to Cincinnati to visit his married daughter, they regarded the good silver dollars of her price with shuddering horror as a sinister kind of blood-money. Nevertheless, they were greatly refreshed and comforted by an excellent dinner at the Limestone tavern, and they set off in company with their friends in a state of subdued cheerfulness and determined hope.

The captain wore his uniform, since they travelled light, and were able to carry only such luggage as each might tie within the compass of a large pocket-handkerchief. The professor's suit of mouldy black broadcloth looked oddly out of keeping with the luxuriant savagery of the forest scene, yet his spare and wiry frame was capable of supporting exertions and fatigues which might have caused a giant to complain. David strode crashing through the underbrush with a superb contempt for fallen logs and mud-puddles, and his hair was like a golden fleece in the sunlight, but Shiloh appeared almost a part of the wilderness itself in the fantastic simplicity of his tattered garments and the bright profusion of his uncovered locks. He sped swiftly forward like a natural force, a sapling tree made animate, a wave, a moving cloud, and such an exaltation made his blue eyes luminous that the others wondered to behold him, and forbore to protest against a pace most difficult to follow.

"Mebbe I can beat you on the highroad, Shiloh," said David with an admiring grin, "but there ain't never been nobody could walk on broken ground so fast as you."

The yellow dog loped at their heels, and his joyous barking echoed like laughter through the forest aisles. Now and again he would turn aside from the path to chase a muskrat or a rabbit, and then Shiloh would reason with him gently and with logical precision on the subject of clemency and the duties of the strong towards the weak, supporting his brilliant argument by morsels of brown sugar, of which the animal was inordinately fond.

Towards nightfall they approached a settler's cabin; it occupied a clearing in the dense timber, and was neatly and picturesquely constructed of rough logs. A field of Indian corn surrounded this rude sylvan retreat, and a potato-patch lay close to a tiny orchard of peach- and apple-trees. Tall sugar-maples shaded the dooryard, and in this sheltered spot a thin young woman sat spinning, her sombre eyes fixed upon the ground.

At the sound of the travellers' footsteps she looked up startled; a painful flush dyed her cheek with duskier crimson, and she put her hand to her breast in a gesture of alarm. Three ragged children who were playing in the dusty grass at her feet drew closer to their mother's knee, and all four stared at the newcomers with the wide frightened eyes of defenceless animals.

Shiloh stepped forward with his most engaging smile, and a simple word of reassurance; the woman immediately lost her look of terror, and the children came shyly nearer to gaze in fascination at the stranger, whose consoling beauty shone through rags as humble as their own.

"Land sakes, how you skeered us," said the woman in a flat lonely voice; Shiloh noticed that her wide defenceless eyes were full of lost and lonely darkness.

"Reckon you can have some bacon and pone; I can't accommodate you with no chicken fixin's," said the woman sadly in response to their courteous request for supper. Nevertheless, she provided them with an ample and not unsavoury meal, and the interior of the cabin proved to be comfortable and clean. The woman seemed to take a mournful pride in her domestic efficiency; she smiled at Shiloh's compliments to her plump pretty children, and explained that their ragged attire was merely a concession to their preference for making mud-pies.

"Can't keep 'em decent nohow," she complained. "They've got good linsey and cotton dresses that I wove with my own hands, but they wear 'em out like so much cobweb. Same with stockin's; it's knit, knit, knit all the time and naught but holes to show for it. As for shoes, I tell my old man that we ought to get 'em shod like Tom and Jerry there; they wears out a heap of sole-leather in a year, and my old man gets sick of playin' shoemaker."

"But think of the priceless dower of independence which you will leave to them, and to your children's children," cried Shiloh fervently, and the woman flushed with pleasure, and allowed that that was true, and presently she was telling proudly of her marvellous success at candle-making, and of the very superior quality of her maple sugar, which Shiloh tasted with keen appreciation. And while the captain and the professor praised the livestock and the noble growth of Indian corn, Shiloh and David sat on the floor in front of the fire of cedar logs, and David gave the boy his willow whistle, and showed him how to whittle jackstraws out of wood, and Shiloh made a brown paper boat for the two little girls to launch in their mother's washtub.

"Lordy, if here ain't my old man back from the store already!" said the woman suddenly, as a fair-haired giant burst into the warm room, and stood transfixed by amazement at sight of its cheerfully crowded state. His six-foot-one of brawn and muscle was precisely measured to fit Shiloh's preconceived notion of a pioneer, and he was cruelly disappointed when this prodigy laid several neat parcels of tea and coffee upon the cabin table of unvarnished pine; the carcass of a bear flung down upon the hearth would have seemed so much more in keeping with the man's appearance.

Introductions were speedily performed, and the frown which marked the farmer's brow was dissipated in the general merriment, in which the capering children joined with spirit. Good feeling prevailed; the host produced a five-gallon keg of whisky, and his wife fried another round of fresh eggs and flitch for the entire company.

"Swapped that batch of butter and chickens for a heap of store tea and coffee and good liquor," said the man complacently. He explained that these were the only commodities which were not produced upon the farm itself, and the travellers wondered at the resourcefulness of this sturdy freeman, who squeezed from the primitive world about him such plain abundant plenty.

"But it's powerful lonesome, powerful lonesome," he admitted, with a searching look into his wife's serious dark eyes. "And we gits the aguey in the fall pretty regular, me and Susan, though the young 'uns are right healthy, and we manage to struggle along. It's full twenty miles to the store, and further still if we wants to go to meeting; 'tain't often as we gits to see company like this of an evening, convenient to our own fireside."

Shiloh was in an ecstasy of admiration for the independence of this forest home; his eyes blazed brighter than the woman's best dip candles as he expounded his theories of freedom and enlarged upon the joys of privacy. The farmer and his wife exchanged occasional glances of scepticsm or surprise, but upon the whole they were immensely flattered, and so encouraged that they talked for an hour past their customary bed-time about the possibility of purchasing another cow and entertaining the preacher during the next revival.

The travellers slept on the floor in front of the comfortable embers; their kind host and hostess would not hear of their occupying the corn-crib. The following morning, after a generous breakfast of mush and milk and frizzled bacon, the wanderer set forth once more upon their journey, with manifold expression of gratitude and esteem. Shiloh left a veritable flotilla of paper craft floating upon the soapy bubbles of the washtub, and the children's round blue eyes were full of tears as they kissed him farewell.

"But you must really have these young people instructed in the simpler branches of knowledge, such as reading, writing, and ciphering," he said solemnly as he shook the farmer's horny hand in parting.

"I won't have no child of mine hurtlin' away his time like that," answered the man with good-tempered scorn. "Now honey," he admonished his elder daughter, patting her corn-sill curls, "say good-bye to the gentleman nice and polite, and don't act like a little scairt rabbit. No, sir," he went on decidedly, "the boy kin git a bit of book-larnin' later if he keers to, but my gal ain't never gwine to be high-larnt if I kin help it; nothin' spiles a woman for marriage like larnin' how to read."

"I am myself somewhat weary of the intellectual woman, confessed Shiloh, thinking of Jane Williams's delicious ignorance and of the calm grey-eyed frigidity of his own domestic blue stocking; at the same instant he experienced a pang in wondering whether those eyes were dark with loneliness by the shore of Lerici Bay.

The Orphan Angel

5

THIS shadow fled like a blur of smoke across the golden mirror
of Shiloh's mind, a shiver of impermanent sorrow leaving laughter in its wake, a ripple on sunny water. For the day was too
lovely to be marred by regrets or forebodings, and Shiloh dreamed
happily of a time when his grey-eyed Mary should have joined
him in the primeval forest, and of the delicate flotilla of fairy
ships, folded from her finest cream-laid, hot-pressed notepaper,
which should set sail for their child's delight upon a washtub full
of rainbow bubbles, under the cloudless sapphire sky of freedom.

There was no peace in Shiloh's mind; its nature was a changing brightness, and often its agitations were divine. That morning, as he trod the forest paths, his spirit was quickened by a
singular certainty of joy; a species of angelic possession set fiery
lightnings round his brow. As he went forward through the trees
this emanating fire was made actual in words; he spoke them
scarcely above a whisper, and yet their echo filled the woods to
overflowing.

Indian summer still prevailed under the impenetrable leafage
of the forest; here no storm could blow, although the sun might
filter down in motes of amber to warm the lower air. But overhead, where the tall tree-tops took the full rigour of the west,
there was continual sound and movement, like the multitudinous
hurry of the sea, and the rich profundity of autumnal colour was
radiant in the wind.

Along the broad buffalo-streets, and through the tangled bear-
brakes, between walls of white oak and tulip-trees, the four
friends proceeded to the professor's wedding. A holiday mood
possessed them; each sang such songs as memory and use made
possible, so that while David roared with sonorous lungs of
Greenland and the whale-fish, the captain hummed meditatively
of The Pride of the Valley, and the bridegroom himself apos-
trophized Beauty's Eyes in a thin tenor. In this curious sym-
phony Shiloh's voice was audible as a single taut and glittering
string, drawn to a thread of sound, vibrating yet never broken.

Brother Lizards

At intervals the jocular yelping of the dog rattled from the under-brush like the bark of a snare-drum.

As evening rose in azure smoke from the trodden leaves of the forest, the professor found that his own and Shiloh's swifter pace had carried them somewhat in advance of the others; he paused to listen for the footsteps of his companions, and was suddenly aware of the words of Shiloh's song.

> "The golden gates of sleep unbar
> Where strength and beauty, met together,
> Kindle their image like a star
> In a sea of glassy weather!"

"A bridal song," said Shiloh smiling: "I made it in celebration of the mutual happiness of most beloved friends; its words are a good augury, yet I will make you another for yourself alone, before to-morrow."

They camped that night by a ford of the Licking, which shimmered among small white stones as numerous as a Milky Way. Winter was in the air at last; the great fire they builded warmed a darkness brittle with frost. The flame, nourished upon fat pine and cedar, grew upward in a formidable splendour like the trunk of another tree; its solid column stood between the oaks and beeches, touching the moss and ivy berries with coraline light, and seeming to support upon its summit a canopy of arching boughs tufted with mistletoe.

"Seemingly ain't a goldarned Injun left around this neck o' woods," lamented David as he cast a pine-knot upon the blaze. "This is a sightly spot for an ambush, and this fire can be seen for miles around, I reckon, yet here we sit as safe as a passel of old wives at a prayer-meeting. It's plumb ridiculous, Cap'n; even a bear would liven things up a bit, but I ain't seen nothing bigger than a jack-rabbit since I quit Boston."

"Personally, my young friend," said the captain, thoughtfully impaling a slice of chipped beef upon the point of a stick, "I can well dispense with the excitements of crushed ribs and cloven skulls. There may indeed be a bear or two in the cane-brake behind us, if you care to investigate its recesses, but the

Shawnees and Piankeshaws are happily shyer than in Simon Girty's days. I wish I might accommodate you with a supper of pemmican and parched corn, but you must be content with these substitutes." He straightened the tin coffee-pot upon its stones, and gave his attention to the sizzling beef.

Shiloh was pleasantly weary; a league of Kentucky mud-hole and buffalo-trace was more strenuous than the thirty smooth green miles between Marlow and London. He leaned against a fallen tulip-tree; the coffee in his tin cup was boiling hot, and sweet with maple sugar. A lazy suspicion persisted in his mind that David had laced it with fiery liquor from his flask; in calm defiance of his principles he did not greatly care. He ached with sleep; there was a musical confusion within his brain with whose falling rhythms he was half familiar.

"It is the sound of the sea," said Shiloh to himself, closing his sea-blue eyes against the electric brilliance of the flame. He had forgotten the steady rushing of the wind among the tree-tops, which indeed were far removed above the hollow where he lay. Now it appeared to him that waves instead of withered leaves were moving over him upon the currents of the air.

"I must write it down before it blows away," he said to himself absurdly; with one long hand he groped among the fallen leaves for the bit of brown paper which had contained the maple sugar. His head ached a little with sleep and the imminence of the music; he leaned upon his elbow in the extreme firelight and scribbled on the scrap of paper, to which a few moist amber crystals still adhered.

"There, Lackland, is your Epithalamium," he said presently; he slipped the folded paper into the professor's hand with a shy secretive haste, and turned upon his back with a sigh. In five seconds he was fast and profoundly asleep; the professor looked at him and wondered how he could slumber so peacefully in the radiant heat from the cedar logs, whose sanguine colour made the silvered locks of his hair into a fantastic wreath of flames.

"Looks like a salamander, or maybe a chameleon, doesn't he, Lackland?" said the captain with a queer smile. He stood staring down at Shiloh, and twisting his rusty beard with meditative fingers.

112

Brother Lizards

"Read, Lackland, and see what the chameleon has to say about marriage," he proposed at length.

The professor unfolded the paper and read, pausing first to admire the pretty drawing of a forest tree wherewith the manu script was embellished.

"It is — rather an astonishing production," he murmured uncomfortably. "As a poem, I should pronounce it to be of the high est merit, but I should hardly care to show it to Miss Lillie upon the eve of our wedding."

The captain took the paper and perused it with reflective care instead of returning it to the professor he deliberately put it into his own pocket-book.

"I'll keep this for the poor boy," he said with decision; his eyes were again upon Shiloh's sleeping figure, and both David and the professor observed the curious melancholy of his look He had been wearing his ragged army greatcoat slung nonchan lantly over one lean shoulder; now he removed it, and with a brusque embarrassed gesture tossed it upon the ground.

"Tuck it round the confounded critter, Davy," he exclaimed irritably. "Damned long legs of his, stretching miles from the logs; probably freeze before morning. Yes, that's more like it; suppose his hair won't catch fire while he's asleep. And now brother lizards," said the captain with a stupendous yawn, "let' to our rustic couches, because for my part I'm abjectly sleepy and crosser than David's mythical bear."

Nevertheless, the captain lay awake long after the others were absorbed in their respective dreams of Shawnee warriors and rose red brides; at intervals he unfolded Shiloh's bit of brown paper and reread it carefully by the light of the diminishing embers At such times his face was illuminated by a brightness which seemed reflected from the uneven lines upon the paper, com mensurate with something clearer and stronger than a dying flame, and his look, as it strayed to Shiloh's slight and motion less form, was full of grave affection and concern. At last he slept, but not before he had determined to venture into the deli cate and mysterious reticences of the other's mind with a salty cordial of excellent advice.

"For," argued the captain sagely to himself, "even if he isn't the particular mad crusader I believe him to be, he'll never last in this wilderness; the first bout of chills and fever will shake him into kindling-wood."

With which kindly but mistaken foreboding the captain turned upon his side and slept, while the words of Shiloh's Epithalamium made an ocean music in his dreams.

6

"Shiloh," asked the captain in the crisp beginning of the next day, "why on earth don't you go home to your friends?"

The translucent clarity of early morning was in the sky; it filtered milkily among the tree-trunks, blanching Shiloh's countenance to a waxen mask. The captain was amazed to see how the increasing light scooped hollows around the shining eyes and set lines upon the corners of the lips.

"No," said Shiloh sharply and rather angrily, "no; I shall not go home until I have done what I set forth to do."

Then he stared suddenly at the other, stared with those bright and hollow eyes, and spoke again in a changed and gentler voice.

"But how is this — home to my friends?" demanded Shiloh. "Are not you and Lackland my friends?"

"Of course, my dear fellow," the captain assured him kindly; a pang of compunction visited his heart upon the instant, in observing how his question had altered Shiloh from yesterday's creature of warmth and hardihood into a pitiful difference and pain. He knew that there was suspicion and revolt in the variable brilliance of the eyes, and he wondered what hateful trap had closed upon the brain behind them. He was sincerely sorry that any careless words of his should have rendered this contrivance effective and set Shiloh wincing from the clutch of invisible fangs, and now his one desire was to undo the evil work.

"Of course we are your friends, with all our hearts," he repeated. "And for this very reason we have sometimes feared that you must be lonely in a new land, that you must often grieve for the older friends you've left in Italy and all the rich amenities of your former life. I know little enough about it, to be sure,

Brother Lizards

but either it's made you what you are, Shiloh, or else you've shaped it like a bright shell to fit your soul; in either case it's better than the dog's life you've been leading here."

Shiloh stared at the captain incredulously; his astonished gaze shifted from the captain's solemn face to the comfortable antics of the yellow dog; he looked at the fluttering colour of the camp-fire and at the powdery hoar-frost melting on a scarlet leaf.

"It does not seem to me a dull or arduous existence," he said softly. "As for my past fortunes, they have been happier than I deserve; my regrets are all for my own shortcomings. Neverthe-less, you are wrong about my soul; it has clothed itself in no rain-bow shell; rather has it stifled in something narrow as a coffin, and obscure. This was of my own shaping, and by heaven I have lived withdrawn into its shadows like a tortoise under his horny shield; often I have felt the outrageous weight of the world upon my back. A sudden cataclysm split that armour; I emerged into a new element, a volatile compound of sun and sea-water and eccentric liberty, and in this I have contrived to swim and fly and scramble across half a continent, to the immense benefit of my health and spirits. You speak of a dog's life; I am at a loss to understand you. We live like wild deer or a free company of eagles; a finer life it is impossible to imagine. Don't send me home, Appleby; I don't want to go home; I want to go to the professor's wedding."

"And that you shall, by graminy, or I'm a double Dutch-man!" cried David furiously, standing with clenched fists at the captain's shoulder. His face was crimson under the bronze; the visible muscles of his arms were like knots of copper cable.

Both Shiloh and the captain burst into a shout of laughter; the deep rumble in the captain's throat was thunder to the light-ning of Shiloh's eyes. The professor regarded the scene with decorous surprise.

"Don't murder me, Davy," the captain finally found breath to implore. "I promise to let him attend all the weddings west of the Alleghanies, and he needn't go home to his Italian palace unless he chooses. Shiloh, my dear boy, I admit I was mistaken; if you like us as well as all that, I have nothing more to say."

"I should hope not, Captain Appleby, sir," David interposed

115

. . .
indignantly. "Fair made my blood boil the way you was both-
ering and hectoring of him, and him so humble and polite and
asking your leave, by jingo, as gentle as a lamb. He hasn't to ask
nobody's favour to go to no weddings so long as I'm on deck,
and as for his turning back to them goldarned fever-smitten
heathen climes, I'll break the neck of the man that says he must.
Didn't I fish him out of the bloody ocean with my own hands,
and him as white as a new sail in moonshine, and ain't I seen
him come to life, and grow strong and spunky as a young catamount? Think he's a-going to be let fall back into whatever hell
was hurting of him? Not while I'm here to learn the reason
why!"

"David, David, moderate this ebullition of loyalty, or you
will be the death of me!" the captain entreated through his
laughter. "I have no intention of arresting your friend's natural
development of mind and body; on the contrary I am unaffect-
edly fond of him, and far from condemning him to fever-smitten
climes, I mean to force him to swallow several ounces of quinine
before the day is out. In regard to the relative salubrity of the
Bay of Spezzia and a Kentucky cane-brake, I dare say it's a ma-
larial six of one to an aguish half-dozen of the other, but never
mind; Shiloh shall dance at this wedding, and there shall be
cakes and ale for everyone."

"In so far as the sadly limited means of Mr. and Mrs. Lillie
may permit," amended the professor nervously.

Shiloh was quite helpless with laughter; he leaned against a
tulip-tree and wept for mirth. David's loving ferocity, the captain's amiable sarcasm, and the professor's bewilderment appeared equally amusing. He had been vaguely and courteously
grieved by the captain's good advice, but now all remembrance
of reality was swept away in a warm hightide of animal spirits.

"Thank you, David," he said brokenly. "I am truly grateful
for your championship, but I do assure you, my dear fellow, that
the captain and I are not at daggers drawn as you seem to suppose. I won't ask you to apologize to him for your impetuous
words; his feeling heart will already have forgiven you; I must,
however, request you to shake his hand in amity before we eat
our breakfast. That's my brave Davy; that's my seven-at-a-blow

shepherd boy. Now give us all a smile and a cup of coffee, and we shall know you are yourself again."

David, his face still glowing like red metal above the emotional furnace in his breast, managed to clasp the captain's hand without rancour; he felt ashamed of his heat, and mortified by Shiloh's levity. He shook his thick gold hair in stubborn disapproval before he spoke.

"All very well to laugh and carry on like that," he muttered with an ominous frown, "All very well to laugh and holler like a fool, only where'd you be now if it weren't for me, and where'd your sickly skeleton bones be bleaching? 'Tain't often as I remind you of that, Shiloh, but you know it's give me a sort of right to look after you, and see as nobody harms you, and you don't plumb forget to take care of yourself. Storms and sharks I've saved you from before this, and deacons and yaller fever and Mr. Daingerfield on dry land, and now mebbe it's going to be Injuns and bears and murdering bandits. If I spoke hasty to the captain, 'twas a long of me being bothered about you, and afeared you'd slip back to your Eyetalian troubles if he didn't leave you be in peace. And then," said David gruffly, "you talked so pitiful about wanting to go to the wedding, like you was a little boy and the captain a cross schoolmarm, that by tarnation I just clean boiled over like a hot sugar-kettle!"

"I know, Davy, I know!" cried Shiloh consolingly, clapping him on the back. "Come now and eat your bacon; everyone understands and everyone loves you for your excellent impulses. Believe me that I am not unmindful of my debt to you; I only wish I might repay it in kind."

"Aw, that's nothing," grumbled David, deluging Shiloh's tin plate with an excessive quantity of bacon-grease.

"But seriously, Appleby," Shiloh said to the captain a little later, while they were scrubbing the dishes with sand preparatory to bundling them into their packs, "I am eager to convince you of my good faith; my heart is in the search which David and I have so romantically begun, but over and above the dream of finding Silver, our journey has been a singularly happy progress into that forgetfulness for which my spirit longed. I have explained to you the curious circumstances of my life; a letter may soon reach me through the Commercial Bank of Louisville, whither Captain Ffoulkastle promised to forward all correspondence. I think it is as yet too soon to hope for word from Italy, but a prosperous voyage may so expedite matters that I shall know my fate within a few weeks. God grant that it may not be a mandate sentencing me to lifelong solitary exile; if I dared to imagine that she will join me in the innocent wilderness! But enough of that; I must bear with fortitude those things which cannot be mended short of Utopia. For the present I am fortunate; I neither remember nor attempt to prophesy, but am content with the propitious hour. Be patient with me, my friend, and permit me to deceive myself in transitory peace."

"With all my heart; I'll worry you no more, Shiloh, with sage advice," answered the captain emphatically. "You know your own business best, I dare say, and even if you don't, it's none of mine. There's always fifty acres of bounty land waiting for you in Pike, if you care to join me there; otherwise I'll wish you luck and God-speed on your wild-goose-chasing, and say good-bye. But first there's the wedding; we must all be merry for that, and just to avoid the possibility of a funeral, do let me persuade you to sample old Doctor Appleby's quinine-and-whisky cocktail."

"Oh, very well; if I must I suppose I must," said Shiloh, laughing with a wry face as he swallowed the fiery bitter dose. "You're determined to make a drunkard of me in spite of my principles, but we must all render some slight sacrifices to friendship, so here's to your best health in sanative gall and wormwood!" He drained the cup and put a fragment of maple sugar into his mouth; its taste of spring melted tenderly against his outraged palate.

V

REFUSE THE BOON

Miss Rosalie Lillie was seated upon the wood-pile in an attitude of negligent grace; her fine eyes were fixed above the distant tamarack-trees in contemplation of some winged chimæra of the mind. A gold pencil-case was suspended by a delicate chain around the lady's creamy throat; a notebook peeped from the pocket of her blue satin apron, and a gilded album lay within reach. Under a furred cloak her attire was frail and silken; she wore thin-soled bronze slippers, and her hands were encased in gloves of primrose kidskin.

Miss Lillie was a singularly lovely girl; her features were regular and her figure tall and classically formed. She had a rich abundance of chestnut hair and her velvet eyes were the colour of purple-brown pansies. She looked very expensive and unsuitable against a background of enormous forest trees and ragged rail fences; the smoky November sun picked out the Italian cameo upon her bosom and increased the splendid damask of her cheek.

The reversed fortunes of the Lillie family had subdued their material welfare to the level of a log cabin, but this cabin was both neat and commodious, and the hand of refined taste had set a few late-blossoming plants in its circular flower-beds and draped its narrow windows with ruffled muslin curtains. The expanse of

119

turf before the house had been entirely cleared of underbrush, and a modest vegetable-garden lent an air of respectability to the back premises; nevertheless the scene offered a melancholy contrast to the suave and regal creature now rudely enthroned upon the wood-pile.

Miss Lillie lifted her Spanish guitar from an adjacent pine-knot; she smoothed out its scarf of yellow silk with a pensive hand, and then idly strummed the opening chords of some rhapsodic love-song.

"Heigh-ho!" said Miss Lillie aloud, in time to the music, "heigh-ho, alas, I would that he were come!"

Her pansy-coloured eyes suddenly overflowed with facile tears; at the bottom of her heart she knew that she did not call upon the professor in this apostrophe. Beyond the oaks and tamaracks the sunset flared ominously into crimson and then ebbed away in gentler fluctuations of light; Miss Lillie saw the forest as a vast tapestry from which a paladin upon a snowy charger must presently emerge; even now she could hear the iron harmony of hoof-beats approaching to her magical undoing.

She raised her head; her chestnut ringlets fell about the fine carnation blushes of her face. A sound was indeed audible; she knew it for a trampling of footsteps along the logs of the corduroy road.

The sky was luminous now, but its rose reflections had subsided into pallor. In the cabin someone kindled a lamp; its illumination fell like mild domestic moonlight across the fields of pumpkins and Indian corn. Rosalie held her breath, waiting for a dawn of miracles to divide the forest with its ecstasy.

She saw the thorny underbrush violently shaken; lamplight in golden rain fell from its leaves to confuse her. A yellow creature like a goblin fox ran from beneath the bushes and frolicked on the lawn; it lifted its tawny muzzle to the appearing stars and barked with a sharp hylactism, and the woods echoed with airy cynic mirth.

A tall figure strode from under the oaken archway where the corduroy road debouched upon the fields; the pupils of Rosalie's eyes dilated into velvet black, and her suave deep pulses skipped a beat, for the striding figure, which moved so quickly among the little wigwams of the gathered corn, was assuredly not her fiancé the professor. At first, and for no reason save that he walked so lightly, and that his head was bound with a coronet of hawks' feathers, she believed the man to be an Indian brave; the fear which should have followed upon this wild imagination was absent from her heart. Then, as he came within the radius of lamplight, she perceived the sunburnt fairness of his skin and knew instinctively that his dazzled eyes were blue. He stared straight into the bright windows of the cabin; he must have stumbled against the scattered logs of the wood-pile if she had not spoken, in a hurried breathless whisper without words.

"I beg your pardon, Madam; I had not observed you in the obscurity of dusk," he said at once with exquisite courtesy.

Miss Lillie was enchanted by his accent and by his easy grace of manner; it was clear to her that a disinherited prince stood among the monstrous flame-coloured fruit of the pumpkin-field. She saw with pity and passionate indignation that the royal garments were extremely ragged, and that the delicate nobility of the brow was stained with dust. Yet did the eminent nature of this gentleman emerge purely from the casual tarnish of misfortune, and to the girl's vision the rough hawks' feathers were a proper diadem. Along the corduroy road the footsteps of a company of courtiers drew near with an effect of multitude; in truth David's tread was constitutionally heavy, and the captain and the professor were sadly tired.

"Oh sir," said Miss Lillie with feeling, "I do not know who you may be, but you must not pass our humble dwelling without accepting its hospitality for your weariness! My father and mother would never forgive me if I allowed a distressed traveller to proceed into the unknown uncheered by such warmth and sustenance as we can offer. I do beg that you will share our supper, and even spend the night if your engagements will permit."

The gentleman bowed slightly, his long fine hand upon his heart; he laughed in a light-minded manner a little out of keeping with the air of romantic poverty which Rosalie found so tragically poignant.

The Orphan Angel

"My dear Miss Lillie," he answered politely, "surely no other engagement of mine can rival in importance the charming necessity of attending your wedding ceremony."

Rosalie felt herself grow cold and faint with disappointment; she could not tell what fantastic hopes had painted arabesques upon her mind for a moment. She was silent in the dull vacancy of her thoughts; she looked at the stranger to see whether there was any mockery in his laughter, and realised through a queer stupidity of pain that his smile held nothing but good-will and ingenuous pleasure. At that instant the professor approached across the darkening field; she submitted to his embrace with stiff pretended gestures of affection.

Her voice to her own ears was thin and artificial with despair, but indeed she managed to enact surprise and delight so prettily that the deception was precise enough for truth, and both Shiloh and David shared the professor's profound belief in his proven happiness. The captain glanced keenly at the animated face of this handsome girl who was about to marry his friend; he and David were quiet while the other three chattered excitedly of the journey and the wedding and the wicked price of wax orange-blossoms in Louisville. David's mind was full of awed admiration for Miss Lillie's classic beauty and elaborate grace; the captain's reflections were more critical and perhaps more melancholy.

"But Rosalie, my love, how imprudent of you to sit perched upon a wood-pile this particular chill November evening!" cried the professor with ill-concealed approbation of such engaging eccentricity. "I fear that you will most certainly contract a severe cold as the price of your poetics. Of course it is all very complimentary to me, to find you thus disconsolate and longing for my arrival, but next time you are moved to song I trust it may be by our own warm fireside, dearest girl. Meanwhile here is Shiloh, who has himself some talent for original composition, and who will doubtless furnish an elegant extract for the famous album; eh, Shiloh, what say you to a little rhyme-capping after supper in honour of the glad occasion?"

A strange expression, compounded of ironic mirth and some graver, wilder pang, flitted across Shiloh's countenance; it was visible only to the captain, who believed he could unriddle its

Refuse the Boon

secret with a mad conjecture. He said nothing, but he looked at Shiloh as if he also, among the cloudier regions of the soul, perceived that gentleman as a disinherited prince.

" But la, sirs, of what am I thinking, to detain you here in the bleak twilight while we chatter about literature? I protest I am but a poor hostess, and my parents will scold me unmercifully if I delay another instant to introduce you to them. Sometimes I could swear I was moonstruck; I fall a-dreaming even over my fancy-work, and Mama warns me that at this rate I shall never finish the sweet hearts'ease slippers I am making for poor Papa's Christmas. You are a poet yourself, Mr. Shiloh, and no doubt you can feel for me in my sad giddiness; the comfort is, such moods are partially divine, but you will not persuade my dear mother to credit this heresy, least of all when I allow the wild-plum marmalade to boil over upon her immaculate hearth, as I did this very morning."

Miss Lillie addressed this lively monologue to Shiloh, turning the velvet splendours of her eyes upon him as she led the way to the cabin in a rustling hurry of satin petticoats. Shiloh's nerves were clean and sensitive as a child's after the fresh ascetic rigours of the forest, and he was painfully affected by the lady's musical voice and by the scent of patchouli which pervaded her garments. Of her discourse only two words were made evident to his senses: the thought of wild-plum marmalade was innocently pleasing to the imagination, but he chose the flower rather than the fruit as truer cordial for the spirit.

" Hearts'ease is my favourite flower," he said pensively. " I wish very much that I possessed a pair of slippers worked in hearts'ease; my friend Hunt had such a pair once, I remember, and they were extremely beautiful."

Rosalie caught her breath with rapture; the death-knell of Mr. Lillie's Christmas hopes was sounded in Shiloh's idle comment. Already in fancy she felt herself tenderly sorting the Berlin wools suitable for the production of an artistic masterpiece; the violet and the purple threads flowed softly through her fingers as she dreamed.

The lighted doorway of the cabin swung wide to receive the travellers; their host and hostess stood within its warm low frame with a lavish fire behind them and welcoming hands reaching out into the shadows. Shiloh found himself drawn into a comfortably glowing room; he sank into the corner of a settle and stared about him rather dizzily. A small pretty lady was embracing the professor; a tall stately gentleman was pounding the captain upon his stiff rheumatic shoulder-blades. David stood sheepishly by the hearth; he was blushing hotly, and his eyes followed Rosalie with looks of fatuous delight.

Miss Lillie was not unaware of the sentiment she had awakened in the breast of this nautical-looking person in the pea-jacket; the fact that the sentiment burned in an unsuitable quarter failed to deprive it of its entire charm of incense. Her vanity was soothed, and while she watched Shiloh from the rolling corner of a fine dark eye, she did not scruple to enslave David by a variety of ladylike enchantments.

"Mama, this is Mr. Shiloh, who appears to have come all the way from Italy to wish us joy upon our wedding-day!" she cried with a nicely modulated trill of laughter. "Didn't Lackland tell me that your home was in Italy, Mr. Shiloh? Ah, how I envy you the noble treasures of art with which that country must abound! Now I am quite sure you must be shockingly fatigued after your long journey; Papa must mix you a sherry cobbler at once, unless you prefer to drink whisky, like our dreadful Kentuckians."

Shiloh rose and bowed to the small pretty lady, who was evidently Miss Lillie's mother; she took his hand very kindly in hers and looked at him with gentle curiosity; for a moment she did not speak, and he was grateful for the pause. Her silence made a fragile peace in the centre of confusion; he noticed that, although her colours were all warm and velvety like her daughter's own, her little features were quite different, soft and blunt and childishly unformed. When finally she spoke it was only to express some simple anxiety as to his immediate comfort. Her voice was low; her southern accent blurred it sweetly into singsong. Shiloh blessed her for an assuaging antidote to the conflict of impressions which surrounded him.

The room was large, and presented an anomalous appearance upon closer view; the puncheon floor was covered with braided rugs, and there was a buffalo-skin before the hearth. Along the whitewashed log walls were hung a number of water-colour views of the French Riviera; curtains of glazed chintz concealed a recess, and the gilded strings of a harp glittered in the firelight. A splendid pier-glass, its carven frame spotted with damp, occupied the space between the windows. A marble-topped table of vermilion boule was piled with sheet music; a fowling-piece was suspended over the rough stone chimney, and rows of books crowded the shelves on either side of it, their rich morocco bindings contrasting strangely with the unplaned yellow pine.

The air was full of the thick opulent fragrance of food and drink; Shiloh could smell sherry, and frying ham, and a queer tart flavour which he later recognised as pickled cucumbers. He felt unhappy; his strong desire was to be gone into the cold conventual sanctuary of the forest. He drifted back towards the fire and sat down in the corner of the settle; he closed his eyes and tried to think of the extremest peaks of Monte San Pellegrino. Rosalie's velvet stare was pressing heavily upon his closed lids; the scent of patchouli came again to his nostrils, and he stifled in its syrupy fog.

2

"Better drink this, Mr. Shiloh; it'll do you good," said Mrs. Lillie's light voice at his shoulder. She put a sherry cobbler into his hand and stood regarding him with a look of mild perplexity; it was plain to him that like a dutiful child she waited for his approval of her offering. Her presence was like a small tender screen between his perturbed sensibilities and the intensity of her daughter's lustrous gaze.

Shiloh took the drink with a murmured expression of gratitude; he sniffed at it suspiciously while pretending to taste it. He was very thirsty, but he would infinitely have preferred to slake this longing in a bright tin dipper of spring-water or a foamy measure of new milk. Nevertheless, being at the limit of his endurance, he drank.

The mixture was smooth and palatable; Shiloh was reminded

of the negus brewed by Hogg behind the charmed oak of University College. Its gracious flavour medicined his mind to an immediate calm; he thanked Mrs. Lillie again and more fervently.

"That's a sweet boy," thought Mrs. Lillie with sympathetic interest. She attached no importance to paladins and princes; there was an orphaned quality in Shiloh's smile which smote her malleable heart with a peculiar pity. "He needs a mother, poor lamb," thought Mrs. Lillie, who was at most some ten years Shiloh's senior. "Rosie shouldn't be casting sheep's-eyes at him; it's positively indecent, with Lackland in the room, and the dear innocent himself half dead with sleep."

Aloud she said simply, "Why, I'm certainly glad you like it, Mr. Shiloh; it's nice sherry cobbler. Mr. Lillie used the last of his manzanilla to make it, except a dozen bottles he's saving for the wedding. We don't have many luxuries nowadays; I wish we could have enjoyed the pleasure of your company in our old home in Louisville. This is a terrible change for us all, of course; not but what I sometimes feel there are compensations even in the direst poverty, but then, it's very difficult for poor Rosie; the child has such a fastidious nature."

Rosalie's attention was momentarily diverted by her fiancé's gift of an engraved thimble; the professor was explaining that the pretty implement had been his mother's, and the lady was experiencing no little difficulty in forcing her square rosy fingertip into its thin gold cup. Mrs. Lillie, with a soft mouse-like furtiveness of motion, slipped into the vacant seat next to Shiloh; through a vertigo of sleep he noticed the delicate frosty threads in her chestnut hair and the faint lavender fragrance of her grey merino gown.

"Sometimes, Mr. Shiloh," said Mrs. Lillie, clasping her small hands in her lap and talking very fast in her tender shadowy voice, "sometimes I'm truly thankful to be poor, for my own part; it saves me such a world of trouble and domestic care. I wonder whether a boy like you can possibly realise what it means to a woman to have a popular hospitable husband and a beautiful ambitious daughter just growing up; I give you my word, Mr. Shiloh, that in Louisville three years ago we seldom sat down to table under twenty, and that doesn't include birthdays and holidays and political entertaining, and although the society is very select and almost worthy of your European standards, you know what gentlemen are, and then of course the drinking too, not that I'm narrow-minded, but naturally one has to regard the china and napery as part of a good housekeeper's duty, and although I made it a point never to complain to Mr. Lillie, some of his friends were sadly inconsiderate, particularly as his port was famous from the Cumberlands to the Barrens, and even in a slave state service is very unsatisfactory, and I suppose it was a dreadful calamity to have forty-six banks fail completely, and God knows what the legislature will do, but for myself I regret nothing but the conservatory, and when I think of poor folks starving that appears sinful, and just before the panic of eighteen-nineteen no fewer than four duels were fought in Louisville on Rosalie's account alone, she has her father's aristocratic nose but I believe it's rather her lovely eyes that explain it, and this is a remarkably quiet district, and I have enjoyed the peace and tranquillity beyond words to express, and now it's to be the professor after all, and if she hadn't gone to school with Miss Fuller whose mother came from Wilkes-Barre it would never have happened, and perhaps it's all for the best, only when I let her go East last April I thought of someone a little more comfortably settled, but he has a soul attuned to poetry as she says and an uncle in Congress so I dare say it will end quite happily."

Shiloh had been dreaming of a famous port between the Cumberlands and the Barrens; he saw it as a glassy harbour of pure quicksilver, bright between devouring jagged jaws of headland. Peace and tranquillity; a quiet port in a storm; its delicious waters drowned him in their deepest blessing.

When Mrs. Lillie stopped talking, the amazing silence woke him with a start; he stared wildly about him, ruffling the hair above his brow into wisps of dark and silver. His fingers touched the coronet of hawk's feathers, and he snatched it off with an exclamation of apology; he felt all at once savage and uncivilised and grimed with dust. He looked helplessly at the stains of clay and leaf-mould upon his slender hands.

The Orphan Angel

"You'd like a bath, wouldn't you, Mr. Shiloh?" asked Mrs. Lillie with clairvoyant lovingkindness; Shiloh heard the saving words with passionate relief.

"If there were any lake or sequestered pool in the neighbourhood, I should be most grateful for directions which might enable me to find it . . ." he began, but his hostess cut him short with a sound of gentle mirth.

"Good gracious, my dear, you'd catch your death," she said laughing. "All the ponds will have ice on them to-night, and I can't have my poor guests frosted to match the wedding-cake. There's a big laundry tub in the out-house, if you're no prouder than my husband's ruffled shirts, and I can have plenty of hot water for you in a moment. My last batch of soap wasn't particularly successful, but it's better than nothing even if it didn't come from Paris. Edmund," she called to the professor, whose Christian name was thus for the first time revealed to his friends, "you and Mr. Shiloh are going to have a bath in the laundry tubs before supper; please do the honours of our establishment to the best of your ability while I put the kettle on with the captain's kind assistance."

"Really, Mama, how excessively indelicate!" cried Miss Lillie in a fever of rose-red shame.

Among the curling azure steam-clouds of the out-house Shiloh relaxed in the luxury of cleanliness; the hot water and the harsh brown soap appeared almost wickedly effete in their perfection of comfort. He eyed the fresh linen laid upon a yellow-painted chair with sensuous delight.

"I feel like a Roman emperor, Lackland," he said happily, in the vigorous exercise of a rough huckaback towel.

"You look more like a red Indian," replied the professor with some asperity. He had observed the singular interest which Shiloh seemed to have aroused in Miss Lillie's maidenly bosom, and he was by no means pleased by this phenomenon. He was far too fair-minded to hold his friend responsible, but he was only human, and his voice was sharp with annoyance and chagrin.

Shiloh noticed nothing; his weariness was miraculously fled, and he felt preternaturally hungry and intelligent and cheerful.

Refuse the Boon

An absurd fancy visited his mind; his recovered vitality forced it into lively speech.

"I should like for supper," said Shiloh ridiculously, "a large mutton chop and a lost fragment of Sophocles and a pretty woman."

"Ahem," answered the professor with an acid smile. "I should be inclined to think you had already acquired the latter commodity."

"Oh, you mean Mrs. Lillie," said Shiloh with such translucent innocence that the professor had perforce to believe him while swallowing a private pang of jealousy. "Yes, is she not a charming person? I really think she liked me; I perceive her nature to be simple, but exquisitely sympathetic, candid, and pure. It is a type but too infrequently met with in this brutal mechanical age; I think I shall ask her for some bread and milk instead of those large alarming cucumbers I saw set forth in a cut-glass dish. Will she be offended if I refuse to eat virulent green cucumbers?"

"Of course not, you idiot," the professor replied impatiently. "Those were only pickles and relishes; you're not compelled to eat them, but you'll find them very excellent if you care to try. Rosalie has frequently spoken of her mother's pickles; you may have watermelon rind or limes or young spring onions if you are afraid of cucumbers."

"No thank you," murmured Shiloh, a look of unearthly terror widening his eyes. "I had far rather not make the attempt. Curious, are they not, these customs of the country? You will scarcely credit it, but in Italy young women of good family actually eat *garlic* . . ."

"Disgusting!" said the professor. "And what, pray, has such a depraved habit to do with cucumbers?" He spoke as sourly as if the most astringent of Mrs. Lillie's conserves were already wrinkling his palate, and Shiloh permitted the subject to languish into silence while struggling with the Gordian problem of his bootlaces.

In the large room of the cabin their host received them with a fine sleek blend of mockery and pompous rhetoric, mingled smoothly like his sherry cobblers. He was cast in the noblest Roman mould, but bilious-coloured and arid as a desert sand-storm;

it was evident that his desiccated frame must require a constant stimulating dew of punch and negus. His mannered speech was suavity itself, but he had the hot and violent eye of an irascible elderly stallion. One pictured him within the mahogany precincts of the counting-house, or splendid in the senate-chamber; his well-shod feet appeared to spurn the puncheon floor with instinctive scorn, and all his gestures threatened to demolish the cabin walls into abject heaps of match-wood.

After a massive meal of turkey and ham and hot waffle cake, crowned by quantities of custards and tipsy-parson and enlivened by much witty conversation, the company gathered about the profuse comfort of the fire; a superb set of ivory chessmen was produced from behind the flour-barrel, and the captain and Mr. Lillie gave themselves up to the high intricacies of the Allgaier gambit.

The cold turquoise forget-me-nots of Rosalie's new thimble hovered fastidiously over the rich furry colours of the Berlin wool; Tyrian hearts'ease burgeoned upon slippers grown conspicuously narrow for a father's gout. Now and again her refulgent gaze slid with velvet demureness to Shiloh's feet; easy tears clouded her enchanted vision to perceive with how preposterous an elegance his ankles emerged from the dusty hobnailed boots. She hummed softly to herself, and bent her curls above her sewing.

Mrs. Lillie was netting a little purse of pearl-grey silk; minute and glittering particles of steel were looped along its surface like a fall of dewdrops. "Nothing to put in it except my lucky silver levy and some pennies," she said, laughing.

The professor had found his lady's album; a pinch of jealousy peppered his delighted pride as he exhibited its marvels to his friend. Shiloh was sympathetic, but sleep had once more enveloped him in a wizard's mantle; he was vague and pale, surveying the scene giddily from the platform of a dream, and his weariness was a visible veil across his eyes.

"Oh, charming, charming," he repeated, swallowing the yawn he was too courteous to confess.

"You see," said the professor, turning a leaf upon which a poem was freshly inscribed with a quill pen below a dainty vignette of a pair of children playing battledore, "this was composed upon the wood-pile this very evening; she copied it while we

were at our — ahem — ablutions. Is she not a girl of truly astonishing talent? "

Shiloh blinked, sighed, and read; Rosalie, watching him
closely, was soothed and flattered by the profound sadness of his
face.

" Ah, she has called her poem ' Hearts'-ease,' after the slippers,"
Shiloh murmured politely, staring at the words through his
Delphic veil of sleep.

> " Thy tender syllables suggest
> A Paradise denied to me;
> Within this wasted, wounded breast
> The heart awakes uneasefully.

> " Hearts'-ease! If Heav'n but hear my prayer
> Thy pensive blessing I shall have
> When, purple upon proud despair,
> Thy blossoms glow above my grave! "

" A very pleasing set of verses," said Shiloh without irony;
his wild and delicate mind was singularly uncritical in such
matters, and the simplest expressions of melancholy were ever
germane to his taste.

" Won't you write something of your own, Mr. Shiloh? "
asked Rosalie with unaccustomed timidity; she dipped the long
quill pen in her best Indian ink and laid the open book upon
Shiloh's knee.

Its gilded satin covers were plump as pincushions; Shiloh
was quite sensible of their weight, and of the fact that their
glossy fabric was impregnated with the scent of patchouli. His
weariness seemed intolerably augmented by the task required of
his imagination.

" Anything; something you've already written, and can remember," the professor added in humane recognition of his
comrade's pallid and bewildered looks.

Shiloh stared down at the virgin page, and the quill trembled
and shook in his hand as though it were still a portion of some
aërial wing; then he lifted his eyes, which passed blindly by
Rosalie's sleek loveliness to rest upon her mother's half-averted

face. The quill was poised and eager, alert for a leap into immediate blue; suddenly Shiloh's hand relaxed, and the feather wavered to the floor.

"I am sorry," said Shiloh faintly; "I am too tired to invent rhymes; I trust you will forgive me. Perhaps I can recall an appropriate trifle; do you happen to understand Italian? This was composed for a lady's album; it is quite in the album style."

"Alas, no," Rosalie replied regretfully. "French and German I know very well indeed; I have always been complimented upon my French accent, and Papa has taught me a smattering of Spanish for my guitar. But Italian . . ."

"A little," said Mrs. Lillie; "Petrarch's sonnets; when I was a girl." Her shadowy drawling voice was so low that only Shiloh heard her.

He picked up the pen and began to write. When he had finished he handed the book to Mrs. Lillie with a smile; the orphaned quality of his smile was more than ever evident to her pity, and she immediately began thinking about blankets for the spare bed, and wondering whether or no the best linen sheets had been properly aired.

Nevertheless she felt a mild curiosity concerning the Italian words traced upon the album's page; she perused them carefully, pleased to find that she had no difficulty in deciphering their meaning. At her shoulder Rosalie's warm presence was somehow stormy and inimical.

> "'Buona notte, buona notte!' — Come mai
> La notte sara buona senza te? . . .
> La notte quando Lilla m'abbandona. . . ."

"How sweet!" said Mrs. Lillie gently. "Thank you, my dear. And now I think we had better all go to bed. Edmund, will you conduct the gentlemen to the attic? Mind the ladder, Mr. Butternut; it's a sad makeshift, but I'm sure your sailor's agility can manage it. I hope you will sleep well, Mr. Shiloh; pleasant dreams to you; good-night, good-night."

Refuse the Boon

3

THE rhythmic beat of rain upon the roof woke Shiloh; the corn-husk mattress whispered rustlingly beneath his slender restless bones, which ached with weariness along their tightened nerves. He lay still, marvelling at the darkness and at the singular imminence of the rain, whose sound was so contiguous to his mind that his fingers groped for drops against his cheek. He knew, through some exquisite cognition of the body, that it must be morning; he was puzzled by the thick obscurity, and alarmed by a sense of imprisonment. He felt that he was suffocating, and, thrusting the hysteric mists of terror from his face, he leaped up with a muffled cry. A mysterious engine clattered to the floor; both wood and iron echoed his surprise, and a faint light entered to explain the gloom.

" Knocked over the pitchfork, by graminy, and the old lady's best patchwork goes trailing in the dirt! " exclaimed David's reassuring bass; Shiloh perceived the dim glimmer of his friend's head upon a near-by pillow, and realised that he himself was shivering upon the edge of a large bedstead, rudely curtained by a succession of quilts fastened to the rafters. A ghostly dawn penetrated this screen, and showed the attic strewn with a curious agglomeration of objects; three chests, an old-fashioned spinning-wheel, and a number of reels and swifts crowded the space between the two mattresses occupied by the captain and the professor. Shiloh's bed was placed immediately below the peak of the roof, upon whose surface rain drummed continuously; the wooden frame of the bed was still covered with a sylvan grain of bark, and its twisted proportions seemed to have shaped themselves in a spontaneous miracle of growth. Shiloh thought it a fit couch for a dryad; he was faintly troubled by David's mighty limbs disposed beneath the blankets, and by the nautical air which his friend retained even among the arboreal convolutions of the bedposts.

" But it isn't an air, it's a smart gale," remarked Shiloh meditatively, wondering why David had never married a mermaid.

133

The Orphan Angel

"Wet day for a wedding," yawned the captain, rolling over upon his side and dispatching a dusty boot in the general direction of the professor's head. "Not but what your prospective parents understand admirably the art of excluding cold and damp by means of spirituous armour, God bless 'em."

"Spiritual armour?" said the professor in a voice of sleepy wonder. "Oh, no, I am quite irreligious; mine is the scientific mind, you know. Besides, my people were all Presbyterians, and I was taken to church at far too early an age. But I've been reading the marriage service, and upon my soul the thing's poetry, Appleby; it's equal to Dryden. 'In the time of man's innocency . . . mystical union.' Is it not prodigiously fine?"

"Detestable shackles," Shiloh cried indignantly, "garlanded with the most tremulous and tender flowers of speech!"

"But I calculate as how there'll be fiddlers," added David. "And certainly you'll allow that the victuals and drink are elegant."

"Which remark blends with the welcome scent of Mocha to remind us of breakfast," said the captain, rising and shaking himself like a lean earth-coloured hound.

At least three out of the four companions bumped their foreheads against the low-hung attic roof, but presently by the light of a long twelve a certain state of order was retrieved from among the tangled heaps of coats and shoes upon the floor, and they descended the stick ladder into the warmth and bustle of the living-room.

Mrs. Lillie provided them with a large iron skillet and a quantity of boiling hot water and strong brown soap, and setting these cosmetic luxuries on a bench beneath the eaves of the house they contrived a mild degree of cleanliness in common. There were plenty of huckaback towels; Shiloh found a great silky square of fine damask tucked under his arm, and vaguely perceived that his hostess had placed it there.

"I embroidered six dozen especially for my Louisville guest-chamber, but the ciphers are very hard upon the eyes," she told him seriously.

He shaved with one of Mr. Lillie's beautiful slim French razors; he felt deliciously soothed and tranquillized as he sauntered to the spring between the soft cold curtains of the rain. He knelt and splashed the water in his face, and then drank of its chilly sweetness; it was a delicate and cordial wine, and he loved it better than all the golden manzanilla borne on galleons out of the Old World.

"And now if I might only have tea for breakfast instead of coffee, I should be quite content," said Shiloh to himself as he returned through silver November mists to the cabin door.

A thin and flowery fragrance saluted his ravished senses as he entered; it pierced the bacon smell like a filament of crystal, and Shiloh saw a round blue Canton tea-pot upon the table, and a noble tea-cup flanked by jugs of cream. Wreaths of jasmine-blossoming smoke ascended towards the ceiling, veiling Mrs. Lillie's pretty countenance in a becoming gossamer.

"This is really too kind of you!" he cried happily, hastening to her side.

4

MESSENGERS, in the nimble likeness of a regiment of ragged boys, were immediately sent forth over the neighbouring country to summon guests to the wedding; it was not until three days later that a sufficient company were assembled to lend the affair its final social and religious grace.

The skies were once more calm and brilliant; a last autumnal haze, withdrawn before the cruel steeliness of winter, rendered the horizon blue as heaven itself. The cold was as yet slight and brittle, breakable by the noonday sun into splinters of air clear as ice and sweet as sugar. It was early afternoon; an afternoon formed by a benevolent god for lively pastoral rejoicing, for dance and song and the innocent relish of creature comforts.

Happily all such were now at hand; no Venetian carnival or Maypole dance upon an English green could have presented a more vivacious motley to the eye. Here were fine gentlemen and fair ladies from Louisville, in cashmere and velvet and rich seasonable furs; here were farmers from the next clearing and mountaineers from the distant Cumberlands, in coonskin caps and buckskin gaiters, with their wives and daughters in linsey-woolsey,

The Orphan Angel

and copperas and blue plaid homespun. Here was an itinerant Baptist preacher from Maine who looked like a starving Hebrew prophet, and an Episcopal clergyman from Cincinnati who looked like a corrupt Roman emperor. The gathering overflowed into the fields; the grass-plot before the house was pied and variegated like a tropical garden. Shiloh gazed about him in stupefaction; he hated the crowd and the clamour, and yet he was fascinated by the improbability of the spectacle, and by the wild beanstalk speed of its sudden growth.

On the sunny sheltered side of the cabin the fiddlers were already tuning their instruments, hugging the battered honey-coloured fiddles to their breasts and whispering affectionately to the tense and nervous strings. Within the firelit living-room a long table was laid with warm and heartening viands and generous bowls of punch and sangaree; Mrs. Lillie was babbling of syllabubs against her husband's reiterated insistence upon gin-sling and juleps. Shiloh had never in his life seen so many baked hams and roasted turkeys; he was visited by a fleeting recollection of the breakfast-table at Field Place during the Christmas holidays, and the ghosts of cold pheasants and visionary rounds of beefs rose vaguely in his memory.

The soft preparatory wailing of the fiddles charmed him; he remembered Hogg's little apologue of the interrupted country dance and the enraged musicians.

"Do you know," he said to David, who was staring wide-eyed at the impressive scene, "I have come almost to believe in the truth of this fable; my friend was eloquent in his account of how I devoured all the rosin which these poor fellows had provided for their bows."

"And you might have done so, at that, Shiloh," David assured him, grinning. "Ain't we all seen you eating spruce gum, or licking the tar off pine trees same as a cat licks cream?"

He heard a gentle voice at his shoulder; Mrs. Lillie was behind him, her small face pink with some secret poignancy of alarm. Shiloh saw tears in her pretty eyes.

"Oh, my dear boy," she said quickly, "I shouldn't ask you such a thing, I know, but I feel sure that although such a recent friend you are a true one, and you would have great influence

136

over her if only you would be so kind as to try. Now if you'll just go back of the chintz curtain at the end of the cabin you'll find poor Rosie with her wedding veil on and in her white satin which has turned out better than one could have expected but crying her eyes out and I can't think why except that she says nothing will induce her to marry him but perhaps if you reason with her you can persuade her and oh, Mr. Shiloh, I do entreat you to make the attempt for her father and I can do nothing."

A preternatural brightness of fear flashed into Shiloh's eyes; he would more willingly have fought the fiercest beasts at Ephesus than have been called upon to penetrate behind the chintz curtain into the privacy of Miss Lillie's passionate distress. At the same time he had a painful conviction that it was impossible to refuse this request.

"I am afraid I shall be rather worse than useless," he said with desperate calm, "but of course, if you believe I can be of service, I shall be most happy to assist you to the best of my powers."

Shiloh lifted the chintz curtain with a visibly trembling hand; he tapped timidly at the whitewashed log beside it, and a tear-drenched contralto murmur permitted him to enter the little recessed dressing-room.

The window at this end of the cabin was so tiny that two tall candles of deer tallow burned above the makeshift dimity flounces of the toilet-table. Miss Lillie sat upon a low stool; she regarded herself steadily in the depths of a round mirror which hung like a circle of shadow between the candles. The tarnished gilt festoons framed a countenance no longer suave and smooth and rich with carnation blushes; Rosalie had been crying, and her eyelids were smudged and reddened by her tears; for the rest she was pale and by no means beautiful in her grief. Nevertheless Shiloh liked her better than he had before; he wished that she would not scent her garments with patchouli, but he was profoundly touched by her evident trouble and confusion.

"I suppose you have come to laugh at me," she said defiantly; Shiloh was convinced that this was the language of madness or delirium.

"Good God, for what do you mistake me?" he cried in sincere horror. "I have only come in the forlorn hope of helping you, of comforting you for a sorrow I do not in the least comprehend. It was your mother's thought; if I intrude, pray tell me so, and I will immediately leave you."

"Please, please do not leave me," said Rosalie in a voice of humble entreaty. "It is a respite; it is a passing interval of peace; if you have any pity, you will not hasten its inevitable conclusion."

Shiloh, with an involuntary sigh, seated himself cross-legged upon the floor and prepared to be patient; the tuning of the fiddles sounded enchantingly free and far-away, like a chorus of magical grasshoppers.

"Why do you not desire to marry my excellent friend Lackland?" he inquired politely. "I quite understand all the theoretical objections to matrimony, but in this case the partner of your life will be a man of such high conscientiousness and noble tolerance that I confess I am at a loss to account for your extreme agitation."

Rosalie turned her eyes upon him; their pansy-colour was darkened to a dreadful despairing intensity of black. She gazed at him fixedly for a moment, and the blood was congealed in his veins; he saw the amazing anger of her eyes, and they seemed to him the unlighted sockets of a dream of bedlam.

Suddenly Miss Lillie uttered a piercing shriek, and fell into a fit of violent hysterical weeping, crumpling the delicate laces of her veil against her vehement tears.

Shiloh remained crouched upon the floor; slowly the blood was withdrawn from his face, leaving him so pale that every freckle was distinct and surprising against the fairness of his skin. He was frightened half out of his wits, and his astonishment was somewhat in excess of his fear. His hands became very cold; he could not have stirred a finger to save himself from destruction. The noise and passion of the scene were infinitely strange and horrible to his shrinking mind; he would have closed his eyes if he could, but he was incapable of exerting himself by the quiver of an eyelash.

His relief was sharp and painful when Mrs. Lillie came into the room; he returned to life in her reassuring presence, the blood flowed agonisingly along his frozen veins, and his teeth chattered in his head.

138

Refuse the Boon

"Rosalie, control yourself at once!" cried Mrs. Lillie with unaccustomed crispness. "Can't you see that you are alarming Mr. Shiloh? Dry your eyes immediately, and I will fetch you some elder-flower water in which to bathe them, for you look neither more nor less than a fright, and the rector has been waiting this half hour, having come all the way from Cincinnati to learn that you are an ungrateful girl, to say nothing of poor Edmund."

Rosalie had never before been addressed with an equal severity; the spoiled child was so far astounded by the Spartan rigour of her mother's tones as to find them an effectual tonic against the hysterics. She did as she was bid quite meekly, only casting toward Shiloh's motionless form a glance imploring and to him inexplicable.

"The unhappy creature is suffering under some furious visitation of acute mania," he thought sadly; the little dressing-room was very hot, and he longed hopelessly for fresh air and the cheerful company of fiddlers.

"Run along out of doors, Mr. Shiloh," said Mrs. Lillie pleasantly. "I should never have sent you in here in the first place. Rosie's upset you, and no wonder, but there's a nice cool west wind blowing and you'll soon feel better out there among your friends. Now don't sit there staring at me, but get along, like a dear boy."

Shiloh rose obediently to his feet, and without a word walked lightly, swiftly, and rather unsteadily from the enigmatic chamber into the blue and windy afternoon.

"So," said Mrs. Lillie to her daughter, "I suppose that is the explanation of your behaviour. Thank heaven he doesn't suspect a thing, poor lamb; I'm not so certain about Edmund."

"Mama," cried Miss Lillie tragically, "how can you be so cruel? It is positively inhuman for a mother to mock a daughter's desperate unhappiness. Cold words and cynical reflections: is this all you have to offer me in my hour of trial?"

"I have some nice elder-flower water, Rosie, and one of your father's clean pocket-handkerchiefs. Now, my dear little girl, stop crying and answer me one question. Do you really mean not to marry Edmund, since in any case you can't marry — somebody else?"

The Orphan Angel

Miss Lillie considered this problem for the briefest possible instant; the colour deepened in her cheeks, and her eyes grew bright with a contrary fire. Her mother observed with satisfaction that pride was rapidly repairing the ravages of grief upon the damask of her fine complexion.

" Certainly I should prefer to marry Edmund, if only in order to leave this detestable spot," she announced decidedly. She thought of the amenities of the eastern seaboard, and of the Philadelphia Assembly, to which Edmund's maternal aunt had promised to introduce her. She determined upon peach-coloured silk of the best quality, and felt sure that the trustees of the college must inevitably see eye-to-eye with her in the matter of Edmund's salary. " I must have been mad; of course I will marry him," she repeated, looking all at once extremely handsome.

" You must have been mad, dear; now let me arrange your veil," murmured her mother sympathetically. Rosalie submitted humbly to a second sleeking of her profuse tresses; she caught sight of herself in the glass, and realised that she was beautiful again.

Indeed, something of veritable madness had tinctured the hope which she had recently indulged; this infatuate conceit had followed Shiloh from the room, and Miss Lillie now discovered herself to be in cool possession of all her faculties, yet burning with the additional lustre of emotion. Her loveliness appeared actually augmented; faint purple shadows lay beneath her eyes, and her cheeks blazed under the frosty laces of her veil. She arranged the wreath of waxen orange-blossoms above her untroubled brows with hands that trembled not at all.

5

ALTHOUGH Miss Lillie's fingers trembled not at all, but moved composedly in unison with her pulses, Shiloh had drunk the cup of trembling, and found it poison for the spirit. His knees shook beneath him as he walked lightly from the ambiguous chamber; he did not in the least understand the nature of the scene enacted there, but he was profoundly moved by a sense of something

Refuse the Boon

sinister and equivocal in the air of the little room, lit dimly by its two tall candles of deer tallow. The atmosphere had been but too literally exhausted, and he suffered a corresponding prostration of soul as he staggered into the clear immaculate wind.

David ran to him at once; the honest fellow's countenance was crimson with alarm. He caught Shiloh by the elbow and hurried him to the sheltered side of the cabin, where sound flowed liquid and honey-sweet from the hollow fiddles.

" What in tarnation have they been a-doing to you, Shiloh? " he asked angrily, " and where have you been hiding all this goldarned time, and why do you look as if you'd seen a million mildewed graveyard corpses? Have you met old Jasper, or have you catched the ague, or has someone been hurting of you, just in order to get his skull cracked against this pretty little fist of mine? "

" No, David," said Shiloh mildly. " I am very grateful to you for your kindness, but it is quite unnecessary to crack any skulls this afternoon. Nobody has been hurting me, yet I have a hideous conviction, impossible to explain, that I have been hurting someone else. Let us not speak of it any more; let us leave for Louisville this very minute. Come with me now, David, while we are as yet unobserved; I have a great desire to push on to Louisville to-night, and the evening is beginning to fall, and I wish we were miles away from all these noisy and terrifying people."

" Aw, Shiloh, ain't we even going to wait for the ceremony or the Virginia reel? " David inquired with pathetic eagerness; Shiloh could not resist the dog-like entreaty of his eyes.

" Oh, very well, my dear fellow; of course we will stay," he said laughing, while inwardly his mind cried with weariness like a child confused by glare and clamour. " We will stay for the wedding and the country dances, and then, since that silver feather of a moon must be fire to-night, we will go forth into the forest together after dark. You will come with me, will you not, my best David? I wish we were alone again, and hastening upon our truer quest."

" That I will, by graminy, and with all my heart! " cried David exultingly. " I like the cap'n and the professor real well, but I'm getting almighty sick of 'em, I'm bound to confess.

141

The Orphan Angel

Scared blue I've been that you'd kind of weaken, Shiloh, and go off to those blasted bounty lands in Illinois, to breed fine upstanding young republicans like the cap'n says you should. And then where'd I be, I asks you, and where'd Silver be, and where'd you be yourself but tied down to a log cabin and a truck-patch and a passel of squawling brats? Oh, that ain't you, Shiloh, and 'tisn't me neither; we're for the raging wilderness and a life of bloody adventure."

" I trust so, sincerely," Shiloh agreed with gentle gravity.

" But oh, looky, Shiloh, here she comes, looking brighter and shinier than the first run of Kennebec salmon! " shouted David in excitement, clutching Shiloh's arm and nearly breaking its narrow bones. " There's Miss Lillie, or Miss Rosie as I call her to myself, and I swan she's the prettiest lady I ever see in all my born days, by cracky! "

Rosalie indeed appeared a perfect idealism of a lovely bride; anger and elder-flower water had smoothed all trace of tears from her brilliant lips and eyes. She glowed and undulated across the lawn in a billow and froth of whiteness; her skin had the suavity of the glassy blossoms about her brow, but it was richly stained with blushes where these were blanched and cold. She looked unreal, yet solid and deliberate as a statue; she might have been a noble wax doll, fashioned to delight some giant darling of the skies.

" Ain't she elegant? " David persisted, and Shiloh nodded without speaking. He was deeply relieved by the evident re-establishment of Miss Lillie's powers of self-control, and the mysterious sense of guilt which oppressed his heart to physical pain was sensibly lightened by the fine spectacle of her magnificence.

" What's she coming out here for, 'stead of being married all proper in the parlour? " wondered David, echoing the question in many curious looks and whispered comments.

" I protest I must be married out of doors, Mama," Rosalie had said as she applied a final delicate bloom of rice-powder to her glowing cheeks. Her mother knew better than to dispute the fantastic point; the girl was sane once more, but a dangerous temper simmered below the polished surface of her calm.

" I'll see what I can do with your father and the rector; he

Refuse the Boon

likes your father's sherry, so he may be amenable by now," said Mrs. Lillie humbly. " Of course you'll catch cold, but it's your own wedding, and I suppose you must have your way."

" In this, at least," replied Rosalie, with a bitter compression of her bright and curving lips.

When at last she crossed the rough grey lawn upon her father's arm, the guests acknowledged an admiration greater than their shocked astonishment. Edmund Lackland stood waiting for her, tranced in quiet idolatry; Rosalie had never been so evidently the vision which lies beyond all metaphysics and astronomies.

" ' Ever remain in perfect love and peace together. . . .' Might it not be true, Davy, and were it not beautiful if it were true? " asked Shiloh in an awe-struck whisper. He was, as always, profoundly impressed by elevated language; he had tried quite sincerely to detest the ceremony, but the pure high heavens touched with pearly light, the first flower-coloured evening stars, the music of the solemn exhortation, proved too much for his prejudices. By the time Rosalie and Edmund were pronounced man and wife, Shiloh was almost persuaded to be a Christian.

Nevertheless, his graceful presence was conspicuously lacking among those who embraced the bride at the close of the service, and the captain caught him gazing wildly at the pretty scene with the look of a slim and mettlesome horse who goes in scornful terror of the curb.

" What's up, Shiloh? " asked Captain Appleby, who knew, with precision and a certain wicked pleasure. " Don't you intend to salute the lady? I never thought to see you so ungallant; her eye is upon you, my boy, and a remarkably reproachful eye it appears to be."

Shiloh blushed, and endeavoured to edge his way through the crowd to a more retired portion of the field. His efforts were circumvented by Mr. Lillie, who invited him to join the country dances then in progress, at the same time courteously offering to introduce him to several charming girls from Louisville. Shiloh was apparently trapped; on one side loomed the stately proportions of his host, brandishing a sherry cobbler in either hand; on the other side at least six lusty young women fluttered and giggled alarmingly. Behind him was Rosalie; in front of him a row

143

of corn-shocks and a rail fence presented various barriers to escape.   •

The events of the last half-hour had strung his nerves to the breaking-point; Shiloh suddenly decided to go free at all costs, and, casting convention to the four strong winds of heaven, he dived between the corn-shocks and vaulted buoyantly over the rail fence. Mr. Lillie stared after him in dignified surprise; the eyes of the six young ladies from Louisville were round blue moons of amazement at his heels.

Shiloh paused among the pumpkins only long enough to pronounce an exquisitely polite but somewhat incoherent speech of apology; then he caught sight of David in the charitable distance, under the shadow of brown winter oak-trees. Shiloh turned and ran; if he had been running for his life he could not have achieved so passionate an energy as now possessed him in the pursuit of liberty.

6

LIBERTY eluded him among the delicate tawny grasses of the field; it flew visibly, a slender streak of light like a running hare; it fled before his longing, incredibly nimble and divine. Its silver scut flashed between the furrows of the next field and was gone; Shiloh stood beside David laughing and out of breath. The lovely thing had escaped him for the moment; it had vanished along the narrowing meadows of the distance, but its trace would be phosphorescent in the moonlight, and he would follow it in an hour or two.

Meanwhile he was very happy; he looked back over his shoulder and beheld the wedding dwindle into a bad dream. David put a cold metallic object into his hand; he perceived it to be a large duelling pistol of antique design, newly primed and redolent of raw gunpowder. He grew suddenly conscious that he was in the midst of a group of ragged men and boys; David appeared to be the honoured comrade of them all. Shiloh was favourably impressed by the intelligent democracy of their demeanour; he was pleased by their rough garments of homespun and Kentucky jean, and by their thin hawk-faces, which, variously tanned and freckled by the sun, preserved a uniformity of feature and expression. They wore the aspect of a tribe of fair-haired savages; Shiloh knew at once that they were hardy, humorous, and daring.

"We're a-shooting at that there mark, Shiloh, and you can have the next try if you've a mind to," David explained kindly. "Osbert's gone back to the cabin for a deck of cards for targets; it's pretty good sport at fifteen paces. See, we stick 'em atop of that stake yonder; Dan'l here's the best of the lot so far, but I lay you can lick us if you like. This here's a fine family; Kilpatrick their name is, and they come from Barrens, and their father's known as Squire Johnny, and he used to be a schoolmaster, but was forced to quit on account of fighting such a power of duels. These pistols as Bob loaned me has killed several gentlemen back in Barrens. At first they said they was white folks and me a Yankee, using the word ' Yankee ' kind of abusive-like, but we fixed that up quite friendly after a little argument, and now we're all serene. Come on and have a shot while it's light enough, for the sun'll set afore we know it."

At this instant Osbert arrived with a pack of greasy playing-cards; the ace of diamonds was inserted in a cleft at the top of the stick, and Shiloh assumed his station at precisely fifteen paces from the mark. With an air at once nonchalant and vague he took aim and fired; the card quivered upon its rigid stem, and David saw that the pip had been cut meticulously from its exact centre.

"Neat as if you'd gone and done it with a pair of scissors, by jiminy! " he cried with a whoop of triumph. " Always knowed you was a wonder, but I admire to see it proved public to the satisfaction of all and sundry! "

A stranger of distinguished and commanding appearance, who had been idly loitering upon the outskirts of the group, seized the opportunity to approach Shiloh and felicitate him upon this small victory of skill. The man had a splendid pair of black mustachios and wore a tall top-hat and an overcoat richly lined with astrakhan.

"Allow me to congratulate you, sir," he said in a mellow powerful voice. " You are a magnificent shot; I should like to try my own luck against you on a wager."

145

The Orphan Angel

Shiloh, who knew that this tribute of praise was grossly exaggerated, accepted it as a simple instance of civility. He was slightly embarrassed; one of his transitory blushes imparted a look of touching innocence to his open brow.

"I thank you, sir; it is nothing, and I am convinced that you could easily excel me," he said shyly, in the manner of a schoolboy detected in some ingenuous piece of mischief.

The ingratiating stranger was convinced of exactly the same thing; as a matter of local history he had already excelled so many people in that particular neighbourhood that the advent of Shiloh appeared truly providential to his mind.

"How much are you agreeable to bet, sir?" inquired the gentleman in the astrakhan collar with unctuous eagerness.

"I have no right to wager money, from a common store subject to my friend David's modest necessities, upon so hazardous a chance as my poor proficiency at target practice," explained Shiloh politely. "I shall, however, be most happy to determine our several degrees of excellence by an amicable trial of skill."

He was completely unprepared for the corrosive flood of profanity which burst sulphurously from the stranger's writhen lips; if an actual volcano had spattered the sweet autumnal herbage with malignant fire he could scarcely have been more mortally appalled.

"I am at a loss to understand how I have offended you, sir," he said quietly; his sense of spiritual decorum was outraged, and he spoke with tranquil contempt, but inwardly he was shivering with distaste and indignation. He laid his hand upon David's arm in order to restrain him, and David was amazed at the iron strength of that thin brown hand, and at the energy of anger implicit in its touch.

"I'll bash your damned dirty little head in!" the stranger shouted raucously, advancing upon Shiloh with clenched fists; his face was distorted into a grotesque mask of fury, and its gargoyle shape was stained to the ugly purple of a bruise.

"I'll bash your dirty little goddamned head into a bloody pudding!" he yelled once more, and David drew back, ready to strike a swift defending blow.

He was too late; before he had doubled up his fist into an

146

effective weapon Shiloh had struck instead; the stranger lay in a bulky crumpled heap upon the ground, and Shiloh was examining his own knuckles with an air of astonished concern.

"I do assure you, David, that he seemed to run straight into my hand!" said Shiloh with a sweetly reasonable smile, opening his large blue eyes and looking fully as dangerous as a new-born babe.

"We hope you've finished him, young feller, and no mistake!" cried the Kilpatrick family in happy chorus, capering about the body of their fallen enemy. "We all of us jest naterally hated Simon Hanna, and he was the wickedest sneakingest villain around these parts, as our dad can tell you. Now he's dead, and the widow and orphan can begin to sit up and take notice. As for you, you're a real genuine public benefactor, and we crave the honour of shaking you by the hand that done the deed!"

Shiloh appeared much confused by these manifestations of popularity; he continued to smile and to blush, while exchanging cordial handclasps with all his new friends from lean gigantic Daniel to goblin Osbert. It was pleasant to be regarded as a romantic champion of freedom, but he felt faintly sorry for Simon Hanna, and the flayed knuckles of his right hand were excessively painful in the strong Kilpatrick clutch.

"Do you really think he is dead, Davy?" he wondered anxiously, while David examined the prostrate foe with quick ungentle competence. "I had no idea that it was such an easy matter to kill a man; I suppose I should be overcome with remorse, but he was such a disagreeable person, and his manner was so gratuitously rude, that I cannot entirely regret having struck him. I hope, however, that he is not really dead, though I shall be sorry to disappoint my young friends the Kilpatricks."

"Aw, Shiloh, of course he's not dead, the cowardly dog," grunted David disgustedly, with his ear to Mr. Hanna's loudly labouring chest. "Can't you hear him puffing like a grampus, and don't you see he's as red in the face as a drunken turkey-cock? Takes more than a tap from your skinny fist to kill a beast like that; not but what you landed him one in the jaw very neatly, and a pleasure it was to see you do it. Clever and handy you always was, and quick as buttered lightning; I could teach you a trick or two in no time that would learn you to box blue-fiery rings around a lumbering hulk like him. Now we'd better be clearing out of here afore he comes to; he's an ugly customer, and if we want to fetch Louisville to-night we must be getting under weigh."

"It does not precisely agree with my notions of fair play to leave a vanquished enemy unconscious upon the field of combat," said Shiloh with a troubled sigh. "It is true that I am very eager to be gone, yet I should prefer to feel certain that this unhappy creature remains in charitable hands. May I count upon the goodness of your hearts, and will you not succour him if it becomes necessary?" he asked the Kilpatricks with a charming trustful smile.

"No, sirree, we ain't a-going to succour no rascals like Simon Hanna," Daniel announced with cheerful ferocity. "Kicks is all he'll ever get from us; he's lucky if he doesn't get a bullet between his shoulder-blades one of these fine winter evenings. We likes you and we honours you, but you're a plumb fool if you tries to be charitable to that kind of trash. He ought to be squatched out and wiped off the face of the earth; now leave him lay, and that's too good for him. If you'll come along home with us we'll give you some wholesome liquor and make you known to our old dad; he'd be proud to meet the man that laid Simon Hanna low."

"It's real good whisky this time, too, though a little raw and indigestible through being a new batch," added Bob hospitably, "but it does the job just as well for all that, and we'll have you roaring drunk by midnight, I can promise you, young feller. Dad's damned pleasant company in his cups; he knows a power of comical songs he didn't learn in Sunday-school."

"Oh, thank you, thank you with all my heart for your delightful invitation, but I must really be going to Louisville," said Shiloh in a low agitated voice, wringing his hands with nervousness and moving rapidly away in the direction of the deeper forest.

David followed him, making frantic signs of farewell to the Kilpatricks, who stared after the departing pair in speechless be-

Refuse the Boon

wilderment. Daniel scratched his freckled forehead and spat; Bob trundled Mr. Hanna's top-hat along the dusty ground with the toe of a reflective boot.

"Well," said little Osbert at length, breaking a silence pregnant with dismay, "they was a couple of crazy lunatic Yankees that didn't know good liquor when it was offered 'em gratis, but I'll say this much for 'em; they knew how to punch people in the jaw, didn't they, Dan'l?"

A groan from the recumbent Simon Hanna seemed to attest the truth of the lad's statement; Daniel caressed his own chin, and whistled gloomily as he gazed after Shiloh's swiftly diminishing form.

"You hold yours, or I'll do it for you, young Osbert," said Daniel with dark emphasis; he had been immensely impressed by Shiloh's personality, and it took a vast quantity of whisky to wash away the memory of his disappointment.

"He was a raging murderer, and no mistake," he told his father in one of the evening's intervals of comparative sobriety. "Wild-eyed he was, when he rushed on Simon, and fierce as a regular Shawnee, but I took a powerful fancy to him, and I would of liked to call the man my friend. Oh, sir, he was a proper ring-tailed squealer, if ever I see one; I wish we had him here, though I reckon we'd seem pretty tame company to him after the foot-and-hand, tooth-and-nail, claw-and-mud-scraper, knife-gun-and-tomahawk sort of massacree as he's accustomed to. 'Tarnal death to me! But he was a gentleman, and his name was *Fight!*"

7

"David, if I am called upon to drink any more whisky I shall inevitably go mad," said Shiloh with passionate solemnity as he sped across the rough ploughed fields towards the forest.

"Better steer clear of Louisville then, my lad," David replied grimly, making certain that his own flask was snug in its accustomed pocket. "Seems to me that your easiest smoothest course would be to learn to love the stuff like I do, but since you won't nohow be reasonable and human, my advice to you is to keep

149

running wild in the woods like the b'ars and catamounts, and not go near no towns, where folks is naterally drunk and friendly in spirit. Darn it, Shiloh, I think the world of you, as well you know, but it beats me why your habits are so eccentric and savage-like sometimes. Not drink whisky! Why, man, it ain't even decent, the way you go on about liquor, and it ain't suitable to a brave lively feller like you, taking up this tarnation teetotal attitude, and by graminy I wouldn't hardly think it of you, Shiloh, and I blush for you, I swear I do. Ain't you never heerd of civilisation afore this? "

" Frequently," answered Shiloh with becoming meekness. " I have heard many hard things of it, and more of myself as its invincible enemy. But perhaps you do not fully understand, my dear good Davy, the stupendous difference between our present shocking industrial system, and the high golden age of Greece. That was civilisation in its noblest form; this is merely . . ."

" Aw, stow it, Shiloh," rejoined David crossly. He was bitterly chagrined at parting with his new-found friends; loyalty forced him to accompany Shiloh wherever that fantastic creature chose to roam, but at least half his honest heart was in the Kilpatricks' cabin, among the merry fumes of corn.

He repented of his asperity, however, when he saw Shiloh droop his head and wither visibly into sadness, and his next words were amiable and reassuring in proportion to his pang of self-reproach.

" You crazy little scalawag, don't look so goldarned miserable," cried David with a burst of laughter. " Mebbe I was kind of crabbed just now, but I was thinking as how we might have had a rare old time with the Kilpatricks to-night, 'stead of traipsing off to the wilderness. Still, that's what we come west for, I'll allow, and I ain't a-going to scold you no more, Shiloh. By jiminy, we've both of us been forgetting about Silver and all we was calculating to do for the poor critter! "

" I never forget," said Shiloh seriously. His eyes were luminous with that peculiar fire which invariably informed them at the mention of Silver's name; they blazed like mortal stars in the soft monotonous twilight, and David stared at him marvelling, and perhaps a thought afraid.

Refuse the Boon

"I been forgetting all I owes to him," he whispered to himself. "I been forgetting Silver, and Jasper dead and gone along of me, and the strange salvation of my soul that come to me when I brought Shiloh back to life in place of him I'd murdered. God forgive me if I ain't forgetting my vow, to follow him faithful through the world. Well, I'll say no more of whisky and such-like luxuries, and by golly if he wants to drink water he shall, or I'm a double Dutchman!"

His small blue eyes were full of tears as he turned to Shiloh and slapped him jovially upon the back, and his loud voice was shaky with an emotion other than mirth.

"Too late to make Louisville to-night, my hearty," he said. "We'll find one of these here crystal springs as you're always talking of, and pitch our camp in the depth of the wood, to give you a chance to get your bearings, like, and fetch your breath in peace and quiet. You're plumb wore out with crowds and carryings-on; you wasn't never meant to mix much in society, I reckon, for all your pretty manners."

"I believe you are right, David," replied Shiloh, with an involuntary sigh of relief.

Nevertheless his conscience smote him in remembering Captain Appleby and the professor, and he realized that there was something of cowardice in this sudden dereliction of friendship. He thought of the happy hours spent over the pages of Laplace, and of the smiling bounty lands of Illinois, and for a moment he paused in his wild-swan flight, and trembled with indecision. Then another and more curious memory shook his mind, and he smelled once again the mingled fragrance of patchouli and melted deer tallow. The recollection rendered him quite faint; he hurried onward, quivering with alarm, into the cool revivifying solitude of the wood.

A singular circumstance now forced itself upon his vague attention: his footsteps were a lighter echo of David's ponderous tread, but ever behind these a second more insubstantial echo sounded, a noise frail as the rustle of a skeleton leaf, and far away. At first he thought that the faithful yellow dog had left the noble beef-bones of the wedding-feast to follow them upon their journey; then he knew that the rhythm of the delicate scampering was familiar and human. A woman was running after them through the forest; her footsteps were very small and pathetic under the infinite arch of the darkness.

"No matter who it may be, we must wait for her," he said to David with perfect firmness; his heart, however, tried its best to escape from his bosom and be gone into silence and safety.

"But who in thunder can it be, and why are you so scared, Shiloh?" asked David in perplexity. "You appear to be scared green, and yet it can't be nothing wuss than a woman that's following us; don't see why you're so almighty scared o' women."

They stood together beneath the vaulted canopy of trees, heavy with mistletoe festoons; Shiloh was shivering, and David caught him by the elbow to steady his evident trepidation. The footsteps approached; they sounded peculiarly soft and harmless in the gentle secrecy of dusk.

"What on earth's the matter with you, you crazy catawampus?" asked David somewhat impatiently. "Goldarn me if you're not the looniest lad this side of Bedlam, mixing up with Simon Hanna as calm as a summer sea, and then throwing a fine conniption fit of terror 'cause a poor weak woman comes a-lolloping after us like a rabbit. 'Tain't nothing but a plain ordinary woman, I tell you, you silly innocent, so quit shivering, and speak polite to the lady when she catches up with us, for she won't take it as no compliment the way you're going on."

"Good God, it's only Mrs. Lillie!" breathed Shiloh thankfully; he stopped trembling, and went forward with a courteous eagerness to meet the small dishevelled form of his late hostess, who now emerged from the mysterious forest aisles.

"Oh, Mr. Shiloh, I do hope you will forgive me for running after you so unceremoniously!" cried Mrs. Lillie in an exhausted little voice. "I do hope you will forgive me, my dear boy, and I quite understand your wishing to leave the wearisome confusion of the wedding, but I had one or two trifles that I had meant to give you, and I could not bear you to go off all alone like that without a word of farewell, so I took the liberty of following you along the southern meadow, and of course I know it is very unconventional, but you see you had forgotten your bundle, and I thought with the winter coming on, and you being accustomed to a warmer climate, that I had better in spite of appearances."

The poor lady was in a pitiful state of distress; her pretty pearl-grey silk was torn, and her small imploring face was streaked with dust and tears. She carried the dilapidated gypsy bundle in one hand; the other held a neat brown-paper parcel and a pair of red mittens.

" I knew that most of Mr. Butternut's belongings were in the pockets of his pea-jacket," she went on anxiously. " And then, he's used to roughing it, but with you it's different, and if any little comfort could possibly be helpful, I should be so very happy, though to think of your spending Christmas among the red Indians is almost more than I can bear, but be that as it may, I brought you a packet of tea, because I know you're fond of it, and a few of my cucumber pickles to remind you of our pleasant times together, and I think that's all except hard-boiled eggs and radishes, and oh, of course the muffler which is around my own neck because I had so much to carry and you do forgive me, don't you? "

Shiloh was overcome with gratitude and remorse; the thought that he had actually fled from this tender creature was almost intolerably pathetic. To be sure, he had feared another in the approaching footsteps, but now he sought by every means in his power to restore some measure of confidence to Mrs. Lillie's frightened spirit. He took the red mittens with a murmured word of thanks and stood gazing affectionately at their donor, who in her turn gazed up at him with large adoring eyes.

" I do appreciate, far more than I can express, your amazing kindness to a lonely traveller," he said gently; the orphaned quality of his smile was starrily apparent in the twilight, and Mrs. Lillie loved him with a double adoration.

" We've heard about Simon Hanna," said Mrs. Lillie humbly, " and it was exactly like you, and wonderfully heroic and brave, but I do hope you'll be a little more careful about the savages, and I meant to ask you whether you had plenty of quinine and calomel, because being so far from a doctor, and perhaps with a tendency to colds, and O Mr. Butternut, you will take care of him, won't you? "

"I aim to do so, ma'am, to the best of my powers," replied David rather haughtily. He was excessively bored by Mrs. Lillie, and a little jealous of her.

"And now good-bye, and may God have you in His holy keeping, my dear boy," said Mrs. Lillie in a breaking voice. She took Shiloh's slender brown fingers in both her small white hands; she looked as if she were going to kiss his finger-tips, but only an invisible tear touched them in the silence.

Shiloh was painfully affected by her unconcealed sorrow; he wished very much to comfort her, if it were possible to do so without abandoning his own pursuit of liberty and peace. He tried to think of some simple consolation, and his wild and worried blue eyes fell upon the neat parcel of provisions, which had dropped unheeded to the ground.

"Would you not like Davy to make you a cup of tea before you leave us?" he inquired solicitously. "Davy makes excellent tea, and it might refresh you for your long homeward walk. It is quite chilly in these woods; I am sure a cup of tea would be both beneficial and delicious. Have you the flint and steel, Davy? because I can collect enough dry sticks in a moment to make a very cheerful little fire."

"Ain't no spring in sight, far as I can see, and how can you brew tea without water?" grumbled David obstructively. He need not have taken the pains to discourage Mrs. Lillie; her spirit was already completely shattered, and she smiled wanly and shook her head in response to Shiloh's benevolent suggestion.

"No, no; I really couldn't; I have not a particle of appetite, and besides, I must be getting back to my guests, and supper at six, and most of them counting on my special apple pandowdy, and nobody understands the Dutch oven but myself," she murmured desolately, turning to go.

In the dusk she was no more than a silky grey wisp of farewell; David himself was moved by her pitiful futility, at point to vanish into even less.

"If a swig from my flask could be any comfort, ma'am . . ." he muttered shyly.

Mrs. Lillie paid no heed to him; she took Shiloh's hand again, but now a thin gossamer suggestion of hauteur had fallen insensibly over her manner, rendering it at once formal and childish, so that she was like a little girl bidding a polite good-bye to a birthday party of ogres and warlocks. Behind this veil of exemplary civility her soft unhappy hazel eyes glinted with a feverish desire to be gone into nothingness.

"Good evening, Mr. Shiloh; I wish you a very pleasant journey," she whispered; tears shone along the spider-web thread of her voice; the obscurity of night received her as its own.

She fled with the quiet scampering haste of a squirrel or a field-mouse; the rustle of her going was almost unbelievably delicate and brief. High among the tree-tops the ghost of an echo trembled in the pale remaining leaves.

"Poor lady! I have a melancholy suspicion that her life is overshadowed by some vague but painful tragedy!" said Shiloh sadly, seating himself cross-legged at the base of a gigantic oak. "It would have been impracticable in the extreme to have attempted to join her fortunes to ours, and yet I am not wholly satisfied with my own conduct in the matter; I do not entirely approve of Mr. Lillie as a husband for this vulnerable creature. It is very distressing; I wish we might have solved the difficulties of her future."

"Aw, shucks, Shiloh, 'tain't none of our business!" cried David robustly. "Women, women; I know 'em! Wanted to be a mother to you, I dare say; wrap you up in red flannel and feed you on calomile pills and Queen Anne, drat her. Sooner I get you away from all that kind of Miss Nancy hanky-panky the better it'll be for your everlasting good. Weaken your guts, that's what women do; it's women as have taught you to drink chiny tea instead of decent whisky. 'Take care of him,' she says to me, indeed, as if you was a baby; she must be plumb off her head, the silly old hen!"

"Really, David, you are unnecessarily severe," murmured Shiloh absent-mindedly, crouching upon the frosty fallen leaves and staring rather forlornly into the hollow darkness; he felt unnerved, and uncomfortably chilly. The knitted muffler was hunched ridiculously about his ears; his uncovered hair stood on end like the feathers of some tropic bird dismayed by cold and brutal winter.

"It's not women; it's people; it's the whole hellish society of men," he said bitterly. "How is it possible that one of so weak and sensitive a nature as mine can run further the gauntlet through this world of cool ferocious malice?"

"Your coat's just rags and tags; we'll buy us some hunters' leather jackets in Louisville," replied David tactfully. "Now you look around for firewood while I find the creek; I can hear it a-gurgling among the stones at the bottom of this little gully. Then you can have your blamed cambric tea and I can have my grog, and we'll see what Mrs. Lillie give us for our supper."

8

A few moments later the scene was fabulously altered: Shiloh perceived a pleasantly circumscribed paradise in the small warm cavern of firelight which his friend had conjured out of blackness and despair. The pine boughs flung crackling streamers of pure yellow flame against the dark; David was already weaving other boughs into a screen to windward. The night smelled of spice and balsam and burning leaves.

"Don't this beat all their grand goings-on to blazes?" asked David triumphantly as he affixed the battered tin kettle to a gypsy tripod of crossed sticks.

Shiloh unwrapped Mrs. Lillie's brown-paper parcel; it was full of hard-boiled eggs and slim ice-coloured winter radishes; there was the wing of a fried chicken, and a few translucent slices of ham. She had remembered the salt; she had also remembered the crumbly lumps of maple sugar for his tea. His eyes brimmed with tears as he beheld these evidences of her loving kindness.

"Sort of thin fare for a cold night," was David's ungrateful comment. He plunged his hands into the vast unfathomable pockets of his pea-jacket, and drew forth an enormous chunk of streaky bacon and the better part of a roast wild turkey.

"Is that mustard in the old lady's package?" asked David eagerly. "Good; devilled turkey legs ain't by any means to be despised as victuals, by graminy. You sharpen a stick, Shiloh, while I finish thatching this here shack agin a possible blizzard."

Refuse the Boon

Shiloh was completely happy again; he sipped sweet scalding tea out of a tin cup, and the exquisite warmth of the fire flowed upward from his toes as the hot tea flowed downward from his throat. He nibbled a crisp icy radish, and allowed David to attend to the devilled turkey.

" I am amazed to discover that I am excessively tired; there was something peculiarly unrestful about the atmosphere of Mr. Lillie's home, although his hospitality was generous to a fault," said Shiloh mildly, masking a yawn behind his slender fire-reddened fingers.

" Didn't suit you nohow; that was plain to be seen from the very word go," David answered judicially. " Can't exactly figure it out, but there was something disagreed with you terrible in the air of that farm; you was getting all peaked and unearthly-like, same as when I fust seen you. Lord, you look another man already in this nice little snug neck o' woods."

After an excellent supper, Shiloh amused himself by turning one of the choruses from the *Antigone* of Sophocles into English lyrical verse; this exercise of the poetic faculties rendered him deliciously sleepy by eleven o'clock. He fell into a light doze, soothed by recurrent waves of music from the inner convolutions of his own mind, now ringing like a sea-shell with harmonious cadences.

He was quite unaware of David's protracted absence; he woke suddenly, disturbed by the loud approach of some great beast that shuffled through the underbrush. The thing was dark and harshly furry; its gigantic shoulders were humped beneath a sinister spiked dream of Burnham Wood. Shiloh was sure that the creature was a bear; he was pleased to observe how curiosity overcame fear in the confusion of his senses.

The beast drew near; Shiloh leaped to his feet, prepared to sell his life only at the price of the most desperate and determined resistance possible to his tense and active frame. A pair of grimly bearded arms embraced him; then all at once they were recognisably David's, and David himself was laughing under a shawl of shaggy hide.

" Thought we might kind of enjoy a good old buffalo-robe to-night; there's liable to be a regular black frost afore morning,"

The Orphan Angel

cried David, flinging his savage burden upon the ground. It lay like a wounded animal; Shiloh could fancy it ambushed to spring with the springing flames.

"Reckon I skeered you, didn't I?" asked David cockily. Shiloh was slightly annoyed; he recovered his toppling dignity by the little effort of a smile.

"Did you kill it?" he inquired amiably. David was enchanted by this fantastic theory of his exploit.

"I'll be switched if I didn't shoot it with a pea-shooter, and it with an elegant felt lining and all!" he chuckled, displaying the thick glossy fur mounted upon dark blue cloth of the richest and most durable description. Shiloh was impressed, but he was also troubled.

"But if you stole it from someone, Davy, that person must presumably go cold to-night," he said with profound anxiety, staring at David with large and solemn eyes.

"Stole your gran'mother; borrowed it, you mean, my lad," his friend replied jauntily. "And that feller won't be cold to-night, I can promise you; he's laying dead drunk in Mr. Lillie's kitchen at this very moment, and there's a roaring fire not a foot from his coat-tails. More likely to be roasted, he is; it's a real act of charity to take this here contraption and keep it safe till morning. He drives the stylishest oxcart in the county, and this robe is one of a pair, one to cover the straw cushions and one to cover the folks as rides on 'em. Now don't you go wrinkling your forehead and ruffling your goldarned crazy hair, but into the shack with you, and roll yourself up in this grand old buffalo-hide, and you won't know nothing till you smell frying bacon at sunrise."

When they were actually within the balsam-scented warmth of the shelter, with the heavy fur drawn up to their chins, David spoke once more, but very drowsily.

"This beats cock-fighting, don't it, Shiloh?" he asked in the accents of an absolute contentment; in the firelight his countenance was like a copper mask of peace.

"Presumably the comfort and tranquillity of our present situation must indeed be far superior to that peculiarly stupid and barbaric sport," said Shiloh in a voice impregnated with the gentle lenitive of sleep.

Refuse the Boon

He lay watching the lovely diminution of the flames; they flickered softly along the reflecting surface of the fallen leaves, which still held some of the colours of fire in their delicate decay. The night smelled of spice and balsam; the smoke of the burning leaves was sweeter than incense. Shiloh was very happy; he knew this happiness, and savoured it upon his tongue with the exquisite bitter taste of wood-smoke, before the hypnotic dark overwhelmed him in oblivion.

His mind fled lightly and dizzily in front of the advancing wave of sleep; he drew Silver's miniature from his pocket, and gazed at the shagreen case by the diminished glimmer of the pine logs. He was too tired to open the case, but he could see quite clearly, behind painted shark-skin made magically transparent, the small pale face and the eyes suffused with darkness, like the patterned eyes upon the wings of moths.

A few frail snowflakes floated nonchalantly down; the fire subsided into tender rose-red ashes, and Shiloh slept, his lips against the little shagreen case.

VI

PASTORAL GARAMANT

"Ain't we never going to have no adventures?" asked David plaintively the next morning as he finished the last bit of bacon. The weather was warm again; no faintest trace of snow lingered upon the tiger-coloured leaves about their feet, and the sun was an incandescent shield behind the eastern fringe of tulip-trees. The buffalo robe was flung to one side, and the friends were in their shirt-sleeves, stretched at ease within the thermal influence of the awakened fire.

Shiloh had plunged into the stream before breakfast; it had been vehemently cold, but its fierce electric iciness had washed the cobwebby worries from his brain, and now he felt clean and strong and sanguine as he faced the daybreak. The bright blood was sentient under the sunburn on his cheek, and all his muscles were confident and happy; his eyes were almost savage in their brilliance. It was impossible to imagine him disheartened or ill; David looked at him with unconcealed approval, and filled the tin cups with potent boiling tea from the kettle.

"You seem ready and willing to lick your weight in wildcats, Shiloh; when do you reckon we'll get a chance at a scrap?" persisted David stubbornly.

"Soon, I hope, since your soul is set upon it, Davy," said Shiloh with a smile. " But meanwhile I have a small piece of news for you, not wholly lacking in elements of excitement." He drew the miniature from his pocket and opened the case; instead of turning to the portrait his attention was engaged by the circle of gold wherein the ivory was mounted.

" You see," he explained at last, while David watched him fascinated, " the back of this setting opens like a locket; there is a bit of paper within the space concealed. I found it this morning, before it was really light; I wanted to see the picture, but in the obscurity I found myself staring at the other side, and then I observed a little crack along its edge; finally I succeeded in prying it apart with my thumbnail, and this is what I discovered."

He handed a torn fragment of paper to David, who seized it avidly, and squinted with furious curiosity at the blurred inky characters upon its surface.

"'Jasper Crooks,'" read David slowly, "' Bumbolow's Tavern, Louisville, Kentucky.' Yes, but who's Jasper Crooks? Our Jasper, that I murdered aboard the brig, was Jasper Cross; do you calculate as how this is the same fellow with another name, Shiloh? "

" Assuredly it is the same person, Davy," explained Shiloh eagerly. " In fact, I think I can perceive the origin of the change; Crooks means precisely Cross if you spell it in the Latin manner, C-r-u-x. Doubtless one or the other of Jasper's names was assumed, in some stress of danger or disgrace. It is all very romantic, and I was quite sure you would be pleased; this will simplify our search considerably, now that we have an actual address in Louisville."

" I should say it would, by graminy! " cried David jubilantly. " Well, if that isn't the goldarndest piece of luck that I ever heard tell of, and just as I was beginning to be kind of mad 'cause we had to go to Louisville to find your old Eyetalian letter at the bank and all! Not that it'll be there for a month of Sundays, by my reckoning, but that doesn't matter now, with clues and false names and everything fine and sort of secret-like. I declare, Shiloh, you're a regular bloody wonder; haven't I always told you so? "

" You have been more than kind in your appreciation of my

virtues, Davy," Shiloh replied modestly. "But in this instance it was merely a singular bit of good fortune which guided my fingers to the scrap of paper. And now, if you will return the buffalo robe, I will occupy myself in stamping out the fire and tying up our bundles; I confess I am unwilling to meet any of the Lillie family this morning."

"Guess I'll just drop it in the road where somebody's sure to see it, and not go near the house myself," said David uneasily. "'Tisn't so much the Lillies as I mind seeing as Captain Appleby; I feel kind of ungrateful when I think of all his kindness, and yet I'll be switched if I want to go and populate Pike county, as he calls fathering a passel of babies. Do you reckon we've used him shabby, Shiloh, or is your conscience clear about the captain?"

"Not entirely, I must admit," Shiloh answered sadly. "I am heartily ashamed of my inability to go back to the cabin and bid good-bye to them all, decently and frankly; my only excuse is that I detest farewells and that I am convinced that an interview with our friends would so affect my nerves as to render me incapable of continuing our journey to-day. And that," said Shiloh pensively, "would surely be a thousand pities; I am certain Captain Appleby would forgive me if he understood my present predicament."

"You hate anything as cramps your wild free goings-on, don't you, Shiloh?" inquired David with sympathetic interest. "Anything like a cut-and-dried hide-bound plan makes you downright miserable, I can see. 'Tain't easy to put words to what I mean, but you seem kind of scairt and jumpy soon as anyone tries to stop you going where you want to."

"You are perfectly right, David." Suddenly Shiloh looked rather haughty and desperate; his eyes had the brightness of a fawn's, and yet there was something of the panther in his air of pride. "I know I am a fool, my dear fellow, but you are amazingly right; any infringement of my personal liberty makes me sick with revolt. Nevertheless, I confess it is a fault; I shall learn better, I suppose, before I die."

"Aw, Shiloh, but why should you?" protested David loyally. "I like you best this way; I like you being so spunky and owdacious. Shouldn't want to be the man to stop you to-day, by cracky; don't seem as if nothing could, the look you've got in your eyes."

Shiloh was accessible to the flattery of this honest praise; he had been more than human if his eye had not brightened and his brow flushed upon the word. He shrugged his slim shoulders, seeming to cast some burden from them as he did so, and stared up into the luminous blue; then he laughed and leaped to his feet.

"I go on until I am stopped, and I never am stopped," cried Shiloh rather crazily, beginning to stamp out the remaining embers of the camp-fire.

Sparks flew into the air and whirled around his head like a swarm of parti-coloured bees, golden and tawny and vermilion; he stood in the midst of the swarming sparks and laughed. He looked a creature of fire, a fierce and subtle flame; even his wild and tattered garments were transfused by a curious effulgence, and upon the locks of his hair particles of light had fallen from the cloud of burning wings.

2

THEY stopped at noon by a great beaver-dam to eat the ultimate scrap of turkey; David drained his flask, and rejoiced to think of the good distilleries of Louisville. Shiloh discovered an enormous grapevine, thicker than a man's arm, among whose withered leaves a few bunches of grapes were still concealed; these were sun-dried and sugary as raisins, and he found them a very palatable dessert. He was further enchanted by the appearance of a huge snapping-turtle; he seemed to detect a sinister wisdom in the reptile's gleaming hooded eyes which charmed his imagination to dreams of prehistoric monsters. The parakeets had flown south, but many smaller birds chattered in the genial warmth, and the squirrels and chipmunks leaped like streaks of silver and ruddy lightning along the branches of the poplars and tulip-trees.

Another four miles brought the friends to the first houses of the town; to eyes accustomed to the cane-brake and the tomahawk improvement, the courthouse with its portico and spire loomed splendid in the distance. They inquired their way of a civil stranger in broadcloth and a beaver hat; presently they stood upon the steps of the Commercial Bank of Louisville, looking savage and unkempt in the shadow of its neatly pointed brickwork.

"You could thump me round the earth with a crab-apple sooner'n get me inside that green door, Shiloh," declared David firmly. "It seems so kind of prim-like and respectable that it makes me feel like a mad yaller dog. Reckon I'll go hunt for this here Bumbolow's tavern, and come back for you in half an hour; I'll be setting on these steps waiting for you when you finish talking to the old codgers in there. Beats me how you got the guts to face 'em, in them trousers, but then you never did care nothing for appearances, as the saying is."

David sauntered off happily in the direction of a swinging sign setting forth the virtues of Hope's Celebrated Whisky, and Shiloh, with a somewhat nervous air of bravado, laid his hand upon the shining brass doorknob of the Commercial Bank. He was faintly embarrassed by the fact that his boots were in a shocking condition and his blue jean shirt in holes, but far more powerful was the fear that disagreeable news was ambushed behind the smart green paint of the door-panels.

He felt quite light-headed with relief when a supercilious clerk informed him that there were no letters for Mr. Shiloh; only a sense of duty drove him to demand audience with some higher official.

"My dear sir, I trust I invariably recognise a gentleman when I see one," said Mr. Townley, unbending in the chaste mahogany comfort of his private sanctum. It was true; he had offered Shiloh a rich black cigar before he even glanced at the note of introduction with which Mr. Lillie had insisted upon providing his young friend. Shiloh promptly declined the gift of the unctuous Habana, but he was touched by the courtesy of his reception. The leather arm-chair was very grateful to his ascetic bones; he knew he was in danger of falling asleep, lulled by the pleasant laziness of Mr. Townley's voice.

"Unfortunately it is quite out of the question that a letter from Italy should reach Louisville for another six weeks," said

Pastoral Garamant

Mr. Townley with a condoling shake of his fine iron-grey head. "Of course the post will travel much faster than you have walked a like distance, but then you must allow for the two voyages across the Atlantic, and that, be your ship the swiftest Yankee clipper ever launched, must inevitably take time. I'm sorry, my boy, so far as you are concerned; tidings of your wife and child are now your one desire, I know, and it grieves me to have to dash your more sanguine expectations. My advice to you is to stay in Louisville until the letter comes; our posts are excellent; in fact nine mails arrive weekly and are distributed from the post office. I would most gladly find you some employment in our town during your interval of enforced inactivity; if it were not an impertinence I might suggest private tutoring, since Mr. Lillie says you are an elegant classical scholar. Also, if you liked, I could put you into the Bank; I am sure you write a legible clerkly hand, and are clever at figures, eh, Mr. Shiloh?"

"You are more than kind, but really I fear I am unable to avail myself of your generous offer," murmured Shiloh diffidently; Mr. Townley thought him a very sensitive and mild young man, but the fantastic creature's mind was inwardly vivid with rebellion. He was determined not to be trapped in a counting-house or a schoolroom, and the thought of the Italian letter was strangely hateful to his spirit.

"Is it possible that I do not wish to hear from Mary?" he asked himself in honest horror; then suddenly he knew the truth, and shivered in a nakedness of soul. He had never wanted to hear from Mary; his cold dread of being scolded transcended all the other and more romantic emotions which Mary's accusing grey eyes could arouse in his bosom.

The knowledge neatly stripped a layer of self-esteem from a soul always susceptive to the point of agony; Shiloh was visibly shaken, and Mr. Townley thought him in the chilly fit of a remittent fever, and unlocked the cellarette with humane intention. His guest declined the whisky with determined politeness; the chill was moral rather than physical, and its passing left a frosty ache not to be warmed by creature comfort.

"Still a bit agueish, aren't you? This sultry autumn weather has played the devil with us all," said Mr. Townley kindly, swallowing a therapeutic draught with an appreciative grimace.

Shiloh stared appalled at the spectacle of his own soul; the sunny afternoon was black with grief and shame. Nevertheless he experienced a certain sharp relief in knowing the worst about himself, and he resolved to discipline his weakness with the utmost rigour and severity. He rose to his feet, wan but indomitable.

"' The Magus Zoroaster, my dead child, met his own image walking in the garden,'" said Shiloh solemnly; Mr. Townley was more than ever certain that the man was in the grip of a tertian fever.

"I shall remain in Louisville until the letter arrives," Shiloh continued resolutely. "All other business must give place to the sacred duty of providing for the happiness of those I love; for the happiness of those I love." He repeated these concluding words no less than three several times; Mr. Townley began to believe that his young friend's ague had already been modified by an enormous remedial dose of whisky.

Shiloh was filled with an honourable desire to make amends; he saw himself waiting patiently and soberly for Mary, while David took the adventurous future to himself. He wondered which of Mr. Townley's suggestions would inflict the most exquisite retributive justice upon his spirit; the thought of teaching Latin to children was distasteful enough, but he fancied that the endless columns of figures in the ledgers of the Commercial Bank might be the fitter trial of his fortitude.

"Can you really find me a position in the bank?" he asked politely, hugging the dreadful resolution to his heart as if it had been a wolf-cub; under cover of his pride the Spartan boy was torn and bleeding.

"I am quite sure I can; it may not be a position of responsibility as yet, but the dignity of labour is apparent in the faithful efforts of the humblest clerk in our employ," replied Mr. Townley guardedly; he had no immediate intention of trusting this eccentric stranger beyond the limits of simple computations with a quill pen.

"Of course," Mr. Townley continued with helpful eagerness,

Pastoral Garamant

"if you decide to push farther into the west your letter can be forwarded in time; I mean if you will leave a definite address, in some accessible part of the country. People," said Mr. Townley vaguely, "do go west, particularly in the spring. But undoubtedly your safest plan is to remain in Louisville."

"I know," said Shiloh with a sigh and a shudder; the invisible wolf-cub was devouring the very core of his heart, and the memory of Silver's ivory face was extremest torture. With a shock of amazement he realized that she might even now be in Louisville; nevertheless she seemed to his depressed imagination infinitely farther removed than when a quarter-world had sundered them by thousands of savage miles.

As a matter of ironic fact, no letter was on its way from Italy; no letter had reached the grey-eyed widow in her Pisan solitude. Mary still believed herself to be a widow. In her sleeveless gown of black velvet, cut low to flatter the lovely marble of her bosom, she sat like an immemorial effigy of grief in the midst of the noisy household of the Hunts at Genoa. Pisa and San Terenzo were places of the past; England shimmered distantly through sea-born mists, and the world was sorrowful. Captain Ffoulkastle was neither a knave nor a fool; he was merely dead. The *Witch of the West* had gone down with all hands aboard three days out of Boston Harbour, on the seventh of September, 1822, and Shiloh's letter to his wife had gone with her to be obliterated for ever in the bitter green depth of the sea.

Therefore the excruciating division of Shiloh's soul was all for naught; he need not have suffered as he did in resolving to remain in Louisville. He was free to depart; free to return to Italy, or, less commendably, to set forth upon farther travels even beyond the moon.

"I shall stay," he said rather breathlessly, turning to go. "I must find my friend, and acquaint him with this new decision, but in the morning I shall present myself at your door, prepared to accept whatever employment I can obtain. For the moment, then, farewell; to-morrow we shall meet again."

He spoke with some degree of agitation, and Mr. Townley still wondered what disorder of body or of mind might account for his singular behaviour. The banker took off his silver-bowed

167

spectacles and rubbed them with a red silk handkerchief; when he put them on again his curious guest had disappeared.

3

SHILOH found David sitting upon the steps of the bank eating gingernuts; he looked flushed and cheerful in the rose-coloured light from the west.

"Good news, Shiloh!" he cried at once, offering Shiloh the choice of an apple or a handful of gingernuts from his capacious pockets. "Leastways, mebbe you won't call it good, on account of us having a little matter of another three hundred miles to go, but I've seen this blasted old curmudgeon Bumbolow, and spite of him being most god-almighty drunk on Jamaica rum he remembers Jasper plain, and Jasper's pa and ma, and Silver herself, when she was nothing much more than a yaller-haired baby. Jasper come here to Bumbolow when he fust run away from home, along of the old man being a family friend, like; he run away when he was fifteen, but they didn't none of them live in Louisville; they come from St. Louis. Now quit glaring at me with them blue saucer eyes of yours, and listen careful; I know it's kind of confusing to strangers, but I reckon we can walk it if we ain't got the steamboat fare, and for my part I'd admire to push on to something a bit wilder, for this town's too niminy-piminy prim to suit me nohow with all these here brick houses. Strike me silly if I've seen an Injun yet; bloody-wild ground they call it, but it's too bloody tame for me. Not but what the whisky's real good, which they say as it's our bounden duty to drink, with the water so downright poisonous; you must lay off that blasted tea as long as you're in Louisville."

"I dare say I shall do very well if I do not omit the precaution of Chincona," said Shiloh sadly; he felt that it would require more than an infusion of tea-leaves to hearten him against the cold flood of melancholy overwhelming him at the sound of Silver's name. "If the water is really so unwholesome, however, I may take a glass of white wine with my supper. But Davy, I don't understand; is Silver then in St. Louis, as you call it?"

Pastoral Garamant

"Well, so far as that old bellowing Bumbolow can reckon, she must be," David assured him; Shiloh had a horrid vision of his own image balancing the ledger in the Commercial Bank of Louisville while David went on a journey alone, with Silver at that journey's end.

"You see," continued David eagerly, "seems as how her pa was a Frenchman, a regular scoundrel he was and the perfect spit of Jasper, and he was some kind of a river pirate and robbed a power of honest folk, murdered some too I reckon, and then at last the Injuns got him, and served him right, but it was hard on his innocent wife and children, and so Jasper gone wrong, and Silver was left an orphan along of her ma dying of sorrow and starvation, and the poor lady was Spanish, and from foreign parts, and always homesick in St. Louis, and her husband beat her, and she never could get properly warm in winter, and her life was a perfect hell until death released her, and then here was little Silver all forlorn, and I calculate as how it's a tarnation lucky thing we come west."

"And Silver is really destitute and in trouble!" cried Shiloh; the blood beat in his pulses, and his voice quivered in accord with them.

"I should just say she was, by graminy!" was David's delighted rejoinder; it was plain that he accounted the circumstance of Silver's poverty in the nature of a personal triumph.

"'Tain't that I want the poor girl to be unhappy," he explained in the next breath, "only it would seem kind of loony and outlandish if we'd 'a' come all this goldarned ways without any rhyme or reason. But now it's all straight sailing, and we know we done right to come, and there's nothing to stop us leaving immediate for St. Louis to rescue her from misery."

Shiloh was silent; he had not the heart to dash in the slightest degree David's golden and chivalric dream, and he felt a curious reluctance to admit in words that his own part in their adventures was over for ever. David noticed his pallor and dejection and ascribed them to hunger, by which natural pang these symptoms were undoubtedly augmented.

"Talk about sorrow and starvation!" cried David. "You're the living picture of 'em now; if you could see the face on you

169

you'd die laughing. Why, you crazy son of a musket, won't you never learn no sense about your victuals? Come and get something under your belt; you ain't had nothing all day but a scraggy neck of turkey. There's elegant venison at the tavern, and mutton chops sizzling as beautiful as music."

Shiloh permitted himself to be led in the direction of the tavern, which was not Mr. Bumbolow's establishment, but a nearer and more cheerful hostelry. In spite of his melancholy he was not wholly unconscious of the salutary effects of a hot supper upon his drooping spirits; the planed venison was very savoury, and the ham and beefsteaks, hissing from the gridirons, were excellently tender and cooked to a turn. He wondered precisely how wicked he had been in abandoning the Pythagorean diet while travelling; he took another small slice of venison and decided that the lapse was forgivable.

"Peacock always said well-seasoned," murmured Shiloh, wielding the pepper canister with no uncertain hand. "And perhaps after all I will have a pint of some very light white wine, since you assure me that the water is so pestilential; I have no desire to fall a victim to the hepatic complaint which the landlord informs me is most prevalent in this insalubrious clime."

There was no light white wine to be had; Shiloh was forced to content himself with half a bottle of Marsala, of which David consumed the major portion. Nevertheless he felt warmed and comforted; he began to speculate upon the post office facilities for forwarding letters from Louisville into the farther west.

"Time to be getting on to Bumbolow's; I told him we'd be there by seven," said David, fortifying himself and the Marsala with two fingers of neat whisky. It was the moment for explanations, but Shiloh said nothing; he cracked a fine walnut and finished his glass of wine in complete silence.

4

WITHOUT, the night was starlit, and sweet with tonic frost; a brisk pace was indicated by the freshening wind. David made his way with admirable precision through a tangle of lampless streets;

finally he knocked three times upon a sagging door, which was opened by an elderly man of sinister appearance.

"Come along in and set down by the fire, young fellers," said this individual in an unpleasant snuffling voice; his crooked smile disclosed long yellowish teeth, and the gleam of his eyes was vulpine under bushy brows. Shiloh felt an immediate antipathy to the man, which the touch of a cold claw-fingered hand did little to dissipate.

"Don't be turned agin him, Shiloh, for pity's sake, just because he ain't pretty," whispered David as they filed into the inner room. "He's been a pirate and an outlaw by his own account, and he don't pretend to no special holiness, but he's got the very news we want of Silver, and I reckon he ain't a bad sort when you come to know him."

A good fire of hickory logs burnt upon the cracked stone hearth, and the low-ceiled room was warm with candlelight. In spite of scaling plaster and cobwebbed shadows the place had an air of comfort after the darkness and the sharp whirling dust of the streets. Shiloh saw that two or three quiet drinkers were gathered about a small table in the corner; the settle by the fire was empty, and towards this pleasant refuge Mr. Bumbolow now led them, with a secret look and a portentous shake of his scant grey whiskers.

"Easy now, easy now," said the old man huskily; he shuffled to a cupboard and returned with two thick tumblers of whisky, which he placed in front of the friends. "Don't you go a-talking at the top of your blasted lungs about Jacques la Croix, like you was to-day, young feller, or you and me'll be in jail afore we can say knife. Christ strike me blind if I don't wish I had a dollar for every murder he done in his time; blood-money it would be and no mistake, and a bloody bastard I'll call any man as contradicts me. But drink up, young fellers, and ask your questions, and whether I'll tell you any lies or not depends upon how civil you speak and how well you hold your liquor."

"But the name's not la Croix, Mr. Bumbolow; it's Cross or Crooks, as I was a-saying this afternoon," began David, but Shiloh hurriedly interrupted him.

"It's all the same, Davy; I see precisely how Jasper derived his different pseudonyms from the original form. Please go on, Mr. Bumbolow; we are most eagerly awaiting your valuable information."

"Valuable indeed," cried Mr. Bumbolow bitterly; "yes, and I suppose I must part with it for nothing to a couple of lousy beggars who can't even pay for their drinks! " Tears came into his eyes, and he smeared them away with the back of his hairy hand.

"We can pay you well for the drinks," David reassured him. "We're poor, but not so poor we have to spunge on you for them, by graminy. As for the tidings of Jasper, if you was his friend you ought to be ready and willing to aid his sister to the best of your powers."

"Friend! " repeated Mr. Bumbolow still more bitterly. "Yes, I was a true friend to him, as God is my witness, and a true friend to his father before him, and all I ever got for my pains was cheating and abuse from the pair of 'em, curse their dirty souls to hell. Think of me, a lonely old man a-trying to earn my living in a strange unfriendly town, and Jasper probably master of a ship by now, without even the gratitude to send me a pound of tobaccy from foreign parts."

"Jasper's dead and gone, as I told you," said David solemnly. "It's little Silver as we're trying to find; won't you help us, if only for her ma's sake as you used to be so fond of? "

"Fond of her! Fond of her, d'you say, young feller? Chris'-a'mighty, that ain't no proper way to put it; I plumb worshipped her, I did, and if I ain't done all I'd 'a' liked to 'a' done for her little gal, 'tis along of my years and my poverty, and not for lack of heart! Oh, Dolores, how I loved you in them days gone by! "

Here Mr. Bumbolow placed his yellow-grey head among the whisky-glasses on the table before him, and gave way to unaffected grief. The spectacle, while it jarred upon Shiloh's keen æsthetic sensibilities, touched him nevertheless to an uneasy pity; the old man was drunk and ridiculous, but he was palpably sincere.

"I do entreat you, sir, to believe in our friendship and in our tender care for Silver; we have every intention of succouring her, if that assurance can at all console you," said Shiloh, nervously patting Mr. Bumbolow's ragged shoulder. The old man heeded him, and, raising a blotched and haggard countenance, stared half incredulously into the other's large and innocent blue eyes. His own eyes were rheumy with the slow difficult tears of dotage.

"You ain't a-figuring to do her no harm, young gentleman?" he inquired slyly, moved to an unwonted formality of address by Shiloh's courtly manner and that romantic air of his no tatters could obscure. "You ain't a-figuring to ruin her, perhaps, or cast her into prison along of her daddy's crimes? 'Cause if you is, old Tom Bumbolow'll have a word to say, I reckon, that'll fair scorch the hide off you. But no, young gentleman, you can't be so sinful as to aim to ruin little Sylvie; I can't a-think it of you, with them blue-chiny eyes of yours a-looking at me, and I'm a-going to trust you and to tell you all."

"Good God, Mr. Bumbolow, pray divest your mind of this hideous suspicion!" cried Shiloh, pale and luminous with horror. Mr. Bumbolow was convinced, and smiled an incredibly crooked smile.

"Well, young gentleman, Silver as you call her, or Sylvie as her daddy called her, speaking it French-like, or Maria Solidad de Sylva, as her ma called her and the priest christened her, must now be twenty-one years old; when last I heerd of her she was fifteen, but that's five or six years ago, afore Jasper runned away to sea. At that time she was apprenticed to a French milliner in St. Louis; the shop was on the rue Royale, or Main Street as they names it now. Her father was a blasted scoundrel, a Canadian trapper known as Jacques la Croix, who made his money by piracy and murder; her ma was a Spanish lady, some kin to Governor Piernas as I've heard tell; how she come to marry so much beneath her has always beat me, but marry him she did, and bore him a family of children what mostly died in infancy; Jasper and Sylvie was the youngest and the only ones as lived to grow up."

"Why did Jasper take the name of Cross on shipboard, and call himself Crooks in Louisville?" asked David; the point was one that continued to trouble him.

"Reason enough, young feller, reason enough, if you'll listen and mark my words," replied Mr. Bumbolow with some asperity.

"In the first place, his daddy was a pirate, with a price on his head when the Injuns killed him; in the second place Jasper himself was no plaster saint, as I've been a-telling of you. Lit out with his sister's savings when he bid her good-bye, and then runned away to sea from this very tavern, with my cash-box under his arm; reason enough if ever I'd caught him! "

"Tarnation mean, I call it," said David indignantly; the reflection was soothing to a conscience burdened, albeit lightly, with Jasper's premature demise.

"God-a'mighty mean, I say," agreed Mr. Bumbolow with feeling, " and I for one can't hold it agin you that you cracked his skull by mistake; lucky kind of a mistake for all concerned. But Sylvie, little Sylvie, she's a different kettle of sugar; the black and the white of it, was that pair of twins, and even in her cradle she shined beside his sulky shadow like a star."

"And what," asked Shiloh, his soul vibrating with his voice, " what colour are Silver's eyes, Mr. Bumbolow? "

"Well," Mr. Bumbolow answered judicially, drinking up Shiloh's whisky with an air of slow satisfaction, " well, that's a bit of a poser, young gentleman; reckon you'll have to find out for yourself. Dark they was, leastways when she was twelve years old, but whether grey or brown or hazel I don't rightly know and I wouldn't like to say. She was as fair as corn-silk, and soft and bright, but about her eyes I'm uncertain; you'll have to see them for yourself."

"I cannot do that," said Shiloh desperately, looking at David; " I am unable to go to St. Louis." He closed his eyelids upon some darling vision, and set his lips into a narrow resolute line.

"Oh, Shiloh, what crazy lunatic idea has got a-hold of you now? " David's cry was angry and amazed, but not so lamentable as Mr. Bumbolow's.

"I knowed it! " wailed the old man bitterly. " I knowed you never meant to help her like you was pretending! Too much of a fine gentleman, I dessay, to mix yourself up in the affairs of a poor little orphan like Sylvie; leave her starve, you will, while you drink and carouse, and pass by on the other side of Jordan like Pontius Pilate! Yah, you lily-livered bastard, I

174

know you! " He choked over the dregs of Shiloh's whisky in the hurry of his indignant speech.

Shiloh stared from one to the other of his two accusers; he was hurt and bewildered by the violence of the attack, and his consciousness of innocence was so strong as to render him inarticulate. He knew, with terrible clarity, that he was relinquishing his own desires in remaining in Louisville, and that this was the course of sacrifice and self-discipline; the trick of circumstance which made it appear otherwise was a sharp temptation, and his eyes were brilliant with pain as he replied.

" Really, David," he said at last, and haltingly, " you do me an injustice; it is not a crazy idea, but my simple duty; I must wait for the Italian letter. And you, Mr. Bumbolow, who have thought fit to shower me with vulgar abuse, you also are singularly unjust, since I seek only some means of benefiting Silver without abandoning my other responsibilities. Davy shall go to St. Louis in my stead; he shall take all our money, and do what he can to help this child to happiness; for my part all my dearest hopes go with him."

He ceased, and David was silent, knowing some portion of the fever in Shiloh's heart, compounded alike of childish disappointment and archangelic rage; Mr. Bumbolow was not so scrupulous, and his voice was once more raised in furious protest.

" Davy, is it, indeed, to go in your stead? " he asked sarcastically. " And a pretty plan, too, I must say, to send her brother's murderer to the poor gal, all unsuspecting as she'd be, and trustful, a-laying of her little hand in his blood-stained fist without a-dreaming of the dreadful truth. No, my fine young gentleman, it's you or nobody as goes to St. Louis, and if you doesn't go Sylvie will most likely perish of starvation, for her ma was always delicate, and she wasn't more'n a little whiffet of a thing as I remember her, God bless her golden curls! " He wept, and David looked miserably guilty beneath his lachrymose regard.

" Not but what it wouldn't be proper enough for this young feller to come along if you was there to break the thing to her gentle-like and explain as how he done it accidental and without malice," Mr. Bumbolow went on more mildly. " But now, sir, I

The Orphan Angel

ask you fair and honest, could you expect a tender-minded little thing like Sylvie to take money from her brother's murderer? No, no, young gentleman, you're the lad as must do the deed, if it's to be done; as an old family friend I have a word to say, and I say it plain and emphatic: it's you or nobody! "

"The old man's right, Shiloh; 'twouldn't be noways decent unless you was along," said David wretchedly; he looked so dimmed and disheartened that the very gold of his hair was tarnished, and Shiloh longed to kindle him into energy again.

"But that is prejudice and superstition," murmured Shiloh with white lips; the temptation was stronger now, and the child and the archangel wrestled mortally within him.

He was dizzy with conflict; he had two souls, and not to save them both could he have disentangled the soul of light from the soul of shadow. He strove upon a pinnacle above the world; some prince of the powers of the air had borne him there, and this creature was a burning part of his own soul. Above him the rays of the sun were spread like golden wings.

Now there were wings about his head, the wings of eagles and the darker wings of vultures; his own wings beat upward into flame. Below the broken clouds a lucent prospect floated half-revealed; this was the other side of the moon; this was the silent silvery reverse of sorrow, the lovelier thing than love. Below the mortal weariness of conflict the valleys of the moon lay deep.

He strove for ever upon the pinnacle, among wings of light and shadow; then a starry fire pierced his side, and he was falling, falling among stars. The archangel was fallen, and all the loosened feathers of his wings were stars that fell with him. The air was wild with stars; they were thick as snowflakes about his head, and he was falling into the other side of the moon.

He fell headlong, not into the other side of the moon, but into Mr. Bumbolow's tavern in Louisville. "Lucifer, son of the morning, how art thou fallen! " he said absurdly, and knew that David was shaking him by the shoulder and that the air was full of sparks and ashes in a sudden draught from the chimney.

"Wake up, Shiloh! " cried David rather crossly. "Goldarn it, man, you can't go to sleep now; you've got to decide. Are you

176

going to St. Louis, or ain't you? Wake up, for the love of Moses, and don't sit staring at me like a loony or a ghost! "

" I have decided," said Shiloh from the hollow of his dream. His voice was cool and quiet, but inwardly he was trembling with exaltation. "I have decided to go to St. Louis, to find Silver. I was mad to doubt it; I must go, and go to the end of the world if need be, searching until I shall find her."

5

" LET us not lose ourselves in distant and uncertain plans, but rather systematise and simplify our motions, at least for the present. It would be very delightful, to be sure, to travel by water, but obviously the expense is beyond our slender resources."

" I reckon it's Shanks' mare for us, Shiloh, all the way to St. Louis," David replied regretfully, eyeing the steamboat *Independence* with unconcealed longing. " Don't suppose we'll have the luck to fall in with no more arks like the cap'n's, neither, and though I'd admire to try my hand at paddling an Injun canoe again, 'twould be a matter of months with the current agin us and all that. Yessir, we got to walk it if we're a-going to make it afore the New Year. Gawd, I wish we'd 'a' had the cash to go cordelling upstream! "

The river-front at Shippingport was bright with traffic; the cries from deck and pilot-house were musical in David's ears, and the November air was amber wine. Nothing appeared difficult or dangerous on such a morning; to swim, even to fly seemed natural to the brave, and Shiloh was on mercurial tiptoe to be gone. The two early miles from Louisville had raced along an excellent turnpike; the rapids lay like a dancing glacier in the dawn, and the friends had walked down Tarascon Street to the levee singing " Shannandore " at the top of their exulting lungs.

" Come, Davy; we'll cross by the ferry and be off into the wilds," said Shiloh, for whose imagination the northern road traversed a fabulous map of primæval forest. David lingered by the water-front; the names of the steamboats charmed him, and as he caught the flashing sunlit letters one by one, he pondered

The Orphan Angel

upon the relative nobility of these golden appellations, *Tamerlane* and *Vesta, Eagle, Rifleman,* and *Rising State.* At the same time he looked with something like contempt at the wingless ships whose paths were fixed and narrow along inland waters, and for a moment he was homesick for the trade-winds.

The crossing of the river was over all too soon; they were on a broad clear road again, with the image of Silver at the end of it. In a little wood by the wayside they cut themselves sticks from the young and living trees; David's stick was hickory, and Shiloh's a straight black shaft of cherry, speckled like a snake. Their bundles swung light enough from these, and the yellow sunlight was warm upon their backs. Behind them, down the sparkling distance of the water, someone was singing a sad song in a high and merry tenor; the melancholy notes were bloomed with joy, as a bunch of dark grapes may be frosted with brightness.

"Oh, love was the 'casion of my misery;
Now I am bound, but once I was free!"

"Oh, once I was bound, but now I am free!" sang Shiloh like a mocking echo, altering the refrain to his own mind.

In the Commercial Bank of Louisville a snub-nosed boy was unfastening the green shutters while Mr. Townley arranged the documents and ledgers upon his immaculate mahogany desk. In the fly-blown parlour of the tavern, Mr. Bumbolow, who had breakfasted upon Jamaica rum, wept bitterly because he could not remember whether a child's soft eyes were shadowy brown or hazel under the silver-gilded tangle of her hair.

It was a day for auspicious adventure, a day of angelic crystal dreaming over innocent earth; it seemed a pity to Shiloh that the morning disclosed nothing more mythical than a travelling pedlar and a lost liver-coloured hound. Nevertheless, a lively splendour informed the very air, and spiced the somewhat meagre buttermilk and roasted potatoes of their noontide meal in a farmhouse kitchen. The frugal repast was pleasing to Shiloh's fastidious conscience; afterwards he snatched half an hour's sleep above the pages of Æschylus, while the back-log crumbled in

Pastoral Garamant

the chimney and the kettle hummed. He had an enchanting sense of laziness, as he sat there, drowsily aware that David was chopping wood for the farmer's wife in a frenzy of native skill.

"These folks is proper Yankees, from down Portsmouth way," he told Shiloh when the other joined him by the woodpile. Shiloh rubbed his eyes, partly to dissipate the trance of slumber and partly in admiration for the gleaming antics of the axe, which smote the log and loosed upon the air a flight of chips as buoyant as feathers.

"Easy as cutting butter with a hot knife!" cried David with a magnificent scorn for his own prowess. The dazzling steel flashed down once more, and left the pointed end of the log as cleanly wrought as though it had been finished with a chisel.

The neat white houses of New Albany were left behind; the twelve cool windy miles to Greenville flowed smooth as water through the afternoon, Indian Creek and Blue River were crossed in falling sunshine, and even the long twilight road to Fredericksburg was comforted by a crescent moon. They were very tired when the first candles of the town shone warm and yellow under the lonely silver of the sky; they had walked thirty-four miles since daybreak, and the way had been stranger than the way between Marlow and London, or the steep and wooded trails among the hills of Castine.

"We was plumb fools to come so far, but I'll allow as you can lick the hide off us all a-walking," said David, collapsing under a giant sycamore tree and loosening the buckskin laces of his boots with a vigorous groan. "Dunno how you manage to keep it up so slick an' chipper, for I'm clean tuckered out myself. I wish we was to supper in that elegant shingled house a piece back along the road."

Shiloh dropped lightly down upon the golden leaves beside him; he knew he would be stiff and sleepy within' five minutes, but this first instant of suspended motion was still volatile with speed, and he felt exquisitely cock-a-hoop, and livelier than a hawk compared to David's twelve-stone-twelve of solid weariness. A divine levity informed his mind; he wondered whether the stuff of his body were subject to the same laws of gravitation as oppressed the mortal earth, and rejoiced to fancy his very flesh and blood more subtle than terrestrial air.

"A certain form of uncaptive balloon," he murmured happily, aware that the sycamore leaves were comforting and warm beneath a frosty dust of dew. He put his bundle under his head for a pillow and abandoned his faculties to slumber.

"Don't turn back, Davy, it's an unfortunate omen, and quite unnecessary," he said; through a descending veil of sleep he perceived that his friend had risen and was about to reconnoitre the surrounding country. "I had far rather sup in a hovel upon the forward line of march than retrace our steps to yonder commodious mansion. Only, my dear good Davy, pray beg our prospective hosts not to prepare any pork for our entertainment; I am amazingly tired of pork, and even bacon begins to bore me a little. Shall I be very discourteous if I decline to eat bacon?"

"You do beat the Dutch for impudence!" grumbled David, moving off in the direction of the village, where dusk was coloured genially by kitchen fires.

Shiloh was stiff and cold as a winter snake when David waked him twenty minutes later; he crawled meekly enough towards the white clapboarded cottage which his friend pointed out to him in the twilight.

"I fear we have somewhat overestimated our capacity for sustained effort," he admitted sorrowfully. "Our wings are most effectually clipped; we cannot fly so far to-morrow; we are geese, and perhaps not even wild geese at that, Davy." He looked profoundly serious as he flapped his arms in a vaguely aëronautical gesture.

"I'm pretty damn wild when I smell that pot-pie," David replied with passionate conviction.

"Now see here, Shiloh," he went on, pausing upon the threshold of the humble dwelling, "these folks ain't in any ways grand or stylish, like Miss Lillie and all that, but they come from my own neck of woods in a manner of speaking, though it's more Vermont than Maine, and I'd thank you to be extra civil in your dealings with 'em. Not but what you ain't always polite and pleasant; you're gentry, I know that, only don't go mocking of 'em even in your heart of hearts, or I shall guess it somehow. You told me you wouldn't eat no pork, and naturally this give 'em the notion to start with that you was a Jew or a Papist or such-like, for I says my friend won't eat no pork, and they says is it religion or just plain dyspepsia, and laughed, so now you must show 'em that you ain't pernickity nor proud. You may have to swallow just a mite of whisky, just to be friendly, but it won't be much, and the pot-pie is elegant."

Shiloh stared at David in pure amazement; his mind was so innocent of the vanity of birth or breeding that he was actually unaware of this weakness; his prides were all of a nobler lineage. He could not conceive why David should warn him to be kind to David's kindred, and he looked particularly haughty as he replied.

"David, I shall endeavour to conform to an ideal courtesy," said Shiloh in the cool clipped voice of his ancestors.

"To explain a bit more about these here folks," continued David, his hand upon the latch, "Bartlett's their name, but their ma was a Miss Higgins from Maine, and they're regular Yankees to begin with, but Hoosiers along of living in Indiana. People around these parts are all Hoosiers and Suckers, Buckeyes and Corncrackers; funny set o' names I'll allow, but I reckon them as bears 'em ain't so bad neither. The proper southerners calls themselves white folks, same as if the Yankees was niggers, but they don't mean no harm by it; it's just ignorance."

"In the eyes of the virtuous, all men are equal," said Shiloh rather absently; he was very tired, and the fragrance of the pot-pie was rendering him very hungry also.

He entered like a brilliant wraith into a white-washed kitchen full of Bartletts and Higginses; if a ghost were made of fire instead of graveyard mist it might wear for one night the fierce and luminous grace of Shiloh's beauty. Wind and warm autumnal sun had burned him to a flame of energy; even in his weariness there was no languor, and its fever set a more savage radiance upon his lifted brow.

"Lord save us, it's a wild rampaging Osage," remarked

Mrs. Bartlett with admirable calm as she poured the gravy upon the smoking platter.

Shiloh was charmed by his reception; to be taken for an Indian chieftain seemed the perfection of compliment, and the Bartletts' lean and strenuous faces appeared quite gentle in the domestic firelight which flashed so strangely from the splendour of his different flesh. They all looked straight into his amazing eyes and loved him in spite of themselves; the younger Bartletts loved him ironically, because he was so slim and dashing and ridiculous, and their mother loved him bitterly, because he reminded her of her one black sheep, Benjamin, who had run away to sea.

She kept looking to see if it were really Benjamin, while she dished out the pot-pie with Olympian impartiality; she was secretly relieved to discover that the mole was lacking from the left cheek, and that the eyes were blue instead of grey. Benjamin was still her favourite child, but seven years are seven years, and Benjamin had never been respectable, even in Vermont.

Shiloh received a piercing glance from the old lady's deep-set agate eyes, and an enormous portion of pot-pie in token of her approval. He was grateful for her evident solicitude for his comfort, but the food was a dubious blessing; he was quite horrified by the fact that at least half a peck of onions, as well as four young pullets, had entered into the composition of the lordly dish. His hunger was a pungent sauce which made possible a very fair play of knife and fork, and the boiled Indian corn and pumpkin jelly were bland and innocuous to his taste.

"Genuine store tea; none of your spice-wood nor yarb stuff," said Mrs. Bartlett proudly as she tipped the great brown teapot over his empty cup.

"Oh, ma'am, it's done my heart good to eat a real downright old-fashioned meal like this," cried David, drenching his flannel cakes in maple molasses. He looked sentimentally at the custard pies upon the sideboard, and the memory of his home was like nutmeg and cinnamon in his nostrils.

Indeed, David might have been the youngest and the ruddiest of the Bartletts themselves, so plain a kinship stared out honestly beneath straight brows and hair the colour of pine shavings from these square Puritan countenances. Shiloh observed the company silently while he sipped his tea, and was himself observed by all of them, but more especially by one who was neither a Bartlett nor a Higgins, but a widowed daughter-in-law from the marshy bottom-lands down around the Shineys.

She was a delicate ash-blonde creature, with something of Silver in her big bewildered eyes; he looked at her once to learn if this miracle might be, and then looked away to forget her in arrowy and flying dreams.

She had never beheld such another; she trembled in her worn little shoes to see him burn among the stiff automata surrounding him. She had always believed that her husband's family were strong and handsome folk, but now they appeared to her like so many wooden figures with a live man in their midst. A live man or the mortal image of an angel; his eyes were like blue thunderbolts against her soul.

"Dunno what ails ye, Deborah," said Mrs. Bartlett that night, when the sound of sobbing waked her. But she knew very well, and although she had loved her tall eldest son, she did not blame his widow for her alien tears. Benjamin had been his mother's favourite child, and the burning blue-eyed stranger, now sleeping peacefully in the hay-loft, was marvellously like Benjamin.

"Poor Benjamin; he wasn't ever what you might call respectable, even when he was singing in the choir at the First Congregational!" sighed Mrs. Bartlett as she turned upon her tow-linen pillow. "I calculate, when all's said and done, that it's the Lord's mercy this young fellow isn't Benjamin, for the poor lad doesn't look any too respectable either! I must count the spoons in the morning; I must remember to count my wedding spoons."

6

"Twenty miles to Lebanon and cross Silver Creek!" chanted Shiloh some nine days later, as they left Johnson's Settlement upon the first morning of December. The altered season was cold and pale under a pure translucent sky, and last night's dews were now a velvet bloom of frost along the fields. A rosy muffled sun hung low in the virgin east, and the distant trees were feathery as snow crystals against the horizon.

"Snow in the air," said David, and sniffed, buttoning his pea-jacket closer about his splendid chest. "You was a fool, Shiloh, not to buy a leather waistcoat off that Injun in Vincennes; you'll freeze before we fetch St. Louis, in them rags."

"Shall we be there by candlelight?" inquired Shiloh in ridiculous continuation of his chant. He looked romantic and a little mad in a faded blue flannel shirt and a vest of Kentucky jean with most of its buttons missing; a fine new bandanna handkerchief passed under his right arm and was knotted on his left shoulder. This eccentric decoration lent lustre to his poor attire without adding very materially to its warmth; nevertheless Shiloh was obviously pleased with himself, and the sunburnt colours of his countenance were clear and tropical in the winter scene.

"How many miles to Babylon?" chanted Shiloh perversely, repeating his question about candlelight.

"It's Lebanon, you crazy loon, and I reckon we'll get there before dark, seeing as it's a bare score of miles 'stead of the four-score and ten as you're a-hollering about," David replied severely. "Waste your cash on a red-and-yaller bandanner and sing like a certified idjit and catch your death when you could have had a proper Injun jacket for five dollars with beads and foxes' fur all complete!"

"I confess I was unwise to miss so excellent an opportunity to guard against the rigours of the increasing cold," said Shiloh with admirable meekness. "I detest winter; the severity of climate in these northern latitudes is uncongenial to my temperament and my health alike. I wish Silver lived in the south."

"Which I don't neither; blamed glad I am to feel some human Christian weather at last; Thanksgiving day might as well been on the west coast of Africa with that goldarned mugginess. Beats me why you like it hot; you're a funny son of a musket and sometimes I think you come from hell."

Pastoral Garamant

"Sometimes I am quite of your opinion, David," answered Shiloh with gentle gravity.

"Aw, shucks," grunted David, ashamed of his impatience. "You may come from hell, but you're a god-damned decent kind of devil. We can buy all the Injun stuff we want in St. Louis; it's a grand market for that sort of notion, and I'd admire to see us rigged out like a couple of genuwine trappers."

The week had slid by like a painted frieze of small adventures; there had been the amusing incident of the one-eyed Shawnee at Hindostan, and the exquisite evening when the star-reflecting waters of White River had been stirred by a deer's thin cloven hoof. Shiloh had gazed enchanted at the creature's soft fantastic eyes and at the incredible elegance of its ankles, seeing a lovely chimerical image of his own soul mirrored in the moving stream. He had drawn the last crumb of maple sugar from his pocket and approached delicately over the frosted grass; the wild thing had surveyed him for a wizard instant of indecision, and then fled sideways into the twilight.

"It laughed at me; you heard it laugh, Davy," said Shiloh, pensively eating the maple sugar.

There had been a solitary buffalo beyond French Lick, and innumerable foxes, blue, grey, and black, in all the woods along the way. There had been opossums in the gum-trees, and ground-hogs devouring the mast in oaken groves. There had been the thrilling scent of cucumbers which portends a rattle-snake, and once, at sunset, a golden elemental shape which must have been a wildcat had leaped athwart the path. Altogether, Shiloh had known some seven days of sharp elusive happiness; at times he had gone cold and hungry, but at the worst he had gone free, and he throve like a salamander in fiery joy of this. You had only to look at the tawny freckles on his cheek and at the singular colour of his eyes to perceive the strength of his vitality.

"You ain't really civilised, Shiloh, for all your quality ways and pretty manners. We was bloody fools to walk fifteen miles on fried eggs and johnny-cake," young David had grumbled, who resented his friend's innocent attempts at asceticism, and was beginning to weary for Egyptian fleshpots and dressed beef.

The eve of Thanksgiving had found them upon the outskirts of Vincennes; in David's ears the exotic name chimed with melancholy forebodings of starvation for the morrow.

"Don't suppose there'll be a turkey in the whole damned town; these French bastards ain't got no proper idea of religion," he said gloomily.

"What is it, Davy? Some idyllic form of harvest festival?" inquired Shiloh, picturing a village church in Sussex hung with burnished laurel and coraline rose-apples. The memory belonged to his fifth year, long before his prejudice against orthodoxy had crystallized into acute repulsion. He saw the silvery diluted sunlight lie like water upon the scarlet berries, and heard the music that he had not learned to hate flow upward in a cloud of sound.

"It's sermons in the morning, and all your aunts and cousins to dinner, and slews of elegant victuals, and most generally a bit of skating along about afternoon, if your folks ain't too strict and you live in a nice climate like Maine," explained poor David with nostalgic fervour.

"I don't believe I should like it; the skating perhaps; certainly not the aunts and cousins," said Shiloh, and fell silent and a little sad, thinking of Harriet Grove and the holiday parties at which she had danced in a brightness of dawn-coloured tulle.

"Cheer up; mebbe there'll be some Christian families in Vincennes after all," David had encouraged him kindly.

There were few Congregationalists upon the banks of the Ouabache, but David discovered that even Catholics are Christians, and his Thanksgiving did not lack the darling incense of a roasted fowl. His dark-eyed hostess listened to his mournful praise of home, and there was turkey for dinner; wild turkey, stuffed with corn-meal and sausage meat, and pickles and preserves, and beautiful brown pastry shells filled with pumpkin chips and maple syrup.

"French notion of pies, but blamed good, by graminy," David had said with his mouth full. Afterwards there was ratafia from New Orleans, and ginger out of a blue-and-white

Canton jar with a 'dull silver top. "Beats cock-fighting," said David, and Shiloh agreed with him, and left the sweet fierce liquor untasted in the glass.

He was glad enough to be on the road again, and never so happy as when his companion permitted him to dine upon dry bread and apples in a pause by the wayside. Nevertheless, it was fortunate that David looked to his material welfare; otherwise he might have been tempted to subsist entirely upon light and air, flavoured with the sparkle of frost and the fragrance of burning leaves.

" Get that under your belt, or you'll snap in two like an icicle one of these cold winter days," David would say sternly, pointing to some homely hospitable meal, set smoking on the kitchen table of the night's lodging. Shiloh would smile divinely at the people of the farm, and sigh in secret to his own soul, and meekly eat corned beef and cabbage, or flitch and potatoes, or fried chicken and mush, or whatever the woman of the house might put before him. He was a charming guest; sometimes he laughed, but more often he was shy and gentle and rather sleepy over his supper. His courtesy was admirable; he was loved for this, and for the transparent innocence of his gaze. He was seldom allowed to pay for the privilege of sharing the family repast and spending the long dark night in the chilly comfort of the hay-loft.

" Plenty of blankets and buffalo robes, if you ain't too proud to be beholden to the hosses," their host would tell them with a grin, and Shiloh and David were often thankful for the loan as they burrowed deeper into the meagre store of hay.

Shiloh might fall asleep half stunned with fatigue, to wake shivering in a bitter black frost at sunrise, but the amazing resiliency and lightness of his body and the stubborn gaiety of his mind bore him onward into each new day, and by noon he was always slightly drunk with the effervescence of his own triumphant speed. David strode methodically at his shoulder; against the pearly winter landscape the two figures marched like prodigies of nature, David solid as a moving rock beside a gilded frigate that flew under press of sail.

Now upon the ninth morning of their journey they both felt

garrulous and energetic after an excellent night's sleep and a breakfast of hot coffee and griddle-cakes. Only forty miles remained of the long road to St. Louis, and two days more would leave those miles behind them like a smooth and glittering wake. It was an hour for high and extravagant nonsense, and Shiloh chanted a succession of absurd nursery rhymes to a chorus of picturesque profanity in David's profoundest bass.

"'Tain't often as I cuts loose, as well you know, young feller," said David when they paused for breath. "But you can't be raised a sailor and talk pure Sunday-school in the face of a fine fresh breeze like this 'un."

> "All the spirits that stand
> By the naked man
> In the book of moons, defend ye . . ."

Shiloh cried the words aloud; you could not truly say he sang.

> "That of your five sound senses
> You never be forsaken,
> Nor wander from
> Yourselves with Tom
> Abroad to beg your bacon."

"God blast your vitals for a thundering bloody son of a gun!" replied David; he had exhausted the more pungent terms in his vocabulary, and his tone was casual and pleasant; "why in the name of all damnation do you have to walk so god-damned fast? My lungs are busted keeping up with you, and my ears are fair split a-listening to that lunatic chantey. Quit it, Shiloh, for cris'sake, or I'll lambaste you one in the jaw as'll make you hold your hush to hell and high purposes!"

Shiloh looked at him in mild surprise, and perceiving the friendly smile upon his lips, ventured an amiable protest against a violence of language of which he could not wholly approve.

"I do not particularly care for your choice of words, Davy," he murmured softly. "If you were to call me a catawampus, now, I should be overjoyed; 'catawampus' is such an enchanting epithet. But bastard, and — no, but really, my dear Davy, I

188

trust I am sufficiently unprejudiced, but really I had far rather you called me a catawampus."

"Aw, shucks, have it your own way, you crazy bedlamite," agreed David with a roar of affectionate laughter. "You know I don't mean no harm by it; if I did, you'd soon be glaring at me like a mountain lion, same as you did at Simon Hanna when he forgot himself and spoke uncivil!"

"His looks were wild, and devil's blood stained his savage hands and feet . . ." said Shiloh, who was beginning to chant rhymes of his own composition, and to misquote them at that.

Certainly there was a fine barbaric sting in the air that danced along the veins like lightning; the legendary profile of a Piankashaw warrior, sharply cut against the pale horizon, lifted Shiloh's heart with ecstasy. Here was the authentic type of freedom, sprung from the secret womb of this new world like a sudden flower of bronze.

Shiloh's knowledge of the noble redskin was largely derived from the imaginative works of M. Châteaubriand; it is probable that he had never heard of the Wyoming Massacre, or of Bryant's Station, and the benevolent associates of Simon Girty. His brow flushed with rapture to behold the Piankashaw brave, who bestowed a brief contemptuous glance upon the travellers, and disappeared into the distance like a pillar of tawny smoke.

"What happiness," cried Shiloh with innocent enthusiasm, "to observe the free intrepid mien of this man, and to contrast it to its high advantage with the cowed submissive manner of the negro slaves whom I have seen to my sorrow in Virginia and Kentucky! Thank heaven we are now within the boundaries of liberty; often in Louisville my spirits completely overcame me in considering the debasing effects of such bondage upon the human race!"

"'Tain't right, it stands to reason," said David, wrinkling his flaxen brows with difficult thought. "Slavery's agin nature, as I reckon it, but mebbe these here Injuns ain't so grand as you make out, Shiloh; I calculate as how they might be mighty ugly customers if you was to rile 'em. Besides, the niggers seems more cheerful-like, and somehow they got a kind of freedom in their souls, as comes out in their singing, which sounds so queer and far-away on a summer's night. I've heard 'em in Charles-town and New Orleans, down around the water-front; it's blamed queer, Shiloh. Seems like they know about the birds of the air, and about the powers of the air, both good and evil. Reckon it's what they calls an incantation."

" That's beautiful, David; I wish I might have heard them sing that song. And they too could be fierce if you were to rile them, as you call it, and small blame to them if they were. But I refuse to hear my beloved Indians traduced; I shall be-lieve nothing illaudable of them until they have actually scalped me! " and Shiloh laughed, and tugged at his abundant and untidy hair as if to make certain of its immediate safety.

All day the sun hung in the heavens like an heraldic shield, turning from rose to silver and from silver to gold; all day the pure cold atmosphere preserved the frost upon the grass. The travellers went swiftly and joyfully across the hours, which coloured the earth with changing magic and were gone. If any shape of fear or horror lay concealed under the yellow archway of the west, their minds were innocent of its betrayal. It was a very lovely afternoon, and the evening fell as softly as a fall of snow whose flakes are shadow instead of shining crystal.

Shiloh flew upon the pinions of a superhuman happiness; before he came to Lebanon he made a song about the powers of the air both good and evil, and this song was so beautiful that it should have been sung by Lucifer or one of the other archangels if it were sung at all. Shiloh can hardly have been said to sing it; he chanted it rather harshly as it came into his head, and he looked so ragged and barbarous a figure that the song seemed far too fine for him. He was like a savage hunter who has caught a star of heaven in a net spread for wild-fowl; now upon the pinions of an archangelic happiness he carried the star with him along the road to Lebanon.

VII

WILD SPIRIT

THEY reached St. Louis at the end of the next day, having walked twenty miles under a striped grey sky that spat and clawed at them in feline warfare of rain and sleet. Their clothes were in ill case for such inclemency, and they were drenched to the bone and shivering with cold in the first hour of their journey. By all the laws of nature they should have contracted the severest of chills; perhaps the unreasonable speed of their progress may have saved David from a chronic rheumatism and Shiloh from an attack of pleurisy. By eleven o'clock they had their second wind, which strove quite successfully against the far greater one which issued roaring from the clouded north, and when at last the sunset lifted a few shaking spears of light athwart the gloom, they were no more than half frozen and completely cross as the result of this protracted battle with the elements of storm.

David was cursing between gritted teeth; Shiloh clenched his own teeth even tighter to keep them from chattering, and thought longingly of the Indian's leather jerkin. His flannel shirt was like wet sea-weed against his skin, which he imagined must have turned green and silvery as a fish's beneath the cruel fall of water from above.

The Orphan Angel

His feet still moved swiftly and evenly along the streaming road, but his mind had lost its flying lightness; he felt numb and stupid with cold, and for a moment he hated the whole world. He saw it as a monstrous beast, lying drowned and weltering in rainy blood under an assault of arrows from heaven; he saw the world as a dead beast, and winter issuing dragon-like from the north in an armour of frosted scales. He knew not which he hated most bitterly: the carrion body of the world, or the dragon hungry to devour it.

" Oo, how I hate the cold! " he said in a thin voice that whistled like the wind itself. Then around a bend in the road he beheld the river; for a crazy instant he thought he looked upon the sea, but in that same instant the clouds lifted and the remoter shore was visible, far-away and wavering like a mirage in a veil of rain. Shiloh stood still and gazed across the river, which washed the monstrous image of despair from his soul in a torrent of noble calm.

Its calm was that of undisputed power; it was not smooth, for the storm had lashed it into turbulence, and yet it laid a strange tranquillity on Shiloh's eyes as it stretched before him in the evening light. It was coloured tenderly enough by this, and coloured too by all the miles of living earth which it had taken to its flood, so that it was neither grey nor brown nor ruddy, but something of all three, mixed and made faint to opalescence by the sunset.

They crossed in a small keel-boat managed by two French-men; the fellows were fantastically clothed in brightly dyed shirts and fringed leather breeches, with blue woollen scarves wrapped around their long black locks, and as they talked and gesticulated they seemed as singular and savage as a pair of parakeets. Shiloh was very happy again; he stood upright in the bow of the boat and drank the flying spray with rapture. The wind lifted his hair to wings, and he was no longer cold; it was impossible to believe that he had ever been cold or tired.

Upon landing in St. Louis they repaired at once to Yostic's tavern at the corner of First and Locust streets; Mr. Bumbolow had given them a letter to its proprietor, and they were kindly received in spite of their disreputable appearance. Perhaps Mr.

Wild Spirit

Bumbolow had mentioned their remaining store of silver dollars; perhaps Mr. Yostic was the benevolent spirit which his outward semblance so heartily suggested. Be this as it may have been, before their drenched garments had dried by the fire they were provided with an excellent hot meal and a bowl of steaming negus, and when they finally set forth into the darkening town their hearts were high above a friendly warmth of creature comfort.

They were going in search of Silver's milliner; the address was written in Mr. Bumbolow's crabbed script on a bit of brown paper. " Madame Clothilde, rue Royale "; so it was written on the bit of paper, but the words " rue Royale " had been blotted out, and " Main Street " scribbled in their stead. Mr. Bumbolow was growing old, and it was often hard for him to remember that the streets of St. Louis had changed the ancient regimen of their names.

" I suppose we must learn to call her Sylvie, David; she will not wish us to call her Silver any more. But I shall always think of her as that, and Silver Cross is a lovelier sound than Sylvie la Croix."

" What's her real name, Shiloh? I mean the name her mother gave her; Spanish-like it was, and too stiff and stately for a little girl, same as if you was to call a pretty catboat ' Victory ' or ' Constitution ' or some such frigate-name."

" Oh, that was a very stately name indeed, Davy; stately and saintly too, and musical, but perhaps a trifle like the plaster statues of the virgin in a Spanish cathedral," said Shiloh laughing. " Maria Solidad la Croix y de Sylva; that's a ridiculous mixture of tongues, and fit for the Tower of Babel, and yet it's charming in its way, and pitiful. The child of a French Canadian cut-throat and a Castilian lady; how romantic and dangerous an heritage! " Shiloh shivered, as if this romance were a danger to his own heart. " Saint Mary Solitude," he said, twisting it into English, and suddenly the double meaning of the words smote upon his heart and turned him pale.

"Mary Solitude; Saint Mary Solitude," he thought dizzily, seeing the darkly wooded shores of San Terenzo as plainly as though they had been painted within his eyelids. The Italian letter fluttered from among the cypresses, winged like a dove or the little white owl called aziola. It passed the long wine-coloured waves of the sea, and the steep and glassy waves of land whose crests were mountain-tops. It hovered over Louis-ville, with an olive branch in its beak, and he was three hundred miles from Louisville, and dreaming of another Mary Solitude.

"But I shall always call her Silver Cross," he said aloud, and David wondered why his voice laid an audible sadness upon the words.

They had plain directions from the tavern, and they found Madame Clothilde's shop with no greater trouble than the re-wetting of their shoes in a dozen large puddles along Main Street. The milliner appeared in response to their repeated summons; she proved to be a tall gaunt woman with the ghost of a moustache upon her grim upper lip, and Shiloh was reminded of Eliza Hitchener and the Good of Mankind.

"Sacred name, is this a suitable hour at which to disturb honest working-people?" grumbled Madame Clothilde in the accents of martyrdom; it was no more than seven o'clock, but the travellers' appearance had quickly convinced her that they had no honourable intention of purchasing a Spanish lace shawl or a bonnet imported from Paris by way of New Orleans. She lighted a single disapproving candle in the gloomy cavern of the shop, and faced them with a very black frown.

Shiloh's blue eyes caught the beam and shone like two good deeds in a world of bandboxes and dusty bolts of ribbon; his face emerged clearly from the surrounding shadows, and the candlelight danced in motes of radiance over a delicate mask of supernatural gold.

"Name of God, what can two ragged leetle Yankee tramps want with a fashionable modiste? Is it perhaps an Indian muslin robe, or a Leghorn hat with ostriche plumes?" cried Madame Clothilde, and cast her eyes to heaven, but her ill temper was strangely fled, and she permitted them to question her concerning Silver with no further marks of indignation than an occasional groan, or a shrug of her angular and ex-pressive shoulder-blades.

Wild Spirit

"Sylvie? The little Sylvie la Croix? But naturally I knew her; have I not often rapped her knuckles for taking such crooked stitches, and for never basting her seams? If you will believe me, she would not wear a thimble; what is one to do with a girl who will not wear a thimble when she sews?"

"It is impossible to say, madame," replied Shiloh diplomatically, thinking that by far the best course would be to kiss the pricked forefinger of the milliner's apprentice called Sylvie la Croix. "But what, precisely, have you done with her, all without a thimble as she is? It is to discover this that we have come to St. Louis."

"I have done nothing, except to scold her now and then, always for her soul's good, and to teach her to trim bonnets with taste and discretion," said Madame Clothilde with an air of conscious and acidulous virtue. "But what that wicked old man has done with her is another matter; you had better demand from Monsieur Saint-Ange an account of his stewardship, my little cabbage, and not come bullying decent milliners out of their beds." She wrapped the folds of a red flannel dressing-gown about her bony limbs in the manner of a Roman matron answering some calumny intended for Cæsar's wife.

Shiloh experienced a pang of horrid fear; the name of Saint-Ange must cover a very hellish angel of the pit if one half the suspicion in Madame Clothilde's tones were justified. A pulse began to beat in his temple as he asked a question in a cracking whisper.

"For God's sake, what do you mean, madame? Do not torture me, I beg of you, but tell me what you mean."

"Nothing, except that Sylvie has gone to California by Monsieur Saint-Ange's advice, and that for my part I cannot approve of the step," said Madame Clothilde with dignity.

2

"To California!" cried Shiloh and David in one breath of amazement; a slight quality of nightmare seemed to move the atmosphere of the little shop, and Shiloh felt his hair prickle with cold surprise. The figure of Silver was once more remote and tiny at the end of a long road; it shone minute and brilliant as some sacred doll in a niche above a vast cathedral nave, among a multitude of candle-flames. Tears of weariness and disappointment came into Shiloh's eyes, and made the true candle-flame prismatic and cruciform like a thorny star.

Even David was disheartened; he took Shiloh's hand in his, gripping it with kindly violence, and the two stood together in the silence of a bad dream.

"But it's real, Davy; it's only too real and ineluctable," said Shiloh at last, and David understood at least half of his bitterness.

"You see," explained Madame Clothilde, who herself saw quite plainly that they were blinded and confused by wonder, "it is the little one's rich relatives who have taken her so far away; a fine piece of luck if only they are good to her. I doubt it, in my sad knowledge of life, but of course there are occasional miracles. But then these excellent Coronels were always proud and overbearing, and poor Sylvie is so much their inferior in birth, with her blood of a river-pirate and a murderer, that they cannot help despising her be they never so Christian in intention. Ah, it is all very sad, and I advised Saint-Ange against it from the first, but what would you? He is a stubborn man, and the Coronels promised great material advantages for the child."

"But who is Monsieur Saint-Ange, and why had he authority over Sylvie's happiness?" inquired Shiloh with nervous indignation; he longed to discover an object for the holy and somewhat hysterical rage which was shaking him to the marrow.

"Ah, he is merely an old man with a passion for interfering in other people's affairs," said Madame Clothilde more mildly. "Indeed, I suppose he would be harmless enough, though sufficiently mad, if he had not acquired an ascendency over Sylvie's youthful mind which has resulted in her undoing. Would it not be better to be a milliner's apprentice in an honest hard-working household like this than a drudge in the palaces of the wicked aristocrats? The dogs! They will tear her to pieces between them, like as not, and gobble the poor rabbit up without grace before

meat; it makes my blood boil even to think of it! " Madame
Clothilde's principles were sternly republican; she had left
France as a romantic girl, while yet the Revolution was in its
unbloodied infancy, and her hatred of the rich was only equalled
by her high talent for securing them as customers.

" Perhaps I should do better to sell slippers, in case these great
ones should lose their heads one fine day! " she would remark
to her intimates; nevertheless she numbered the first families
of St. Louis among her patrons, and the bonnets she made
them were a subtle inducement to pride.

Now she spoke with such fire that Shiloh was alight in a
moment; the picture of Silver as a small snow-soft rabbit being
devoured by wolfish dogs was too much for his composure, and
he cried aloud upon all the powers of gentleness and courage
as he besought Madame Clothilde for news of Silver's present
home.

" Is it really possible that she is a drudge? That they may
beat her, or tyrannise over her mind with the nameless cruelties
of the strong against the weak? " he asked in an agony of angry
pity. His agitation was so extreme that Madame Clothilde tried
to make him sit down and drink a soothing cup of camomile tea;
she was truly distressed when he insisted upon striding back
and forth between the counter and the front door and wringing
his hands like a madman.

" Calm yourself, my poor child, I beseech you; you will have
a frightful migraine after such a crisis of the nerves," she told
him when he began to tear his hair; her firm tones tranquillised
him a little, and he summoned sufficient resolution to frame a
coherent question as to the actual circumstances of Silver's going.

" Sit down and cease wringing your hands, and I will tell
you all I know," Madame Clothilde promised him; he sank
into a chair and listened quietly enough, with his forehead
against his clenched fists and his elbows on his knees, but even
in the dim light it was very evident that he trembled.

" It was like this, but you will find it difficult to understand
all the family names," Madame Clothilde began. " You have
heard much of the infamy of Jacques la Croix, but perhaps you
do not know that Sylvie's mother was a distant relative of

Governor Piernas, and that she had cousins in Spain and cousins in California and cousins in New Orleans. These Coronels were no kin to the governor, nor yet to the de Sylvas; they were her mother's people, that is to say Sylvie's grandmother's people, and they have been settled in California for some hundreds of years, I believe. One of the daughters came to New Orleans and married a de Sylva; Sylvie's mother was the fruit of that union, or the flower, for she was far more like a white flower than anything so rosy as an apple or a peach. Both the de Sylvas and the Coronels cast her off when she in her turn married Jacques la Croix; of course it was a very bad match, but families should hang together, and for my part I hold that they were unnecessarily severe. Poor Dolores; his murdering cheating ways were too hard for her, and his death the final disgrace. At last she died of grief and shame, leaving Sylvie and that mad sheep Jasper to the mercy of myself and Monsieur Saint-Ange. That old fool claims to be of the same blood as Saint-Ange de Bellerive, the friend of the great Pontiac; personally I doubt it, but at least he and I were by far the most respectable of the children's friends, and we did all we could for them, which was not much, for we are not rich like the arrogant Coronels of California."

"Would to heaven she had never left your kindly sheltering roof! How could this Saint-Ange permit such a tragical mistake to involve a child that he has cherished?" asked Shiloh in a broken voice.

"Ah, you may well wonder; I think he regrets it now himself, particularly since he has come into a little legacy. He is a fool, but I pity him; he worries constantly about the girl now she has gone. It was Jasper's disappearance that decided him; he always said that he had failed with the boy, and how could he be sure that the girl was safe from disaster? She was safe enough in my shop, but he is a snob, and a sycophant, and when the Coronels sent word that one of her cousins was in New Orleans, and that we were to dispatch Sylvie to him at once, the old gentleman scratched the money together somehow, and sent her off by steamboat down the river. Poor rabbit, she looked very pitiful in the little hood and cloak that I had made her;

Wild Spirit

dark blue with a scarlet lining it was, and a good durable English cloth, but she was crying so bitterly that I was afraid she would spot it. One can never be certain about these smooth-finished materials, and of course as usual she had lost her handkerchief and had to borrow mine! "

" But you said California, ma'am; you ain't going to tell us that Silver's gone around the Horn? " asked David in a sort of terror; the picture of the dark blue cloak and the borrowed handkerchief turned all his bones to tears.

" Yes, you good-for-nothing, that is precisely what I am about to tell you," Madame Clothilde answered shortly; in spite of her democratic ideals her heart rejected David in favour of Shiloh's quality of the exquisite and the finely-bred.

" Assuredly she has gone around the Horn, unless indeed she is drowned," she continued relentlessly; then Shiloh's shuddering groan touched her to pity and she spoke more gently as she turned to him.

" Do not despair, my dear; I suppose she is in California by now, and alive and well, though probably homesick for her old Clothilde," she said with tonic cheerfulness. " Monsieur Saint-Ange can give you more information; you had far better go to him at once. There is no need to distress yourself so cruelly; all may yet be well, and it is useless to torture your mind with these forebodings. Go to him; he is kind, and no more a fool than most men of his age. I have not clearly understood what is your true connection with Sylvie, but I am sure that you are her friend, and that you intend her nothing but benevolence."

" We was her brother's friends, and we aim to help his sister if we can," declared David with perfect simplicity; Shiloh felt a momentary shock in considering the special providence which had removed Jasper from life, and he looked a little wanly at David's broad right hand clenched in its casual strength. Then he knew that David had the true inwardness of the matter clear as daylight in his ingenuous mind, and he was ashamed of his misgivings and of the fainting purpose of his soul.

" I hope that you may be able to do so; I care profoundly for the happiness of that child," said Madame Clothilde, still ad-

dressing herself to Shiloh. She thought that he might make a
charming husband for little Sylvie if only he would settle down
in some lucrative business, and earn a decent livelihood.

" For, after all, breeding is something, and he has such singularly beautiful hands," thought the republican Madame Clothilde
as she bade him good-night with a curious and unaccustomed
tenderness unloosing the steely ligaments of her heart.

3

" BUT look a-here, sir," objected David, with a shade of regret in
his manly tones, " if the old milliner's just a plumb idjit, and if
these grand Spanish relations of Silver's is so god-a'mighty rich
and respectable, how the mischief could she be in any need of
help from the likes of us? I'm blamed if I can make it out
nohow."

A night and a day had passed since the conversation with
Madame Clothilde and now Shiloh and David sat at dinner
with Monsieur Saint-Ange in that gentleman's comfortable
dwelling. A recent legacy from a nonagenarian aunt had made
it very comfortable indeed; it was built somewhat after the style
of Colonel Auguste Chouteau's mansion, with walls of solid
stone surrounded by a wooden verandah, and although it was
no more than a miniature copy of the other house its true amenities were equal. The black walnut floor of the salon was freshly
beeswaxed to a mirror which reflected several charming bits
of furniture in the Empire mode, and two exquisite urns of
white Marseilles faïence adorned the mantelpiece.

They had discovered him in this delightful apartment when
last evening's search had led from the shop straight into his impressive presence; he was courteous and kind, and when he
bade them to dinner upon the following day his manner made
them implicitly a pair of foreign ambassadors whom whimsical
fancy had disguised in rags.

" But this should have been all for Sylvie," he had said, with
a gesture which included his padesoy dressing-gown, his decanter of cognac, and his volume of Montaigne, " only for her

Wild Spirit

I should have selected sea-green silk, a thimbleful of anisette, and the latest romance by a pious Frenchwoman."

David had been quite frankly afraid to come to-night, but now he sat at ease, well-fed and flattered into loquacity by his host's attentions, and when he repeated his question it was put to a friend.

"Blamed if I can make it out," he said again.

"Ah, my dear boy, there are other needs than riches, in this little irony of the good God's which we have agreed to call life. Madame Clothilde is of course entirely mad, but she has reason in her fears for Sylvie's happiness. I should have kept the child with me, but I was poor as skim-milk, and how was I to know that I had the honour to be my aunt Alphonsine's residuary legatee? I let her go, because the Coronels are rich and well-intentioned, but now I am sorry, and since I am too old and too rheumatic to go myself, you and Shiloh must go to California. I hope you will bring her back to me; at least you must go, and find out how she is supporting her exile. Is it not so, *mon brave?* " asked Monsieur Saint-Ange, smiling at Shiloh, whom from the first he had treated with distinguished consideration.

During the past twenty-four hours he had acquired the curious habit of looking fixedly at the young man and murmuring, to the ghost of an operatic melody, the song of the minstrel Blondel: " *O Richard, ô mon roi, l'univers t'abandonne!* " It was plain that he, no less than Miss Lillie and Captain Appleby, regarded Shiloh in the glamorous light of a disinherited prince. Indeed, he would have begged to lend him the raiment proper to royalty if the other's austere simplicity of habit had not bundled all sarsenet waistcoats and delicate cambric shirts into one contemptible oblivion, and now his gaze was well-nigh adoring upon the spectacle of Shiloh's fastidious lack of interest in *poulet en casserole* and old Madeira.

" *L'univers t'abandonne!* " remarked Monsieur Saint-Ange sadly, perhaps apropos of Shiloh's really shocking boots.

"Is it not rather I who have abandoned the universe? " asked Shiloh, in his charming faintly Italianate French.

"Possibly, by escaping from its prison, which is a captivity of more than Mohammedan rigour," agreed the old gentleman.

201

The Orphan Angel

"And that is a very excellent reason why you should not abandon Sylvie to the severity of the Coronel dungeon. Oh, I am by no means to be taken literally, and doubtless the child has plenty of bodily liberty and nourishing food, but in this fine household of her cousins she must of necessity be a sort of little Cendrillon. How can an old and stupid godfather — who, alas, is not a wizard — turn her tatters into spun glass? Do not hesitate, *mon prince;* she must be weary of waiting in the ashes."

"You have not forgotten that I am already married, my friend?" asked Shiloh somewhat nervously; he was pale with excitement, and the slices of chicken upon his plate were quite untasted.

"I have not forgotten, *mon prince,*" answered Monsieur Saint-Ange with mysterious brevity.

"I am no prince of chivalric legend, but a wretched creature without durable virtue, and the slave of an enchantment. Did you ever read *The Tempest,* monsieur?"

"No, my dear, I never did, and now I probably never shall. I do not admire Shakspere," said Monsieur Saint-Ange with an intellectual honesty truly Gallic.

"It does not matter; there is a creature in *The Tempest* . . . but how can my own poverty and incompetence hope to serve the lady of this fairy-tale?"

It was clear that Shiloh was profoundly depressed; he wore the air of an unlucky angel fallen into a pit digged for the toughest and most horny-skinned of fiends. His countenance was blanched as though he bled in secret from some mortal wound, and above the luminous pallor of his brow the tossed hair showed a silver side like stormy willow leaves.

"I wish you would eat your dinner; you may serve Sylvie far better if you have not first starved yourself into a consumption," said Monsieur Saint-Ange rather impatiently.

"I am sorry, monsieur," murmured Shiloh politely, and turned a trifle paler as he cut a slice of chicken into two pieces and neglected to eat either of them. The recollection of several lovely ladies had taken away his appetite.

Several lovely ladies; seven imprisoned princesses. Melissa of the honey-sounding name, and Silver sitting among the ashes

202

of her California exile, made the seven of the fairy-tale, added to those others out of the past. Always he had meant to be so wise and valiant, but all the princesses were still in prison, and he was a wretched creature and the slave of an enchantment.

The first of the ladies was little and slight, a child, a school-girl truly; her face was veiled in such a manner that he dare not look at it. She was Harriet; he had intended to rescue her from parental tyranny and the horrors of Mrs. Fenning's school at Clapham. He had been nineteen years old at the time and a philosopher, so that he had a rational disdain for knight-errantry, but she had wept bitterly, and her tears had been April rain-drops upon apple-blossom skin. There was never anything else that did not actually flower in a garden quite like Harriet's face, but such flowers are perishable, and alas . . . his mouth grew cold with an approaching faintness, and there was the taste of river-water upon his lips.

Mary was another child; *thou child of love and light!* She was all white and flaxen, but lighted like an alabaster lamp from within, and the shadow of her dark-grey eyes was clear as light itself. He had loved her and he would for ever love her; he had meant to rescue her from a cruel stepmother in green spectacles, and from the loneliness of unfulfilled desire; he had taken her away, and at first she had been happy. Yet he knew that he had often grieved her, and of late there had been a silent anger burning at the heart of her beauty. At Lerici, by the shores of the bay of Spezzia, she had burned with silent rage, and her white and golden flesh could scarcely veil the flame. Translucent flesh, and too mysterious soul; doubtless he was a fool not to understand, but this darkness was bitterer than the depth of the sea.

Claire was a child; a spoiled child once, and charming as a tiger-kitten. He had tried very faithfully to stand her friend, but her fierceness was untamable by any pity; it was not pity or friendship that might have tamed her heart. He had been gentle with her as a brother, and all to no purpose; he had been patient, though such was not the natural pulse of his blood, but patience could never content this Claire, for whom even love was lacking in flavour unless it were spiced with ferocity. Poor tiger-kitten, miserably trapped in the household of Professor Bojti at

The Orphan Angel

Florence! Now he could never set her free to frolic up and down the parti-coloured jungles of a dream.

Emilia Viviani was a captive dove; *poor captive bird, who from thy narrow cage* . . . there was no profit in the memory of that illusion. *I think one is always in love with something or other; the error lies in seeking in a mortal image the likeness of that which is, perhaps, eternal.* So he had written of Emilia, but first he had written of her to another tune, the veritable music of the soul . . . *but true love never yet was thus constrained* . . . *it overleaps* . . . *like lightning with invisible violence* . . . *and makes free* . . . *makes free* . . . *the limbs in chains* . . . *the heart in agony* . . . *the soul in dust and chaos* . . .

It was impossible to eat the liver-wing of the chicken while he remembered Emilia. There were chains of deathly weariness upon his limbs, and he would have given ten years of his life for a breath of free heaven to cool his forehead. The room was very hot.

Jane's hands were always cool. That was the expression of her inmost spirit, a cool and delicate spirit, not profound, but sweet as cream in a dairy. This lady had never been imprisoned, or, if she had, so long ago that her smiles had forgotten it; it was Edward who had freed her. But suppose . . . of course it was all a vision and a mirage . . . suppose that somewhere within her spirit there had lain a secret of divinity far sweeter than clover-scented cream, a sleeping warmth, an unawakened Psyche. It was too late ever to know this thing; the Psyche must lie unawakened now, with cool hands folded over her secret.

Melissa of the honey-sounding name was still a child, and happily this child was safe in the keeping of her father's friend. She was the least of all the ladies; she was only fourteen years old. She was far safer in her present keeping; to free her would have been to cast her forth into premature sorrow, into a midnight ravenous with wolves. It was better to have left her quietly in the shining moonlit room, and to have come away without a word, with only the ghost of a kiss, a little pulse of sighing air . . . such kisses die . . . but live . . . *but live within the sense they quicken.*

He closed his eyes, those eyes of burning and incredible blue

Wild Spirit

which Melissa had loved more than he might ever know, and without their singular illumination his face became no more than a thin trivial mask; a death-mask it might have been, white as plaster under the sunburn, with hollow temples and tormented lips. His beauty was put out like a snuffed candle; if one were critical one saw that his nose was slightly ridiculous and that he had a great many freckles.

Neither Monsieur Saint-Ange nor David was critical; the first observed that his young friend was looking profoundly fatigued, and the other that civilisation never did agree with Shiloh nohow, and that he'd be switched if he could figger it out, but the poor boy appeared to have the shakes and he reckoned they'd better take to the road again.

" Crazy goings-on," grumbled David aloud. " Leaves good victuals on his plate and sits there like a graven idol, and it's no time at all since he was tearing along a-hollering at the top of his lungs, strong as a hoss and stubborn as a mule."

" Do be sensible and drink your wine; you need not talk if you are tired, but it is a pity not to drink such excellent Madeira," said Monsieur Saint-Ange to Shiloh.

Shiloh did not answer him; he was thinking of Silver. Six lovely ladies had gone glimmering through his mind in twice as many minutes, and although they had faded very softly into oblivion he was shaken by their going. The seventh still inhabited the future; he could not deceive himself into a longing to return into the past. The past was fair but tragical; a sickness fell upon his heart when he remembered it.

The future was different; a clear heaven-coloured wind blew out of the west, and its stars were of a purer brilliance. This seventh lady was far away, but not in the tragical past; she was set in a niche of the future. Like a saintly doll she glittered in a niche of stars, and yet she was the little figure of the fairy-tale, with ashes in her silver-golden hair and tears in the moth-wing darkness of her eyes.

" But I am afraid that I am an excessively poor hand at rescuing people," said Shiloh, and opened his own eyes upon reality.

It is necessary to confess that Monsieur Saint-Ange cared

only for the immediate relief of Shiloh's melancholy; in the religious city of St. Louis he was a placid infidel, and he troubled not at all about marriage and Mary as he dispensed hot coffee and humane advice for the comfort of his young friend's spiritual prostration. He was a kind old man, but he had no child, and he was lonely among the good burgesses of St. Louis. Shiloh's courtesy and eccentric grace had won him beyond reason and morality, and now he was all for flinging Sylvie's bonnet over the windmill if the gesture were medicinal to his favourite's pain.

He was horrified to perceive the ravages of care upon the beloved countenance; he put a great deal of sugar into the bitter black coffee, and poured out a generous measure of cognac to fill the cup. He gave Shiloh a small portion of cream cheese and a peach preserved in white brandy; he would have given him the moon if that delicacy had been obtainable, and he had every intention of giving him his heart's desire, if that desire chanced to be Sylvie la Croix.

"You must go to Sylvie, *mon prince;* I cannot explain my conviction, but nevertheless I feel that you must go," he said with emphasis, eager to catch the returning colour of joy in Shiloh's face. It was forthcoming, with a kindling glance of animation, and Monsieur Saint-Ange continued, "If it seems that she requires a husband, why not our gallant David here? Name of a dog, is he not good enough even for a princess?"

To himself he whispered that it would be better to be Shiloh's mistress than the other's wedded wife, and that either were a happy fortune for the daughter of Tomahawk Jacques la Croix. Truly he was a kind old man, but he cared little for the opinions of a world which he had studied to despise, and Shiloh had shown a subtle and comprehensive knowledge of his adored Montaigne.

Shiloh only wanted the support of such an assurance; he forgot the spectral visions of the last half hour, and when he had drunk the coffee and eaten the peach he felt much recovered. In spite of his fierce liberty of conscience he was curiously dependent upon Monsieur Saint-Ange's approval, and now with a sigh of exhaustion he relinquished his mind to the counsels which he longed to hear and to believe. His body, ever sensitive to the agitations of his soul, relaxed to peace, and he sipped a little of the Madeira and stared drowsily at the rainbow flames upon the hearth.

4

" I ADMIT," said Shiloh, "that we are in a slight pecuniary distress."

The scene was unchanged; only the augmented fire and the pattern of frost upon the window-panes showed that the season had advanced. It was seven days later, and the three companions were once more seated about Monsieur Saint-Ange's hospitable board, whose polished walnut surface reflected a number of cut-glass decanters and an English earthenware tea-pot. Shiloh had at last persuaded his host to let him drink Bohea instead of Madeira or ratafia punch.

" But my dear boy, I have already explained to you that I shall permit you to go to California only as the guests of my late Aunt Alphonsine," replied Monsieur Saint-Ange; then, perceiving a slight but significant stiffening of the innocent contours of Shiloh's countenance, he proceeded more cautiously. ." Oh, I know that you are very well able to go without that poor lady's assistance, but consider what an inestimable favour you will be conferring upon me in thus consenting to further your journey in some degree of comfort and safety, by means of the material aid which my deceased relative is so anxious to bestow. I know that you are honourable, and I suspect that you are obstinate, but surely you will not refuse to borrow the price of a pack-mule? "

" Then," said Shiloh, evading the issue by another question, " I take it that you and Davy have decided against the Horn."

" Aw, Shiloh, you ain't never done it, and you don't rightly understand how goldarned slow it can be," protested David. " I been to Valparaiso twice, and I'm sick of them lousy vessels a-wallering in Cape weather. I been through the mill, Shiloh, ground and bolted, and I don't want no more of it than I can

help. I come west to see Injuns and buffalo and such-like varmints; you don't see none of them rounding the Horn, no, not
so many as you'd meet right here in St. Louis. Let's go over-
land, for the love of Moses, and get some fun for our money."

"Of which precisely twelve silver dollars remain," said
Shiloh, taking them out of his pocket and placing them carefully
in the centre of the dark mirror of the dining-table.

"And you can't get a decent pack-mule for less'n . . ." David
began, but Monsieur Saint-Ange stopped him with a warning
glance. David filled his glass with neat ratafia and whistled
thoughtfully between his teeth, his eyes upon the silver dollars.

Shiloh was not listening; he too stared at the twelve silver
dollars and appeared to dream. His demeanour was noticeably
subdued; it lacked that sharp and charming hint of the fantastic which marked it at its animated best.

He was attired in a white linen shirt unbuttoned at the
throat and a suit of shabby black merino; these garments had
belonged to the days of Monsieur Saint-Ange's respectable poverty, and there still lingered about them a faint atmosphere of
gum-camphor and erudition. Their prim antiquated cut en-
hanced their present wearer's look of youth and pathos; David
was painfully reminded of the perishing creature whom he
had drawn from the sea upon the night of Jasper's murder.
Here was the uncanny phantom come again, in place of the
dashing scarecrow of every day; here was the sign, the portent,
the messenger of salvation. Even the crumpled collar and the
books bulging from the pocket were the same; the bright and
dark supernal attributes were dimmed by custom and
brotherly use, but David felt his heart grow cold with the recollection of his vow.

"I been forgetting," he said to himself, "I been forgetting
how I dragged him back from death to save my own eternal
soul, when mebbe he'd 'a' rather died, when mebbe life's too
damned hard for him. Well, if he's set his heart on rounding that
there bloody Horn, I'll go with him; I'll go with him to the ends
of the earth, to fight, die, work, beg, or steal hosses for him, by
graminy. He may make a dog of me if he likes, or a nigger, or

a back-log, or a dinner; I've took a vow, and I mean to keep it in spite of hell and high purposes. But all the same I hope he ain't set his heart on that there lousy old Horn."

Monsieur Saint-Ange regarded Shiloh with an affection quite unmixed with awe; he vaguely regretted having lent him the merino suit, since its cut was too scholarly for a prince. The boy's shining singularity was tamed by its decorum; he wore the air of nothing more miraculous than a young revolutionary poet or a romantic student of the arts, and one saw that he was suffering from a slight but annoying cold in the head.

"I do most heartily detest this cruel weather," said Shiloh rather crossly, and poured out another cup of tea.

"Beats me how you can feel that way about it," replied David. "It's just nateral weather for Christmas time, seasonable and healthy, and I like it a sight better'n summer. Ain't you downright thankful to quit sweating like a hoss and puffing like a grampus, and hear the snow go scrunch under your boots agin when you walk? St. Louis's an elegant spot to my way of thinking; we might sort of hang around here all winter, and light out with the trappers in the spring, or mebbe we might settle down in one of them holes in the mountains with some of Ramsay Crooks' or General Ashley's men, and go west by way of Oregon when the snow melts. A power of them has done it lately; I was talking to one of these French bastards only yesterday, and they do have a god-a'mighty lot of larks in the winter-time. Wisht you could see it like that, Shiloh; don't wintering in a hole in the Rockies appeal to you none at all, with the cards and the drink and the singing, and an Injun wife if you was to fancy her?"

Monsieur Saint-Ange began to laugh, very quietly and courteously; the picture conjured up by David's words was exquisitely humorous to his imagination. Shiloh did not laugh; he took one of his host's fine linen handkerchiefs from his pocket and gravely blew his nose; then he shivered slightly and shook his head.

"No, Davy; I am sorry to appear selfish, but really I should prefer to go south if it were possible. I hate winter, and the

American winter seems to be particularly severe. I have not been warm since I reached St. Louis, except of course by Monsieur Saint-Ange's charitable hearth."

"It ain't possible, Shiloh; leastways not except you mean the Horn. That's south, I'll allow, but I reckon you'd find it a damned sight colder'n St. Louis. Still," said David with a dedicated sigh, "if you've set your heart upon that lousy Horn, the Horn it'll have to be, by graminy."

"Do not be alarmed, Davy," Shiloh hastened to reassure him, "I have really no desire to round the Horn; my true preference would lead me south by way of Santa Fé."

"For cris' sake what are you a-talking about Santa Fé for, Shiloh?" cried David indignantly. "That ain't got nothing to do with California; you only show your ignorance when you talk like that. Far better get to Oregon in early spring, and take our chances of a Yankee schooner as would land us down the coast."

"Possibly," said Shiloh, not in the least as if he meant it. "But there are two Americans called Workman and Spencer who went from New Mexico to Los Angeles with a Spanish caravan, and who are now trading in Santa Fé. The road is open to the venturesome and, after all, the road lies south. I feel certain it must be comparatively warm in Santa Fé."

"Well, of all the plumb foolishness . . ." began David, but Shiloh interrupted him by drawing several folded newspapers from his pockets and spreading them upon the polished surface of the table.

"You see," said Shiloh somewhat diffidently, "I have endeavoured to inform myself by means of the public prints. Here are three copies of the *Missouri Intelligencer;* I found them at the tavern, and I have derived both pleasure and profit from their perusal. Allow me to read you this extract from the issue of October eighth; its tone is more optimistic than those of the preceding reports, which speak forebodingly of starvation and murder."

"'The arrival of the greater part of the company under the superintendence of Colonel Cooper from Santa Fé, happily contradicts the report afloat a few weeks since, of their having been

210

robbed and left in a starving condition. . . . Many have also returned who comprised the party under the direction of Captain Becknell. Those of both these parties who remained at Santa Fé — among whom is Captain Becknell — may be expected in a few weeks.'"

Shiloh read these words in a tone of quiet satisfaction; he handed the other newspapers to David, and waited smilingly while his friend's slow forefinger followed the lines of print.

"Well?" said Shiloh at last, and in a voice of triumph.

"Well?" asked David with a deliberate lack of enthusiasm; there had been nothing in the letters from Franklin and Fort Osage to modify his low opinion of the Santa Fé plan.

"But Davy, surely you perceive the manifest superiority of this mode of travel!" cried Shiloh excitedly. "Only consider its numerous advantages; the economy, the novelty, the surprising adventures! 'It is becoming a familiar operation for our citizens to visit this capital'; thus the *Intelligencer* of September seventeenth, and I have myself heard the same tale from a member of Jacob Fowler's party, who returned to Missouri last July. This man is in St. Louis at present; he is an excellent fellow, and he assures me that the thing is possible."

He looked so absurdly impractical and mild in the black merino suit and crumpled linen collar, so delicate and gentle, so patient under the affliction of a cold in the head, and so preeminently unfitted to cope with the realities of danger, that David almost laughed aloud. The burning spirit who had travelled at his side across half a continent was obscured by the dull garments and the duller infirmities of civilisation, and David forgot the fiery impulse of Shiloh's body in contemplating its slight proportions, now immobile within a borrowed coat.

"You couldn't never do it, Shiloh," he exclaimed rather scornfully. "You're crazy if you think you could, but I always known you was crazy. Why, you idjit, ain't I heard about that trail from my friends of the Rocky Mountain Fur Company, who wouldn't go near it for a mint of money, and don't I know it's god-damned awful? Bare hills and howling blizzards, and deserts and sand, and murdering Mexican bandits and horned toads and grizzlies and Iatans and all such devilish varmints, and no water, and you get so's you're thankful to chaw the very mules' ears for thirst, and false ponds a-hovering in the skies, and all manner of horrors! Oh, you couldn't never stand it, Shiloh, never in this world!"

"But how ridiculous, Davy!" said Shiloh with an equal scorn. "Of course I could stand it, and what is more, I shall. It is my irrevocable decision to go by way of Santa Fé; you have been ludicrously misinformed as to the conditions of the journey, but doubtless the deception was unintentional. Perhaps you have received an erroneous version of Captain Becknell's attempt to cross the desert instead of following his former route to Saint Michael, but you must not permit such nonsense to prejudice you against a course upon which I am resolutely determined."

"But why, Shiloh, why in the name of all tarnation?" David was really angry; the good dream of the hole in the Rockies, with cards and whisky and Indian wives, had lain very close to his heart, and Ashley's men had been eloquent in praise of these things. What had this dreadful desert journey to reveal in exchange for the long months of idleness, the buffalo beef and trappers' butter, the mountain bread fried in a kettle of boiling fat, the winter lodges buried deep in snow, the pure spring waking in northern woods, spring woods alight with birches? David was really angry.

"Because I detest the cold, and should very much like to be warm again," said Shiloh calmly.

"You're a fool, a pesky little fool, and I'm sick of your crazy notions!" David told him violently; he had forgotten his vow.

5

DAVID's mind was burrowing into a hole in the Rockies, with a dozen of Ashley's men; he saw the pine logs clear upon the hearth, the clean decks of cards, the noble kegs of liquor, the bags of pemmican. He heard the roof creak under its weight of snow; he strode to the door, and the snow lay upon the world under another fall of moonlight. For months the snow possessed the world as the deep sea possesses a drowned continent; David heard its whispering silence through the winter nights. Within his dreaming mind months passed in a single minute; he was drowned in winter, and then he heard the sliding rush of snow upon the roof as warm rain touched it, and he knew that this rain was spring. There might be violets and bloodroot in the northern woods, such flowers as grow in the woods of Maine; there might even be a flower whose true name is arbutus. The people of New England have given it another name; David called it mayflower, and his mind made it into a symbol of his home.

"A pesky little fool!" he cried again, and smote the table with his fist until the twelve silver dollars leaped like trout above a dark pool.

"That happens to be an unwarranted insult, Davy, and I look to you to retract it."

Shiloh rose to his feet and stared at his friend with cold blue eyes.

"They are both of them fools, and children," said Monsieur Saint-Ange to himself. "As for 'pesky,' I do not know, since the word has no meaning for me, but they are a delightful pair of fools, and I am afraid that they are going to quarrel."

Indeed, Shiloh and David were now regarding each other with looks of anger and distaste; Shiloh's eyes were the colour of midnight in the haughty pallor of his face, and David was deeply flushed and panting. For the moment they were utterly estranged; David's ruddy and flaxen countenance appeared to Shiloh the very personification of detested winter, while David beheld Shiloh as some hateful brother to the Gila monster and the horned toad of the Cimarron desert.

David jumped to his feet and glared at Shiloh from beneath a twisted knot of tow-coloured eyebrows; Shiloh threw back his head, and the locks of his hair seemed to bristle like the fell of some slender savage beast. They doubled up their fists; they began to edge very delicately around the table, at the same time murmuring, in soft perfidious voices, a number of curious and disconnected words.

"Snow," said Shiloh, "cold; hideous unnecessary cold. For months on end; worse than England; worse even than Scotland

The Orphan Angel

Shut in a cabin, endlessly; cards and whisky; greasy Indian women; whisky and women and bacon-grease. An edifying spectacle; soothing to sensitive nerves. And incidentally, cold; the lowest circle of hell; eternal cold. Why did I go to Italy, David? Ah, you don't know, do you? Would you like me to tell you, quite quietly and politely? "

"You would, would you?" David replied with apparent gentleness. "Going down into a lousy desert and dying of thirst to cure a cold in your head! Sensible; that's what it is; nice and sensible, and the spit and image of a pesky fool. Snakes and grizzlies and Iatans, and worse'n that, and you the worst of the lot. Aw, come on, and quit staring at me with them crazy eyes; come on, I say, and I'll learn you a little about them bastard desert trails!"

"But how kind of you, David; how very, very kind!" said Shiloh sweetly. "Only do you really believe that you are fitted to impart knowledge to your intellectual superiors? Because, do you know, I am strongly inclined to question your ability to teach me anything. And 'learn,' of course, is an intransitive verb; not that it matters, but these barbarities of language must excoriate the ears of all persons of sensibility."

"Hold your infernal hush, you blasted son of a gun," answered David in a furious whisper. "Language, is it? How about your own language, which I'm sick to death of hearing of it, with all them everlasting long words and lunatic expressions as'd make a cow laugh and drive a Christian crazy? You're a pretty one to talk about language now; you could be took up anywhere and jailed for most of the verbs you uses in an hour."

"Hah!" said Shiloh with withering contempt, and prepared to strike, just as David said "Gr-r-hah!" and raised his mighty fist in a destructive gesture.

Monsieur Saint-Ange stepped between them with perfect composure; he laid his left hand upon Shiloh's breast, and his right hand upon the splendid muscle of David's shoulder, and he could feel the several beating of their two hearts, one light and rapid like the heart of a flying creature, and the other shaken by a heavier and stronger pulse.

"This imbecility is unworthy of you both," he remarked

214

pleasantly. " Besides, there is really nothing to quarrel about;
Shiloh's plan is not so warm or David's so cold as you appear to
imagine. I dare say the hole in the Rockies, properly unventilated,
may afford a far more salubrious climate than you are likely to
encounter upon the Arkansaw in December. Settle it as you
please; the only intelligent solution is to remain in St. Louis until
spring, and that of course you will not do. Only don't kill each
other over the question of the points of the compass; leave that
office to our friends the Iatans."

" Yessir," said David obediently; he dropped his arm and un-
clenched his fist with a great sigh.

" I beg your pardon, monsieur," said Shiloh with an air of
bewilderment; he blinked his eyes as if he had just been roused
from melancholy slumbers by a word of command.

" Sorry, David," said Shiloh, and David answered him, " Aw,
I'm sorry; 't's all right." They looked at each other shyly and
rather miserably; Shiloh gave a short embarrassed laugh, and
David began to whistle very loudly through his teeth.

" We'll go your way, Davy," said Shiloh suddenly; David
stopped whistling for a moment and grunted a stubborn negative.

" You're the skipper, and Santa Fé's your port," declared David decidedly, and returned to his interesting interpretation of
" Shannandore."

" My God, are you now beginning to quarrel the other way
about, in the pursuit of altruism? " cried Monsieur Saint-Ange
with a groan. " You may argue all night, I suppose, having determined to be unselfish, and I confess that the prospect bores me."

" By amicable debate we may soon arrive at a solution . . ."
began Shiloh, but David had already taken one of the silver dollars from the table; he spun it glittering in the air, and spoke.

" We'll toss a coin for it, sir; reckon you're plumb sick of us
wrangling, ain't you? No, Shiloh, we ain't a-going to argue it
out by no god-damned light of reason; you got to try your luck
on this here dollar, my boy, and look sharp about it. Now, then,
here she goes; is it the bird or the lady? "

" Tails! " cried Shiloh as the coin flew upward; he said it partly
from a generous desire to leave the goddess for David, and partly
because he admired eagles.

The Orphan Angel

"And tails it is, by graminy!" admitted David with commendable good humour, as the silver circle came to rest over its own reflection in the polished walnut.

"Chance," murmured Shiloh, "the merest chance. It doesn't seem quite fair to Davy," but he was glad when Monsieur Saint-Ange assured him that it was. Shiloh felt a passionate inclination to go south, and he did not really believe that there was black ice on the Arkansaw, or snow in the passes above Santa Fé.

"But you will have your winter, Davy, and plenty of it, and Shiloh must learn to wear a buckskin shirt and to button it properly," said Monsieur Saint-Ange laughing. There was an ironical spark in his sherry-brown eyes, and the surface of his mind was brightly rippled by hilarity, but in its colder depths he was afraid.

Monsieur Saint-Ange was a philosopher; he knew the limitations of his own will, and he made no attempt to dissuade his young friend from a project which his maturer judgment condemned as foolhardy. Nevertheless, even with an ironical laugh upon his lips, he stared rather unhappily at Shiloh as that eccentric creature drank his seventh cup of tea in a trance of quiet excitement.

"How obstinate he is, he who appears so mild and tractable!" said Monsieur Saint-Ange to himself. "And how reckless, he who appears so reasonable! I cannot keep him in St. Louis; I have neither the force to save him, nor the stupidity to believe he will survive. He will die upon these cursed trails between here and California; he will die of cold or thirst, of starvation or the tomahawk; it is a hideous certainty, and I can do nothing. I marvel at my own folly in encouraging him to think of Sylvie; I have sent him to his death. I cannot keep him here; I cannot even put him aboard ship; I cannot purchase safety for him. Well, I shall lose him, as I have lost my poor little Sylvie; it is my misfortune to have conceived an affection for a vagabond. And yet, one sees his superiority at a glance; the hands, the brow, the preternatural intelligence! It is a pity, but it is impossible not to love him."

"Be careful, *ô mon roi;* the heathen may truly cast you into prison this time," he said to Shiloh, and hummed the song of the minstrel Blondel in a voice grown dry and thin as thread-paper.

Wild Spirit

6

Next day the three friends set forth into the snow-bloomed brightness of the early afternoon; there was that ineffable frosty glitter
in the air which belongs only to a winter season of full sunshine.
It was pleasant to feel the feathery crystals crunch into ice under
a heavy boot, and pleasant to perceive the quickened breath made
visible in frozen plumes of smoke. David trod the new pavement
of Main Street as though it had been a quarter-deck; he had
neatly cleaned and mended his clothes, and he looked a very able
seaman indeed beside the slighter figures of his companions. His
breadth of shoulder and mighty chest would have split the borrowed great-coat which suited Shiloh so well and made him
appear so elegant, so melancholy, and so austere. It was a distinguished garment of dark blue broadcloth, and Monsieur
Saint-Ange insisted that the cut had always been too narrow for
him; certainly it was quite unworn, and Shiloh derived great
comfort from its excellent fit and from the warmth of its lining.

He carried a hat in his hand; it was a beautiful pearl-grey
beaver, and he would gladly have consented to wear it as a tribute
to Monsieur Saint-Ange's sense of decorum; unfortunately it was
so much too large for him that its brim would have rested lightly
upon the bridge of his nose. He did not honestly regret this circumstance in spite of the keen wind whistling through his uncovered locks; the sun was bright, his cold was better, and Shiloh
had never been fond of wearing a hat.

"But I think I should rather like a coonskin cap," he said
happily, thinking of his friend who had come from Kentucky
with Jacob Fowler. "Jeremiah has kindly consented to sell me his
squirrel-rifle; I have had remarkable luck with it in shooting at
a mark."

"Yes, I'll say that one thing for you, Shiloh," growled David,
who would have said a thousand at need, "you're a goldarned
good shot; don't know how you come to be, potting at sticks with
pistols, or killing these here preserved birds as you was telling me
about when you was a boy; I don't blame you for not taking to

it, for it always sounds to me like pickles and jam. But I'll be switched if you ain't a natural-born good shot."

"Oh, no; not particularly," Shiloh answered, but he was profoundly flattered, and he thought affectionately of the squirrel-rifle which Jeremiah had consented to sell him.

"We will buy many coonskin caps for this journey," said Monsieur Saint-Ange with an indulgent smile. "Yes, many coonskin caps and buckskin breeches, many moccasins, much powder and ball, and a superfluity of squirrel-rifles."

Monsieur Saint-Ange had never been a grandfather, but now he felt rather like one as he observed the flush of joy upon his young friend's countenance. He had always desired to give pretty things to Sylvie, trifles of ivory and tinsel and swan's-down, and he had always been too poor. Now that at last he had plenty of money, Sylvie was far away; she fluttered far beyond the power of silk and spangled nets to draw her back again, and the money was so much base metal, heavy and comfortless and dull. It was like the dusty straw in the fairy-tale, lacking a princess to spin it into gold; Monsieur Saint-Ange was thankful that Shiloh needed a coonskin cap and a quantity of powder and ball. The old man smiled his stiff ironical smile, thinking how strangely these barbarous things were substituted for the shining scented toys which he had always longed to give to Sylvie.

It was the end of the first week in December, and already a holiday spirit seemed to pervade the atmosphere. The sharp gaiety of the winter day was clear to every sense; the sun was an intolerable brilliance in the west, the sky was a blue sparkle over the paler sparkle of the snow, all sounds were mingled in a brittle music, and the sting of the frost was no more acute than the fragrance of burning logs. Somewhere within one of the great stone houses on Main Street a fiddle-string quivered, and there was a smell of cider royal in the air.

Shiloh realised that the scene was livelier and more changeful than any he had beheld since the black curtain of hurricane shut Italy from his view. He was pleased by the varied aspect of the crowd, where ladies and gentlemen of evident breeding appeared in curious contrast to lean trappers from the northern woods, and *coureurs de bois* wild as Pawnees. There were bearded men from the flatboats, and hunters from the Appalachian slopes; there were tall contemptuous Osages and Mandans from the upper Missouri.

"Extraordinary!" said Shiloh, gazing about him with very bright eyes, and walking so fast that Monsieur Saint-Ange found it quite impossible to keep up with him.

Shiloh's expression was grave if inquisitive, but in reality he was in the highest and most effervescent spirits at the prospect of the savage journey imminent upon the morrow. In the first place he was having his own way, which always agreed with his health; in the second place, he and David had lately removed their disreputable bundles from the tavern to Monsieur Saint-Ange's guest-chamber, whose simple luxuries had wrought miraculously upon his nerves to soothe them. He was utterly unconscious of his invariable need for bodily peace and comfort, but he was none the less benefited by the presence of clean sheets and hot water and a quiet library well stocked with the Greek classics.

He and Monsieur Saint-Ange had finally reached an amicable understanding about the practical details of the journey; for the sake of Silver, Shiloh would permit his kind friend to provide David and himself with the necessities of travel. His only stipulations were extreme economy and an admission upon his benefactor's part that the money was merely a loan.

"Mary must of course be in receipt of my income at present," he had said. "If she decides against America, I shall leave her in complete enjoyment of this sum, and manage for myself as best I can."

"We might go into the fur trade, you and me, after we've found Silver and fetched her back here," David had suggested hopefully, thinking of the northern woods.

"You might even attempt authorship, *mon prince;* it is not so profitable as peltries, but I should never advise a person of your fastidious tastes to weary his soul in commerce," Monsieur Saint-Ange had said, thinking of Aunt Alphonsine's inheritance and of the fact that he had no son.

Shiloh had blinked his eyes and ruffled his hair, and said, "Yes; yes; I quite agree," to them both with admirable impartiality, thinking of Jeremiah's squirrel-rifle.

The Orphan Angel

Now as he walked swiftly along the new stone pavement of Main Street, which rang like iron in the glittering cold, he was thinking very happily of salt and dried corn and beans, of pack-mules, and of the high advantages to be derived from a life of danger and adventurous chance. Both his pockets were full of clippings from the *Missouri Intelligencer* relative to the various expeditions which had reached Santa Fé; his head was stuffed with singular details concerning the habits of buffalo and the best way of approaching an Arapahoe village. Jeremiah had been charmingly communicative, and Shiloh had a passion for acquiring knowledge, and an excellent memory.

"I wish you would wait," said Monsieur Saint-Ange, who was sadly out of breath. Shiloh paused obediently and turned to him with a smile.

"I mean until spring; I wish you would wait and start your journey in the spring; it would certainly be much wiser to wait for spring," explained Monsieur Saint-Ange rather fractiously; he was tired, and the fear of losing Shiloh entangled the roots of his mind in chill despair.

"Oh, really there is not the slightest danger," Shiloh assured him with absurd mendacity. "The winter is a most favourable time to travel; Jacob Fowler did not reach Taos until January, and you know he reached it in perfect safety, and Captain Becknell himself, I am informed, intends quitting Santa Fé on the return journey about the middle of December. Doubtless we shall pass him upon the way; I shall be delighted to meet Captain Becknell."

"You'll meet many less desirable characters than Captain Becknell, I am afraid; the average Comanche is not an amiable person," said Monsieur Saint-Ange pessimistically.

"Perhaps not, yet I cannot help honouring his tameless spirit," replied Shiloh, whose own spirit refused to be dashed from its eminence of joy.

"You are aware that the Mexicans kept one of the McKnights in prison for ten years?" inquired Monsieur Saint-Ange.

"Oh, yes, but the change of government has had a most beneficial effect upon their institutions; I understand that there is even talk of a republic," answered Shiloh with an invincible ignorance of fear.

"It does beat me the way you have the whole blasted business at your fingers' ends, Shiloh," said David, who had been largely convinced by the later clippings from the *Missouri Intelligencer* and by Shiloh's native eloquence and energy.

7

By the time the three friends returned to a beechwood fire and a dinner of roast guinea-fowl, Monsieur Saint-Ange felt more than ever like a grandfather, and Shiloh and David had each acquired a complete trapper's outfit of clothes and weapons. The old man had insisted upon purchasing a beautiful new rifle for Shiloh, imported at great expense from a celebrated Philadelphia gunsmith, and provided with the curious innovation of copper percussion-caps.

"You'll probably always prefer your wretched squirrel-rifle," said Monsieur Saint-Ange philosophically, "but you will oblige me by accepting this pretty little engine of destruction; it has a grace and finish which appear to me appropriate."

Shiloh had heard of some Spanish mules which a returned trader was willing to sell at a reasonable price; he had also heard that they could undoubtedly buy their salt from Colonel Cooper at Boone's Lick for the sum of one dollar a bushel. It was truly amazing to realise what a variety of fascinating information Shiloh had received from Jeremiah, and David stared in wonder and respect above the generous comfort of the dinner-table.

"Well, it does beat cock-fighting, the way you rattle off all that crazy stuff like you was born to it, Shiloh," he said, and shook his head as he dispatched the second drumstick of the guinea-hen.

"Of course," said Shiloh, warming to his subject under the influence of China tea, "we might effect a great economy by following the plan of Jacob Fowler, who actually took no provisions with him with the exception of salt, depending upon the purchase from the Osage Indians of the necessary supplies of

buffalo and antelope, dried corn and pumpkins. I understand it
answered admirably in the case of his party, and the less food we
carry the fewer mules we shall be obliged to pack. What do you
think of carrying nothing but salt, monsieur? "

"I have a very low opinion of the idea, my child," replied Monsieur Saint-Ange firmly. "I would far rather buy another pair of
pack-mules and be sure that you will have a reasonable certainty
of beans and coffee. The game you must get from the Indians, or
obtain by your own skill, but at worst you may have beans and
corn-meal to keep body and soul together."

"I suppose," said Shiloh, "that they must be kept together,
and by beans; at least the prejudice in favour of this alliance appears to be universally accepted."

"'Twould be a lunatic notion if they wasn't, by graminy,"
cried David with considerable heat, helping himself to a large
sweet potato which was pleasantly browned and glazed with
maple molasses.

"And to-morrow, or the next day, you will be gone," remarked
Monsieur Saint-Ange with desolate calm.

"I sincerely hope so," said Shiloh radiantly, and then curbed
his manifest glad excitement as he saw the old man's stiff and
bitter smile.

"But I have every intention of returning within the year,"
Shiloh assured him with charming seriousness; it required all
Monsieur Saint-Ange's cynicism not to believe the promise.

Monsieur Saint-Ange was tired and sad; there had been so
many things to do, and he had found them fatiguing in the extreme. They had gone to the Bank of St. Louis, and to John Mc-
Knight's store; there had been long interviews with traders, and
an excited colloquy between Shiloh and a stray Mexican on the
subject of the break with Spain. Now he wished very heartily to
forget his weary anxiety in sleep; the thought of the morrow was
too mournful to be remembered without pain, and he closed his
eyes in a quite unphilosophical pang of loneliness.

"At least you will let me provide you with horses; be reasonable, and consent to this trifling mitigation of your discomfort,"
he said irritably.

"Please don't think me ungrateful; I am most sensible of your generosity, but really I prefer to go on foot," Shiloh replied with mild composure; his manner was like velvet over the metal of his obstinacy.

"Reckon we can do it, sir; you see we ain't exactly new to it, having tramped clear from Boston in two pairs of boots apiece and patches along the road," David explained. "Nobody can lick Shiloh walking, and though I ain't no great shakes myself I generally manages to keep up with him somehow. Don't you bother about us, sir; we shall fetch up in Santa Fé alive and kicking, spite of all the Injuns and god-damned varmints in creation. Hosses ain't necessary, and being brought up to boats I ain't extra clever with a hoss."

"Neither am I, you know; my horsemanship is adequate, but certainly not brilliant," said Shiloh modestly. "I am far better afoot; I can do thirty miles over broken ground and experience no ill effects whatever."

"Yes, yes," answered Monsieur Saint-Ange, "but that wasn't friable soil; you're not accustomed to sand. Well, there's no manner of use in scolding you; you must find out your mistake for yourself. You can always buy a horse of sorts from the Indians, in exchange for powder and ball and blankets, and that is precisely what you'll do sooner or later. It is a pity, because I could have found you a better mount in St. Louis."

All three sat silent for a time, beholding a variety of prophetic visions in the coloured flames; Monsieur Saint-Ange perceived only tragic pictures, while David grinned mysteriously at what he saw, and Shiloh trembled with expectancy. Monsieur Saint-Ange drank Madeira, David drank New Orleans ratafia, and Shiloh drank China tea.

"Good-night, my dear children," said Monsieur Saint-Ange at last. "We are none of us particularly amusing this evening; I think we had far better go to bed. Your candlesticks are in the hall, and I have told Baptiste to light a fire in your room."

It was impossible to speak of the fact that to-morrow night they would be gone; Shiloh was amazed to find himself moved almost to tears as he bade his host good-night. He was torn between pity and an intense desire to go free of all emotional obligations; it was impossible to speak of going, but a profound relief to think that they would soon be gone.

He liked his room, with its air of decorous quiet; he liked the easy-chair before the fire and the little book-cases on each side of the mantelpiece. " But I have never greatly admired French heroic verse," he said to David, taking *Athalie* from its shelf.

Nevertheless he perused it idly, sitting in the easy-chair before the small and jocund blaze upon the hearth; it was diverting to murmur the classic periods to himself in the midst of a fantastic dream of painted Indian braves. He sat toasting his long legs before the beechwood fire and murmuring the solemn couplets of Racine, and all the while he was dreaming of Comanches and the Spanish peaks and the pass above Santa Fé.

VIII

THINGS THAT SEEM UNTAMABLE

"THIS," said Shiloh three days later, "reminds me of our first journey across France. You know we left Paris on foot, with a little donkey to carry our portmanteau; the animal was so feeble that we ended by carrying both it and its burden; we were obliged to sell it at Charenton and purchase a mule in its stead."

"Aw, you mean the time you went with them girls," replied David rather ungraciously; the peculiar circumstances of the adventure had always puzzled and repelled his simple mind. "I reckon you told me about that; they was in black silk dresses, and you didn't have nothing to eat but bread and fruit, and you sprained your ankle and had to buy some kind of a cart to ride in; crazy goings-on, I call it."

"Yes, and I remember that I beguiled the tedium of the way by telling the tale of the Seven Sleepers!" Shiloh laughed; the recollection of his youthful folly amused him and his innocence was unaware of David's Puritan prejudices.

"Well, it's a blamed nuisance having these mules to mind all the time," grumbled David; Shiloh was by no means clever with his slim brown hands, and it fell to David's lot to adjust the Spanish pack-saddles and cinch the broad grass-bandages.

"You're pulling it too tight, Davy; it's cruel to torture the

The Orphan Angel

poor beast like that," was Shiloh's invariable comment, and David as invariably answered, " Aw, shut up, Shiloh, and leave me be; I got to do it like that there Mexican shown me, ain't I? Quit nagging at me, and gimme a hand with this goldarned strap."

David's own fingers were meticulous and strong in the performance of all manual labour; in twenty-four hours he was neatly familiar with every operation connected with the small caravan.

" Reckon you was smart at knotting reef-points 'cause you just naturally liked 'em," he told Shiloh. " You certainly are goddamned clumsy with a mule."

" I suppose I can learn," said Shiloh sadly, and without conviction. The woven straps eluded his light touch, and he was better at feeding and watering the mules, while he murmured to them in the starry flowery Spanish of Calderón's *Autos*.

There were three of these pack-mules: two to carry Shiloh's and David's equipment and one loaded with corn for the animals' own refreshment. There would be very little fodder on the Arkansaw. The mules were small elegant creatures, half burro and half Spanish horse; the Arabian strain made them pleasing to the eye, but their dispositions were deplorable. Nevertheless they were growing fond of Shiloh; they submitted patiently to his ministrations, and poetry did not appear to worry them so much as it did David.

It required Shiloh's wild and vivid fancy to perceive resemblances between the harvest fields of France and this Missouri prairie rough with winter. If he had crossed it in midsummer the landscape would have been bright with briar-roses and musical with doves; now it was nothing but long grey grass and frozen clay. Yet a particular glory clothed the wide horizon and the rolling spaces of the earth; they had the simplicity and strangeness of the sky or the empty miles of the sea.

" Flat as a pancake and ugly as a mud fence," said David, but Shiloh shook his head and talked vaguely of nobility.

The weather was cold but fine, and the roads none the worse for being hard as iron with the frost. The ice on the streams was thin and brittle as yet; the Boone's Lick road followed the course of the river into the central wilderness of Missouri, and the road was passable and the fords not too dangerous. By the

226

Things That Seem Untamable

grace of good luck and their excellent new boots Shiloh and David made the hundred and fifty miles to Franklin in six days.

When they entered the little town everyone perceived at once that they were travellers bound upon some adventurous quest; it would be untrue to say that they strutted, but their mien was proud and cheerful, and they contrived to walk as lightly as though they had not been tired.

"Them two young fellers is certainly all sot up about them there outfits o' theirn," said several elderly on-lookers, and spat not unkindly in the general direction of the approaching caravan.

Shiloh and David were indeed a singularly well-favoured pair in their hunting-shirts of dressed buckskin and long fringed trousers decorated with beads and porcupine quills. Shiloh wore the coveted coonskin cap and David a cap of darker bearskin; their powder-horns and bullet-pouches were slung over their left shoulders, and through their leather belts were thrust large formidable knives in sheaths of buffalo-hide.

"Couple o' beaver trappers making south to the mountains," said some, but others differed, believing that the strangers had a load of steam-loom shirtings, super-blues, and pelisse cloth for Santa Fé. "Kinda late to start," they said, and wagged their beards pessimistically over their whisky.

"The yaller-headed one's a Yankee; easy enough to figger that out, I reckon," observed a much-travelled gentleman from Virginia. "He's what they call a regular down-east Yankee, and a powerful big one at that; I reckon he's been a seafaring man from the rolling walk on him. That there other lad's a heap harder to place; first I thought he was an Injun, the soft way he steps, but I ain't never seen an Injun with blue eyes and freckles. I've took a powerful liking to him, all the same; guess I'll just inquire his name kinda friendly-like and offer him a drop o' liquor."

"Shiloh, eh? That's a mighty funny name, stranger," said the gentleman from Virginia; he was cut to the soul when Shiloh declined a sip from his flask, and yet his powerful liking persisted even in the face of this rebuff, and at the end of five minutes' vivacious conversation he evinced no more than pitying surprise when Shiloh admitted a desire for a cup of tea.

The Orphan Angel

"Well, he brews it mighty strong, anyway, strong as lye, it appears to be, like it would rot the guts out of a copper worm," he explained to his companions; they all confessed that Shiloh was eccentric but agreeable, and most of them were quite pre- pared to forgive him his peculiar taste in beverages.

"Seems like there's something savage in that lad, spite of him being so polite," said the gentleman from Virginia approvingly.

David overheard the words; he looked at Shiloh and nodded with an air of ingenuous pride. It was David's darling weakness to assume the credit for Shiloh's virtues as an adventurer; he experienced almost the creator's sense of power in contemplating this quick and vital creature whom he had saved. Shiloh, drawn moribund from destruction by David's strong right arm; Shiloh, shaking off the trivial harness of civilisation to run wild through a recovered world; these were intoxicating conceits, and sources of the liveliest vanity to David.

And indeed he might well be forgiven for indulging such re- flections, since a magical change was evident in Shiloh when- ever he went free to lead an active and primitive life. Trelawney and Williams had observed the same happy metamorphosis aboard that crank and erratic little vessel which had been their plaything for a summer at Lerici. Now, as David watched his friend even through the critical eyes of the citizens of Franklin, he wondered for the twentieth time if this bronzed and strenu- ous apparition were in truth the same Shiloh who had crouched so forlornly over Monsieur Saint-Ange's study fire in the double misery of a cold in the head and a borrowed coat.

"It's the talk as does the mischief," said David to himself; "the talk, and the fuss, and the bother about women;'that plays hob with Shiloh. Good beds and decent victuals ain't a-going to do nobody no harm; it's the worrying about women as does it, and now, what with the mules and everything, he ain't got no time for women."

The two young strangers enjoyed a gratifying popularity dur- ing their brief stay in Franklin; David's prowess in drinking and in the honourable art of self-defence were both appreciated, and Shiloh's regrettable preference for tea was excused upon the grounds of his excellent marksmanship and his engaging manners. It was generally conceded that David's baritone was an addition to the evening's entertainment, and that although Shiloh seemed kinda shy-like and retiring, he might probably be a ring-tailed roarer in a scrap, and you never knew about them soft-spoken fellers if you riled 'em.

"The big tow-headed Yankee is a mighty nice lad," said the gentleman from Virginia, "but for a right smart regular devil, give me that there little blue-eyed Injun every time."

"You boys is terrible fools to be figgering on getting to Santa Fé on foot," said the oldest inhabitant, who insisted upon calling the town by its original name of Boone's Lick. "Take my advice, which you're welcome to free gratis for nothing, and get a couple of hosses for yourselves afore you reach the Arkansaw. 'Tain't no time of year to start anyways, and what's the sense of acting foolisher than you can help?"

"Thank you," Shiloh replied with his usual courtesy; "we will consider your suggestion." But in reality he was adamant to such whisperings of caution, and every hour his aspect became more eccentric and more elegantly savage, until the very porcupine quills upon his buckskins appeared to bristle with impatient fire.

"Got to be going, or Shiloh yonder'll bust his boiler," grinned David, who had been talking to a steamboat captain from New Orleans.

2

THEY encountered a snow-storm upon the first day after leaving Franklin; David tramped stolidly through its frozen sands, but now and then he would turn and look at Shiloh to see how he was liking it. If Shiloh felt a secret misgiving as the cold wind whirled the sleety crystals about his ears, his outward semblance refused to confess it. He had discarded his heavy boots in favour of greased moccasins, and his blanket great-coat hardly impeded the stubborn rapidity of his stride.

"These here hides are handier than any tent," David boasted late that afternoon as he stretched a couple of deerskins across a frame of willow boughs; but indeed it was David who was

229

handy. The jack-knife he had bought in Boston was still the favourite implement of his skill; he carried a little whetstone in a rawhide case. To Shiloh it appeared that the shelter was constructed with no more effort than David would have given to the proper cutting of a willow whistle.

"Plenty of driftwood a-laying round down by the creek," said David. "Fetch along as much as you can manage, Shiloh; Satan finds some mischief still, I reckon, so don't go pulling the books out of your pocket until after the kettle boils."

The mules were hobbled in a patch of cottonwood, whose leafless tops provided both a wind-break and a supper for the sagacious beasts. "Saves corn," explained David laconically, "and mules seem to find this sweet-bark cottonwood real tasty."

The azimuth compass was in Shiloh's keeping; he derived great satisfaction from plotting their probable course upon a scrap of paper before the sapphire darkness fell across the snow.

"And you could 'a' got that turkey if you'd had your wits about you; now you won't have nothing but what you call everlasting bacon for supper, and lucky to get it," said David, shaping neat patticakes of cornmeal and water and tossing them into the sizzling fat in the pan.

"You are perfectly right, Davy," Shiloh answered penitently; "I could have got the turkey, and quite easily. My wits were sufficiently about me, but at the last moment my heart misgave me, and I forbore to slay the bird. I suppose I shall have to overcome such scruples if I am to provide our camp with fresh game."

"Yessir, you'll have to get over all that kinda nonsense, if you don't want to catch the scurvy," was David's firm reply.

"That particular fowl," said Shiloh with a thoughtful sigh, "had so haughty and aquiline an air that I was awed into a dereliction of duty; I promise to be more ferocious to-morrow."

Even without the luxury of fresh game, the meal was warmly welcome to the travellers; Shiloh had never been so hungry in all his life, and he revised his views on bacon-grease while devouring hot fried corn-cakes with the appetite of a young and impulsive wolf. Nevertheless, although a table was lacking, his table manners remained perfect; unlike David, he did not swear when he burnt his tongue, or confuse the functions of a knife and fork. He ate a quantity of bacon and drank a great many cups of very strong tea, and yet by some queer grace he contrived to do these things in a fashion fastidious and well-bred and incurably polite.

"You're bound as you'll keep your quality ways, and set a good example to the prairie squirrels, ain't you?" David asked with a guffaw. David would always eat with his knife, but after years of forecastle amenities he found his friend's deportment singularly pleasant as a sauce for wilderness bread and bacon.

After supper Shiloh returned to his plottings with a pocket compass, until, grown weary of this exercise, he began scribbling on the other side of the scrap of paper. Thus in a series of minute pot-hooks was mysteriously captured the pure solitude of the skies and of the round plain spread with luminous snow, and this in the brief space of an hour, by the camp-fire's uncertain brightness.

"I understand so well," said Shiloh when he had folded the paper and put it away, "why that red-bearded man in Franklin longed to build his farm in the wilds of the primæval forest; they warned him that he would be lonely, and he replied: 'I wish never to hear the bark of a neighbour's dog.' That, to me, is quite comprehensible, but then I have ever loved all waste and solitary places."

"Well, this must suit you down to the ground then, by graminy," David told him as he unpacked the blankets and buffalo-skins which were to serve as bedding. "It's a bit too lonesome for my taste, and still it's exciting and kinda nice to think about Injuns and such-like, and to hear the wind a-whistling through them cottonwoods. Good-night, you crazy catawampus, and don't forget you gotta kill that turkey to-morrow."

This was the night of the sixteenth of December; by Christmas Eve they had killed several turkeys and encountered a band of wandering Osages from whom they purchased a supply of antelope and buffalo beef. The savages appeared friendly, and Shiloh was deeply impressed by their impassive copper-coloured countenances, with domed and shaven brows and high gaunt noses. He was remarkably clever at making himself understood by means of a few words and many smiles, and he was privately flattered by a belief in his ability to fathom and perhaps improve the mind of primitive man.

"Well, this'll be the god-damnedest Christmas that ever I

spent, not forgetting the one in irons owing to a little mistake on the cap'n's part, and the drunken one in Rio," mused David as he plucked a fine turkey cock which Shiloh had shot for their dinner. "Seems like it's kinda blasphemous to eat this bird in such an un-Christian country, among all these murdering heathen; I wisht we had some cranberries for sass."

"But Christmas is really a pagan festival, Davy," explained Shiloh, who had read John Brand in his youth, "and you know what Pliny has to say about mistletoe."

"I'll be switched if I know a word of it; I ain't never heard the old codger's name before," said David. "I don't specially hold with mistletoe, but I do hold with pumpkin pies. We don't have no mistletoe in Maine, but even aboard ship you'd get a bit of plum-duff for your dinner."

It was a curious Christmas Eve; the stars were solemn tapers burning high above a vast tranquillity of snow, and Shiloh's sensitive spirit was touched to rapture by their influential light. There was a delicate smell of winter in the smoke from the burning driftwood; and the ice on the little creek glittered with specks of silver and gold in the glow of the camp-fire.

"Sightly, ain't it?" said David, with his eyes on the enchanted scene. "But somehow it don't look Christian; sort of ghostly, like there might be uncanny critters about."

"I'll read you a poem concerning such superstitious fancies, Davy," murmured Shiloh in a soft and spectral voice. "Oh, no, it isn't one of my own poems; it isn't in the least my sort of thing."

He took from his pocket a small octavo volume which Monsieur Saint-Ange had given him; most of its leaves were yet uncut, because Monsieur Saint-Ange loved Milton no better than he did Shakspere.

> "'And sullen Moloch fled
>   Hath left in shadows dread,
>   His burning idol all of blackest hue,
>   In vain with cymbal's ring,
>   They call the grisly king,
>   In dismal dance about the furnace blue;
>   The brutish gods of Nile as fast,
>   Isis and Orus, and the dog Anubis haste.'"

Things That Seem Untamable

"'Naught but profoundest hell can be his shroud,'" intoned Shiloh necromantically; he spoke the words in a low unearthly chant, and David felt the hair rise upon his scalp as he listened.

If David had been a Catholic he would undoubtedly have crossed himself; being only a rather careless Congregationalist, he began to whistle between teeth which had a tendency to chatter. A dim and phosphorescent light crept upward from the snow, and along the star-powdered horizon certain figures moved in an ambiguity of darkness. Perhaps they were a company of Osages returning from a hunt; perhaps they carried deerskins and rough white bearskins across their arching saddle-bows. Certainly they appeared very vague and monstrous in the distance; their horses had the equivocal shape of a dragon-brood. Shiloh stared after them in wonder quite unflawed by fear, but David pulled him down into the shelter and swore in a fluent grumble. David had stopped whistling, but he could not stop the chatter of his teeth.

"God damn you, Shiloh, for skeering the hide off me," he muttered. "Them bastard Injuns is bad enough, but that there poem is a sight skeerier, the way you say it. This is the goldarnedest Christmas Eve I ever expect to spend this side of hell."

3

It took them twenty-five days to reach the Arkansaw, and these days were often difficult enough, chequered not only by the inevitable alterations of midnight and noon, but also by black frosts and blinding snows. Yet, taken all in all, the sum of these days was not unprosperous; good fortune flourished in the minds of the friends, a halcyon sunlight gilded the morning skies, and the camp-fire at dusk bloomed like a desert rose. If they made twenty miles before the evening halt they were lucky, since this distance must be traversed in a single span; if the mules had been allowed to rest they would have tried to lie down, and then there would have been no getting them to their feet again without unpacking the load. This apparent cruelty was the source of some anxiety to Shiloh; it troubled David not at all, and he calmly followed the Mexican rule-of-thumb in managing the beasts. It must be admitted that they preferred Shiloh, in spite of his absent-minded manner; he was especially fond of the little bell-mare, to whom he would recite portions of the *Magico Prodigioso* while secretly nourishing her upon his own midday repast of parched corn.

David was as resourceful in the discovery of creeks as though a perpetual hazel wand had burgeoned in his hand, and Shiloh developed a marvellous gift for placating Osages and Pawnees. Some cherub upon a flying star may have held the reins of their luck in his indulgent power, or it may have hung upon David's durable good sense and Shiloh's scintillant intelligence and courage; suffice it to say that this luck continued for twenty-five winter days, and that there was an abundance of sweet water and fresh buffalo beef during all that time.

They shot many turkeys, and once Shiloh killed an antelope and wept over its delicate carcass in the light of a waning moon. He felt less tender about buffalo, but nevertheless he more often elected to purchase supplies from the Indians, and his personal taste inclined to dried pumpkins and maize.

The strange face of this country, the rolling prairie, the limestone bluffs, the streams bordered with cottonwood and willow, had a wild monotony which moved the beholder to sorrow and delight. It was like a landscape seen in a dream, veiled in the loneliness of something lost and forgotten. The clear airs, the shining colour of the heavens, the sunlight flashing from the snows, were not sufficient to exorcise a spirit of melancholy that possessed the scene. Shiloh, who had known such pure extremity of beauty among the glacial pinnacles of the Alps, for whom Italian waters had revealed dead palaces and towers, was nevertheless aware that this broad dominion wore a wonder of its own. It belonged not to the savages who scoured its distance, but to greater and more barbarous powers; its conquerors were the lightnings and the frosts.

Sometimes as a troop of wild horses passed the travellers Shiloh would gaze a little wistfully after their flight, but for the most part he was content to journey as he had chosen, trusting to his human endurance and speed. The fact that these qualities approached the superhuman made his course less arduous; the

Things That Seem Untamable

wings upon his heels were invisible, but it was hard to believe
that they were broken. The Indians he regarded with fearless
curiosity; his amicable sentiments toward both Osages and Pawnees made him unable to understand their hatred for each other,
but by a sort of cool and airy friendship he contrived to win the
suffrages of all.

At length the Spanish Peaks floated in cloud upon the horizon,
and they beheld the Arkansaw rippling wide and shallow between banks of white sand. Above the low bluffs with their
growth of willow a few tall cottonwood-trees stood naked against
the evening sky.

Shiloh and David camped that night on an island in the river,
crossing by a crazy bridge of flags and rushes. An old Indian fort
sheltered them from the increasing wind; it was circular in shape
and builded of logs laid one upon another. About it a tangle
of grapevines still held some dried and frozen grapes, and
within the fort a rude spit had been erected over the ashes of
ancient fires.

"I should like to live forever in this charming and romantic
spot!" cried Shiloh with his eyes upon the shining mountains,
but David wagged his head and looked nervously at a blue feather
of smoke to westward.

At midnight a fantastic clamour tore through the tranquillity
of sleep; Shiloh waked to a confusion pierced with loud and violent cries. There were sounds of horses splashing through the
river, and a fitful shimmer of torchlight on the willow-trees.

"They've got the mules," said David in his ear, "and I reckon
they've got us too. Grab your gun and keep quiet."

There was really nothing else to do; Shiloh crouched on the
pile of buffalo-skins and watched the monstrous spectacle through
the door of the fort. It was a brilliant nightmare painted upon
obscurity; his senses were quickened by amazement, but he did
not remember to be afraid. He caught sight of slim bronze bodies
striped with firelight, of faces savage with vermilion and plumbago, of the bloody nostrils and insensate eyes of stallions prodigious against the shattered dark.

Then there was a sudden diminution of noise; long furious
execrations of farewell faded into stillness, and a portent loomed

in the low doorway of the room. Shiloh perceived that the creature was an Indian; his gigantic height and the rich trappings of his robe were manifest even in the shadow which hid his countenance from view.

" That there fellow's an Iatan, Shiloh; easy now, 'cause them's the worst of the lot," whispered David in a hurried breath.

Shiloh rose to his feet and advanced to meet the visitor with tolerable composure; he was not frightened, but a certain pulse of awe slowed the beating of his heart and made his hand cold upon the cold steel of the squirrel-rifle. He held out his other hand to the Indian, who accepted it without a word, and stood waiting in impassive silence; his clasp was iron around Shiloh's slender fingers.

" Greetings and good fortune to you," said Shiloh steadily, in a phrase he had learned from the Pawnees.

It is possible that the words annoyed the Comanche because they were spoken in an enemy accent; it is possible that he had intended from the first to murder Shiloh and David for the sake of their small possessions. He had just saved the mules from a band of Pawnee horse-thieves; the scalps of some of these were even now reeking at his warriors' belts. He stared haughtily at Shiloh as if the pleasant speech had been a blow; his face was still obscured, but the chill implacable anger of his soul was evident in the altered air. Shiloh felt the thing, quick and flickering as a snake's tongue; it brushed him, and he shuddered to the marrow of his bones. He was not afraid, but horror laid a light reptilian touch upon his spirit before he spoke again.

" Surely there is no reason why we should hate each other, you and I," said Shiloh politely. " I have done no harm to you, nor you to me; let us each go upon his way in peace."

The Indian dropped Shiloh's hand; the casual gesture was harsh with contempt. " You are a thief and the brother of thieves," he said insolently. " You have stolen goods from the White Father, goods which that great chief intended for me. If you do not make restitution I shall kill you, torturing you first as a punishment for dishonesty."

" But how ridiculous; of course you cannot mean what you are saying," replied Shiloh; indignation caused his eyes to radiate blue lightnings upon this savage who thought fit to insult a friendly stranger with absurd uncivil words.

"You shall see how truly I have warned you," said the Comanche with scorn; he seized Shiloh's arm in a grip of inflexible metal and twisted it with peculiar ferocity.

Shiloh fought like an agile tiger-cat to escape; his gun was torn from his grasp in an instant, and he strove with bare hands and the courage of a blinding rage. There was a sanguine mist before his eyes, and the blood beat in his head like a madman's hammer. He was dimly aware of David at his back struggling with a score of painted devils; the hellish picture caused him to redouble his own attack upon the giant Indian. He strained against a Minotaur; the odds were so unequal that it hardly needed the onslaught of a dozen other warriors to bring Shiloh to his knees. He struck wildly and yet more wildly; there was a strange sound in his ears, and he knew that he sobbed with fury and exhaustion. The pang of anger against himself was his last conscious thought; a darkness full of dizzy stars descended, and like a comet he was whirled into oblivion.

He awoke to a darkness without stars or firelight; his forehead was cloven with a cruel shattering pain, and he felt as sick as if he had been crossing the Irish Channel in a storm. By an effort of will he mastered the horrid vertigo and gazed about him; slowly his aching senses pierced the gloom, and he perceived David huddled in the farthest corner of the fort; his brow rested upon his folded arms, and he was swearing and weeping in the same desperate breath.

Shiloh sat up; the outrageous pain within his skull seemed to split it asunder as he moved. The sickness rose to overcome him like a cold green wave of the sea; his forehead was damp with its loathsome dew. He clenched his hands and fought it as he had fought the Indian, and luckily with more success; in three seconds he was able to speak in a voice which David recognised.

"I lost my temper, didn't I?" asked Shiloh with sincere interest. "Did they scalp us, Davy? My head feels precisely as if I had been scalped, and there is a quantity of blood upon my hair."

"Reckon you was tomahawked but not scalped this time," replied David in a hoarse and shaken whisper. "God damn them bastards to the everlasting pit, we didn't do nothing, and they've beat us to a pulp and took us prisoner, and now they're fixing to burn us or some such lousy plan. I told you how it would be if we come south among them varmints."

"I am extremely sorry if I have brought disaster upon us, Davy," said Shiloh with a sigh; he felt quite unequal to an argument, and David's vehemence increased the frantic throbbing in his temples. "I suppose I should not have lost my temper with that unpleasant person with the vermilion stripes upon his cheekbones, but really I could not support his impertinent accusations for another moment. When he caught hold of my arm I was unable to bear the indignity; his behaviour was most offensive, Davy, and I confess that I struck him. I hope you will forgive me for my natural exasperation."

"Aw, I don't blame you, Shiloh; you couldn't have done different, not with him talking sassy and calling you a thief and all that," David admitted. "Quit worrying, Shiloh; I reckon we was bound to hit something like this from the first. Mebbe we can manage to give them devils the slip; I've been figgering how we can do it, but I got such a goldarned crack on the head that I can't think very clear yet."

"Neither can I, Davy; everything seems to have acquired an annoying trick of circular motion, and certainly I have a shocking headache," said Shiloh; the travail of consecutive thought made him feel so ill that he lay down again upon the buffalo robes and closed his eyes. In five minutes he was asleep; his dreams were troubled and somewhat feverish, but the poignancy of his misfortunes was mercifully softened by these slumbers, and David forbore to wake him from his brief repose.

4

WHEN Shiloh awoke for the second time the milk-white winter dawn was staining the gloom with soft and delicate light, and David was sitting up and swearing loudly into the new face of the day. Shiloh's head still ached violently, and he was infuriated to discover himself so far prostrated by pain and loss of blood that the least exertion appeared laborious in the extreme. He would have preferred to leap to his feet with a spirited war-cry and rush into the Comanche camp like a mad avenger; by straining every nerve and sinew he actually contrived to lean upon one elbow and look about him.

"Well, I see you're not dead yet, y' crazy catamount," said David with a grimace which might have been a grin upon lips less cut and battered out of shape. "One of them lousy sons o' guns come in here a minute ago and turned you over with the toe of his moccasin, kinda contemptuous-like; I reckon he thought you was done for, and he went out again with a few tender words to me about how they was fixing to burn us along about breakfast-time if the fine weather holds. They wouldn't leave us be like this if they calculated as we could talk to each other, so don't go roaring like the bull of Bashan and bringing 'em in here to lambaste us."

Shiloh felt that it would be quite impossible to roar like a bull, or even like a sucking dove; the idea of being burnt before breakfast affected him with an unpleasant qualm of nausea. "'Fiend, I defy thee! With a calm, fixed mind, all that thou canst inflict I bid thee do,'" said Shiloh bravely, but in rather a faint voice.

"Which remark don't butter no parsnips," replied David with some impatience. "First place the bastard can't hear you, and second place it wouldn't do no good if he did; he'd go on piling that brushwood and driving that stake cool as a cucumber. You can hear 'em out there arranging things as bright and cheerful as if it was the county fair and trotting-races instead of bloody murder; we got to act quick if we don't want to be smoked like a couple of hams."

"What course would you suggest, Davy?" asked Shiloh. "I am willing to adopt any plan which recommends itself to your judgment, although I am afraid I shall not be much help to you, as I seem to be somewhat dizzy."

"Yes, and you got a right to be, by graminy," David assured him. "Looky here, my lad, don't you know as you've got a hole in your head as I could lay two fingers in and that you're the spit and image of Lazarus out of the tomb? You're doing mighty well to be alive at all, after the clip that devil fetched you when you busted him one in the jaw."

The Orphan Angel

This remark had a tonic effect upon Shiloh; very softly he touched the wound above his brow and stared curiously at the blood upon his fingers. "It appears to be a considerable aperture," he murmured proudly.

"Sure it is, and you must have a skull like cast iron," David told him, and Shiloh felt much better, and equal to the chances of escape.

He examined David by the snow-reflected light which filled the room, and observed that his friend's sunburnt countenance was yellowy-white and streaked with dust and gore; a large bruise about the left eye was already assuming hues of azure and purple. Shiloh wondered how his own face showed in the pearly flicker of dawn; he concluded rightly that he was very pale, that his abundant hair was wildly disarranged and matted over his wound, and that a great deal of blood had trickled down his brow and cheek.

"We're a pretty pair, ain't we, and fit to skeer a Christian into fits?" asked David, laughing at Shiloh's inquisitive scrutiny.

"Well, at least we are amazingly cheerful under the circumstances," Shiloh answered; he marvelled that it should be so, and could not help experiencing satisfaction in the knowledge.

"You see, Davy," he said with a sudden flash of insight, "neither you nor I really believes that he is about to be burnt alive; if we did we could not regard the prospect with any degree of equanimity. We expect something to happen; some miracle from heaven or some surprising act of courage from ourselves. At the same time we are rather pleased by the romantic character of martyr and heroic victim; if they actually burn us we shall not like it at all."

"Reckon you're right, Shiloh, but we're a-going to make a try at getting away before they roast us, ain't we?" David inquired. "Now, my plan is something like this: let's you and me pretend to be sorta weak and discouraged-like when they takes us out of here and drags us towards the stake; then just afore they ties us up let's make a dash for it and hop into the river. Ten to one they'll get us with their god-damned arrows, but anyways we'll give 'em a run for their money."

"It sounds," said Shiloh, "like a truly admirable plan." He

was strengthened by the slight promise of freedom; excitement stimulated him as brandy might have heartened a less volatile spirit, and suddenly he was animated and resolved upon escape.

At that moment a shadow fell athwart the doorway and a tall Comanche entered with noiseless tread; Shiloh sank back against the buffalo-skins and succeeded in appearing upon the tragic point of death. His extreme pallor and the bloody wound above his brow aided him in the deception; he was further served by the fact that he was still rather faint and agitated from the events of the preceding night. The savage regarded him with placid scorn; he grunted contemptuously and pulled Shiloh to his feet with a single movement of his muscular arm. Then he turned to David with a muttered word of disdain; Shiloh leaned against the rough log wall of the fort and shook with pride and furious defiance.

David rose and tottered to the centre of the room; he looked sufficiently ghastly to make his assumption of weakness quite convincing. He swayed drunkenly and clawed at the Indian's athletic shoulder; the man was completely deceived, and grunted once more in cold and grim amusement. A second Comanche appeared at the door; his comrade jerked his thumb towards Shiloh, and the newcomer strode over to the ensanguined and dishevelled figure which drooped against the wall.

Shiloh had not forgotten the plan of escape; the hope was clear and kindling in his mind, and he strove to overcome the anger which convulsed his soul and vibrated in all his nerves. If the Comanche had moderated by a hair's breadth his insolent demeanour, if the spark of contempt in his opaque dark eye had been a shade less evident, it is possible that Shiloh might have acted with discretion and restraint. But he had had no breakfast, his head throbbed with sickening pain, and the Comanche's manner was excessively rude; Shiloh was unable to support the intolerable instant, and he lost his temper with the blinding impact of an electric thunderbolt.

"Come with me, you cowardly little dog," said the Indian in his own language; Shiloh did not understand the words, but their meaning was hideously plain to him in every insulting inflection of the other's voice and in the snaky glitter of his gaze.

Suddenly, and with the most startling effect, Shiloh straightened his thin body to its fullest height and glared into the Comanche's chill black eyes with eyes of burning blue; his lips writhed in a haughty smile, and he walked swiftly and steadily across the room to the open door; the sunlight fell sharp and silvery over his wounded forehead as he went.

"Go to the devil," said Shiloh to the amazed Comanche. "I am perfectly well able to proceed to my death without your impertinent assistance, thank you."

"Aw, now you've done it and no mistake; the fat's in the fire now, Shiloh, and that's no figger of speech neither!" cried David in the accents of despair.

Shiloh knew that he had flung their chance of liberty to the wind; he saw it whirled away like a feather down that unreturning stream of air. He had been guilty of this delirium in order to save his pride intact from the hands of the savage; he did not really regret the madness now that it was accomplished.

"Sorry, David," he threw back over his shoulder as he stalked into the unclouded morning.

David did not believe him; he understood his friend too thoroughly to mistake the supercilious cock of the head and the inspired lightness of the feet, and he realized that the moment was one of peculiar felicity for Shiloh.

Shiloh paused in the doorway of the fort and surveyed the scene without; he saw that the little island was thronged with Comanche warriors, and that the near-by shores of the river were covered with a vast concourse of men and horses. The atmosphere was clear and cold; the Indians' particoloured blankets appeared as moving fires in the sun, and their weapons glittered and rang in unison with the choral solemnity of their gestures. Against the pallid tints of sand and snow and frosty willow-trees the barbaric pageant lay uncoiled like a gorgeous snake.

Immediately in front of Shiloh, and in the centre of a ring of painted braves, a great stake had been driven into the snow; brushwood and faggots were piled about its base, and its appalling significance seemed already to cry to the unstained and smokeless heavens.

In the midst of this prodigious show of cruelty and power, Shiloh stood composed and firm; his eyes were singularly brilliant, and about his lips a small delighted smile mocked and saluted the puissance of his enemies. He was still pale, but his very whiteness was a luminous challenge to the swarthy countenances around him; he carried the blood-stained colour of his brow like a chivalric banner. The human vanity which had revolted against insolence, the defiant pride which had rejected hope, fell from him in that instant; he was a spirit of pure courage as he faced the Comanche braves.

They recognised this fortitude and respected it; he was actually permitted to walk unattended through the circle of warriors and to reach the dreadful stake alone and in silence. He had forgotten the brutal throbbing of his wound; he felt strong and triumphant and happy. He told himself that he was about to die, that certain minutes of execrable pain must be endured by his defenceless body, in which mortal pang his soul need have no part; he was glad to know that he was not afraid.

He submitted quietly to the binding of his hands with a leathern thong; other thongs were passed about his waist and ankles, and he was strapped securely to the stake. He saw David a long way off, struggling in the grip of two giant Comanches; his friend's broad hands were pinioned behind his back, and an agonised devotion filled his eyes as he looked at Shiloh. The secret alien faces of their foes were dark and immobile between them.

" Shiloh," called David across the intervening space, and Shiloh knew by his voice that he was very angry, " I couldn't do nothing to save you this time; you want to die, Shiloh, and I've known it all along; you wasn't really hankering to live, ever, and now you've got your god-damned crazy way and I hope to God you're satisfied at last! "

"David," said Shiloh, "perhaps you are right, you are often right. But please forgive me, David; even if it is true, you must forgive me."

David began to cry, noisily and without dignity; he was heedless of the scornful warriors at his shoulder, and Shiloh understood that he was beyond caring for a little thing like pride.

Shiloh stood with his back to the stake; he stood erect and noble in the sunlight, and now he was not conscious of his bonds. He thought of Prometheus, and of Laon's funeral pyre; in a sort of gentle philosophic trance he watched a trivial thread of smoke curl upward from the brushwood about his feet.

The thin translucent feather flew some signal to the assembled throng; in a moment an abominable clamour broke out among the Indians along the shore; a flight of arrows whistled bird-like about Shiloh's head, and the air was full of cries and violent wings.

He had preferred the silence; he was sorry that he was not to be allowed to die in quiet torment among the flames. Slowly he became aware that the smoke had thickened before his face, and that an arrow quivered in the stake above him. Even as he saw it, another arrow pierced his arm with a slender fiery sting; he regarded its plumed shaft with wonder.

There was a difference in the clamour along the shore; the cries were varied and increased by some new emotion. Shiloh was astounded to behold a score of moccasins trampling out the fire at his feet; as the smoke cleared he knew that his bonds were cut, and that the fallen arrows lay upon the ground like innocent dead birds whose wings are broken.

Now suddenly he felt the cruel ache of the wound over his temple; again he was conscious of the pains of mortality. He was visited by a horrid conviction that he was about to yield to a disgraceful faintness in full view of the Comanches; he believed that death were infinitely more desirable than this humiliation, and he was sincerely thankful for the stake firm behind his shoulder-blades. For the second time that morning he put forth a preternatural effort and regained mastery of himself; he woke his spirit from its swoon; he stiffened all his sinews; he raised his head to stare around him.

5

A slim boy mounted upon a cream-coloured pony was watching him from the circle of braves; the lad appeared very proud and comely in a sleeveless tunic of soft white buckskin and long fringed leggings covered with an arabesque of beads. Across his forehead he wore a band of silver, and there were silver bracelets upon his arms and sea-shells in his ears.

Things That Seem Untamable

"Good God, sir," said this young person coolly, reining in his pony with one slender hand, "you look precisely like the pictures of Saint Sebastian which the Spanish padre used to show me when I was a child; I protest that you are the veritable image of Saint Sebastian. If these silly fellows have made you suffer, depend upon it that they shall be punished as they deserve. Permit me to remove that arrow from your arm; it must be most uncomfortable."

Shiloh had no real prejudice against Saint Sebastian; that romantic martyr of the Christian mythology was not uncongenial to his secret mind. But the stranger's casual tone annoyed him, and he was further irritated by the debonair and somewhat dandified manner which winged the words with gaiety. He drew himself erect, and his eyes flashed rather fiercely as he replied.

"It's very kind of you, of course," said Shiloh, "but I think I can manage for myself, thank you. These friends of yours have displayed a senseless enmity towards me for which I am at a loss to account, but the folly and depravity of the human race have ever been my despair, and I suppose my misfortunes were inevitable in this savage land."

"Oh, but by no means, my dear young man; you are quite mistaken about that, I assure you. The Indians are uncommonly pleasant people for the most part, and you are certain to like them when you become better acquainted. I regret extremely that these hobbledehoys should have attempted to burn you, but they are little more than ignorant children, and I know you will bear them no malice for their inconsiderate outbreak."

"Really, I cannot agree with you upon that point," Shiloh answered. "I feel that I have very just cause to be offended by their conduct; they are adult, and entirely responsible for their uncivil behaviour. If you possess any authority over their nature, I trust that you will employ it to inculcate principles of wisdom and virtue more proper to their years."

"Well," replied the youth with a shrug of his graceful shoulders, "I dare say it is unavoidable that you should experience a passing resentment against these poor foolish Comanches; when you have had your breakfast you will be more forgiving. I don't

245

blame you the least for being cross at present; you look very tired, and I perceive that someone has been striking you with a tomahawk."

"You appear to regard that circumstance as a cause for mirth," said Shiloh with immense hauteur; he stared more closely at the stranger's impudently smiling face, and observed that the boy bore no resemblance to any Indian whom Shiloh had ever encountered.

Shiloh saw that the young stranger had an innocently courageous nose, straight and blunt and childish, that his eyes were brilliant hazel and set very wide apart, and that his short thick hair was wavy and coloured like November beech-leaves. His skin was tanned to a fine even bronze, but there was a rosiness of blood beneath the sunburn which matched the small red lips. He seemed to be about sixteen years old, slim and muscular and moderately well grown for that tender age. His garments were delicate and fresh in a barbaric fashion, and the silver bracelets that he wore were scoured to a moonlight brightness.

"Whatever you are, you are not an Indian," Shiloh told him sternly, "and I cannot admit your right to lecture me concerning them. I have journeyed for a month among these violent people without discovering anything but courtesy and kindness; my own good intentions were everywhere the earnest of my safety. Now, among the Comanches, I have found murder and malfeasance beyond my dreams of hell; it is not fitting that you should laugh in my face when you speak of it."

"Dear me, my good sir, you do take it all very seriously, don't you?" said the boy with a flippant little grimace; Shiloh thought him the most heartless person whom he had ever met.

"You see," the boy continued lightly, "it's purely a matter of luck; my own experiences have taught me that. You were well treated by the Pawnees, and now the Comanches have singed your ankles and cut your head open for no reason at all except that these activities amused them. I, on the other hand, was stolen by the Pawnees and destined for a very dreadful fate; a band of Cheyennes and Comanches rescued me from this, and I have, naturally enough, become deeply attached to my preservers. But let us talk of all this another time; I fear that my chatter is wearying you, and you are quite palpably in need of food and slumber."

Shiloh disliked a certain condescension in the lad's cheerful voice; he would have preferred to refuse the offer, but his endurance was nearly at an end, and through a mist of exhaustion he heard David's voice in his ear.

"Come on now, Shiloh, quit arguing with the young lady and let her give you some nice hot breakfast."

Shiloh gazed at him in bewilderment; David's familiar features grew large and nebulous to his view, and he had scarcely the strength to whisper his surprise.

"What on earth do you mean, Davy?" he murmured dizzily. "There is no young lady here; what can you possibly mean? I see only a boy on a cream-coloured pony."

"Why, you crazy little fool," grinned David, "that there ain't a boy; that's a girl, and a mighty pretty one at that!"

David put out his arm, but not in time; the girl sprang from her pony with a soft and frightened cry. They were both too late; Shiloh had grown white as death upon the words, and fallen forward into the trampled snow, which showed a small red stain where his forehead touched it.

They knelt beside him, and down the face of each the tears were running; they tasted the cold salt tears upon their lips, and these tears tasted of winter and sorrow and the bitterness of love.

"Goldarn you, Miss!" cried David, "why did you have to go and tease and pester him like that, and him so tired? Couldn't you see he was wore to a frazzle with all these hellish goings-on? Seems like you was possessed of a devil or something, Miss, to mock him like you done, and him never able to stand women. That's what I've always declared; Shiloh can't stand women nohow; he's fond enough of 'em, I reckon, but if you'll excuse the liberty, Miss, they wears him out completely, and now you've been and killed him with your devilish mocking ways."

The girl knelt weeping in the snow; she lifted one of Shiloh's hands and kissed it, and the hand was cold and frightening against her lips.

"Oh, do you really believe that he is dead? Oh, do you really believe that he is dead, and that I have killed him by my cruelty?"

she asked David in a small and humble voice. "I am more savage than these ignorant Comanches; I am truly a devil, and I think that I am mad. I spoke to him scornfully because I loved him; I have never loved anyone, in all the years I can remember, and I loved him from the moment I saw him, loved him so that I was wounded by my love, so that it was like an arrow or a sword in my heart, so that I talked like a fool or a devil because my heart was broken by my love."

David was profoundly shocked; in all his life he had never listened to such wild and passionate words, and they were the more indecorous to his mind in that they were spoken childishly and in a small and tearful voice.

"Oh, my darling, my adorable, my beautiful!" cried the girl, addressing herself to Shiloh inanimate upon the snow, "please don't say that I have killed you; please be alive again and say that you forgive me for my devilish wickedness! You can't be so cold-hearted as to lie dead before my eyes and refuse to forgive me; if you will only listen while I tell you how I love you, you will never have the cruelty to die!"

She crouched in the snow; she raised Shiloh so that he lay upon his back with his head against her crossed knees. Her tears fell down upon his dishevelled hair and wetted his closed eyelids, and presently they had frozen into ice which sparkled crystalline against the dark hair and the shut secret eyelids.

A tall warrior approached the girl and laid his hand gently upon her shoulder; she started and looked up into his face with pitiful eyes. She said a few words in the Cheyenne language, and the warrior nodded briefly and withdrew to the river-bank.

"Let's get him into the fort," said David; he was sincerely shocked, but the girl's sorrow and wild regret had touched him with sympathy. He remembered that he had called to Shiloh upon the deck of the clipper ship, and that Shiloh had answered and returned from death; he knew some measure of the grief which shook this singular girl to madness.

"We'll get him into the fort," said David, "and we'll build a big fire and make some coffee; I've got brandy in my flask, and there's lots of blankets and buffalo robes in there where we leaved 'em this morning. There don't nobody need to touch him but you and me; I can't stomach these painted varmints laying a finger on him, and you're a strong girl; you lifted his head as easy as anything just now. Come on, Miss; we ain't got no time to lose a-crying if we wants to save him."

"You are right," said the girl at once; she dried her eyes and assumed an air of composure. "That will be best for the night; to-morrow, if he lives, I shall send for a litter and we can carry him to my father's lodge. Meanwhile I shall dispatch a messenger to bring us such comforts and remedies as our home provides; my father is the chief of the Cheyennes, and he will welcome this stranger with honour and affection for my sake."

"Well, Miss," replied David, "I can't rightly figger it out as yet how a white girl comes to have an Injun for a father, but if you say it's so I believes you, and there's plenty of time for explaining all that after we've got a drop of hot coffee into Shiloh. Now I'll take his shoulders and you take his feet and we'll have him into that there fort as slick as butter."

Several Indian braves rushed forward to relieve the girl of her burden as she stooped and prepared to raise Shiloh's feet from the ground, but she stopped them with an imperious movement of her head, and David knew that she was comforted by performing this humble service for his friend. He lifted Shiloh's thin body from the snow without difficulty; the girl did her part with a look of rapt devotion upon her face, and together they bore the unconscious figure between the silent watchful Comanches into the doorway of the fort. The silver winter sun glazed the white ice of the river with radiance, and David and the girl went slowly and in awe, because they loved Shiloh and feared to know that he was dead.

6

"WILL you forgive me for being rude to you, please?" asked the girl a little later; she knelt at the foot of Shiloh's couch of buffalo-skins, and suddenly she bent down and kissed the toes of his scorched moccasins.

David was boiling coffee over a driftwood fire; he wondered at the softness of the girl's voice and at her gentle and submissive manner. She was completely tamed; not a trace remained of her mockery or even of her passionate self-reproach. She moved about the rude interior of the fort with quiet peaceable steps, and her touch was exquisitely light and cool upon Shiloh's wound.

"Wonderful what love will do," mused David to himself as he added a dash of snow-water to the bubbling coffee. "She was a regular vixen, and now she's mild as a cream-syllabub."

"Will you please forgive me, out of the great goodness of your heart?" whispered the girl again, laying another airy and elusive kiss at Shiloh's feet.

"Of course; but you mustn't, you know," said Shiloh in a low voice; he still felt somewhat brittle and imponderable as he lay upon the couch, and he was not quite sure whether the girl and her kisses were real, or whether he and she and the shaggy buffalo-hides were all floating in a transcendental region of the soul.

"You see, I thought you were a boy, and rather an unfriendly boy at that," Shiloh explained patiently; it was a painful weariness to speak, but he saw that the girl's translucent hazel eyes were full of tears, and he had not the heart to disallow their sacred beseeching question.

"It was my horrid clothes; you couldn't know I was a girl in these ridiculous clothes," she assured him meekly.

"No; it was my own stupidity; I remember that my head ached, and then there was so much noise and confusion, and the smoke hurt my eyes and made me giddy," said Shiloh. "But I was an idiot not to know that you were a girl; you couldn't possibly be anything else, and I feel that I owe you an apology."

"No, no, no; the fault was entirely mine, and now I am going to get you a cup of coffee and to make you stop talking," the girl replied; she jumped to her feet and dried her eyes by rubbing them with her small brown knuckles. She moved with the grace and agility of a panther-kitten, and her golden skin rippled and shone over muscles smooth and quick as running water.

"'Course he'd 'a' rather had tea, but this coffee's more heartening-like on a cold day, as I reckon it, Miss," said David, giving her the tin cup. His prejudice against her was vanishing in the simplicity of his nature and her queer fantastic charm, even as the maple sugar was now melting in the amber warmth of Mocha.

Things That Seem Untamable

"Lucky you was able to get back the mules and the baggage from them lousy—from them I should say cantankerous var-mints, Miss," said David companionably, pouring hot coffee into the girl's cup and his own. "There was things there as Shiloh set great store by, specially some of them books and such-like trash and all."

"I am happy to have been privileged to be of service to him," the girl answered gravely.

7

"It cannot be good for you to hear so many solemn words before you sleep," said the girl that evening, shutting the book upon the *Misticay real Babilonia.* "The priests in Santa Fé compelled me to read these things when I was a mere child; my taste was vitiated by too much religion. If it were the *Galan fantasma,* now! that is amusing."

"As you will; we will read no more to-night, then," replied Shiloh, opening his eyes and smiling at her serious face. "Besides, it must be difficult to decipher the page by the lovely but wavering illumination of the flames. You had far better put the book away and tell me about yourself."

"It will tire you," said the girl, but it was plain to Shiloh that she longed to talk to him, and he was much too soft-hearted to disappoint her.

As a matter of fact he did not greatly care; he was compara-tively comfortable now, and although he was weary he did not wish to sleep. He had been enchanted to discover that the girl read Spanish with fluency and a certain ingenuous music; it was a pity that she did not know Greek, as her voice was both harmoni-ous and clear. Some natural elegance of diction was distinct in her speech, which seemed to hold the vague suggestion of an ac-cent foreign and refined. Shiloh supposed, and rightly, that this was the result of her knowledge of three several tongues.

Shiloh had lately led an existence of such variety and adventure that his enforced idleness was a severe nervous trial to him, and if he had been permitted to choose he would have insisted upon an immediate departure for the Cheyenne camp. But David and the girl chimed in a maddening laughter at the thought, and told him that he would be exceedingly lucky if he were allowed to set forth upon the morrow.

"What, you crazy catawampus, do you reckon as you can get your head laid open afore breakfast and pay an elegant social call on your murderers the same goldarned day?" asked David, and the girl displayed a concurrent mirth as she evolved a remarkably nourishing soup out of venison and wild turkey.

Therefore Shiloh was a trifle bored, and ready enough to listen to her story. He had slept the winter afternoon away, soothed by some decoction of medicinal herbs, and now that he was wakeful he preferred to be amused. The ability to suffer a slight concussion at midnight and to enjoy the dramas of Calderón upon the evening of the same day is possessed by few mortals, but of this demi-Olympian company Shiloh was the shining superior star.

It was the girl and not he who had grown drowsy over the book; now her evident eagerness to confide in him appealed to every philanthropic instinct of his being. "Tell me about yourself," he repeated gently.

"My name is Anne, and I was born in New England," said the girl. "David pretends that he knew from the first that I must be a Yankee; perhaps he did, but that was very clever of him, since I was reared in Sante Fé and have spent the last three years of my life among the Indians."

"Knowed it all the same, Miss, the minute I clapped eyes on you," insisted David. "It's a sort of a look as is hard to explain if you ain't never seen it; up and coming, if I may say so, Miss."

"Well, never mind about that; if we both talk we shall tire him, and I have a great many interesting things to tell," said the girl, gazing fondly at Shiloh; she was ecstatically happy, but even in her happiness she remembered to speak in a mild submissive voice. She was not quite unselfish enough to keep perfectly silent, but at least she did not converse above a whisper, and she frowned most indignantly at David whenever his louder tones interrupted her narrative.

"Anne is a beautiful name," said Shiloh, who rarely forgot to be kind.

"I am glad you like it, as I know no other to tell you," the girl informed him with a radiant smile. "You are to understand that my father and mother both died when I was a child, and that I was adopted by the priest in Santa Fé and cared for out of the charity of his heart. That priest is also dead now; he was a nice old man, though rather too fat; for all that, he was a Spanish gentleman, and he made me study very hard. One eccentricity he had which annoyed me: he would never tell me my father's name."

At this point in the girl's story no scandalous suspicion leapt into Shiloh's mind; most innocently he waited for the truth, and in a moment he had it.

"You see," said the girl, "my poor father was a Protestant missionary; a Congregationalist, I think one calls it, if such a long word can possibly be right."

"That's right, Miss," David told her with an elder-brotherly air. "That's what my folks was; that's the proper thing for Yankees."

"For Yankees, perhaps; not for the inhabitants of Santa Fé," the girl explained. "And certainly my father was silly to attempt to come to Mexico and convert the people; I am afraid my poor father was a fool. The priest was quite charming to me about it, but of course he disapproved profoundly of the idea, and he believed that when my father and mother were killed by the Kiawas on the road to Santa Fé they only received the punishment which they richly deserved. The opinion is possibly extreme, but one cannot blame dear old Padre Francisco for holding it."

"I can," said Shiloh; "I think he was excessively intolerant and cruel."

"Oh, nonsense, although you are an angel to think so," Anne assured him. "You are too good for this world; the padre was an ordinary person, and that is the way people are. It is a pity, but you must get used to it."

"Never!" cried Shiloh, meaning it with all the fervour of his extraordinary soul.

"Now I hope you are not permitting the idea to worry you," the girl said tenderly. "You really must not let my simple story excite you; you will have a fever if you do, and it is all so unnecessary. I have led rather a quiet and uneventful life; a few adventures with the Indians, but that was to be expected."

"Please go on, please," Shiloh begged her; he knew that he would quite certainly have a fever if he listened to her, but the tale was too singular to leave unheard.

"Well, Padre Francisco obtained possession of me from the Kiawas; I was but seven years old at the time, and they had no earthly use for me," the girl went on. "Then he tore my father's and mother's names out of all their books and papers; most of the books he burned afterwards, but I think he kept them for a while out of natural curiosity, and I was fortunate enough to find several of them, and to steal them for my own purposes."

"It was not stealing," said Shiloh. "They were your parents' books to begin with, and the priest had stolen them from you."

"But that is absurd, my beautiful darling," Anne replied. "He was a grown person, and I was a disobedient child; of course I stole the books. You don't think I am ashamed of that, do you?"

"It is perhaps a matter of terminology, Anne," said Shiloh, which meant nothing to the girl beyond the pleasure of hearing his voice.

"I read the books; they were in English, but my father must have taught me to read, because I found I could read them quite easily," continued Anne. "I discovered from certain papers that my father had been a missionary, and I confessed my discovery to Padre Francisco; he was afraid I would feel the disgrace very keenly, but luckily I did not; it takes a great deal to shock me, you see."

"I see," said Shiloh, who could not help laughing. "And what were these terrible books, my child?"

"Oh, they were sermons by Mr. Cotton Mather and Mr. Jonathan Edwards, and hymn-books, and little books about witches," the girl answered airily. "Some of them were rather wicked, I admit, but no worse than the Indians when they are really out of temper. Merely details of damnation and that sort of thing; there's very little difference between that and some of the Comanches' more ingenious tortures."

"We are agreed upon that point," said Shiloh; if the girl had been observant she would have known that he had a fever already.

Things That Seem Untamable

"Yes, but you are far more disapproving of it all than I," she said. "You cannot expect people to be soft-hearted, you see; it simply doesn't happen. Sometimes, yes, and for the few they truly love, as I love you, but not for all the world; not for enemy tribes. I am not soft-hearted myself about the Pawnees."

"I suppose not; the devils stole you, didn't they?" asked Shiloh anxiously.

"They did; they are not really devils, of course, although you are a darling to say so for my sake; still, I shall always consider them an unpleasant tribe, since they intended to roast me at a slow fire. A slow fire; think of it!"

"I can't!" Shiloh replied faintly.

"Well, I dare say that is because you were almost burned yourself this morning," said the girl indulgently, putting her cool hand upon Shiloh's brow; but in this supposition she was wrong. Shiloh was not thinking of himself; he was thinking of Anne, and he did not wish to think of a slow fire.

"Of course the poor Pawnees had a perfectly sensible purpose in stealing me," the girl said cheerfully. "That is, if you believe religion can ever be sensible; sometimes I am myself inclined to doubt it. Aren't you?"

"Often and often," Shiloh told her, with the light of something more than fever burning in his eyes.

"This was quite a simple idea; a little superstitious and silly, but then, what can you expect of ignorant savages? It appears that the Pawnees believe implicitly in sacrificing a young girl every spring; the theory is that this will propitiate the morning star or some such folderol, and that the morning star will send them plenty of corn and beans and pumpkins in consequence. Childish, isn't it?"

"Good God!" said Shiloh; he found it difficult to say even this.

"They treated me extremely well during the entire six months which I spent with them; I was stupid enough not to realise that they meant to kill me, and I had a charming time of it, to be perfectly honest. You see, Padre Francisco had just died, and I rather missed him, and then I was deadly tired of the Mexicans; such dull greasy people, much worse than the Pawnees! I never liked them; I was delighted when the Pawnees took me away. I was

255

The Orphan Angel

fourteen years old; that is two years ago now, of course, and I was still fond of juvenile games. I thought it great fun to play at being an Indian."

"Did you go with them of your own accord?" Shiloh asked her.

"To tell you the truth, I did, and it's very clever of you to have guessed it!" said the girl admiringly, kissing his hand. "But you must never give me away to the Cheyennes; I pretend to them that I always hated the Pawnees like poison. It flatters them, you see, and after all they did rescue me from a dreadful death, but to begin with I thought the Pawnees were delightful people. I went out for a walk one morning in the environs of the town, and met about a dozen of them on pretty little ponies; they looked so straight and tall compared to the dirty Mexicans that when they invited me to visit them I consented at once. They let me run home for my books and my Spanish shawl; in five hours we were miles and miles from Santa Fé, and they had given me a pony and taught me to say my prayers in the Pawnee language."

"Did you?" Shiloh inquired curiously.

"Sometimes; sometimes I said them in Latin like Padre Francisco, and sometimes I said a bit of Jonathan Edwards for a change. Do you think it really matters, my sweetest?"

"Not very much," said Shiloh, thinking that this was a child of nature's most fantastic marriage with a dream.

"And then," continued Anne in a vivacious whisper, "at last it was April, with little white clouds like swan's-down in the sky, and one showery morning I was taken to all the lodges in turn, and given silly pieces of painted wood, which I had to give back again to the warrior at my side, and that was so absurd that it made me cross. Not that I wanted the horrid scraps of wood, but it was such a senseless thing to do, you know. This mummery went on for two days, and then, if you please, I was varnished like a doll with vermilion and plumbago, so that I was half red and half black; fancy what a fool I must have looked! And that is not the worst, my love, if you will believe me; those hateful Pawnees actually intended to hang me on a gibbet and roast me alive over a slow fire; is not the idea in execrable taste? People are amazingly stupid and prejudiced when it comes to religion, or so it has always ap-

256

Things That Seem Untamable

peared to me. Later it seems I was to have been dispatched by means of tomahawks and arrows, but the slow fire is the most disagreeable part of it, isn't it?"

"It is," said Shiloh, to whom the thought was veritable hell-fire.

"I remember it all so clearly; it was an enchanting April day, coloured like my turquoise necklace; the streams were as blue as the skies, and along their edges the willows were turning silver and gold at the tips. Everything was gay and windy; it was such a dreadful waste of time to bother about burning me on a day like that. I was scared, I confess; I felt quite sick, and also very angry, because I did not want to die. That is all, I suppose, except that the Cheyennes came riding up in a cloudy powder of dust and rescued me just as the flames began to look like yellow flowers around my feet. I knew precisely how you felt this morning, my dearest; you see, the same thing had happened to me. Of course I didn't faint, but then no one had wounded me, and I was more frightened than hurt, as Padre Francisco used to say when I was a little girl."

8

SHILOH found it impossible to answer her; it is equally impossible to describe the horror which had sucked his words away.

"So then the Cheyenne chief took me home with him and treated me with the most distinguished kindness," Anne concluded. "His own daughter had recently perished in attempting to tame a wild horse, and as I was almost exactly the same age he soon grew very fond of me indeed. Finally he adopted me as his child; that is the reason that I always refer to him as my father. Probably he is much nicer than my real father was, and certainly he is much stronger and cleverer. He is the most powerful chief in this part of the country, which makes it pleasant for me; you may have noticed that those wretched Comanches were awed out of their wits this morning when I appeared; that is because they know I will stand no nonsense from anyone. That fellow who hurt you is a miserable sort of half-chief; it will be diverting to see what my father will do to him. My father is good enough to consider me fearless and original; I dare say

257

a romantic person might say he doted upon me, but I am not romantic, except of course about you. In a word, the old man adores me; he is sorry that my hair is red and my skin the colour of cream, but that cannot be avoided, although it is a great pity."

She drew a long breath, and kissed the topmost feathery lock of Shiloh's hair.

"I don't think it a great pity to have a skin like lucent gold and hair like a magical bronze bell," said Shiloh; he had recovered his voice, and he employed it benevolently, but it must be confessed that he was very tired.

Anne perceived his state as soon as she stopped chattering; she controlled the passion of love and pity which convulsed her spirit, and went quite meekly to fetch him another bowl of soup. Shiloh lay still; his burning mind shone through his eyes in brightness.

"Aren't you hungry, my angel?" she inquired tenderly, putting a pinch of salt and a small peppercorn into the soup. "Please try to eat it for my sake; I will be so grateful to you if only you will eat a spoonful of my poor soup, which is longing to be eaten by an angel. Now you must not look as if you were going to die; you are frightening me and my little soup out of our lives, because we love you and live only for you. But I warned you that you would have a fever if you insisted upon hearing all that solemn twaddle about Babylon; it is worse even than Mr. Mather's witches. You are to think of the nice funny things I told you, and try to sleep."

"Don't you know as you've been a-harrowing of him with all that jabber about Injun wickedness?" asked David in an angry whisper. "Drat you, Miss, you surely are the queerest girl I ever seen in all my born days! 'Tain't the reading as done it; it's women; you ain't none of you got no sense, if you'll pardon the expression. Taking all that trouble to cook him up a pint of soup, and then spoiling his appetite with horrors; it's downright half-witted, that's what it is!"

"But those were not horrors; those were the everyday facts of my life, and my life upon the whole has been most amusing," said Anne in perfect simplicity and good faith.

Things That Seem Untamable

Shiloh lay and watched her as she moved about the room as gently as a ripple of golden water; he wondered what mystery of soul her merry and casual talk concealed, and then, for no more than a passing instant, he wondered if indeed there were a soul obscured within the sunny glimmer of her body. This last conjecture faded before the visible adoration in the transparent hazel eyes which gazed into his own and were puzzled by their burning. Shiloh knew to whom Anne would say her prayers that night, although the only kiss she gave him was laid lightly and ridiculously at his feet.

" Good-night, my beautiful," she said; " I am going to leave you now, but David will take excellent care of you, and I shall see you at seven o'clock to-morrow morning. They've built a lodge for me before your door, a pretty little lodge all painted with deer and hawks and flying arrows; there's a cross old woman in it waiting to put me to bed, and I must kiss you good-night; I kiss the tips of your toes because I am your slave, your slave who loves you."

" Oh, surely not my slave; you must never be anyone's slave, my child," said Shiloh, but he was too tired to contest the point; she kissed the shaggy buffalo-skin in the place where she believed his narrow feet were hidden.

" A princess to the common people, but a slave to you, my sweet," she said as she vanished into the night, leaping softly through the door with the silent fluent grace of a panther-kitten.

" Good God, what a distressing idea! " thought poor Shiloh; he was shocked by Anne's unenlightened opinions and embarrassed by her humility; he was afraid that she was at once a sincere tyrant and a congenital slave. If such a creature could exist, it were no better than a lovely cockatrice; the fancy bothered him, for by this time he was very feverish.

He was feverish, he was weary, he was troubled by the bright and subtle fire of his own mind; it was like a too-bright lamp shining into his inward spiritual eyes, so that he could not sleep, or rest quietly upon his savage couch.

In a luminous splendour of delirium he saw the events of the preceding hours stream past his inward mind; the thing was like a radiant tapestry unrolled by an enchantment. The

259

The Orphan Angel

torches at midnight, the sparks against the glittering snow, the ripple of light like sunny water where Anne's own body moved, these several magics met and flowed into a single sheet of flame, and for a moment Shiloh believed that the heavens had opened in unnatural dawn.

Then he knew that it was only his memory playing monstrous tricks with his imagination, and he determined to be calm and to forget the Comanches' cruelty and Anne's hazel eyes.

"Might I have a drink of water, Davy?" he asked politely; his extreme politeness was more than David could endure.

"Aw, Shiloh, don't be so god-damned nice about it! If you was to swear at me or something, I'd know you wasn't going to die; I'd know that little hell-cat hadn't killed you with her jabbering. I'd 'a' liked to box her ears, princess or no princess; she's just a little red-headed Yankee like you'd see at any quilting-party and wouldn't bother to kiss, and her pretending to be someone grand's just to get you to take notice of her, I reckon. Aw, I know 'em, I know 'em all too well, and they're a bad lot when they're in love!"

It was impossible not to laugh; his amusement did Shiloh more good than the tin cup of snow-water, most of which David had spilled in conveying it from the calabash to the bed. All at once the world resumed the warm humane proportions of a mortal home; the nightmare was dispersed, and Shiloh was delighted to discover that he could sleep.

"Of course I am not going to die, Davy," he said. "There's nothing whatever the matter with me beyond a slight abrasion of the scalp, and you are aware of the amazing resiliency of my constitution. To-morrow we will go to the Cheyenne village; the change will be beneficial, and in three days I shall be perfectly well. There is nothing to worry about; you will see that I am always right."

"Reckon you are, you crazy critter," muttered David admiringly as he replaced the calabash upon its log and prepared to bank the embers of the fire.

Shiloh drew the miniature of Silver from his pocket; his fatigue rendered the act an effort, and his fingers refused to unfasten the clasp of the shagreen case. Nevertheless it was a

260

comfort to hold the thing against his cheek and to dream the countenance which it concealed. Here was no violence or moving glitter of gold; here were colours silvery and pearly, and the shape of peace. The lips were cooler than snow-water, the eyes were softer than the end of sorrow, and Shiloh was asleep.

IX

THE UNPASTURED DRAGON

SHILOH's was a true prophecy: the morrow's journey performed a miracle of healing upon his light corporeal frame and revivified his mind with wonder. He did not really dislike the motion of the litter so long as he was permitted to gaze about him in silence; the girl walked by his side, but her mien was subdued into a docile melancholy when she perceived his desire for repose. She had dismissed her cream-coloured pony with a flick of her slim fingers, and now she went on foot, with bended head and downcast visionary eyes.

The litter was borne by four warriors of imposing aspect; it was quite evident that they stooped to the unaccustomed service only to humour a princess. They followed the meanderings of the river, and sometimes the way was rough, but fortunately they had but to traverse a distance of seven miles, and Shiloh supported the uneven pace with perfect equanimity. He was warm beneath a covering of splendid furs, and the circumstances of his progress were too romantic to be wholly displeasing to his taste.

Anne had awakened him at dawn with an armful of preposterously munificent gifts; he had tried hard to refuse the red and silver foxes, the velvet beaver, and the rich tawny marten

The Unpastured Dragon

which she carried, but finally her tears persuaded him against his will, and she had the satisfaction of flinging a king's ransom at his feet before she brewed him a cup of tea.

Now he was clad from top to toe in garments of pure white buckskin, exquisitely soft and supple save where their delicate surfaces grew stiff with an embroidery of turquoise beads and scarlet porcupine quills; his moccasins were two intricate patterns of colour. Shiloh was grateful for the cleanliness and comfort, but every ascetic nerve in his body revolted against this elaborate luxury, and he determined to be rid of his grandeur as soon as he was well enough to walk.

Nevertheless he derived a certain pleasure from the fact that he was clothed like a savage prince; he was ashamed of this feeling, but far too honest to deny it to his private mind.

"You are beautiful; so beautiful that you will draw my eyes from their sockets and my heart from my breast to hang at your belt like horrid trophies," breathed Anne in a low religious whisper. Shiloh laughed; he did not believe her in the least, but in truth he was very beautiful as he lay among the suave and heavy furs looking the slighter and the brighter by contrast with that rich and sombre fleece. In his hand he held one long feather of the golden eagle, which the girl had given him that morning; he liked it better than all her other gifts. He thought that he might perhaps wear it in his cap when he was strong again, and rushing over the prairie almost as swiftly as the shadow of a flying eagle.

Anne could not guess his thoughts; she gazed at him sidewise through her thick brown lashes and trembled with the intensity of her love. It was a great deprivation to her to be silent; only the authentic adoration of her soul for Shiloh could have kept her so for more than five minutes. Occasionally she would turn her haughty little head to frown resentfully at some unlucky brave who had disturbed the devotional stillness with a muffled shout; she felt extremely virtuous in spite of her disappointment, and the disapproving glances which she cast upon others consoled her in part for her own suffering.

The cavalcade passed slowly along the shimmering riverbank; the ice upon the river sparkled in the sun. Save for the

braves who carried Shiloh, Anne and David alone of all the
company went on foot; the Indian warriors reined in their ponies
to a gentler pace, and David spoke to the mules in a mutter of
remonstrance whenever they trotted near the litter whereon his
friend lay stretched beneath a covering of sumptuous furs. It
seemed half royal progress, half idolatrous procession; the circumstance that the cherished creature in its midst was a republican and an atheist adds a clear ironic lustre to its image
in the eye of the mind.

At last they reached the outskirts of the Indian village; here
the river widened to a curving basin, and the ice was strong and
smooth as levelled stone. Upon this noble playground a number
of Indian boys were engaged in contests of endurance and athletic skill; Shiloh saw to his amazement that they were stark
naked. He stared enchanted at this spectacle of hardihood; his
own detestation of the rigours of winter made the children's
courage appear transcendent. In reality they were not in the
least disturbed by the cold, having been accustomed since infancy to defy it; the armour of their copper skins was quite
sufficient for their needs. To Shiloh, however, they seemed a
brood of heroes; he thought of Sparta, and blushed among his
comfortable furs. There was that in his nature which invariably
desired to oppose the tyranny of danger and of pain; now his
true inclination was to spring from the litter and dare the torturing elements to do their worst. Had he done so, he could
scarcely have hoped to escape pneumonia; the mental blessing
of a vindicated pride might possibly have compensated him for
this annoyance. The sole reason that he delayed to put the matter
to the test was that he knew very well what David and Anne
would say, and how long and how loudly they would repeat it.

" What a bore it is," he reflected, " that there should always
be someone to make a fuss about these things; I don't mean to
be ungrateful, but I do wish that their affection did not interfere with my personal liberty."

" My dearest love," said Anne at this moment, " we are now
coming to my father's lodge. Here is a headdress of eagles'
feathers; it was taken from an Aricara chief who had come into
our country, and who was very properly murdered by one of my

The Unpastured Dragon

most intimate friends. Let me bind it about your head, my beautiful; it will conceal that hateful bandage, and help convince my father that you are an important person."

"If you insist, my child," said Shiloh. "But I would far rather not wear it; it is stained with fear and anger. Besides, you know I am not really an important person."

"What nonsense," cried the girl indignantly. "Of course you are; the most important person in the world! And only look, there is hardly any blood upon the feathers; they are the feathers of the great gold war-eagle, and each one of them is worth the price of ten excellent horses."

Shiloh sighed as the plumes were bound about his brow; he wished that both the golden eagle and the Aricara chief were still alive and flying above the clouds, or across the cloudy shadows of the plain. The band about his brow made his head ache; Anne had bound it too straitly, but he had not the heart to tell her so. Her hazel eyes were bright with tears; the life-blood of the Aricara meant nothing to her, but the little drop of blood upon Shiloh's bandage drew the life from her own veins.

The Indian encampment numbered some three hundred lodges, and stretched for a considerable distance over the prairie; many dogs and horses roamed at large upon its borders, and the place was populous with dark-skinned squaws and children. Here were gathered the chiefs of the Comanches, the Arapahoes, the Cheyennes, and the Snakes, with a sprinkling of Kiawas among them; this village extended for a mile along the winter banks of the Arkansaw.

Shiloh was borne into the lodge of the Cheyenne chief; his litter was deposited upon the earthen floor, and he looked into the downward-gazing eyes of a tall and grizzled Indian of commanding appearance.

"This is my father," said Anne solemnly. "Father, this is the greatest chief of the eastern world, the King of England's eldest son."

Shiloh flushed with surprise and keen exasperation; the suggestion was too outrageous to be endured. He flung the silver foxes from about him and rose to his feet; impulsive fury tightened his muscles until it hardly needed his hand upon the tent-pole to steady him as he faced the Cheyenne chief. Their eyes were level as they met like flint and steel to make a fire.

" Really, Anne," said Shiloh, " you know perfectly well that your statement is slanderous and untrue. If you understood the moral and political infamy of the house of Hanover you would not presume to couple my name with any member of that house. Pray explain to your father that I am an honourable and virtuous person, or I must decline to trespass further upon your hospitality."

2

LARGE scintillating tears appeared within the aureate hazel of Anne's eyes; her voice was petulant as she answered.

" I only said that in order to make my father fonder of you," she said. " You are dreadfully silly, my sweetest, to be angry with me because of a little thing like that; for my own part I should much prefer to be a king's daughter; my father was a missionary, and yet I never trouble myself about the disgrace, or allow it to depress me. Now sit down like a sensible darling and let me fetch you something to eat."

" Good-day, sir; you are welcome to my house," said the Cheyenne to Shiloh in slow accurate English. " You must not permit this impertinent child of mine to weary you with her vagaries; she is a good child at heart, but excessively foolish. It will give me great pleasure to make you known to certain of our more distinguished chiefs to-night; you must be sick of the society of women and social inferiors."

" Thank you," Shiloh replied; his mind was whirling with bewilderment. " I should of course be glad to make the acquaintance of your friends; I cannot agree to your strictures upon the opposite sex, and I have never agreed to any theory whereby society is arbitrarily divided by certain rules inadmissible to an enlightened mind. At present I am grievously fatigued; may I depend upon your kindness to grant me a brief interval of rest? "

" Good heavens, my dear fellow, my entire household is at your service! " exclaimed the Cheyenne with obvious sincerity.

The Unpastured Dragon

"Ask for anything your fancy dictates; a cloak of golden fox-skins lined with feathers, a milk-white Spanish horse broken to your rein, or a young virgin purer than the April moon; all these await you if you will take the trouble to accept them. Meanwhile, here are peltries from the Canadian mountains and seal-skins from California; I beg you to consider this couch as your exclusive property, unless you should prefer to share it with the fairest maiden of my tribe!"

"But, father, you have not arranged it in the least as I directed!" cried Anne with passionate scorn. "What are all these horrid moth-devoured furs doing here, when I told you there must be nothing but sable and beaver? By the body of Christ, I shall run away with the first horse-thief who importunes me rather than submit to this indignity! I have told you that I love this man, that I adore him with the ultimate fervour of my soul, and yet you dare to spread his resting-place with the mangy hides of nameless animals unknown to decent people! I declare to you, and by the holy cross I mean it with all my heart, that I will strip the skin from my own body and stretch it here for his comfort rather than permit my darling to sleep upon less than perfection, although the difference trembled in the splitting of a hair!"

"Anne, Anne!" Shiloh implored her, "I beg you to measure your words; this is the tongue of madness." He was repelled by her vehemence, and a look of strain and exhaustion drew his sensitive lips together and darkened the clear colour of his eyes.

"Gently, gently, my dear little girl; it is quite unnecessary to become so emphatic about a mere question of bedding; besides, you are embarrassing our guest," said the Cheyenne quietly. "I entreat you to excuse her, sir; her youth was subject to the most deplorable influences, and her education has been woefully neglected. I am endeavouring to correct its deficiencies, but sometimes I fear that the simplest principles of courtesy and self-control are beyond her powers of apprehension. Her physical courage is above reproach, but her mind is undisciplined and moonstruck in the extreme."

"Moonstruck? Of course I am moonstruck," cried Anne immediately. "Moonstruck, sunstruck, starstruck, and struck by

267

the blue lightning of his glance; father, you have seen him, and you cannot be surprised."

"I am never surprised by any of your antics, my child," replied the Cheyenne. "But I will punish you severely if you persist in this frenzy; go to your room, and let us see no more of you until to-morrow. I shall send you seven grains of parched corn and a walnut-shell full of water for your supper; I trust that this enforced abstinence may medicine the temper of your brain."

"Oh, pray don't punish her because of me; I really can't bear that!" exclaimed Shiloh in horror. The joints of his knees became all at once unstable, and he sat down upon the couch and covered his eyes with his hands.

"But who will give my beautiful darling his supper, then?" Anne demanded tragically; she was far too deeply in love to have any appetite, but the thought of Shiloh deprived of her cherishing attentions gnawed at her soul like hunger.

"Why, anyone whom he pleases to select, of course," said the Cheyenne with cool serenity; if he had the least suspicion of his daughter's anguish his face did not betray him into pity. "I suppose he will choose an agreeable virgin for that office, or any other that his desires may relish."

"You won't, will you, my angel?" murmured Anne; she sank down beside Shiloh and laid her tawny head upon his knees.

"You won't; I know you won't," she whispered. "You could never have the heart to marry anyone else to-night, while I am shut up in my horrid stuffy room with seven grains of parched corn and twenty drops of water to console me. Remember me; remember how I love you; promise me that you will not let my father persuade you to marry an agreeable virgin while I am loving you all alone in a cruel locked room whose walls are painted with yellow rattlesnakes!"

"You decided upon that design yourself, Anne," the Cheyenne reminded her. "You said that it was cheerful, and that you liked it because it put you in mind of the garden of Eden. Now get up at once and go to your bed; I cannot have any more of this egregious folly."

"I promise, my child," said Shiloh at the same instant; the

The Unpastured Dragon

words were low, and strung upon a little laugh. " I shall certainly not marry anyone to-night; you may depend upon it that I will remember. I am sorry that you are to have no supper, but perhaps your father will relent when I tell him how very good you have been to a distressed traveller."

He patted the top of her tawny head, that was so like a magical bronze bell that he almost expected it to ring with music under his light touch.

" I don't care about my supper; I care about yours," said Anne in a tearful whisper. " You must be certain not to let them give you any of that horrible roasted dog; I wouldn't eat any dried pumpkins, either, if I were you, because they're rather indigestible. Father will make you smoke that ridiculous pipe; if you're not accustomed to strong tobacco you'll probably feel dizzy. Don't forget that you may have a fever again to-night; make the wretches get you everything you need and don't sit up too late talking to those silly old men; after all, you were severely wounded yesterday and you are entitled to some consideration. It's positively inhuman of father to send me away from you; I alone understand your angelic nature and the peculiar character of your injury, which requires to be kissed as well as treated with cold vinegar compresses; the kisses must not be cold, my beautiful, and in order that you may obtain their true benefit they should be administered every five minutes."

" Anne," said the Cheyenne sternly, " be silent, and go to your room. We have had enough of this disgusting balderdash."

" Oh, please don't speak to her like that! " cried Shiloh. " She is very impulsive, of course, but she has such an affectionate and feeling heart that it is diabolic to rebuff her."

" She is not a baby," said the Cheyenne. " She is nearly seventeen years old; she must be taught to manage her emotions as she manages a refractory horse. Girls who can manage neither the one nor the other come to grief; luckily she has good hands on a horse, but her emotions are unbroken to any curb."

Shiloh remembered with a sentiment of awe that the Indian's own daughter had been killed in taming a horse, and he marvelled at the chill indifference of the voice that spoke of grief.

" Good-night, my love," whispered Anne. She rose swiftly to

her feet, her pliant body springing upward like a flame; her hands were little darting flames about Shiloh's head. If she touched him even very lightly her caress was too fugitive to be realised; she gave him no kiss, but passed from the room like fire blown out by adverse breath.

"Do you think we have hurt the child?" asked Shiloh miserably.

"Not half so much as she has wearied us," was the Cheyenne's cool reply.

Shiloh was grateful for the tranquillity of the empty lodge after the Indian had left him; he stretched his long limbs upon the couch and prepared to question the universe in general and his own spirit in particular. A few minutes of this metaphysical exercise sufficed to wrap his mind in slumbers more profound than the deep peltries in which his bones were laid; he slept soundly, and awoke refreshed and soothed into contentment.

David was standing by the tent-pole and regarding him with a faintly quizzical expression upon his honest countenance. He looked clean and ruddy and restored to his best able-seaman temper.

"They're a-waiting for you in the big lodge next door," he told Shiloh with a broad grin. "Seems like they think I'm your valley-de-shawm or some such dunderheaded foolishness; I ain't invited to their lousy party, and the old codger's been and ordered me about like I was bound over to him for life. It's him as sent me in here to wake you; say the word and I'll tell him as you ain't a-going to come to his god-damned barbecue, for I reckon the food won't be much to your liking."

"I am afraid it would be discourteous to decline," said Shiloh regretfully, sitting up and rubbing his eyes, which were still large and vague with sleep.

"Oh, to hell with politeness if you're tired," David cried. "Only mebbe it might kinda cheer you up a bit if you was to go to their party, just to pass the time, like, and to see all them solemn old mummies setting round in their blankets same as a passel of grandmas in their Sunday shawls, and them handing a long painted pipe about in the silliest way I ever see in all my born days. Grunt like regular hogs, they do, and never crack a smile a-doing it. Guess you better go, Shiloh; you can take along a fistful of parched corn if you don't hanker after hound-dog fricassee."

" I fear that it is my duty to go," said Shiloh, rising from the couch. " I shall of course take you with me; it must be made clear to these people that you are my friend, and that the happiest equality has ever governed the relation of our hearts. I wish I might have a bath before I appear at this tiresome supper."

" You can, my lad," replied David. " There's hot water and oil and white sand a-laying ready for you in the next room, not to mention a new suit of yaller buckskin embroidered in purple, and about a peck of elegant silver jewelry."

" I much prefer these garments which Anne was kind enough to give me," said Shiloh. " The bath, however, I shall certainly take, and that was an excellent suggestion as to the parched corn."

An hour later Shiloh and David entered the enormous lodge where the chiefs were assembled; it needed but a word from Shiloh to the Cheyenne to make David welcome in that company. The word was gentle, but there was a glitter in Shiloh's eyes that convinced the Indian of its veracity.

The chiefs of the Cheyennes, the Comanches, the Arapahoes, and the Snakes were met together for a great feast; the festival was pacific, but it celebrated some bloodier anniversary of conquest. The calumet, passed from hand to hand with ceremonies of grave decorum, was indeed the emblem of peace; the smoke that wreathed the fraternal bosoms' of the savages symbolised a more durable bond. Certain dark and ambiguous objects dangling from the rafters overhead failed to engage Shiloh's flying glances; David observed them, and knew them for what they were; he was glad that his friend's attention was deflected by the solemn ritual of the supper.

" If he knew them god-damned things was scalps," said David to himself, " there's no telling what he wouldn't say or do. Most likely there'd be ructions; mebbe our own hair would be kinda added to the collection afore the night was out. Well, they ain't said nothing about him sticking to parched corn and refusing roasted pup, and I reckon the old fools has the sense to like him; have to be a sight bigger fools than them fellers not to like Shiloh."

3

"My beautiful darling, I have brought you the finest present in the world!" cried Anne the next morning, entering the room with impetuous speed and turning a clever handspring in the centre of the floor.

She was in exuberant spirits, and the softest colours of flame danced in her lips and eyes and informed the texture of her hair. Nevertheless Shiloh's heart sank into his moccasins as he heard her; he was afraid that she had come to offer him her hand in marriage, and it was an invariable agony to his soul to be forced to refuse a favour to a woman.

Shiloh and David were seated quietly in front of a little fire; they were drinking tea and eating crisp johnny-cakes within the circle of its warmth. Anne was a disturbing element, although the element was clear and golden as the flames upon the hearth.

"What is that, my child?" inquired Shiloh; he was exquisitely gentle with her although she had overturned the tea-kettle in her leap to his side. "You know I have already told you, my dear little girl, that you must not give me any more presents; it is quite impossible that I should accept another, but please believe that I love your generosity and thank you from the depth of my soul."

"Oh, but this you must take, my sweet; it is far too splendid to decline!" cried Anne; her gaiety overflowed in a sunny stream of laughter, and she whirled into a fantastic waltz with her own shadow.

"What is this splendid gift, then?" asked Shiloh patiently.

"Why, the life of your enemy, to be sure, my angel!" said Anne with a pure chime of exaltation in her childish voice.

Shiloh set down his tea-cup with a hand that trembled very visibly; he leaned back against the wall of the lodge and regarded Anne with the wide bright eyes of fascination. If the girl had suddenly displayed a serpent's breast under the delicate fabric

272

of her gown, if some loathsome blight had struck her into physical decay, his horror would have been as nothing compared to this repugnance of the heart.

"What can you mean, in the name of God?" asked Shiloh in a shuddering whisper.

"Merely precisely what I have said, my sweet; father has consented to have the man executed at once, and I came straight to tell you the delightful tidings. You see I lay awake all night and cried because I adored you so, and when my father saw how unhappy I was this morning he felt sorry for me and wished to comfort me; he gave me leave to choose whatever precious thing I desired, and of course I wanted revenge upon the enemy of my love. My father is a perfect darling, and I shall never say again that he is cross or unkind."

"Oh, Anne, Anne, do you know what you are saying?" Shiloh demanded with ashen lips.

"It's not so very surprising after all, my angel, although I confess that I feel proud and triumphant because I can give you this beautiful present," Anne continued; her felicity had not perceived that Shiloh was blanched and frozen by her words. "You remember that I explained that the dog was only a sort of half-chief; as a matter of fact he is the son-in-law of the true Comanche chief, and my father had little difficulty in getting him condemned to death. I don't think the old people like him very well; they have often spoken of his selfishness and bad temper. So the whole thing was quite easily arranged, and you need not be afraid that you have made the least trouble for anyone."

"Anne," asked Shiloh, sick with fear of the answer, "is the man dead?"

"You are a funny impatient angel, aren't you?" laughed Anne; her eyes were worshipful as she looked at him. "Do you know, I really believed that you might be vexed with me, and scold me for this? But no, the man isn't dead yet, my sweet; he soon will be, however, and then I shall have proved my love to you beyond a doubt."

"Anne," said Shiloh, "go, while there is yet time, and save this unhappy creature from the fate which your atrocious cruelty has prepared for him."

The Orphan Angel

If every silvered lock of Shiloh's hair had been a rattlesnake venomed with the Gorgon magic, Anne could not have been stricken into a stiffer image of despair. Her light and flexible limbs appeared to turn to stone or bronze; her eyes stared round and empty into Shiloh's, and they were blinded like a statue's eyes. She was too warmly tinted by the sun to grow pale; only her lips ceased to be rosy. All pride and happiness were expunged from her little face, leaving it cold and vacant and forlorn as the ashes of a fire.

She stood upright in the precise centre of the lodge; her hands were clenched and laid against her narrow thighs, her small feet were set close together upon the floor. She swayed very slightly as she stood, not with the supple grace of a living girl, but like a meagre disastrous image broken from its pedestal.

"Anne," said Shiloh, "I am sorry that I spoke so harshly to you just now. You are ill; let David look to you while I go to save this wretched man from death."

Anne shook her head slowly from side to side; her face was quite expressionless and rather stupid. "No," she said to Shiloh, "I will go myself. Please let me go; please do not speak to me again, but let me go."

She turned and walked from the room with languid deliberate steps; her air was curiously apathetic, and she moved as though she were intolerably weary.

Presently she returned and sat down beside Shiloh; she kept her eyes averted from his countenance, and her thin rigid body seemed to shrink from him in pain and terror.

"I have done what you commanded," she said in a breathless tired voice. "I did not mean to offend you, my darling. I loved you; I wanted to be revenged upon your enemy. It was all quite simple; I suppose that I am very wicked, but I do not really understand. This much I know: that you have looked at me in horror and repulsion; it is enough; it is finished for ever."

"Anne, my child," said Shiloh, taking her cold hand in his, "what is finished? I do not know what you mean."

"Why, life, of course," Anne replied briefly; she smiled as she spoke, but her lips were colder than her little hands.

The Unpastured Dragon

"Oh, no; truly it isn't," Shiloh told her; he put his arms around her and drew her to him with remorseful tenderness. "I was wrong, my child, to speak as I did; we were both of us in error, you to injure the Comanche and I to hurt you by the harshness of my words. Let us forgive each other and be friends; I cannot pretend that I was not rather shocked, but I think I am beginning to understand, and I am ashamed of myself for making you miserable."

His voice was so gentle that Anne tried in vain to stop her tears; as well might she have hoped to staunch a wound piercing into the very core of her heart. She began to cry, hiding her face against Shiloh's shoulder.

"Good-bye, my beautiful darling," she said presently. "My father has talked to me of your departure to-morrow; I am glad that you are to have the horses and the stick as a safe-conduct, since you will not accept an escort. He believes, poor old man, that you may return and marry me after you have settled your affairs in California; I know of course that this can never be, but the hope pleases him, because he has taken a great fancy to you, and he sees that I love you with my entire soul. I am not mad enough to dream of such happiness; I am better able to imagine hell than heaven; it is my Puritan inheritance, I suppose. Good-bye, my love, forever; do not forget that I love you. I am your bondwoman; I am your slave; perhaps in heaven I shall be permitted to serve you."

Shiloh had none of that pinched deformity of spirit which hates a love it cannot reciprocate in kind; his nature owned an innocent gratitude for all affection. Now he took the adoration of this singular child with a simplicity which comforted her tears and laid a delicate balsam of peace upon her heart.

He was too noble to hurt her by indifference and too sensitive to humiliate her by pity. "Good-bye, my dear child," he said. "I shall always remember you; I shall always love you, if you will believe it. Perhaps some day I may return; meanwhile there is a brotherly and sisterly pledge between us which shall never be broken."

"You are an angel," said Anne. "Good-bye, my darling."

275

She bent her head over his hands and kissed them; then quickly she stooped to lay a light elusive kiss upon the toes of his moccasins.

"That's my true way of kissing you, my love," she whispered as she went from him.

She went swiftly, like a flame blown out by the breath of doom; the flame was wild and fluttering and torn, but lovely again as a flower and brave as the fringed banner of a forlorn hope. It was a living girl who flew from the room on ragged wings of sorrow, and life was not really over, and the forlorn hope was a hope of heaven.

4

THE REMAINDER of the journey to Santa Fé was marked by many strange adventures, but these were fortunate and rapid in their course, and the two friends reached San Fernandez de Taos without serious mishap. It was obviously unwise of Shiloh to travel before the wound above his temple was completely healed; the fact remains that the hazard was unattended by unpleasant results.

When he removed the bandage for the last time it was evident that, although the scar was so neat as to be well-nigh invisible, a pale miraculous plume of pure silver had sprouted among the locks surrounding it; the circumstance cannot be said to have altered Shiloh's appearance for the worse. He looked an amazingly slim and comely creature astride the splendid horse which the Cheyenne chief had given him at parting.

These horses carried them over certain difficulties which might otherwise have soared into portentous dangers, and the painted stick with its eccentric characters of men and beasts was a sure passport from tribe to tribe of Indians. The Comanches accepted it as a friendly sign, and because the Pawnees had recently consummated a treaty with the Cheyennes, the Pawnees smiled when they beheld the Cheyenne figures carved upon the wood.

The mules were exceedingly useful as pack-animals; now that the snow lay deeper in the valleys and dry and shallow along the foothills of the mountains, it was pleasant to be mounted upon a pair of spirited horses, and Shiloh and David were very sensible of their good luck.

Some few experiences befell them which Shiloh in particular found distressing, but they themselves went unmolested and unscathed through snow-storms and a moiety of peril, and no great white grizzly crushed their bones for the vultures to pick. They found plenty of fresh game of several varieties, and the dried beans and maize wherewith Anne had stuffed their saddle-bags were frequently seasoned with venison and savoury wild geese.

It was disappointing to discover that the Republican Pawnees were not republican but savage in the extreme, and appalling to observe certain of their ceremonies; it is possible that Shiloh's silver feather of hair grew whiter after an evening spent among them. He met with nothing but kindness at their hands, but those hands were so deeply dyed in blood that he was loath to touch them. When he beheld them fling the scalps of their enemies upon the ground and stamp upon them with loud triumphant cries he turned from their lodge to sleep in the snow under the frozen azure arch of heaven. David made a strong shelter from a fallen tree, and their buffalo robes were numerous and warm, but even if he must have stiffened into winter ice Shiloh could not have remained in the lodge.

The Comanches were even worse; there was a nightmare festival into which Shiloh stumbled weary from a twenty-mile ride across the mountains; he could not believe the evidence of his outraged senses as he watched the scene.

A score of Comanche warriors were clad in the barbarous skins of bears and panthers; upon their dark bosoms were suspended necklaces made from the teeth and claws of these ravening beasts. They kneeled in a wide circle upon the floor, crawling upon their hands and knees and growling like the creatures whose rough or spotted pelts they wore. Between them they had laid the hearts of their enemies, cut into small pieces; they showed their hatred for these pitiful trophies of poor flesh by the bestial sounds which escaped their throats; their faces were fixed in a calm ecstasy of malevolence.

Shiloh fled from this revolting spectacle as though all the yelping packs of hell had been close behind him; later he wished to return and chastise the Comanches in a measured anger, but David caught his bridle and compelled him onward into the snowy passes of the hills.

Now did these hills continually rise higher into thin pellucid air, and the wind grew swifter and colder with each advancing hour. At last, upon a morning of fair weather flawless and chill as tempered steel, they crossed the Sangre de Cristo pass and gazed at the great plain beyond it; at their left hand and behind them the mountains ascended into heaven in purity and splendour. No word was said as the friends paused upon the summit of the path to survey this wonder; David blinked at the dazzle of majesty, but Shiloh was like a blue-eyed eagle as he stared into the sun. Some transmutation of glory was performed within his own mind, so that its actual convolutions came to hold the meaning of that crystal universe and to exalt it into a clear abstract perfection of language; there are those who would sell their souls into darkness for a knowledge of the syllables which flowed like a stream of snow-water through Shiloh's mind.

San Fernandez de Taos was a small town of white adobe houses; they approached it by the Spanish road as the Angelus was ringing, and beheld it like a holy city perched against the curtain of a steep blue hill. Once having gained its narrow streets, it was revealed to them as no more than a dusty village; they welcomed it as the end of the day's march and the meeting-place of their mortal kind. David might drink Taos lightning to his heart's content, and Shiloh might ask questions about politics in the fine literary periods he had learned from Calderón; it was good to rub shoulders with humanity again, and the world appeared warm and tractable in the light of a yellow moon to southward.

Contrary to their first expectations, they were not thrown into prison; the alcalde merely demanded the invoice of their goods, and later accepted a trifling gift in lieu of the non-existent document. When he realised that they had nothing to sell he was amazed but sympathetic; Shiloh's manners effected their usual enchantment upon the man, and by seven o'clock he had introduced them to the priest and invited them to a fandango at his own dwelling.

The Unpastured Dragon

The occasion was cheerful, although somewhat shrill and odorous; Shiloh disliked the heat and clamour, but he confessed to a pleasure in the gay and childlike character of the assembly. He made a temperate supper of tortillas and milk; he did not greatly appreciate red peppers, and mescal appealed to him not at all. He attracted the favourable attention of at least twenty ladies, and for a while he talked to these in Spanish with that grave courtesy which gave the last refinement to his charm. Finally he grew tired of this exercise in patience; the last they saw of him that night was the flying fringe of his buckskins and the alarmed scintillation of his large blue eyes.

Shiloh and David slept in a neatly whitewashed room adorned with the image of a saint and a crucifix of brass nailed to a wooden cross. They agreed that they had been used with the utmost hospitality in Taos, and that it would be delightful to be gone along the road to Santa Fé.

"Davy, it is actually beginning to be warm in the sun at its meridian," cried Shiloh three days later, reining in his horse and flinging his coonskin cap to the moderated breeze.

"So it is, but I reckon you'll get too much of the goldarned sun afore you makes California," replied David rather sourly. He had drunk an excessive quantity of mescal overnight in the little hamlet of Elgidonis, and for once he envied Shiloh his devotion to China tea. The luminous glimmer of the distant snows was cool and sweet, but the heat of the sun upon his forehead was distinctly unpleasant.

"Pick up your cap, you crazy loon; it's a fine cap, and we can't afford to go chucking things away like that; a Mexican might give you a good gallon of mescal for that there cap."

"But I don't like mescal," said Shiloh; nevertheless he recovered the cap from the dusty ground, and he was enchanted to observe that the dust was warm beneath his moccasins.

"Well, I like mescal; reckon I like it too goldarned much," David admitted. "It tastes kinda like crab-apple cider we used to have in Maine."

It was perfectly true that the weather was changing with the winding downward road; the nights were still intensely cold, but the noons lay bright under a rain of arrows from the sun which pierced to the lively skeleton within Shiloh's skin and filled his very bones with rapture. He had always hated to be cold; now he was thawed and comforted like a golden snake in the spring-time.

Therefore he was inclined to be pleased with the city of Santa Fé de San Francisco; it wore an air sufficiently southern and outlandish to appear spiritually friendly to himself. The mountain towering to the east, veiled in perpetual whiteness, the cascading stream drawn from its glaciers, the houses pale or yellow against the extreme blue sky, the nameless colour of the aspens whose silver leaves were fallen into dust, these things were acceptable to him by reason of their austral form and atmosphere. To walk upon the flat roofs of the palacio in the cool of the evening was delightful; it was fortunate for Shiloh that the governor had received him as an honoured guest.

The large loud bells in all the churches began to ring for the Angelus; Shiloh was sorry that there was to be a feast and a fandango that evening, with a guitar and a violin, and a vast supper of beef and frijoles and chile, followed by wine from the Paso del Norte. He liked the chocolate, and hoped that he might be permitted to drink only that; the salads of green peppers were also innocuous to his taste. The Mexican ladies looked romantic from a distance, but when he spoke to them he was faintly troubled by the fact that a flavour of garlic still lingered upon lips marked by an epicene pencilling of moustache. He had a suspicion that they wanted to gobble him up with a clove of garlic.

"Davy, I wish we could run away to-night instead of to-morrow," he said to his friend with a plaintive sigh.

"Well, you gotta jabber a powerful lot of Spanish to-night to that old fool of a governor to make him give us a proper passport for California," replied David with his customary good sense. "Besides, by graminy, we need a bit of advice about Injuns, and crossing the desert, and that there canoe and everything; you'll be so took up with the old codger that none of them god-damned women can come a-pestering and a-plaguing of you, thank the Lord."

"I do," said Shiloh pensively, as he turned from the evening stars to the vociferous fandango.

The Unpastured Dragon

"You see," explained Shiloh to the governor as soon as supper was over, "I have always been fond of boats; big boats and little boats, from the frailest cockleshell to the noblest galleon. Therefore your suggestion of proceeding down the Hila river by means of a canoe is particularly pleasing to my mind."

"My dear young friend," said the governor, thoughtfully lighting a cheroot, "I believe that the thing can be accomplished; the Indians have done it often, and if you are going to San Diego there is no manner of use in your taking the northerly Los Angeles trail. But the expedition will be both difficult and dangerous; I wish you would remain in Santa Fé."

"*Vive Dios!*" said Shiloh, who had heard these sentiments so often and from so many different people that he was beginning to weary of their sound. "But I really can't, you know; I never remain very long anywhere, to tell you the truth. I do not wish to appear discourteous, and of course your city is a charming spot, but I assure you that I must leave for California not later than to-morrow morning."

"Very well," replied the governor in a tone of resignation; "you know best about your own affairs, my boy; we shall be sorry to see you go, but I will give you excellent certificates and the most sagacious advice which it lies in my power to provide. Now, touching the matter of the canoe . . ."

In this fashion it came to pass that Shiloh and David set forth next morning under an unsullied sky, with every possible precaution against disaster neatly packed in their pockets and saddlebags. Their brains also were well stocked with admirable counsel, and their spirits rose in affinity with the fine ascension of the sun above their journey.

Shiloh indeed was so happy that he almost believed that his soul had left his body to fly beyond it along the western path; it might return to him at rapid intervals to circle about his head like a swallow, but it flew onward again each time. His happiness was far too swift to be held back by the galloping hooves of his horse; he knew that it had wings to leave the body, and he marvelled at its faithfulness in returning to its cage.

"I'll be switched if I see how you can stand this blazing hell-fire of a sun and never turn one of them crazy grey hairs," grumbled David long before they had reached the Hila river. The sun was not really hot; it was only glassy bright and shadow-less at noon, and Shiloh's bones absorbed it to their marrow. He was beginning to forget that he had ever hated this season of the year. It was now the middle of February; the nights were still freezing, and winter prevailed upon the hills, but on the broad mesas about Albuquerque the thin dry air was delicately cold like wine.

They followed the course of the Rio del Norte southward, turning from it at last to find the young stream of the Hila among the sands. David swore that the land was no better than a barren waste; he would have fled to the water-brooks of the foot-hills with their groves of piñon and cedar if Shiloh had consented to come with him.

"Have you forgotten Silver?" Shiloh asked, and David shook his head and scowled at the horizon.

"There's something horrible a-laying for us over yonder," he said. "Can't rightly figger it out, whether it's a man or an animal or a ghost or just a kinda blurry wickedness, but it's there, and it's a-laying for us."

"Nonsense, Davy; I never listened to such nonsense in all my life." Shiloh laughed; he was in a continual effervescence of health and spirits, and he did not believe a word of David's melancholy predictions.

He loved the chances and changes of their roving life; the strange pale rainbow of the desert colours, the fantastic meals of aloes and beaver tails; he tasted the *miel de tuna* with approval because it was made from the juices of the prickly pear. The Indians of this country were mild and amicable; their festivals were not murderous, and although they looked fierce enough in their varnish of scarlet paint, Shiloh soon learned that this savage decoration was a sign of friendship.

"I think the practices of the Brothers of Light are far more barbarous," said Shiloh, turning pale with the recollection of the thing he had witnessed one midnight near Santa Fé.

Now that they had come to the Hila they remembered their intention of purchasing a canoe from the Indians; finally they

The Unpastured Dragon

succeeded in buying a small boat rudely hollowed from a tree-trunk. They had to pay several beaver-skins and a vast quantity of powder and ball for this, but when they had actually obtained it Shiloh's felicity was complete.

"Ah, this is something rather better than heaven," he said, lying supine in the bottom of the canoe and staring upward at the immaculate azure of the sky.

"Well," answered David, "you won't never make no progress a-laying on your back and looking at the sun with them saucer eyes of yours as ought to have been blinded afore this what with all them lousy books and all."

"What an adjective to apply to Æschylus!" said Shiloh, putting the unopened volume into his pocket and seizing the paddle with a pair of remarkably sunburnt hands.

It was difficult to compel Shiloh's spirited horse to learn the pace of a pack-animal, but by hook or by crook of fiery will the stubborn human creature charmed the beast into submission, and for ten enchanted days Shiloh floated down the surface of the river, living in magical reality the very progress of a dream.

"'Through death and birth to a diviner day,'" said Shiloh in the accents of beatitude.

A day came all too soon, mortal enough and sad, when he was forced to abandon the beloved boat and journey across the desert to the Red river, which the Spaniards call the Colorado. And even now he was happy; he was disembodied from his past and flying into a future which could only be beautiful and kind.

"Blamed if you wasn't patting the god-damned varmint on the head!" David declared when he discovered Shiloh gazing at a rattlesnake with innocent curiosity. Of course the statement was not strictly true, but it had enough of truth in it to make them both laugh uproariously. Nevertheless each slept with a hair riata wound around him, for it was senseless to perish on the threshold of adventure by the malice of a serpent's sting.

These were the days in which Shiloh made a number of little songs which he never took the trouble to transcribe; delightful little songs they were, dealing with snakes and coyotes and the

283

The Orphan Angel

queer burrowing owl which inhabits a hole in the ground. David liked them enormously, and they seemed an agreeable accompaniment to the fall of darkness over the opalescent shiver of light along the painted plain.

David had trapped a great many beavers on the Hila river, jerking their flesh in the pure dry sunshine, and they had plenty of parched corn and beans and coffee in their packs. By the time they reached the grassy prairies and the cottonwoods of the Colorado they had almost forgotten David's nightmare of prophecy.

The gigantic Yuma Indians of the Colorado wore loin-cloths given them by the Christians in the Spanish Settlements of California. This drew the hope of an ending to their journey warmly around the travellers' hearts. These Indians were dark-skinned and strong; they often went entirely naked, and the hair of the women fell to their narrow brown insteps.

David was appalled by their immodesty, but Shiloh thought it a very edifying state of nature, and wished he could have told Mr. and Mrs. Newton about it in Chester Square. He knew that this excellent couple would have shared his own horror at the Yumas' regrettable habit of dining upon the flesh of fatted dogs served without bread or salt.

These men carried bows of tough and elastic wood which the Spaniards call tarnio, fitted with reed arrows of an equal length. Their women wore snail-shells upon the ends of their long black tresses, and Shiloh thought that not even the Witch of Atlas had ever met with stranger creatures of the solitudes.

From these Indians David and Shiloh purchased another canoe; Shiloh was supremely glad of its possession, and as they floated downward towards the mouth of the Colorado, borne by a rapid current between banks of lofty cottonwood trees, it appeared indeed that they were nearing the glad conclusion of their toil. The new leaves of April flickered in the wind.

They floated pleasantly through warm and sunny airs; there was an abundance of beaver meat, and they saw numbers of wild geese and pelicans. So they floated for close upon a hundred miles; David himself was persuaded that their dangers were at an end, and Shiloh existed in a simple paradise of his own contriving which was fresh and innocent as April leaves.

The Unpastured Dragon

He looked upon the face of Silver's miniature every evening before he slept; she seemed the titulary saint of this peacefulness, and her shadowy eyes held lovelier images than sleep or even death.

"'Of neither would I ask the boon . . .'" said Shiloh, as if he had been saying his prayers.

At last they met a great chief of the Yumas who told them by signs that he had been to the Spanish Settlements, giving a very tolerable imitation of the breaking of surf along the shore. This venerable man raised the expectations of the travellers to the point of tears; it seemed a wild and poignant thing to hear this echo of the sea in his voice. He was astonished at the whiteness of their skins, and gazed with awe and admiration at the flaxen gold of David's hair and the ocean colour of Shiloh's eyes.

They floated onward for three days, and then suddenly they knew that the current was against them, and that they were upon the eddies of a tidal river. The knowledge was bitterer than the brine mixed in the swirling waters under their bows.

"We cannot follow the river any longer," said Shiloh. "The governor's map may have been traced by guess-work, but it shows quite plainly that the river flows into a great gulf which is set on the wrong side of the peninsula. We must take the mules and horses and strike across country. It is a pity, but it cannot be helped."

"Away from the river?" asked David. "Aw, Shiloh, surely that's a god-damned crazy plan! It's getting terrible hot, and we can't never last long away from the river." His eyes ached with the fear of leaving the water and the young green of the cottonwood trees.

"If you think there is danger from thirst," said Shiloh, "perhaps we had better set the pack-animals free; perhaps they will seek out a Yuma village, but I hope they may run wild over these plains for ever, defying man. It is a pleasant fancy in the midst of our considerable worries. If you wish, we may start out upon the horses; we can pack enough for a few days' travel on our saddle-bows, and then if the supply of water fails us we can free the horses also; I should be sorry to subject them to the tortures of thirst."

"But how about us ourselves?" inquired David. "Don't you give a rap about the tortures of thirst for us poor critters?"

"It's rather different, Davy," said Shiloh. "We are reasonable beings, and free to choose in this dilemma."

"Well, I ain't free to choose, not with you so goldarned stubborn as you are, unless I was to leave you to your fate, and that I'll never do, so help me God, even if it was deserved, which it ain't, you being the god-damn decentest man alive, if a bit lunatic, and I ain't forgotten that vow, and to hell with everything, I'm a-coming with you, old catawampus," replied David under his breath.

"The thing I can't exactly figger," he said presently, "is whether it's better to take the mules along and walk, and have more provisions, or take the hosses and ride, and so get along at a smarter rate of speed. Seems to me we'd better start with the whole shooting-match, and then see how things work out for us later."

"Very well; I will agree to that undertaking," said Shiloh. "Only we must send the poor things back to the river if we can find no water."

"And keep right on ourselves, no matter what happens?" asked David.

"Of course," said Shiloh. "That is what we came to do, isn't it? To go on until we had found Silver."

"I reckon so," said David. "Yes, I reckon as you're right, but well . . . for cris'sake!"

They filled every available canteen and flask with water, and started early in the clear and exquisite dawn, which turned to a brassy glare by midday. It was evident that they could never hope to carry enough water for the horses and mules; by noon Shiloh was so frantic with pity for their brute thirst that David with great difficulty prevented him from sharing his own portion of water with the animals. At the evening halt they turned the horses loose and watched them dash away in the direction of the river with a feeling of relief, which in David's mind was tinctured with a desperate envy.

"But anyways, we come pretty far to-day because of 'em, and I'm kinda thankful they're a-going to see them fresh green

286

The Unpastured Dragon

cottonwoods above the water again. Reckon the mules can hold out for another day; they're hardier, and mebbe we'll find water by to-morrow night."

But Shiloh could not wait for to-morrow night; he lay thinking how thirsty the mules must be, and he could not sleep, for he was rather thirsty himself, and his imagination credited the poor beasts with the endurance of torture. David was snoring peacefully, but he had piled all the water-bottles about his pillow, and Shiloh knew that he would wake the instant one of them was touched by the stealthiest hand. He rose, and stood looking at David; then he tiptoed very softly to the place where the mules were tethered and unloosed the ropes.

"*Adios, amigos,*" he whispered to them as they disappeared into the hot starry darkness. He had forgotten to remove the bell from about the neck of the little mare; it tinkled sweetly as she ran, and roused David from his slumbers.

"Might 'a' known you'd do it, drat me for a fool," was David's comment. "Well, I could see as you was half out of your wits all day, worrying about it; you was bound to take leave of your senses, I reckon, soon as you started figgering out how the poor dumb critters was a-feeling. Wish I'd 'a' told 'em to give my regards to them cottonwoods along the river, for I'd like goddamned well to get a sight of 'em to-night."

The morning revealed a singular landscape: for miles around them stretched a plain of harsh and salty sand; there was no tree, and no charitable sign of water. They took from the packs the little they were able to carry; already they were tired, for the heat was intense, and in their minds was a sorrowful assurance of ruin.

"I am afraid I rather sacrificed you to the mules, Davy, but I could not bear it another moment, and I hope you will forgive me," said Shiloh.

"You got to forgive yourself, too; it's as bad for you as it is for me," David told him sombrely. The words reminded Shiloh of Sir Philip Sidney, but there was not the pure customary delight in the recollection. The packs were heavy, and the water in the flasks could not last for ever.

"Good God almighty, is that a lake a-shining in the sun?"

287

cried David the next morning after they had walked for perhaps two hours under a blazing sky which turned continually from gold to cruel fire.

" It is; it must be," said Shiloh in a queer hoarse voice. He was very obstinate about not admitting that he was thirsty, but David guessed at his sensations from his own, and he was not surprised at the strange croaking sound of Shiloh's voice.

The water in the flasks had dwindled to a pitiful drop of mercy between themselves and hell, and now they were always thirsty and feverish, with a horrid crack-brained lightness in their heads. The sparkle of the lake in the sun was dizzy and sweet.

It was deliverance; they walked towards it slowly, because they were very tired, but at the last they ran and stumbled to its brink. They knelt down and tasted the water, and it was salter than the waters of the sea. Their eyes, which were withered with thirst like the rest of their bodies, refused them tears; nevertheless they felt their hearts as well as their brains crack within them with a crazy sound of drouth.

" Shiloh, are you thirsty? " asked David in the wide lunatic stare of the next noonday; he knew that he was trying to hurt Shiloh, and he had forgotten why he was doing it. His own torment was so acute that it had set a temporary madness upon his mind, and now for the first time in his life he tried to hurt his friend. There was no water left in the flasks; the drop upon their tongues last night had been hot and poisonous with despair.

" Are you thirsty? " he repeated, and wondered what he was saying.

" Not particularly," said Shiloh in a rustling whisper.

" You know you are, you know you are, and by God you got to admit it," persisted David; he moved and spoke like some dreadful automaton, and all his body was parched and burnt to the colour of dull red earth. Only his hair caught the brightness of the sun in brightness above the stupid agony of his forehead.

" No," said Shiloh, never moving his eyes from the far horizon.

Shiloh himself was shrivelled up into a scarecrow; he was so thin that the slight bones of his skeleton were plain to see, very elegantly formed and neatly articulated under the fragile tissue of his skin, that appeared no more substantial than a dead leaf in the wind.

His eyes were sunken in his head; the blue of the iris was incredibly brilliant in the hollows under the brow.

Last night after they had drunk the last feverish drop of water, they had scraped away the surface of the burning sand to find the cooler soil beneath; in these narrow graves they had lain down stark naked to endure the tortures of hell within their living flesh. David had slept for a few hours; Shiloh had never closed his eyes against the pointed fires of the stars. It was no wonder that his eyes were like consuming fires in their sockets.

Now he never moved his eyes from the far horizon, where a mountain of pure crystal glittered in the sunshine; Shiloh knew that the imponderable cloud of light was real, but it appeared silvery and dissolving as a single snowflake. It was far away, and very far away; it was not given to a mortal to attain such mountain-heights.

He was aware that he was traversing a little hill; he was so weary that it seemed a brutal labour to reach even the summit of a little hill. He climbed this mean eminence and paused because he could go no farther; his heart was knocking against his ribs, and all the veins of his body were filled with hellish flame. For a moment the clarity of his sight was darkened; when he looked at the earth again he perceived a small transparent stream of snow-water flowing softly under the hill. He could not believe his vision.

He touched David's arm and pointed to the water; he was beyond the power of speech, and a fear descended upon his heart lest he should die before he could reach the stream of snow-water.

He went forward lightly and quickly, moved by some obscure courage of the will; he fell down by the side of the water, and looking into it he saw quite plainly not his own face but that of another.

"Arethusa!" said Shiloh in no voice at all; of course he had meant to say Silver, but being very tired he called upon the glimmering image by the sweet name of Arethusa. Then he fainted quietly and lay with his face beneath the cool smooth surface of the stream; if David had not somehow found the strength to drag him backward, he must indubitably have been drowned.

X

DOUBTLESS THERE IS A PLACE
OF PEACE

WHEN the Indians carried Shiloh into the mission of Santa Caterina, the Dominicans all believed that he would die, but David knew better. After they had found the snow-stream there had never been any question of dying; suffering was another matter, and there had been plenty of that in the past fortnight, but Shiloh was alive, and David saw that he intended to remain so until he had come face to face with Silver.

Afterwards was still another question; David had a strange conviction that Shiloh might take it into his head to attempt to cross the Pacific on foot or to jump over a mountain-top or the moon, but for a time at least the silver cord remained unbroken which bound him to the earth, and ultimately it must lead him to San Diego.

For two weeks they had wandered like a pair of scorched re-visitants from hell, over the high passes and along the valleys of the creeks bordered with palms and live-oaks, fainting and falling and rising to stumble onward, but always within touch and smell and blessed taste of water. The Indians had succoured them inter-mittently with roasted mescal and a thin gruel of maize, but their starvation was beyond hunger; it was the shadow of the trees and the chill of the streams which they devoured like bread and wine. David soon regained the admirable power of his muscles, but his mind was shaken as by an assault of devils; Shiloh, who was worn away to a phantom, had never lost the piercing lightning of his intellect or the wildfire of his will. So they were enabled each to help the other during this period of their return to life, but when they entered the Dominican mission of Santa Caterina upon a clear evening of early May the shade of death was still visible over their countenances.

"But the poor boy cannot possibly recover; we must convert him to the faith, and then at least we shall have wrought a cure of the soul, but his body we cannot save," the good brothers told themselves concerning Shiloh. They little knew the gentleman who had come among them; it is difficult to say in which prophecy they were more lamentably at fault. In the matter of the conversion their disappointment was great; the fact that Shiloh did not die also affected them with a mild regret, because already he appeared to be a spirit divorced from the frail remnant of his flesh, and they loved him in a mood of elegy which was sadly wasted upon a living man.

"Told the goldarned idjits you was going to fool 'em yet, and you done it," said David triumphantly the morning they left the mission. His limited Spanish had not permitted him to speak his full mind to the Dominicans, but he had been annoyed by the manner in which they had prayed over Shiloh.

"Of course they were amazingly good to me," said Shiloh, who had been excruciatingly bored by the attentions which his body and soul had received.

They were travelling in a southwesterly direction, with letters for the neighbouring mission of San Sebastian. Their excellent certificates from the governor at Santa Fé had satisfied the military authorities, and they had been allowed to leave without an escort. Now they were approaching the sea-coast, and the surrounding vegetation was rich and paradisal with flowers.

Shiloh had made a truly surprising recovery; he sniffed the air flavoured with salt and honey and felt himself strong again. The skin-and-bone which was left of him composed a light effective engine for speed, and he was so deeply burned by the desert sun that he seemed to have absorbed a portion of its light, so that his fair complexion must hold colours of fire and gold for ever.

The scene was beautiful beyond imagination as they drew close to the shore, having traversed a range of lofty hills; the lower slopes of these were covered with a profusion of blue lupin and pale orange poppies, and as they descended into the green vineyards of the valley they moved in an atmosphere of honeysuckle and jasmine. The orange groves sheltered them at noon, but the wind was always cool from the Pacific, and along the King's Highway to San Sebastian there was no shadow more profound than the sweet shadow of the trees.

By this road, which the Spaniards call El Camino Real, they travelled from mission to mission, coming to San Diego in seven days, gathering wild honey from the blossoms of the mescal and supping on tortillas and fat mutton by candlelight. They reached the cliffs which overhang the sea, high pinnacles on which the waves are poured in tides, and beheld strange monsters, otters and seals and sharks and great whales spouting rainbows in the sunshine. The plains were spread with clover around the port of Todos Santos, where herds of horses and cattle roamed and pastured. This was the road which Junipero Serra had marked out by handfuls of mustard-seed flung along its sides, so that in spring he had walked between walls of yellow blossoms shoulder-high and loud with bees.

When at last they came to San Diego a soldier immediately arrested them, much to Shiloh's annoyance; he observed that the religious orders were more humane than the military. Their passports appeared to impress the corporal, and finally they were ushered into the general's presence. He looked at the certificates and smiled an amiable smile; they realised with relief that they would not be forced to spend the night in a cell among the legions of the Spanish fleas.

"Good," he said to Shiloh. "The governor at Santa Fé seems to have a high opinion of your characters; I trust that you will endeavour to deserve it. You are going to visit Don Narciso de Coronel upon important business; let me advise you to procure some more respectable clothes before doing so, lest he believe you to be persons of no importance whatever."

Doubtless There Is a Place of Peace

So it came about that at five o'clock on an afternoon of warm ambrosial May weather, Shiloh woke from a trance of hurry and fatigue to discover himself proceeding slowly along the gentle acclivity of a hill; he was aware that he was going to the *casa de campo* of Don Narciso de Coronel. He had a delightful sense of leisure and holiday; he had spent the entire morning in preparation for this event, and it had been a dull and wearisome affair to find lodgings where one was allowed to take a bath, and to buy the respectable apparel suitable for a visit to the country estate of a Californian gentleman. Now these details were happily arranged, and Shiloh felt extremely clean and civilised in his exotic new garments.

Exotic they certainly appeared to him; he had sought high and low for a suit with a reasonable English cut, but of course he had been forced to accept the Spanish mode at last. There was nothing else to be had in San Diego; Shiloh was the least self-conscious of men, but he had a light amused notion that he must look rather a fool in this black-and-silver raiment, which was nevertheless the plainest fashion to be purchased in town.

"Unless you dress like a peon," the general had advised him at parting. "And you must not present yourself before Don Narciso dressed like a peon."

Now the truth of the matter was that Shiloh bore not the remotest resemblance to a fool; he looked the most elegant and charming creature under heaven in his costume of a Spanish gentleman, and the fact that he was excessively thin and that his hair was silvered by fever and privation lent a subtle and distinguished grace to his aristocratic appearance.

It may be possible that a woman of sensibility could have beheld him at this moment and failed to fall in love with him; certainly no such extravagant miracle occurred that afternoon. Sylvie la Croix was sitting under a white rose-tree upon the confines of her cousin's garden; when she looked up from her needlework she perceived Shiloh approaching slowly along the road; he carried his broad-brimmed hat in his hand, and the wind was ruffling his hair into eccentric silver feathers. His sense of leisure and holiday had set a smile upon his lips; he was glad to be coming to this place at last, but his heart held no heaviness of awe or

293

sorrow. The ecstasy of the instant was casual and delicious as the discovery of a wild strawberry or a white violet; here was no end to a long and hazardous quest, but the young untroubled beginning of happiness.

2

THE GARDEN was bounded by walls of cream-coloured stucco over which roses of all imaginable tints and fragrances made a tracery of summer, and there were hedges of cypress and beds of heliotrope. The house itself was almost hidden among trees, yellow acacia, and olive and dark evergreen; Shiloh could see its red Spanish tiles and the sun upon its whitewashed plaster. It looked cool and pleasant among the trees, as if it might be a house which peace had taken for a dwelling-place. It was the home of Sylvie la Croix, and Sylvie was sitting under a white rose-tree in the shadow of the cypress-hedge; even in the shadow he could see the silver-gold of her hair and the strange colour of her eyes.

Her eyes were of no known colour under the sun; under the moon, Shiloh believed it were better to say, for there was more of moonlight than of sunlight in their grey-and-golden depth, and more of dusk than of morning in their lashes. These eyes gazed at him from the shadow of the cypress-hedge, and even he, for whom all language was but the instrument of his art, could find no word to tell their colour.

"I believe," said Shiloh, whose manners were always enchanting, "that you must be Sylvie la Croix."

He said it with a smile; such a smile might have broken the heart of a stone to jocund spring-water. To his amazement Sylvie rose swiftly to her feet and ran across the garden into the doorway of the patio; he caught the frightened luminous glance she gave him as she passed.

If Shiloh had been in the habit of swearing he would have declared that he was damned; he whistled softly and unskilfully and walked towards the door of the house in silence. Five minutes later he had introduced himself to Don Narciso de Coronel, and had given him a letter from Monsieur Saint-Ange.

Don Narciso was a little man, very suave and gentle in his

Doubtless There Is a Place of Peace

speech; his tongue caressed the pure Castilian into music. His hair and pointed beard were inky against the pallor of his plump cheeks; his eyes were bright with urbanity and wisdom.

" But how kind of you to interest yourself in the poor child! " he cried with great cordiality after he had read the letter. " She is indeed fortunate to have the friendship of such an one as you, so obviously a man of the world and a person of impeccable breeding. Her own heredity is so deplorable, so tragic on her poor mother's side and so disgraceful on her father's, that I have despaired of settling her in life as I had once hoped to do. My wife dislikes her intensely, my daughters will have nothing to do with her, our friends are unaware of her existence. It is a thousand pities that I ever undertook to look after her; she is what the Orientals call a little white camel upon my hands."

" That is easily mended," said Shiloh rather stiffly. " I have promised Saint-Ange to bring her back to him if she will consent to come. I hope you will trust her in my keeping for the journey; I shall endeavour to acquit myself as a wise and tender guardian."

" I am sure you will, my dear sir," replied Don Narciso, laughing in a manner which affected Shiloh's mind most unpleasantly. " But why should you take all the trouble to carry her back to Saint-Ange? Why don't you keep her yourself? I should be overjoyed to have your superior presence among the somewhat dull society of this town, and I am sure that the climate of California would agree with you. You look rather delicate, you know, and as if the rigours of a northern winter might undo you; you had better settle down in California and take Sylvie off my hands for ever."

" Well," said Shiloh thoughtfully, " I have often considered the advisability of adopting an orphan, and naturally my sentiments towards Sylvie are the most affectionate and benevolent. But my affairs are greatly embarrassed at present, and I believe Saint-Ange were a more suitable guardian than myself for the child."

" I was not thinking of guardians," said Don Narciso in a soft and pensive voice. " After all, you are both young; you are patently a very charming person, and the girl has the merit of being pretty and docile in the extreme. I suggest that you find a small *casa de campo* with a shady garden, and permit yourself that rest and refreshment of the nerves of which you stand so obviously in need. It is evident to me that for this long while your life must have lacked the consolations which only a loving woman can bestow."

"But," said Shiloh, "I have to inform you that I am already married." He spoke haughtily, because he resented Don Narciso's comments upon his personal appearance and was profoundly shocked by the man's impertinence.

"So I supposed," replied Don Narciso. "No gentleman of your distinguished type ever escaped matrimony until his hair was grey; if you had escaped, my poor boy, those locks would not be whitened. I merely intended to propose an amicable arrangement whereby our little Sylvie may benefit by your chivalrous protection and you may find a cook and housekeeper who is also a loving friend. My own reward would lie in the assurance of your mutual happiness and my recovered domestic peace. My daughters are bitterly prejudiced against Sylvie, and my wife declares that it gives her an indigestion only to look at the child's pale putty-coloured hair and eyes like holes burned in a blanket."

"I should have said silver-gold and something else, possibly twilight," said Shiloh loyally. "But if I understand you rightly we are not talking of chivalry or of loving friends: you are plainly suggesting that this unfortunate girl should become my mistress."

He spoke with lofty indignation, and his eyes were cold and blue like Arctic ice. It cannot be denied that Shiloh had for a long time dreamed of Silver with a lover's mind; the thought of a mistress cherished and revered was not unnatural to his imagination or his life, and if another man had proposed the thing the event might have fallen with a different fortune. But Don Narciso was devoid of nobility and of that sensitive kindness which makes the rough world bearable; he was so wickedly eager to be rid of Sylvie and so cynically glad of Shiloh as her seducer that Shiloh shuddered in revolt against the base appeal. If the same suggestion had been made by Monsieur Saint-Ange it might have appeared innocuously romantic, gilded by that refined philosopher's gentle and ironic cast of soul; insinuated by Don Narciso de Coronel, the thing seemed foul and monstrous.

" Come, come," protested Don Narciso with a shrug, " this is very bald language indeed to apply to a poor orphan. Need we always call a fact by its ugliest name? I should prefer to think of my little cousin as the lady of your heart, or your true-love, or your valentine; there are twenty prettier words than the one you have employed."

If Don Narciso had shown Monsieur Saint-Ange's letter to Shiloh there is no telling what might have happened. This letter recommended Shiloh most highly to the Californian's hospitality; it also revealed a delicate suspicion that Shiloh's dearest hopes were set upon Sylvie la Croix. Monsieur Saint-Ange had written in that innocence of the spirit which the bitter cleverness of his brain could never quite destroy; he perceived no harm in the idyllic fancy of a union between these two children of his affection, and if Shiloh had read his exquisite dry phrases he would perhaps have been persuaded to the dream.

But now all was tarnished and polluted by the infamous pleasantries of Don Narciso de Coronel, and Shiloh turned away his countenance from the ruined vision thus unveiled. So by a singular chance a villain bound him to morality, where a virtuous man would have loosed him from its chains.

" I could never take such a cruel advantage of the child," said Shiloh firmly. " I marvel that you can calmly tender such a gift and look me in the face."

" These are very fine words, but they have no real meaning," replied Don Narciso with amusement. " My motives are perfectly disinterested, because you have already told me that you intend to convey Sylvie to St. Louis and return her to her former guardian; in any case I am rid of her, and that is all that matters. I am a soft-hearted fool, and I was sincerely desirous of seeing you comfortable and happy; if you choose to throw away your luck it is none of my business; I am sorry to have been officious."

Shiloh knew that he was speaking the truth; Don Narciso's character was certainly not elevated, but there was no mortal good in being angry with him. Like the rest of humanity, he lived according to his lights; these were not the stars, but no vehemence of righteous wrath could trim their wicks to splendour, and it were a waste of breath to blow them out entirely.

"But how, if I may ask," said Shiloh, because he wondered, "did you think that I could live in California, penniless as I am, and take proper care of Sylvie? "

"Because Saint-Ange writes that it is his intention to name you as his heir; for the present he means to make you a generous allowance in the contingency of your remaining in California. He wants you to return, of course, and yet he says that he is not too selfish to perceive that your own best happiness lies here; if you go back to St. Louis, where Sylvie was born, he could not honourably allow you to possess her; her mother was well known, and the higher circles of society are critical of such open sins. Here she has no position; my wife and daughters have never introduced her to their friends, nor allowed her to claim kinship with them. Her status is that of a governess or companion; it will cause no particular scandal if you seduce her."

"Good God," cried Shiloh, "have I taken leave of my senses? "

" I fancy," said Don Narciso suavely, "that the affecting farewell of which you speak occurred some time ago. Nevertheless you are the most engaging person whom I have ever met; the little fact that you dislike me is of no consequence in my estimate of your merit. Sylvie could not possibly have aspired to the hand of such a man; one sees at a glance that you are well born, well connected; your blood is gentle, perhaps noble, and I should not have been surprised to learn that you were a Spaniard."

" Thank you," said Shiloh crisply, "but I have no Latin blood; I am English." If he had ever been told that his ancestor was that Sir John Hawkwood whose wife was Donnina Visconti he had forgotten it long ago, and his opinion of baronets was not sufficiently high to tempt him to confirm Don Narciso's faith in his gentility.

" Well, I have always had an eye for a grandee; I confess that I am a bit of a snob, and your society would have been most acceptable to me in this neighbourhood," Don Narciso admitted with a sigh. " But you need not trouble to tell me how obstinate you are; you have fixed upon your course, and nothing can turn you aside. It is only such a pity, such a wild and foolish pity;

Doubtless There Is a Place of Peace

I wonder, my poor boy, do you realise all that you are rejecting when you turn away from California? Here is a country beautiful as heaven and far more amusing; here are women like pomegranates and men like Toledo blades; here are splendid horses to make the great land narrow to your impatience, and wine to strengthen you, and all manner of wholesome viands to steady you into health, and such wind and sunshine as might wake a dead man into impulsive ecstasies of living; can you turn from these things, you who are so tired, so desperately tired, and retrace your steps into the petty labyrinth and enigma of everyday? "

3

SHILOH did not answer him; of a sudden he was aware that he was indeed desperately tired. The face of Don Narciso de Coronel became bright with a wicked glittering brightness; his eyes were infernal diamonds for cutting the crystal of another's soul.

"Do you know, my poor boy," Don Narciso continued, " what it is you are losing when you turn away from Sylvie and give her to a desiccated old man to cherish in your stead? The old man will suck a little of her sweetness to prolong his dusty life; he will mean no harm, he will only make spiritual demands upon her, but her sweetness will be drained away; it will be a very horrid tragedy. Then the old man will die, having encumbered the earth too long, and Sylvie will never marry; she will wither into a poor little cobweb of grey sorrow, and all because she loves you, and has been waiting for you ever since she can remember. There she waits for you now, under the same cypress on the lawn; you may know her by the glimmer of the moonlight on her hair, for there is a crescent moon to-night, and Sylvie's hair is silver-gold like its curling gossamer."

Shiloh did not answer him: they stood and faced each other in the low white room among candle-flames kindled by magic on the moonlight-coloured walls. Shiloh stood very thin and erect as he faced Don Narciso, and it seemed to him that the infernal diamonds of the other's eyes were cutting into the quick of his soul as he stood there.

299

The Orphan Angel

"Do you know, my poor boy," said Don Narciso, "what you have rejected in rejecting Sylvie? You have rejected yourself; you have rejected your desires, and your luminous dreaming mind; you have rejected your own soul. It is yourself that you reject in Sylvie, because you love her; you love this child, and when you turn from her you turn from all that is lovely, all that is innocent, all that is the peace of heaven."

"But that," said Shiloh suddenly, "is obviously absurd. You are turning it around, you are twisting it, you are blackening the moonlight and kindling an infernal planet in the nethermost pit to dizzy me. I cannot follow the whirl of this villainy; my mind is swift, but for once you go too fast for me; I know, however, that you are lying, and nothing can turn me widdershins against the power of my own will."

"Very well," replied Don Narciso with a whispering softness of music; "if that is the case, I shall say no more. You have beaten me, my fine lunatic grandee; you have held your own on ground that is mine by heredity and conquest, and perhaps I am not wholly sorry. Good-bye, and may God be with you if you care for His company."

"Who in heaven's name are you?" asked Shiloh with a shiver in his voice.

"You are perfectly well aware who I am," Don Narciso answered him. "Mine was an old name in heaven, and one that you have always admired."

"Good-bye," said Shiloh. "I suppose you are talking nonsense; I am too tired to follow you. I regret having been rude; I have not known what I was saying. Now I will bid you goodnight; to-morrow we must make some arrangement concerning Sylvie, in order to convey her to St. Louis; my friend David will wait upon you in the morning. I have the honour to wish you a very good-night."

"I shall not sleep a wink," said Don Narciso; "I shall be worrying about you, my poor demented child. Now let me send Sylvie to you with a refresco of lemons or a little wine and water. You appear quite exhausted; I am afraid our conversation has been too much for you."

"Not at all," said Shiloh. "You are completely mistaken.

Doubtless There Is a Place of Peace

Pray do not trouble Sylvie for anything of the kind; I am going immediately."

Shiloh turned and went from the room; as he passed into the moonlight he saw Sylvie waiting for him in the shadow of the porch. There was a small crescent moon in the sky which shed no more than the faintest glimmer upon her face, but he knew that she had been weeping.

"Sir," said Sylvie, speaking timidly in English, "is it true that you have brought me a letter from my guardian in St. Louis?"

Shiloh looked into her face; he saw that the nameless twilight of her eyes was intense and translucent with love for him. He saw the delicate pearly colours of her small face, the sweet heart-shape like a petal, the lips cooler than snow-water. He knew that the touch of her lips would be peace against the burning of his eyes.

He looked at her, not daring to speak, fearful lest his weariness should betray him by a word. He tried to send a subtle lightning of farewell from his mind to hers, he tried vainly to put the essence of his spirit into a look and teach her his heart for eternity. It was useless: Sylvie saw only a tall and haggard young man with hollow eyes like holes into the sky; she had fallen in love with this young man no later than five o'clock of that ambrosial afternoon, and it was sad that he was going to leave her without a word.

"Don't go," she said to him. "I wish you would wait for a little moment and tell me news of my home."

He shook his head, shaking his silvered locks into the air; she saw the stars of the sky through his hollow eyes, and he was gone upon the wind from the Pacific.

4

In the freshness of early morning Shiloh sat upon the summit of a hill and stared at the blue waters of the sea below him, where the waves were shattered into rainbows of cold spray against the coloured cliffs, which were deeply stained with ochre and

301

orange and sunny rose. Dark ranks of cypresses were set between him and the east, and the sky's pure azure was unstained by any cloud.

He heard the bells ringing at the mission of Saint James of Alcala, and he wondered whether it might not be good to be a minor brother of an order dedicated to poverty like the Franciscans. He smiled to remember the day when he had walked with Peacock in the green English summer, and, coming to a vicarage with a corchorus in full flower along its garden wall, had all at once desired to enter the church and lead the quiet life of a scholar and a moralist. Peacock had been amazed into laughter; Shiloh had argued mildly that assent to the supernatural part of faith is merely technical, and Peacock had told him that he would find more restraint in the office than would suit his aspirations. Perhaps at that moment Peacock had been right, but now the sound of the Franciscan mission bell shed blessing like a fragrance upon the air.

"'Less oft is peace . . . less oft is peace . . .'" he repeated to himself, staring at the rainbows shattered along the cliffs.

Wrens and swallows were circling about his head, and the wind from the Pacific lifted the locks of his hair into wings. A Spanish brig was entering the harbour; the eagle clarity of his sight could distinguish the separate ropes of her rigging and the particoloured caps of the sailors upon her forward deck. Soon she would be departing for Valparaiso or China or other ends of the earth; there were great mountains in South America, and in China temples and lotus-flowers and the wisdom of a serpent mated with a dove.

He wondered idly whether David had reached the *casa de campo* of Don Narciso de Coronel, and whether his welcome would be worthy of David. For David was an honest boy, and kinder than bread to the hungry; Shiloh knew that David would die for him any plain working-day in the week.

"Aw, I'll go along to the old codger's and fix it with him about Silver," David had said the night before. "I was skeered to when you first asked me, but if you want me to, I'll go for you, and be damned to him for a Spanish galoot that ain't a-going to awe me with no airs and graces. If you've got such a lousy head-ache as all that, I don't blame you for not hankering after another walk to-morrow; I'll go up there instead of you, and you can lay in the sun eating figs and grapes like it was the garden of Eden."

" Perhaps," said Shiloh, " if my head still aches in the morning, I may be selfish enough to do precisely that." But there was no "perhaps" in his mind as he said it; he meant very definitely to send David to the Casa de Coronel to-morrow.

Now it was morning, and David had gone up the dust-bloomed road in a rosy dawn, and Shiloh sat alone upon the summit of the cliffs and watched the past and the future, and the present that was a succession of rainbows destroyed upon the rocks below.

"Reckon I gotta tell her the truth about Jasper, Shiloh," David had said with surprising finality before he departed. It seemed a curious circumstance that David should dare such a decision, at which even Shiloh might have boggled for an instant.

"I wonder, Davy; do you really believe that you must?" he had inquired in some perturbation.

"I reckon it's my simple bounden duty to confess and ask her to forgive me," replied David. "I'll just say to her sorta humble and plain, 'Miss Silver, I was a-fighting with your brother, and I fetched him a clip on the head that killed him, and as God is my witness it wasn't never meant that way, and I'm sorry to the rock-bottom of my soul, and I hope you'll excuse it and be friends.'"

"I see," said Shiloh. "I think you've put it very nicely, Davy; but it may be rather a shock to her, you know."

"But don't I know it all too god-damned well, Shiloh, and ain't that why I'm scared stiffer'n a new tarred rope when I think about going up there alone?" cried David. "Aw, Shiloh, can't you see your way to changing your mind and coming with me? I can see as you feel like hell, but it don't seem natural in you, somehow, to leave me go all alone when the hide's scared off me at the idea."

Now Shiloh had his own motives for wishing David to go alone; it was quite true that Don Narciso's conversation had given him a splitting headache, but a headache could never have kept

Shiloh from performing what he conceived to be his duty, and his heart smote him as he told David a very noble lie.

"I would really rather not go to Casa Coronel again; I find myself exceedingly unwell, and I should only be a nuisance to you and a burden to myself. Go, Davy, and this once without me; after you have seen Silver you will not be frightened."

"Well, I reckon I'll just say to her that I'm in the place of her brother now, and that she's never to feel lonesome nor as if she hadn't nobody to protect her," declared David. "You don't figger it out that there's any real reason why her and me can't be friends, do you?"

"No real reason, Davy," said Shiloh.

"One other thing as I've been fixing to ask you, Shiloh," said David, "is whether or no — oh, I mean if — well, put it like this, sorta — was you — had you — that is to say, what was your intentions to Silver, in the way of loving?"

It was a relief to Shiloh to find that he could laugh, but nevertheless the phrase had a ridiculous poignancy that hurt him.

"'In the way of loving' my intentions are strictly honourable to Silver," he replied lightly. "I suppose there is no use in pretending that I don't know what you mean, Davy; you are asking me whether you have a clear field to win her for yourself if you can. You have; I should begin with the brotherly attitude if I were you, but there is no earthly obstacle . . ." He stopped, and David thought that he must have a very severe headache indeed.

"And I always had a notion that you was fond of her yourself, after you took to carrying her picture in your pocket," said David. "Funny, ain't it?"

"Very," said Shiloh. "I think I will go for a walk, Davy; wear your new clothes and don't forget that you must speak Spanish to Don Narciso. Tell him that you are prepared to take her back to St. Louis, and that you have sufficient money for her passage, and that you are a perfectly competent and reliable guardian for a regiment of orphans. Good luck to you, and don't use double negatives if you can avoid it."

Shiloh had hurried from their lodgings into the virginal dawn; it was very early, and a few stars swam like silver minnows in the violet pool of the sky. The sea was asleep; the waves were flattened and smooth as pearl, and a white mist softer than the breast of a gull rested upon the waters.

Shiloh had slept for perhaps three hours; he wrapped himself in his Spanish poncho and lay down on the dry grass at the summit of the cliff. He lay upon his back and stared at the stars, which presently swam into the invisible; then as the sun rose over the mountains he turned his head to watch it and took the flood of brightness into his eyes without blinking. It was as if a bitter golden balm had washed his eyes and brow; he was aware that his headache had quite disappeared, and that he was no longer unhappy.

He saw David come out of the yellow adobe house and walk quickly up the road which led to Casa Coronel; he would reach the place by nine o'clock. Shiloh had no doubt that by noon David and Sylvie would be friends; he wondered whether it would be one day or seven before they were innocent lovers.

"It is much the best way," he said aloud, and marvelled because he meant it.

5

THERE were many paths that he might take; they were spread fan-wise about him, like the spokes of a chariot wheel or the rays of the sun. Now that the bells were ringing in the mission of Saint James of Alcala he perceived that a little path led inland to the rose-red roofs and white adobe walls. The road to Casa Coronel lay broad and level in the sun; it climbed a hill, but the acclivity was never steep, and the fringe of the road was garlanded with honeysuckle. It would be an easy road to take; yesterday he had walked its entire length in a few hours. There was the road to Italy, which was very long and lay over his left shoulder as he faced the Pacific; to-night the sun would make another path for him along the sea, and pave it with a luminous moving pattern of ripples.

He did not remember that any path led back to Anne; his mind refused that dreadful way, which had burned in naked agony under the sun until death would have seemed a kindly shadow across it. Somewhere among his books, doubled back be-

The Orphan Angel

tween the pages of Sophocles to mark a certain passage in the Antigone, he might one day find the feather of the great war-eagle that she had given him.

Last night he had been tired, but now he was not tired or troubled in any way; he sat under the pale blue sky in the centre of a circle of golden rays, and these were paths leading to the ends of the earth, or little paths leading to a church or a friend or a resting-place. The rainbows under the cliffs broke with a thunderous music among crystal flakes, and the music made words in his mind, but for the moment he was content to let them go free again like sea-birds and to sit above the waters all alone.

He knew that the miniature of Sylvie was in his pocket; he called her Silver to his own mind, and he could have made a song to her if he had chosen, but now she was no more to him than Arethusa rising from her couch of snows. Sylvie must be waking in Casa Coronel, and Shiloh hoped that she might wake in time to welcome David.

He would not take the trouble to draw the miniature of Sylvie from his pocket, but presently he would fumble with his slim brown fingers until he had found a pencil and a bit of paper, and he would catch the syllables that were filling his mind with music; they were wilder than sea-birds, but presently he would catch them quite easily in a little net of pencil-marks. It appeared a godlike prerogative, but for the moment he was content to wait.

His face was thin under the blowing wings of his hair, but its delicate bones were set in pure tranquillity. Only the incredible blue of his eyes, which were coloured like the sea, seemed variable with the sea's own brightness.

"'Less oft is peace . . . less oft is peace . . .'" said Shiloh, but smilingly, as if he loved the sound of the sad words.